The Mercy of Chance

A Pride and Prejudice Variation

By Mary Alice Alexander

TYPOS: As an author, I appreciate readers pointing out where there are typos in my work. Even after editing, reading. rereading, re rereading, ARC readers and copyediting, the odd stubborn typos will remain. I welcome an email letting me know where corrections may be required and appreciate your patience.

Maalexanderauthor@gmail.com

ISBN 1 978-1-966762-99-7 978-1-966762-00-3

For my beloved Douglas, of quiet wisdom and unwavering loyalty,

And in memory of my sweet Alex.

Contents

"…one's happiness must, in some measure be always at the mercy of chance."

Sense and Sensibility, CHAPTER XXXVI

Author's Confession

Dear Reader

- I have taken rather liberal liberties with the law in this tale. Whilst my legal background acquainted me with the dusty precedents and treatises, strict adherence would have made for rather tedious storytelling. Even for someone who was a lawyer, the volumes prove stultifyingly dull. For those brave souls who wish to explore how these matters truly unfolded in the historical reality, I offer these fascinating (if somewhat sleep-inducing) works:

Blackstone's "*Commentaries on the Laws of England*" (London: W. Strahan and T. Cadell, 1783)

Brydall's "*Non compos mentis: or, the Law relating to natural fools, mad folks and lunatick persons, inquisited and explained, etc*" (1700)

Brodrick's "*English Land and English Landlords: An Enquiry Into the Origin and Character of the English Land System, with Proposals for Its Reform*" (Issue 24215, 1881)

Elmer, J. (1872). "*The Practice in Lunacy Under Commissions and Inquisitions. With an Appendix Containing Forms and Costs of Proceedings, the Statutes, and General Orders in Lunacy. A New Edition, with Considerable Alterations and Additions.*" United Kingdom: (n.p.).

Lovelass, Peter. *The Law's Disposal of a Person's Estate who Dies Without Will Or Testament: Shewing in a Clear, Plain, Easy, and Familiar Manner, how a Man's Family Or Relations Will be Entitled to His Real and Personal Estate, by the Laws of England, and Customs of the City of London and Province of York: to which is Added the Disposal of a Person's Estate, by Will and Testament; Containing an Explanation of the Mortmain-act, with*

Instructions and Necessary Forms for Every Person to Make, Alter, and Republish His Own Will: Likewise Directions for Executors how to Act After the Testator's Death …. United Kingdom, author,1792.

Porter, Roy "*Mind-Forg'd Manacles*" (London, Penguin Books, 1987)

"*Reports of Cases Argued and Determined in the English Courts of Common Law*" (Volume 19, 1872)

Suzuki, Akihito, '*Commissions of Lunacy: Background, Sources, and Content*', *Madness at Home: The Psychiatrist, the Patient, and the Family in England,* 1820-1860 (Oakland, CA, 2006; online edn, California Scholarship Online, 22 Mar. 2012), https://doi.org/10.1525/california/9780520245808.003.0002, accessed 20 Jan. 2025.

I trust you will forgive this choice of entertainment over exactitude.

Prologue

The fire in Papa's study stood cold and dark, his leather chair empty. It seemed wrong—Papa was always there in the mornings, a book open on his lap, whilst steam rose from his teacup. But today, the only sound was his coughing echoing from the bedroom above.

"It is a mere cold," Papa said, waving away Mamma's worry as she tried to drape another blanket over his shoulders. His laugh turned into a cough that seemed to rattle the bedroom windows. "I shall be fine in a day."

Elizabeth and her sisters huddled in the doorway. When had Papa ever stayed in bed for the day long? During last year's harvest, when he had worked from dawn until well past dusk, and he still found time to read stories before bed.

"Girls, pray attend your grandfather at breakfast," Mamma said, but her eyes never left Papa's face. The laughter in her voice—the silly giggles that made Papa call her his 'sunshine girl'—had vanished. Her hands trembled as she pressed them against Papa's forehead.

Kitty, the second youngest at nine, clung to her skirt. "But I want Papa--"

"Later, Kitty Cat," Papa whispered hoarsely. His attempt at a smile did not reach his eyes, which burned too bright in his pale face. "Tell Grandpa … tell him we will discuss the south field tomorrow."

Jane, ever practical even at sixteen, tried to guide them away. But Elizabeth lingered, watching how Mamma's fingers intertwined with Papa's, how his chest struggled with each breath. Something cold and heavy settled in Elizabeth's stomach, a dread she could not name.

That night, Elizabeth woke to Mamma's screams. Heavy boots thundered up our stairs—Mr Jones arrived too late. In the hall, Grandpa stood as still as marble, his lined face blank with disbelief. Just yesterday, he and Papa had been planning the harvest together.

"Thirty-eight years old," he muttered. "My darling boy was

but thirty-eight years old." His weathered hand pressed against the wall as if he might fall without its support. In her fourteen years, Elizabeth had never seen him look so old.

Five sisters huddled together in Jane's bedroom, listening to Mamma's sobs turn to screams and back to sobs again. Mary clutched Papa's bible to her chest, her lips moving in silent prayer. Lydia, too young at seven to fully understand, had finally cried herself to sleep in Jane's lap. Outside the window, the first snow of winter began to fall, covering the farm Papa would never see again in clean, unforgiving white.

Elizabeth was employed in walking thoughtfully from the fire to the window, from the window to the fire, without knowing that she received warmth from one or discerning objects through the other. She pressed her forehead against the cold glass, watching the snowflakes dance in the darkness. Tomorrow, the world would expect them to know what to do with death. Tomorrow, they would need to be strong for Mamma, for Grandpa, for each other. But tonight, they were just girls who wanted their father.

Across the side yard, through the swirling snow, Elizabeth saw the lamp still burning in Papa's study window. Someone—probably Mr Hill—had lit it out of habit. It cast a warm glow across the freshly fallen snow, like a beacon calling Papa home. But he would never again sit in that room, never laugh at Mamma's silly jokes, never teach them about the estate ledgers he had only just begun to explain.

The snow fell harder, erasing the familiar shape of the land beneath its blank white sheet. Tomorrow would bring decisions, responsibilities, changes. But for now, she watched the snow fall and remembered how, just yesterday, Papa had promised to take them sledding when winter came.

Chapter One

Elizabeth adjusted her bonnet against the August sun as she accompanied her mother from the draper's shop. The household accounts tucked in her reticule weighed heavily on her mind—the new linen for Grandfather's bed had cost more than expected, but his comfort could not be sacrificed.

"Lizzy, pray attend," her mother murmured. "Mrs Long approaches, and I have not the patience for her particular brand of intelligence today."

But Mrs Long had already caught sight of them, her pace quickening as she crossed the high street. "Mrs Bennet! Miss Elizabeth! Have you heard the news? A young gentleman of considerable fortune has taken Netherfield Park," Mrs Long announced breathlessly, catching Mrs Bennet's sleeve as the latter emerged from the sundries shop. "Five thousand a year, they say." Mrs Long's enthusiasm for the arrival of a young man in the neighbourhood seemed odd at first until Elizabeth considered the lady's spinster nieces. Surely she hoped to 'catch' a husband for one of them.

Elizabeth exchanged a brief glance with her mother, noting the slight tightening of her lips. Before her father's death, such news might have sent Mamma into raptures of anticipation. Now, she merely inclined her head with polite disinterest.

"Indeed. Let us hope he shall prove more attentive to the property than the previous occupant," Mrs Bennet replied. "The house has stood empty overlong."

"He is called Bingley," Mrs Long persisted, clearly disappointed by this moderate response. "A single young gentleman from the north. He viewed the house on Tuesday and was so well pleased that he agreed to take it immediately. His servants are to arrive by the end of the month."

Elizabeth's thoughts turned immediately to the flooding along their southern fields. She traced the mental map of Longbourn in her mind, stopping at the marshy section where Netherfield's boundary met theirs—the same section Grandfather had pointed to repeatedly. He had been concerned about it for months, but without a current tenant to address the matter, and with the estate holder, Mr Sims, long since departed to the West Indies, their options were limited.

"It is most unfortunate that my father-in-law cannot pay his respects when Mr Bingley arrives," Mrs Bennet said. "The damp affects his joints too severely for any social calls."

"But surely some arrangement might be made," Mrs Long persisted. "Sir William Lucas will undoubtedly call upon the gentleman. Perhaps…"

"Yes, perhaps." Her mother's attention had shifted, and Elizabeth followed her gaze to see Mrs Hill hurrying toward them, her expression pinched with worry.

"Pray excuse us, Mrs Long," Elizabeth interjected smoothly. "I believe our housekeeper requires our attention." Elizabeth placed a gentle but firm hand on her mother's elbow, subtly stepping between her and Mrs Long. 'We really must attend to this matter,' she murmured, guiding her mother with the comfortable ease of someone who had performed this manoeuvre many times before. Mrs Long's mouth remained half-open, her next piece of gossip left dangling in the air as they retreated.

Mrs Long's disappointment at having her gossip session curtailed was evident, but Elizabeth guided her mother away without further ceremony.

"Madam. Miss Elizabeth." Hill bobbed a quick curtsy, then spoke in a whisper, her back turned to Mrs Long. She was well aware of that lady's legendary penchant for gossip. "I beg your pardon for interrupting, but dear Mr Bennet has taken a turn. Miss Jane sent me directly."

Elizabeth's hand flew to her throat with familiar dread. "How severe is it, Hill?"

"He was most insistent upon reviewing the harvest in the stable yard this morning, although Miss Jane tried to persuade him to wait. Then his chest seized up something dreadful. Miss Jane has sent for Mr Jones."

"And where is Mary?" Mrs Bennet asked, already gathering her skirts to quicken her pace.

"Reading to Mr Bennet from one of his philosophy books, madam."

"The western field yields," Elizabeth said with a sigh. "We were calculating them before I accompanied you to town. He was most eager to compare them with last year's figures."

As they hurried through Meryton's High Street, Elizabeth noted her mother's tense expression. "You are thinking of Mr Collins's letter."

"His expressions of concern for Grandfather's health grow more pointed with each correspondence." Mrs Bennet's voice was low, and her expression pinched. The constant drum beat of intrusion from the heir to the estate's entail was a source of worry. "We require more time, Lizzy. Your grandfather…" she trailed off.

"I know, Mamma."

They walked in silence for several moments before Mrs Bennet spoke again. "This news of Netherfield—perhaps if things were different, I would have thought only of the marital prospects such a neighbour might represent, as does Mrs Long."

"And now we think of drainage and boundary agreements." Elizabeth attempted a smile. "How our concerns have altered."

"Necessity has made farmers of us all," her mother replied. "I daresay, when Mrs Long mentioned his five thousand a year, I did wonder…" She shook her head. "But we have no time for those considerations. Not with your grandfather's health so precarious and the estate requiring constant attention. Sir William's friendship has proved invaluable these past years, but we cannot forever depend upon the kindness of neighbours." Sir William's introductions had opened doors that remained firmly shut to a widowed woman and her daughters, but Elizabeth had noticed his hesitation growing longer with each encounter.

Elizabeth sighed. Her once-smooth hands now bore the telltale calluses of one who regularly worked alongside her tenant farmers, not with embroidery patterns. She well knew that their situation grew more awkward with each passing season, as her grandfather's infirmity kept him ever more confined to Longbourn. In their dealings with the neighbours, their precarious acceptance was palpable. Mr Long's eyebrows rose, just perceptibly, before directing his response to his steward instead of to her. Just yesterday, Mr Goulding, a neighbour of long-standing, had the temerity to examine his pocket watch with pronounced deliberation mid-conversation, before turning abruptly to address a tenant on matters of the estate—as if she, the daughter of a gentleman, had suddenly become invisible in proper society.

Elizabeth squeezed her mother's arm gently. "We shall find a way to secure an introduction to Mr Bingley. As tenant at Netherfield, he will see that the water table must be resolved before winter rains begin."

"Yes." Mrs Bennet's chin lifted in the faintest elevation, the same subtle gesture Elizabeth had observed each time her mother faced a challenge after father's passing. "Sir William might be persuaded to facilitate the connection, given the practicalities involved."

As they hurried toward Longbourn, Elizabeth spared one last thought for the mysterious Mr Bingley. Perhaps she ought to think of some plan for introducing her family. Dear Jane deserved to find an amiable husband. But Hill's worried expression suggested more immediate concerns required their attention. Thoughts of eligible young men quite fled her mind in favour of Longbourn's needs.

Chapter Two

The house came into view, solid and familiar against the clear sky, its Portland stone gleaming honey-gold in the late morning light. The light August breeze stirred the tops of the elms along the drive, carrying the sweet scent of newly mown hay from the south field. Gravel crunched beneath their shoes as they approached, the sound as familiar to Elizabeth as her own breath.

Mrs Bennet smoothed her expression as she mounted the stone steps of Longbourn. Hill opened the panelled oak door and Mrs Bennet and Elizabeth stepped into the foyer and handed their bonnets to the faithful housekeeper.

News of Mr Bingley and Netherfield must wait. The present crisis required all their attention. They had learnt these past five years that tomorrow's possibilities meant little when compared with today's certainties.

"I shall review the western field calculations with him immediately," Elizabeth said as they mounted the steps. "He will rest easier knowing the work continues."

"You indulge him too much," her mother replied. Her tone held no real censure.

"He taught us that responsibility to the estate must come first," Elizabeth said simply. "I would not have him think us neglectful of his lessons."

"Mr Jones has just left, Mamma. He left some draughts and directed Cook to make up some beef tea. He urged Grandfather to rest, but…" Jane said.

"But he insists the estate will not manage itself," Elizabeth finished. "I shall bring the account books to his bedchamber."

Jane and her mother conferred in low tones. News of Netherfield's new tenant must indeed wait. Their situation at

Longbourn diminished steadily with the passing months, for their grandfather's declining health marked the approaching hour when the estate must, by law of entail, transfer to Mr Collins—leaving the ladies to economise ruthlessly and cultivate what connections remained to them else they be cast upon the charity of relations, Mr Collins's impatience grew more evident with each letter. Perhaps, in another life, she might have viewed the arrival of a single gentleman of fortune as an exciting social prospect. But that luxury belonged to young ladies whose futures were not bound to the land as securely as theirs.

Elizabeth secured the correct ledger and ran up the stairs to her grandfather's chamber.

"Has Netherfield been let at last?" Elizabeth started at her grandfather's unexpected greeting.

"Your mother will have heard the news in the village," he replied, his voice growing fainter. "Five thousand a year, they say. A decent sum, if prudently managed." His eyes drifted closed. "We must secure an introduction. That border requires considerable attention.

His voice trailed off as Mrs Bennet entered the study, her steps quick but controlled. Mary rose to greet her, speaking softly. "His breathing eased somewhat with the draughts once we returned him to the study, but he remains agitated about estate matters."

"As ever." Mrs Bennet sighed. "There was a time when Thomas and I found his dedication amusing. Now I find myself wishing he had your father's ability make sport in the face of life's trials."

Elizabeth smiled faintly. "Father always said Grandfather achieved enough seriousness for both of them."

"Indeed." Her mother's expression softened momentarily before returning to its practical mien. "It is well that Mr Jones has left draughts. Have you been reading to him, Mary?"

"I have tried. He keeps asking for the ledgers and mentioning the property line with Netherfield." Mary hesitated. "He was speaking about a new tenant?"

Mrs Bennet moved to check on her father-in-law, her fingers lightly tested the pulse at his wrist. "So Mrs Long said. A young London man with five thousand a year, apparently, although I am more concerned with whether he might prove a better steward than the previous tenant."

Mrs Bennet straightened as she tucked the shawl securely around her father-in-law's thin shoulders.

Mr Bennet patted his daughter-in-law's hand. "Thank you, Frances. I will be well. I regret going to the barns this morning.

"There is no perhaps about it, Mr Bennet. The barns do not require your attendance, but we do. Now let's settle you with some beef tea. Our girls will take care of the ledgers, as they always do. Although I sometimes wonder what life they might have led had their father lived to see them all properly established in society."

So do I, Elizabeth thought, although she kept the sentiment to herself as she made way to the writing table. Grandfather's mind remained as keen as ever in estate matters, his judgement as sound as it had been these sixty years of stewardship. Yet his body betrayed him, turning even a morning's work into an ordeal. They relied upon his guidance absolutely, which made it all the more difficult to persuade him to husband his strength. Each time he pushed himself too far, it undid weeks of careful recovery. Matrimonial prospects and social niceties—the concerns that might have occupied a normal family of five daughters—seemed increasingly like luxuries they could ill afford. Longbourn's priorities remain paramount.

"This quarter's returns exceed last year's by a fair margin," Mr Bennet said, his voice firm despite his pallid countenance. "Although we must consider—" He broke off as another cough seized him.

"Grandfather, please," Elizabeth murmured. "Let us resume after you have rested."

"The decisions cannot wait, child. The grain merchants will require our answer by the month's end." He reached for the ledger with a trembling hand.

Mrs Bennet stepped forward. "Perhaps we might review the figures whilst you take some refreshment? Jane has just sent word that Cook has prepared that beef tea you find tolerable."

Her father-in-law's sharp eyes met hers. In them she saw the same keen intelligence that had guided Longbourn through drought and plenty, war, and peace. "You believe I overtax myself, Frances." His lips lifted into an affectionate smile.

"I believe your guidance is essential to these decisions, sir. Which is why we must ensure you are strong enough to see them through properly." Mrs Bennet smoothed his shawl, her familiar movements soothing as she subtly observed his pallor and his breathing,

He subsided back in his chair, a slight smile touching his lips. "You have learnt to manage me very well, my dear. Very well indeed." His gaze moved to the window, where the autumn sun slanted across the park. "The south field must be addressed before the frost sets in. The drainage—"

"Is proceeding exactly as you recommended," Elizabeth assured him. "Mr Robinson agreed to begin the work yesterday, following your specifications to the letter."

"Good. Good." He closed his eyes briefly. "You may send for that beef tea, Frances. But bring me the ledger where I can see it. And tell me what news you heard in Meryton today. One must keep abreast of local matters, even when confined to one's study." He smiled teasingly, then settled back in his favourite soft chair, his legs extended toward the warming hearth.

Mrs Bennet pulled the bell cord. If discussion of Mr Bingley's arrival at Netherfield would distract Grandfather from estate matters for a time, perhaps they might achieve both rest and social intelligence. Perhaps he would allow her to place a blanket on his lap.

The breakfast room at Longbourn was awash in early autumn sunlight. Jane poured tea whilst Elizabeth toasted bread, then spread on butter, both tasks performed with the automatic efficiency of long habit. Mary sat comparing two volumes of agricultural reports, whilst Kitty sketched a new design for the kitchen garden. Even Lydia, normally restless at an early hour, was occupied with copying measurements from their mother's household book.

"Sir William called yesterday," Mrs Bennet announced, accepting her tea from Jane. "He brings intelligence of Netherfield's new tenant."

"I am still amazed they finally found someone willing to tolerate those atrocious drainage problems." Elizabeth enquired, not looking up from her toast. "The lower fields have been flooding the lane to Meryton every spring. Not to mention the overflow in the autumn nearly to the kitchen garden."

Mrs Bennet gave Elizabeth a quelling look. "A Mr Bingley has taken it. Sir William says he means to arrive before Michaelmas."

"That gives poor Mrs Nichols barely a fortnight to make the house habitable," Jane said. "Cook says her sister, the charwoman at Lucas Lodge, heard the roof needs considerable work. The attics might be water damaged."

"He brings a substantial income, they say. And a party from London." Mrs Bennet continued.

"Then he can well afford to be a proper landlord," said Mary, marking her place with a finger. "These reports show the damage poor drainage can do to neighbouring properties. He ought to be a responsible member of the neighbourhood..."

"A young, single gentleman," Mrs Bennet added with studied care, watching her daughters' reactions.

"Poor man," said Elizabeth with a slight smile. "Already the neighbourhood must be arranging his future. How many eligible young ladies between here and London will be throwing themselves in his path?"

"Lizzy," Jane reproved gently. "We must not prejudge him."

"Lady Lucas will put her girls forward directly," Lydia predicted with a worldly air that sat oddly on her fifteen years. "Charlotte said Maria has a new blue gown made up."

"It signifies very little to us," said Kitty practically. "Since Grandfather cannot call, we shall not be among his earliest acquaintance."

"But Sir William has offered to convey our good wishes when he pays his respects," Mrs Bennet said. "He understands our situation."

"Sir William is all kindness," Jane murmured. "Although I wish we did not require his accommodation."

Elizabeth glanced at her sister. "It is not ideal, but we cannot alter it. And truly, what signifies a new neighbour when compared to the south field drainage? Which, Mamma, Grandfather insists must be addressed before--"

"Before the frost, yes. I have not forgotten." Mrs Bennet glanced at her daughters in turn, then unfolded a letter. "Mr Collins writes again."

A brief silence fell over the breakfast table. Even Lydia's pencil stopped scratching.

Elizabeth set down her toast. Her appetite quite fled. "What does our esteemed cousin require this time?"

"He expresses his deep solicitude for Grandfather's health," she began, with her brows lifted in incredulity. Mrs Bennet's tone remained, even though her fingers appeared to tighten on the paper. "He enquires whether we have considered his suggestion about engaging a male steward."

"The cost of the steward he suggested would consume nearly half the estate's annual income," Mary said, closing her agricultural report. "And would hardly know the estate's needs as well as we do after five years' management."

"Besides which," added Jane quietly, "Grandfather would never accept it."

"No, indeed." Mrs Bennet folded the letter with precise movements. "Sir William and Mr Phillips have both offered their opinion that the estate has never been better managed. Even Lady Lucas remarked upon the improvement in the home farm's yields."

"Yet Mr Collins persists in believing six women are unable to balance household accounts," Elizabeth said. Her voice held more weariness than bitterness. "I warrant he has never balanced a ledger in his life."

"It signifies little what Mr Collins believes," said Jane, ever diplomatic. "So long as our neighbours continue their support. Sir William's kindness has been invaluable."

"Although I wish Charlotte need not always make excuses for why her mother cannot invite us to their musical evenings," Kitty remarked, adding another neat line to her garden sketch. "As though we might forget our position without reminders."

"Lady Lucas means well," Mrs Bennet said, "but she has her own daughters to consider. And with Maria just turned sixteen…"

"She fears our situation might taint her daughters' prospects," Elizabeth finished. "As though misfortune were catching."

"Like a fever," Lydia added with a grimace. "Although I notice they were glad enough of our advice when their roses developed rust spots."

"Lydia," Jane remonstrated, "they have been kinder than many. And Sir William's friendship has protected us from worse gossip."

"Indeed," said Mrs Bennet. "We must remember that most of our neighbours have treated us with great consideration, given the peculiarity of our situation. The Longs still call regularly, and Mrs Goulding always includes us in her garden parties."

"Where we are seated with the dowagers and spinsters," Kitty muttered.

"Better that than not invited at all," Mary pointed out. "And they do purchase our preserves and honey, which adds to the household income."

Elizabeth's expression softened as she regarded her younger sister. Mary had developed a remarkable head for business these past years, tracking every penny that came in from their various small enterprises. At eighteen, she managed the still room and poultry sales with an efficiency their father's grandmother would have approved.

"And yet," Mrs Bennet spoke with composed deliberation, "we cannot depend forever on neighbourly kindness. Mr Collins's letter, unwelcome as it may be, reminds us that our position here is not permanently secured."

"Unless one of us makes a brilliant match," Lydia suggested with a trace of flippancy. "Perhaps this Mr Bingley will prove our salvation."

"Lydia," Elizabeth began, but their mother interrupted.

"We shall secure our position through competent management and careful stewardship," Mrs Bennet said firmly. "Just as we have these years past. Although I will not deny that advantageous marriages would provide security, we cannot rely upon the mercy of chance to ensure our happiness." She rose from the table. "Now, Jane, you must see to the laundry accounts, and Elizabeth, your grandfather, will expect you in the study at ten. Mary, Kitty, did not Hill mention something about the quince preserves?"

As her sisters dispersed to their various duties, Elizabeth lingered over her cold tea. The arrival of yet another of Mr Collins's letters had cast a shade of despondency over their morning, yet Elizabeth considered Lydia's jest about Mr Bingley with more serious purpose. How would a new neighbour of consequence alter the delicate balance of local society? If he proved a responsible landlord, the improvements to Netherfield would prove salutary to all the surrounding estates. More significantly for the Bennets, his arrival would reveal how their neighbours chose to present the Bennet family to newcomers. Elizabeth considered, with no small degree of vexation, that their reception by Mr Bingley might well determine how the neighbourhood should regard them. Her fingers tightened around her teacup as Charlotte's words from yesterday echoed in her mind: "Mr Bingley's circle will reset the social order in Meryton." The implication had been clear enough—their position rested upon the most uncertain foundation. Would this stranger's judgement turn the balance further against them? Elizabeth set her cup down with more force than intended, causing the tea to slosh over the rim. Jane glanced up, her eyebrow raised in silent question. They shared the horror of being regarded as five unfortunate spinsters in the making, awaiting their cousin's eventual succession to the estate.

If only Grandfather were well enough to make that first, crucial call upon Netherfield's new master. When his health had permitted him to venture into the neighbourhood, his very presence had served as a reminder that Longbourn remained under the guidance of its rightful master, not merely maintained until some gentleman should take charge. His commanding figure, though latterly supported by a walking stick, had carried the authority of five decades of land management. Now, with Grandfather largely confined to his book-room by his increasing infirmity, the ladies of Longbourn were subject to scrutiny that bordered on impertinence.

Chapter Three

The bell above Mr Brown's shop door jangled as Elizabeth and Jane entered the cobbler's establishment. The familiar smell of leather and polish greeted them, along with the rhythmic tap-tap of Mr Brown's hammer from the back workroom. It was their regular quarterly visit to settle the Longbourn accounts—a task that had once been Grandfather's responsibility, but that the sisters now managed themselves.

"Mr Brown?" Elizabeth called, placing her reticule on the counter. Jane moved to examine a display of shoe buckles, her fingers lightly tracing the silver designs.

The tapping ceased abruptly. A moment later, the cobbler emerged, wiping his hands on his leather apron. His expression shifted subtly when he saw them—the polite smile not quite reaching his eyes. Elizabeth noted how different this reception was from the effusive welcome he had once given their grandfather.

"Miss Bennet. Miss Elizabeth," he acknowledged with a short nod. "I was wondering when someone from Longbourn might appear."

"We have come to settle our quarterly account as we always do on quarter day. Midsummer day is Tuesday next," Elizabeth said, her brow furrowed at the tradesman's cheek. She reached into her reticule for the household ledger. "I believe the amount was seven shillings and sixpence for the work these past three months."

Mr Brown drew himself up, not meeting her eyes as he reached beneath his counter for his own record book. The leather-bound volume showed wear at the corners, stained with the marks of his trade.

"That was the amount," he said slowly, turning pages with a deliberate motion. "However, there are now additional considerations."

Elizabeth's fingers stilled on her own book. "Additional considerations, Mr Brown? I have the detailed accounting here of all services rendered—Grandfather's boots resoled, new half-soles for my sisters and mother, and the repair to Cook's walking shoes."

"Yes, well," the cobbler said, adjusting his spectacles, "leather prices have risen considerably. The work on your grandfather's boots required additional attention."

Jane moved closer to the counter, her expression mild but her eyes sharp. "My sister and I examined the boots ourselves, Mr Brown. They required standard resoling, which was quoted at five shillings."

"With all due respect, Miss Bennet," Mr Brown said, his look suggesting he felt very little was due, "a lady's understanding of leatherwork is necessarily limited. The quality of work required for a gentleman's riding boots—"

"Is precisely what we specified, and have always specified," Elizabeth interjected, her voice cool but steady. She noted the slight reddening of the man's neck, the way his fingers tightened on his ledger. "The same quality of work you have provided Longbourn for the past fifteen years, at the established rates."

"Times change, Miss Elizabeth," Mr Brown replied, his voice taking on a patronising tone that set Elizabeth's teeth on edge. "And with Mr Bennet so rarely seen about, certain… adjustments must be made for the risk involved."

"Risk, Mr Brown?" Jane asked, her voice gentle but her eyes suddenly sharp.

The cobbler shifted uncomfortably. "Well, with no gentleman overseeing the accounts—"

"I see," Elizabeth said, closing her ledger with a decisive snap. The action drew Mr Brown's startled gaze. "You fear we may not honour Longbourn's debts because no male hand guides our pen. Is that your meaning, sir?"

Mr Brown's face flushed more deeply. "I simply meant that without proper—"

"Longbourn has settled our accounts in full, promptly each quarter for since my father's death and a century before that," Elizabeth continued, her voice level despite the indignation burning in her chest. "Not once has Longbourn failed to honour its commitments to Meryton's tradesmen. Yet you now suggest an additional…what was it? Consideration?"

"Three shillings," he mumbled, not meeting her eyes.

"Three shillings above the usual price," Elizabeth repeated, letting the unreasonableness of the amount hang in the air. "Nearly half again the cost."

Jane leant forward; her voice was soft but carrying clearly in the small shop. "Mr Brown, my sister manages Longbourn's accounts with the same rigour our father and grandfather always employed. Any… irregularities would be noted not only in our books but in the quarterly review our grandfather and our Uncle Phillips conduct of the estate's finances. Sir William approves their work."

The mention of Sir William—a customer whose social standing far exceeded Longbourn's—caused the cobbler's expression to falter.

"Perhaps," Jane continued with a smile that somehow managed to be both kind and unyielding, "you might consult your previous records? The rate has been consistent for three years.

Elizabeth opened her reticule again and withdrew a slip of paper. "I have here your own invoice from last quarter, in your hand, Mr Brown. The one you presented to me personally. The rate is identical to what we expected to pay today."

She placed it on the counter between them, the cobbler's scrawled figures facing him accusingly. Outside the window, Mrs Long slowed her pace, her curious gaze drawn to the scene within the shop.

Mr Brown's eyes darted to the window, then back to the Bennet sisters. Something in their steady gaze—Jane's gentle but unwavering, Elizabeth's sharp and direct—seemed to make him reconsider.

"There may have been … a misunderstanding," he said

finally, turning back several pages in his book. "Yes, I see the standard rate here. A confusion with another account, perhaps."

"Perhaps," Elizabeth agreed, making it clear she believed no such thing.

Mr Brown stiffened his posture. "Seven shillings and sixpence will be quite correct."

Elizabeth counted out the coins carefully, placing them on the counter one by one, the soft clink of metal on wood punctuating the uncomfortable silence. When she finished, she pushed them forward.

"Our receipt, if you please," she said, waiting as Mr Brown reluctantly wrote out the documentation with a scratching quill.

As he handed the paper over, a slight tremor shook his weathered fingers. "The boots will be ready next Tuesday for Longbourn," he added, now more deferential.

"Excellent. Miss Catherine will collect them," Elizabeth replied. "And Mr Brown, we value your craftsmanship and Longbourn's long association with your shop. May I expect our future dealings will remain as straightforward as they have been these past five years?"

The cobbler nodded stiffly, unable to meet her steady gaze.

As the sisters stepped back into Meryton's High Street, the autumn sun warming their faces, Jane released a small sigh. "That was … uncomfortable."

"But necessary," Elizabeth replied, tucking the receipt into her reticule. "If we allowed his 'considerations' to pass unchallenged, soon every merchant in Meryton would attempt the same."

"Still," Jane murmured, nodding politely to Mrs Long as they passed her, "I dislike confrontation."

"As do I," Elizabeth admitted, adjusting her bonnet against the breeze. "But Grandfather was right about one thing—respect in business must be earned continually. Even when one's hands lack the authority of a gentleman's signet ring."

She flexed her right hand consciously. Her father had always worn the Bennet family ring when conducting estate business. He used it to seal agreements and correspondence. When he passed, Grandfather put the ring away, unwilling to take it back. For Elizabeth, the gravity of that responsibility now rested on her shoulders instead, invisible but no less real. The Bennet ring was stored with Mamma's jewellery, never to be worn again.

"We still need to stop at the milliner's for Lydia's ribbon," Jane reminded her, eager to move past the unpleasantness.

"Indeed. And I expect no 'additional considerations' there," Elizabeth replied with a small smile. "Mrs Hilliard has five daughters of her own to support. She understands our position better than most."

As they continued down the High Street, Mr Brown appeared at his shop door, watching them with a thoughtful expression. She lifted her chin, meeting his gaze directly before turning away. Small victories, she reminded herself, were still victories. And in their current circumstances, even maintaining the status quo required constant vigilance.

They were, after all, gentlewomen who had taken on the direction of an estate–a task that the neighbourhood, and society at large, believed rightly belonged to a man, preferably one who had been to university and knew how to shoot game birds. That they did so under the supervision of an elderly grandfather now rarely seen, even at church services, only added to the general sense of impropriety. Elizabeth recalled with particular displeasure how certain ladies would pause in their conversation as the Bennet sisters passed, only to resume their whispered observations once they believed themselves out of earshot. It was as though by taking up their responsibilities they had somehow shed their status as a gentleman's daughters. Even Mrs Long, who had been among their mother's particular friends, now regarded them with a mixture of pity and uncertainty that Elizabeth found far more galling than outright censure.

Not all the citizens of Meryton were so critical. Sir William Lucas, in his role as the village's most prominent citizen, did his best to smooth their path, but even his hearty endorsements carried a measure of concern that vexed Elizabeth considerably. "Capital!" he would exclaim, upon hearing of their latest agricultural improvements. "Capital indeed! I am amazed that you ladies manage so well without … well, it is capital indeed."

The Bennet sisters might be anomalies in the eyes of society, but in the practical matters of Longbourn's survival, they were proving their worth.

Elizabeth had overheard Mrs Harrington tutting to Mrs Long over tea, "not quite the thing." The phrase, delivered with such delicate emphasis, seemed to capture perfectly their uncomfortable position: neither genteel young ladies waiting decorously for marriage, nor tenant farmers who knew their place in the social order. They existed in a liminal space that the neighbourhood had not yet learnt to navigate. Was it possible that Mr Bingley's arrival might provide some improvement to their uncertain status?

Should he choose to acknowledge them as gentlewomen, to call again at Longbourn and receive them at Netherfield, it would serve as a powerful signal to the neighbourhood. Should he instead treat them with the same uncertain distance that characterised their current social interactions, it would only confirm what many already whispered–that the Bennet sisters were to be pitied and tolerated until such time as "proper order" could be restored to Longbourn.

Elizabeth found her grandfather already at his desk, the morning light falling across the leather-bound ledgers. His eyes remained sharp behind his spectacles.

"I have received another letter from our dear cousin, Mr Collins," he said without preamble.

"From Mr Collins! And what can *he* have to say?" Elizabeth took her accustomed chair at his right hand. The position had been her father's once, she remembered. Before him, he had told her often, her Aunt Eleanor had sat there, helping to manage the estate.

"Full of unctuous concern for my health." His tone was dry. "And sage advice about the necessity of male guidance for the estate."

"He again suggests engaging a steward."

"He does indeed." Grandfather closed the ledger before him. "He has just the man in mind. This steward would report to him on all our decisions. Keep him informed of our methods and allow him to meddle before his time. Perhaps he would like to bear the expense himself rather than deplete the coffers of the estate to pay for his spy."

"I am certain he fears his inheritance may slip through our incompetent feminine fingers without a masculine hand to guide us. Might the steward he recommends be, by happy coincidence, his particular friend?"

Grandfather's lips twitched. "Your father's wit and Eleanor's sense. A formidable combination." He opened another ledger. "I wonder that our cousin does not consider the cost of a competent steward. Perhaps he believes it a worthwhile investment to halve our income to keep us from ruining his future prosperity altogether."

"His last letter to Mamma suggested we might prove more agreeable to his advice if we properly understood our feminine limitations." Elizabeth spoke lightly, but her grandfather's expression darkened.

"Did it indeed? What limitations might those be? The same ones your Aunt Eleanor suffered when she revolutionised our crop rotation? Or perhaps those your grandmother demonstrated whilst managing the farms during war years?" He shook his head. "Mr Collins sees what he expects to see. Like his father before him, he cannot comprehend that a woman's understanding might extend beyond ribbons and lace. The fool was insistent we sell that parcel near Oakham Mount, which is not even part of the estate in entail." Grandfather ran his finger down the column of figures. "The same land my father worked. The same methods my sister Eleanor helped refine, before…" He paused. "She had a unique gift for making even fools think themselves wise whilst guiding them to sensible action. Mr Collins would have gone on unknowingly following her advice whilst believing it was his own idea."

Elizabeth often heard tales of her aunt. Each one revealed a little more of the woman who had helped shape Longbourn's prosperity.

"When your grandmother died, Lizzy," her grandfather continued after a moment, "I thought the heart had gone out of this place. Your Aunt Eleanor proved me wrong. She breathed life into these chambers once more. Then, when we lost her…" He shook his head. "I feared your father would never recover his spirits. Yet he found your mother, and laughter returned to Longbourn once more. Your mother's happiness became his greatest object." His hand still rested on the ledger. "Now you and your sisters keep its heart beating. Mr Collins cannot understand that. He sees only what he wishes to."

"His February letter was most illuminating on that point," Elizabeth said. "Particularly his horror at learning Jane had negotiated the new lease for the Lodge."

"Ah yes. He felt certain we had been cheated." Grandfather selected another ledger from the neat row before him. "Show me the Lodge figures, my dear. I believe they will prove entertaining."

Elizabeth opened the book to a page marked with her own neat hand. "Jane secured terms a full ten percent above what Mr Morris initially offered."

"Just as your Aunt Eleanor would have done. She taught me early that a sweet smile and a sharp mind need not be enemies." Her grandfather adjusted his spectacles. "When your father was young, Eleanor insisted he learn every aspect of estate management. 'A man may have stewards,' she would say, 'but he must understand the work himself.' I have attempted to instil the same principle in you girls."

"Although I doubt Aunt Eleanor imagined her lessons would be put to such use by her great-nieces."

"Perhaps not. But she would have approved." He gestured to the page. "Now, speaking of lessons, explain to me how you calculated the projected yields for next year. Mr Collins's last letter contained several suggestions about crop choices that display his comprehensive ignorance of both agriculture and arithmetic."

Elizabeth suppressed a smile. "He did seem particularly concerned about our decision to expand the sheep fold. We 'ought not interfere in nature's plan for expansion of the herds.'"

"As he was about the new drainage scheme last year, and the hop fields the year before," her grandfather said drily. "Each time predicting disaster, each time proved wrong by the results." He patted the ledger. "Facts and figures, my dear. They speak louder than any gentleman's assumptions."

"I believe his latest objection stems from learning that Mary oversaw the hop fields." Elizabeth turned to the relevant pages. "He seems to feel it an unfeminine pursuit for a young lady of eighteen."

"Ah yes. It is far better she spend her time on fancy work and fashion plates." Grandfather's eyes gleamed with remembered mischief. "Although he was notably silent after receiving our accounts showing the profits from last year's harvest. Mary is adept at such calculations, is she not?

"As you knew she would when you set her to studying agricultural reports at thirteen."

"I provided the opportunity. The interest was her own." He smiled. "Just as Kitty's eye for design revealed itself in garden planning, and Lydia's enthusiasm found its proper channel in animal husbandry. Given room to grow, young minds will seek their natural direction."

"Although I doubt Mr Collins would approve of Lydia's expertise with the breeding lines of our sheep."

"Mr Collins would have us all behaving according to his narrow understanding of propriety. I have seen too many capable women dismissed by foolish men," he said quietly. "Your grandmother. Your aunt. Even your mother, whom some called merely a pretty face with a ready laugh. All of them proved their worth, given the chance. I mean to ensure you, and your sisters have that same chance, whatever Mr Collins may write in his letters. Thank Heaven your father had the sense to marry a woman of practical intelligence, whatever the gossips might have said about her youth and high spirits. She rose to every challenge with Thomas's affection and support. Your mother's management these past years has proved her worth."

Beside them half listening as she checked calculations, Kitty bent over the garden plans beside Grandfather's chair, her formerly ink-stained fingers now protected by the cunning half-gloves Mamma had devised. "For a lady must maintain her appearance even whilst maintaining her estate," as she so often declared. The afternoon sun caught the practical yet elegant fabric, one of many small ways their mother had helped them meet their responsibilities and maintain their social position.

"Mamma would be mortified if we sent out last year's yield calculations without fully accounting for the new drainage work," Kitty said, looking up from her figures with a grin. "She would tell me I was throwing away our bargaining position with the grain merchants."

"Indeed, I would!" came their mother's voice from the doorway, where she had paused in her daily rounds. "I do not forget how well the vegetable yields have done since you implemented your new methods. I want him to fully appreciate that my daughters are not playing at estate management."

Grandfather's expression held both pride and amusement as he regarded his daughter-in-law. Where once she had chattered about officers and wealthy bachelors for her daughters, Mrs Bennet now proudly introduced them as "my Jane, who has such a way with the tenant farmers" or "my Kitty, who has doubled our kitchen gardens."

"Your mother," he said, adjusting his spectacles, "has developed quite a talent for estate matters herself. I believe she drives a harder bargain with the merchants than any of you."

Elizabeth smiled at the observation. Their mother's expertise in household management had expanded to encompass the larger concerns of the estate. Her circle of acquaintance now served to keep them informed of market prices and neighbouring estates' innovations, whilst her talent for social manoeuvring helped smooth the way for her daughters' unconventional roles.

"Now, speaking of business," Grandfather tapped the page

Kitty had been studying, "What did you say about tracking weather patterns against our previous harvests?"

Kitty launched into her explanation with quiet confidence, supported by both her grandfather's wisdom and her mother's fierce pride. They had come a long way since the days following Papa's loss. Then, Mamma barely left her bed, so distraught she could not manage to order a meal. Grandfather insisted that they would manage the estate together, and they had found purpose in the work.

He closed the ledger. "Now then. Show me the arrangements for the south field. And you might tell me what you think of young Robinson's suggestions about the water course. I find I value your opinion on such matters quite as much as I once valued Eleanor's."

From Elizabeth's perspective, no higher praise could be given.

Chapter Four

Elizabeth stood at the stone marker that separated Longbourn from Netherfield lands, frowning at the water pooling around its base. The recent rains had overwhelmed the old water system, and now their improved south field was sending excess water directly onto Netherfield's lower meadow. Not, she reflected, the most neighbourly way to introduce themselves to Mr Bingley.

She had walked out early, hoping to devise a solution before the problem grew worse. Her grandfather reminded her that water flow required careful observation, and the morning light showed the problem most clearly. So intent was she upon measuring the depth with a fallen branch that she did not notice the approaching rider until his horse's hooves sounded on the path just across from her.

"Madam." The tall elegantly dressed gentleman's voice held modulated concern. "Are you in distress? These paths can be treacherous after rain."

Elizabeth straightened, mud on her boots forgotten as she met his grave expression. She recognised him immediately as the sort of well favoured, wealthy gentleman who believed every woman required rescue from the smallest inconvenience.

"You are very kind, sir, but I am quite well. I am simply observing how the water gathers here."

His eyebrows rose. "Water courses? Surely such matters are better left to…" He paused, apparently seeking a polite way to say, 'men who know about such things.'

"To someone with experience in estate management?" Elizabeth suggested pleasantly. "I assure you, sir, I am quite capable of measuring water depth without requiring rescue."

The early sun illuminated Mr Darcy's impressive figure, his

fine London coat fitting in a way that suggested nature had favoured him as much as his tailor. The sharp line of his jaw tightened with disapproval, finding it oddly compelling despite his evident censure.

"These paths are treacherous after the rain," he said, his voice rich despite its clipped accent. Elizabeth's brow rose without thought. He undoubtedly believed himself the very model of gentlemanly attention. "A lady should not venture here alone." His gaze dropped pointedly to her mud-spattered hem.

Elizabeth felt her cheeks grow warm, although whether from irritation or awareness of his scrutiny, she could not say. "How fortunate then, that I am quite accomplished at navigating treacherous ground," she replied, lifting her chin. The movement drew her eyes to his face, which managed to be both stern and to retain something pleasant about his mouth when he spoke. "Whilst I appreciate your concern, sir, I have particular reason to understand this water flow."

He shifted in his saddle, then she thought, he appeared to come to some decision. Dismounting, he tethered his horse and approached the marker. "At least allow me to guide you to more suitable terrain," he said, extending his arm with a courteous gesture in sharp contrast with the judgement still evident in his expression.

Elizabeth hesitated, compelled to consider how a gentleman could manage to be simultaneously so attractive, and so insufferable.

"What I am attempting to explain, sir," Elizabeth said with greater volume and diminishing patience, "is that our improved south field drainage appears to be flooding yonder meadow, which now belongs to Mr Bingley. As I have some responsibility in the matter, I would prefer to comprehend the extent of the matter myself."

That caught his attention. "You have responsibility for flooding at Netherfield?"

"I have responsibility for Longbourn," she corrected.

"I am Mr Darcy of Pemberley," he announced with magnificent hauteur. "Mr Bingley's intimate friend and adviser in estate matters. And you are?"

"Contemplating," said Elizabeth sweetly, "how best to

inform you that whilst you have been offering to rescue me from the mud, you have been speaking to the person responsible for designing the drainage works that created it."

He stared at her, his expression shifting from gallant concern to confusion. "I beg your pardon?"

"I am Elizabeth Bennet of Longbourn, sir." She indicated the water's path with her branch, "Which is the estate bordering Netherfield causing this flood to descend onto our neighbour's fields. And whilst I appreciate your concern for my welfare, I am rather more concerned with how our drainage channel appears to be introducing a water flow that is overwhelming this meadow. Unless, of course, you might swoon if addressed by a lady on matters of drainage?"

He paused, visibly reordering his assumptions. "You speak of drainage with unexpected… familiarity."

"Unexpected in a lady, you mean?" Elizabeth kept her tone light, though she noted his discomfort with some satisfaction. "You may depend upon it, sir, water flows with equal predictability regardless of whether a man or woman observes it."

"You mentioned improvements to the south field?"

"Yes. We implemented this channel last spring." Elizabeth indicated the water's path. "It has proved most effective for Longbourn's fields, although perhaps too effective, as you see."

"We?"

She was certain he suggested he imagined she meant some male relative had done the actual design work.

"My grandfather, my sisters, and I. Although I must credit my Aunt Eleanor's original notes on water management. Her observations from the wet spring of 1783 proved remarkably useful when we designed the works."

Darcy stood quite still, studying her with an intensity that might have been discomfiting had Elizabeth not been so amused by his obvious mental struggle.

"You have studied water management?"

"Among other aspects of estate maintenance. Of late

drainage has become something of a particular interest. One might say it flows naturally from other concerns." She smiled at her own small jest.

A reluctant answering smile touched his lips before he caught himself. "And your grandfather encourages such studies?"

"He insists upon them. Although perhaps you find it all highly irregular."

"I…" He glanced at the water, then back at her face. "I find myself reconsidering certain notions I had previously held." He stepped closer to examine the marker. "Would you explain your observations about the water flow?"

Elizabeth noted that he seemed truly attentive to her explanation, asking several intelligent questions about gradient and soil composition. His obvious understanding made his initial condescension somehow even more vexing, yet she enjoyed their discussion, nonetheless.

"Your solution seems sound in theory," he said finally. "Although the implementation may prove challenging."

"Do you always phrase your agreement so cautiously, Mr Darcy?"

His eyes met hers, and she was surprised to see genuine warmth there. "Only when my entire understanding of a situation has been thoroughly overthrown in the space of a quarter hour."

"Then perhaps I might overthrow it further by suggesting that the gradient here closely resembles one my Aunt Eleanor addressed at Longbourn's north corner. She devised a flow of stepped channels that reduced the water's force whilst directing it to where it might prove beneficial rather than destructive."

Darcy's expression sharpened with interest. "Stepped channels? Similar to the Roman aqueduct principle?"

"Precisely so. Although on a much humbler scale, naturally. When the water falls in stages, it carries less silt with it than water flowing directly downhill. She disguised the channels with plantings to maintain the land's aesthetic appeal."

"At Pemberley, we faced a similar challenge with runoff from the higher grounds." His voice had lost some of its earlier censure as he stepped closer, the morning air carrying the gentleman's scent. His hand elegantly gestured indicating the slope of the land. "Our solution involved a series of collection pools feeding into the ornamental lake."

"Ah, but you have the advantage of a lake to feed. Here we must consider…" Elizabeth's words faltered as he bent to examine the water flow she was indicating, bringing his broad shoulders level with her gaze. She forced her attention back to the matter at hand.

"Yes?" The quiet prompt carried genuine curiosity that softened his customary hauteur.

"We must consider the meadow's intended use." Elizabeth was pleased to find her voice steady, despite the warmth that crept up her neck when he straightened to his full height beside her. "Mr Bingley may wish to graze sheep here, in which case too much water retention would be detrimental to the health of the flock."

His eyebrows rose, and Elizabeth felt a flutter of satisfaction at having surprised him. "You are knowledgeable in the care of sheep as well?"

"My youngest sister would be horrified to hear you question it." Elizabeth allowed herself a small smile, noting how he watched her expression. "She manages our flocks and takes particular pride in our breeding lines. But regarding the drainage - what is your opinion on clay channels versus stone?"

"Stone proves more durable, although the initial expense is greater." As he surveyed the area, the sunlight brought out the strong lines of his face. His posture brought to mind a Roman statue she had once lingered over—elegant, unadorned, and quietly arresting—although she flushed at the thought and nearly missed his next comment.

"The soil here appears to have significant clay content naturally. Have you observed any shifting in wet weather?" He turned toward her, and she glanced away, hoping he did not catch the flush she felt on her cheeks.

"Some, although less than one might expect." His attention

had shifted fully to their discussion, his earlier disapproval forgotten in their shared interest. "My grandfather attributes it to the underlying chalk bed. We discovered its extent when sinking the new well two years ago."

Darcy nodded. "That would provide stability. At Pemberley…" He caught himself. "But perhaps you would find it tiresome to hear about another estate's water management."

"On the contrary, sir. Sound principles of drainage remain sound regardless of their location. Pray continue." Elizabeth turned back to catch a small smile cross his face.

She shook herself. Pure folly, of course—she might as well admire a painting in a gallery. Gentlemen of his consequence did not seriously consider impoverished gentlewomen who spent their mornings measuring drainage ditches, no matter how well they understood water management. Still, she thought with private amusement, if one must discuss soil composition with anyone, it might as well be with a remarkably fine figure of a man.

"If we were to begin the stepped channels here," he indicated a spot several yards up the slope, "the natural contour of the land would aid our purpose."

"We?" Elizabeth raised an eyebrow at his presumption, although she had to acknowledge the merit of his suggestion. "No doubt Mr Bingley's friend has better occupations than helping his neighbour's granddaughter plan drainage solutions."

His grave expression flickered again with something like amusement. "You may be certain, Miss Bennet, I take a pointed interest in practical improvements. At Pemberley--" He stopped himself. "No doubt you have already divined my tendency to speak of my estate at the smallest provocation."

"As any proper landowner should." Elizabeth drew a rough sketch in her notebook, adding measurements. "I suspect your collection pools at Pemberley are rather grander than what we might attempt here."

"Good principles of design need not depend upon grand execution." He moved closer to observe her sketch. "If you angle the first channel thus--" His gloved hand reached toward her notebook, then withdrew. "That is, if you would permit the suggestion…"

"I am not so proud as to reject sound advice, Mr Darcy, regardless of its source." She adjusted the angle on her sketch. "Although I must consult my grandfather before proceeding. His experience with this land spans fifty years."

"A valuable resource indeed." He straightened, resuming his more formal bearing. "Might I enquire… that is, would your grandfather be willing to discuss the broader implications of these improvements? As Bingley's friend, I take an interest in Netherfield's management."

Elizabeth suppressed a smile at his careful phrasing. No doubt he found it awkward to request a meeting through a lady he had discovered measuring mud depth. "I shall convey your interest, sir. Although I should mention that my grandfather's health does not permit him to receive visitors regularly."

"Ah." He looked momentarily discomposed. "What would you recommend then…"

"He would be pleased to speak with you if he is able. I generally review such matters with him each morning at ten in his study." The invitation slipped from her lips before she could fully grasp its implications, and a warmth crept up her neck. "That is, if it would not be beneath your dignity to discuss estate management with a lady present. Or more likely, several ladies."

The transformation of his countenance fascinated her. His mask of aristocratic reserve melted away, replaced by something more enigmatic - a subtle softening around his eyes, a slight quirk at the corner of his mouth that signalled amusement, or perhaps something warmer. He released a fraction of the tension in his jaw as he considered her words. His dark gaze held hers for a moment too long to be entirely correct, and she felt an inexplicable flutter in her chest.

"Miss Bennet," he said, with such an intimate note that her breath caught, "you have thoroughly disabused me of any notion that estate management should be the exclusive province of gentlemen."

He bowed formally, but there was nothing formal in his look. "I would be honoured to contribute to your deliberations." His elegant fingers flexed at his sides as he straightened, as though reaching for something - or someone. The thought sent an unexpected shiver down her spine, one not borne of the morning's chill.

He mounted his horse with barely an effort and rode away. Elizabeth reflected that whilst Mr Darcy of Pemberley might be the last man in the world she could ever expect to marry, he might prove a useful resource in solving their drainage problems. Her grandfather would enjoy matching wits with him, at least.

Chapter Five

Darcy had risen with the larks, determined to inspect Netherfield's boundaries before Bingley eventually stirred from his bed. The autumn mist lay thick as wool upon the lower meadows, the damp air heavy with the scent of fallen leaves and wet earth. His mount's hooves made soft, sucking sounds in the sodden ground as he rode, rendering a thorough assessment of the estate's condition rather more challenging than he had anticipated.

That he was in Hertfordshire at all was an accident of chance and necessity. Bingley's letter had come six weeks prior, urging him to visit: "*You must come to Netherfield at once, Darcy. Caroline insists the estate requires your expertise, although I suspect she wishes to escape town when the season has ended. Do say you shall join us - I am quite at sea with all these agricultural matters.*"

Darcy had declined twice, citing urgent business at Pemberley. In truth, his reluctance stemmed from his sister's delicate condition. Georgiana's spirits had plummeted in the aftermath of her near catastrophe with Wickham, and her composure had given way to a melancholy that troubled him deeply. He had scarcely left her side in the months following the incident at Ramsgate.

"Brother, you must go to Mr Bingley," she had insisted one evening, her eyes downcast as her fingers moved listlessly across the pianoforte keys. "I know you have refused him twice on my account."

"Your wellbeing is my primary concern," he had answered, standing rigid by the instrument. He studied her closely. Was that a tremble? Did she not seem frailer?

Georgiana straightened and nearly met his eye. "That is precisely why you must go." Her voice, although soft, carried a singular firmness. "I am certain you are disappointed in me, although you are too kind to say it. I would prefer some solitude to reflect on my mistake." She had stumbled over the word, her fingers slipped from the keys.

"Georgiana, you are not to blame. I ought to have protected you, to tell you of the danger—I could never—"

"Please," she had interrupted, something she had never done before. "Mrs Annesley will attend me. Your hovering only reminds me daily of my foolishness. Mr Bingley needs you, and I," she had drawn a steadying breath, "I need to prove to myself that I can manage without your constant attention."

Her words had struck him with the force of a physical blow. That she could imagine he was disappointed in her, rather than in his own failure to protect her, was unbearable. And yet, perhaps distance would indeed serve them both. With great reluctance, he had acquiesced.

"*I shall attend you after Michaelmas*," Darcy had written finally to Bingley, duty to his friend and sister both overcoming his resistance. What he had not foreseen, however, was how thoroughly a chance encounter would disturb his composure and overthrow all his careful plans for the visit.

"Yet, Mr Darcy, the sheep did prosper remarkably well in this pasture," Miss Elizabeth had said, her eyes bright with barely concealed amusement at his evident surprise. "Perhaps you find it strange that a lady should speak of such matters?"

"Indeed not, Madam. I find it…" He had hesitated, watching the wind stir loose curls about her face. "…most uncommon."

"Uncommon? Or unseemly?" The arch of her brow had challenged him.

Now, as he rode back to Netherfield, the memory of her impertinent smile and remarkably fine eyes haunted him. Miss Elizabeth Bennet. He turned the name over in his mind, along with the disturbing recognition that he had behaved like a pompous fool. His thoughts drifted briefly to Georgiana—how different these two young women were. His sister, all gentle compliance and now wounded self-doubt, Miss Elizabeth, all confident opinions, and challenging wit. He wondered if some measure of the latter's spirit might benefit the former in her recovery.

"You see here, sir," she had said, opening her notebook with capable hands, "where the channel must be cut to drain the south field adequately." Her sketch had been precise, her understanding of gradient and construction thorough. The angle of the light had caught the intelligence in her eyes as she had explained her great aunt's innovations. His mind drifted from her cogent words to admiration of her graceful form.

"Your expertise does you credit, Miss Elizabeth," he had managed stiffly.

She had looked up at him with that same challenging smile. Without a word, she forced him to rethink his words, his prejudices, and his privilege.

His horse shifted beneath him now, sensing his distraction. Darcy realised he had drawn rein at the top of the rise, staring back toward Longbourn without conscious intention. From here he could see the south field she had mentioned, its careful drainage works evident even at this distance.

"Perhaps, Mr Darcy," her words echoed in his memory, "you might find that capability may exist even where you least expect to find it."

"I shall call tomorrow to speak with your grandfather about these improvements," he had told her, striving to maintain his dignity despite the mud clinging to his polished boots.

She looked up at him through her lashes, the very picture of genteel deference, save for the gleam in her eye. "How fortunate that my grandfather shall have the benefit of your expertise. Although I hope, sir, you will permit me to attend? I find myself quite unable to resist any conversation involving mud and mathematics."

The memory of his stammered response made him grip his reins more tightly. His mount tossed its head at the sudden pressure, the leather creaking in protest.

Caught between amusement and discomfiture, he was

uncertain whether he was being laughed at or laughed with. The wind caught at her spencer, and she adjusted it with an unconscious grace that made him forget, for a moment, that they were discussing drainage channels. A gentleman's daughter who understood property maintenance as well as any steward. Who had not simpered or flirted or shown the slightest indication that his consequence impressed her. Whose beauty rendered him quite unable to maintain his habitual aloofness in her presence.

"Your attendance would be…" He had paused, searching for a word that would neither condescend nor reveal too much. "Most instructive."

"Instructive." He caught the amusement in her eyes. "How proper of you, Mr Darcy. I warn you—if you mention Vitruvius' theories on hydraulics, my grandfather may keep you until supper. Are you prepared to defend your position on the relative merits of ancient versus modern methods?"

He fought an unexpected smile, his natural gravity wavering in the face of her jest. The wind stirred the surrounding leaves, bringing with it the scent of damp earth and autumn. He caught a sweet floral note and unconsciously leant forward towards its source.

Catching himself, he straightened up quickly, and he responded stiffly. "I bow to your superior knowledge of the danger, Madam. Although, Vitruvius would have approved of your careful attention to gradient."

"Mr Darcy! Nearly a compliment?" She caught her bonnet against the morning breeze, but not before he caught sight of lush dark hair. "I must mark this day in my almanack - a man of fashion deigning to discuss Roman architecture with a country miss." She had seemed more amused by his discomfort than awed by his position.

Tomorrow he would call at Longbourn—at a proper hour, naturally—to discuss water management. He would treat the situation exactly as he would a meeting with any steward or land agent, though he doubted any steward had ever possessed such fine eyes or such a penetrating way of seeing through his deliberately maintained façade of superiority.

The leather of his saddle creaked as he shifted uncomfortably at the memory. His sister Georgiana's latest letter lay in his pocket, its pages crackling with each movement. Perhaps Georgiana's new enthusiasm for mathematics might be applied to a new study of estate accounts. Such an occupation now seemed less a charming peculiarity and more… but no, he must not pursue that line of thought. But here, amid the autumn mist and mud, he had no ready category for this bewildering young lady.

The morning air grew heavier with moisture, promising rain. He touched his horse's flank, turning back toward Netherfield. The sooner he finished his inspection, the sooner he might review his own estate's water management. One should avoid being found wanting in practical knowledge when discussing such matters with a lady of evident expertise.

"Until tomorrow then, Mr Darcy," her parting words haunted him still. "Do come prepared for a most illuminating discussion of drainage channels." Her arch expression, her light and pleasing figure, her evident intelligence. It all shattered his expectations. In a London drawing room he would have attributed her wit to flirtation. His reason had no way of placing this young lady in his accustomed understanding of the world.

"Well met, Darcy! Already been out surveying my domain?" Bingley's cheerful voice greeted Darcy as he entered the breakfast room. "Tell me, did you find everything in proper order?"

Darcy hesitated. The drainage issue ought to be mentioned, yet he felt strangely reluctant to discuss the circumstances of its discovery. "There are some matters requiring attention. The lower meadow--"

"Charles, you cannot imagine how tedious it is here without decent company." Miss Bingley spoke over him, as she swept into the room, her carrot orange morning dress an assault upon the eyes. "Mr Darcy, how fortunate that you have returned. I was telling my brother that a man of your understanding must find our local society quite beneath notice."

"I have not begun to make the acquaintance of the neighbourhood," Darcy replied stiffly, accepting tea from the footman.

"Acquaintance?" Miss Bingley's eyebrows rose. "You cannot possibly have encountered anyone of consequence on your morning ride. I am told the local gentry are quite…" She paused delicately. "Provincial."

"Come now, Caroline," Bingley protested. "Sir William Lucas called yesterday and seemed a pleasant enough fellow. And he spoke of several good families in the area."

"Did he?" Miss Bingley settled herself where she might best display her figure to advantage. "I suppose there might be one or two acceptable connections. Although I cannot imagine anyone of real cultivation residing so far from town. Mr Darcy, you must find it vastly different from the society you enjoy in Derbyshire."

Darcy recalled the skilled way Miss Elizabeth Bennet had sketched the water channel gradient. There had been more genuine cultivation in that simple demonstration than in all of Caroline Bingley's practised accomplishments.

"The neighbourhood appears to have some interesting features," he said.

"Oh! You must tell us what you observed on your ride." Miss Bingley leant forward eagerly, displaying what she undoubtably imagined to be an expression of intelligent interest. "Although I cannot imagine what could interest a man of your discernment in these rural byways."

"Primarily drainage concerns," Darcy said shortly, then turned to Bingley. "The lower meadow shows signs of water accumulation. You may wish to consider improvements before spring."

"Drainage!" Miss Bingley's horror suggested he had mentioned something impossibly vulgar. "Dear Mr Darcy, you cannot mean to discuss such matters at breakfast. Are there not more elegant topics? I long to hear your opinion of the new exhibits at the

Royal Academy. I have been reading the most fascinating treatise on the Italian masters…"

Darcy doubted she had read any such thing. On the rare occasion when Miss Bingley encountered the written word, it was generally in the form of titles on fashion plates or gossip in the newspaper. Unbidden, his mind made a contrast with Miss Elizabeth Bennet's earnest interest in her subject. There had been no affected poses as she demonstrated the gradient with her branch. Even with mud on her hem, she had shown more natural elegance than Caroline Bingley would ever achieve with all her studied grace. Not, of course, that the comparison signified anything beyond his professional interest in estate management.

"But tell me about these drainage issues," Bingley interrupted his sister's artistic raptures. "Sir William mentioned something about innovations at Longbourn improving the local water management considerably. Their methods might be worth examining."

Darcy stiffened at the estate's name, but Miss Bingley was already speaking.

"Charles pray do not become obsessed with agricultural improvements before we have even properly settled. We are here to better our social standing, not to become farmers. Mr Darcy cannot wish to spend his entire visit discussing ditches better left to labourers."

"On the contrary," Darcy blurted, "a complete understanding of estate management is essential for any landowner. Technical knowledge need not preclude elegance of mind." He shook his head. Why had he permitted Miss Bingley to irritate him? He ought to remain silent.

"How fascinating," Miss Bingley drawled. "I am sure Mr Darcy's experience with estate management must vastly outshine any local knowledge."

Darcy took another sip of his now tepid tea to avoid a reply. He knew better than to engage with her. Let her imagine what she would. He had no intention of discussing his encounter with Miss Elizabeth Bennet until he had better categorised it in his own mind.

Even then, he did not wish to involve Miss Bingley in the conversation.

Miss Bingley continued her efforts to dominate all discourse at the table as Mr and Mrs Hurst joined the others in the breakfast room. Darcy arranged his features into a neutral expression and doggedly consumed his meal, all the while removing his mind from the premises. His thoughts drifted to convincing Bingley to go to Longbourn on the morrow, without revealing his utter confusion at the young lady he had encountered in the fields. Bingley was a sociable fellow, so likely it would not take much convincing, but it would be well to prepare him for the discussion of topics that were far from familiar.

"I cannot imagine you would wish to associate with them, Mr Darcy."

The mention of his name in Miss Bingley's strident voice broke through his contemplation.

"Pardon me, I was not attending. With whom?" Darcy spoke in the cool, detached manner he reserved for social-climbing mushrooms, not that Miss Bingley would notice.

"The neighbouring estate- Longwood or whatever its name is. It is, according to Mrs Harrington, occupied by a most unnatural collection of women, who run the farm like field hands, although they are supposed to have been born gentlewoman. Worse than bluestockings, they are labourers!" Miss Bingley's eyes flashed with a sort of hungry delight, as though denigrating some unknown local misses was the height of pleasure.

Darcy paused, fixing Miss Bingley with a cool stare. He reminded himself that he would not allow her to nettle him. His mind's eye conjured an image of Miss Bingley, knee deep in a drainage pool, her ostrich feathers wilting as she attempted to assess the water flow to Netherfield. He nearly smiled at the idea.

"I cannot image what possible harm might befall me should I encounter such ladies." His measured speech was at odds with the palpable sense of danger that had prickled his skin whilst he bantered with Miss Elizabeth Bennet. Perhaps not harm, but surely some manner of discomposure would attend the interactions.

Miss Bingley blinked and assumed a blank expression. Darcy imagined he could see some sort of mechanism rotating behind her eyes as she endeavoured to make sense of his remark. No doubt she wished to rail against his exposure to such unnatural creatures, but then might she appear to doubt his vigour? Should she suggest he would be somehow unmanned by women who understood that their dinner did not walk into the kitchen fully prepared, but that there was effort involved in the production of vegetables, grains, and beasts? Miss Bingley would no more consider the many labours that brought her fricassee to her plate than she would take a branch and measure the water level and silt in….

Darcy dragged himself back to the present. Miss Bingley appeared to be about to resume her diatribe- he rapidly rose, setting his serviette on the table.

"Would you be so kind as to join me in the library, Bingley? I have some information about the matter I was speaking of earlier which you ought to hear."

Darcy followed Bingley into the library, closing the door firmly behind them. The room was well stocked with shelves if not with volumes. The crackle of the fire made a stark contrast to the clatter of breakfast and Miss Bingley's ceaseless chatter. Bingley, ever amiable, looked at Darcy with mild curiosity.

"I must tell you of an encounter I had whilst surveying the drainage issues." He paced before the fireplace, his boots silent on the thick carpet.

"Good God, Darcy, you look positively unsettled. Have you found the situation worse than expected?" Bingley's cheerful countenance showed genuine concern.

"No… not precisely worse. The drainage itself is quite manageable, although it will require cooperation with our neighbours at Longbourn. But it is the nature of those neighbours that I find… remarkable." Darcy paused, choosing his words with care. "The estate is run by five sisters, as your sister mentioned."

Bingley's eyebrows rose. "Truly? There must be a brother or

uncle…"

"There is a mother and a grandfather who I understand is quite elderly. But it appears that the sisters themselves tend to the estate. Before you echo your sister's sentiments, I should tell you they appear to be doing a creditable job of it."

Bingley leant forward, his curiosity piqued. "Caroline is rather vehement in her opinions. Some of the local people think their involvement in farm matters is… unseemly."

"The neighbourhood appears divided. Some, like your sister, view their labours on the estate as unseemly. Others…" Darcy recalled the respectful way Sir William referred to Miss Elizabeth, "seem to have accepted their unconventional approach. They maintain the appearance and manners of gentlewomen whilst possessing practical knowledge that most ladies of their station would consider beneath them."

Bingley's eyes twinkled with curiosity. "The Bennet ladies seem to be quite the topic of conversation with the neighbours. I have heard the eldest Miss Bennet praised as a great beauty. What have you heard of her?"

Darcy hesitated, choosing his words with care. He had not yet mentioned his encounter with Miss Elizabeth that morning, and he was not sure why he felt compelled to keep it to himself. "I have not heard much talk. From what I understand, the Misses Bennet are unconventional, but intelligent."

"Well, I for one am intrigued. Shall we ride over tomorrow morning?"

Darcy gave a curt nod, his expression unreadable. "I believe it would be… prudent to consider all available expertise. Mr Bennet's understanding of the land could be valuable. Although I have not yet had the pleasure of a proper introduction, I understand he is homebound. We would need to call at Longbourn to meet with him."

Bingley's smile widened. "Well, then, it is settled. We'll ride to Longbourn tomorrow and introduce ourselves. Who knows? Perhaps Miss Bennet will prove to be as incomparably handsome as the neighbourhood says. I must admit, I am rather curious to see for myself."

"Yes, tomorrow would be most suitable. Although perhaps we should prepare ourselves for a rather different sort of morning call than we are accustomed to making." Darcy chose his words with care. "Our primary concern should be the drainage issues. If we can work with Mr Bennet in resolving them, it would be of benefit to the entire community. The productivity of the land affects the local economy, after all."

Bingley nodded, his expression turning serious. "You are no doubt correct. It is the neighbourly thing to do. Perhaps our paying a call will put paid to some of the more unkind rumours about the Bennet ladies. It is a shame if their mere industriousness is met with such criticism."

Darcy's lips pressed into a thin line. "Very well. I shall make the necessary arrangements. And Bingley--" he paused, his voice taking on a quieter gravity, "--it would be wise to approach the matter cautiously. Your penchant for pretty faces is well known. Tread with care."

Bingley smiled, "Of course, Darcy. I will follow your lead."

As Bingley rose to leave, Darcy remained seated. He was not accustomed to feeling so… unsettled.

Chapter Six

The early autumn sun slanted through the windows of the small sitting room at Longbourn, casting golden patterns across the worn carpet. Kitty and Lydia had pushed aside the small table and chairs to create a makeshift dance floor in the limited space available. The carpet had been rolled away, leaving the scuffed floorboards free for their careful steps. They moved in careful patterns, counting steps under their breath.

"One-two-three, one-two-three," Kitty murmured, her brow furrowed in concentration as she worked to recall the order of steps of the allemande. "Was it right foot or left after the turn?"

"Left, surely," Lydia replied, demonstrating with a graceful step that belied her common occupation among the sheep pens. "Mrs Gardiner showed us last Christmas, do you not remember? She said the London version has an extra flourish at the corner."

They had been practising intermittently for three days, ever since hearing of Mrs Goulding's planned assembly from Charlotte Lucas. Between their regular duties—Kitty's work in the kitchen gardens and Lydia's with the livestock—they had seized every available moment to refresh the dancing skills that had grown sadly neglected with disuse.

"Do you think many gentlemen will attend?" Kitty asked, adjusting the worn ribbon she had pinned to her everyday dress to simulate evening attire. "Charlotte said her cousin from London was visiting—a lieutenant in the militia!"

"An officer!" Lydia's eyes sparkled with remembered enthusiasm. "Perhaps we will have another regiment quartered here. Was there not one some time ago?"

"Six years ago," Kitty sighed, executing a turn with more speed than grace. "After Papa died."

The brief shadow of memory passed quickly, overcome by

the excitement of potential festivities. No sister had attended a quarterly assembly in nearly two years—and that had been at Lady Lucas's annual summer gathering, where they had been relegated to the area where the dowagers and spinsters were gathered.

"I shall wear my blue muslin," Lydia declared, twirling to make the skirts of her work dress flare. "We can let out the seams a bit—I have grown since last summer."

"And I shall borrow Jane's cream ribbon for my hair," Kitty added, already envisioning herself in her best gown, which had been lovingly preserved for the rare social occasions they were included in. "Do you suppose Mamma will allow us rouge? Just the tiniest bit?"

"Miss Lydia! Miss Kitty!" Hill's voice interrupted their dancing as the housekeeper appeared in the doorway, basket of mending in hand. "Whatever are you about? Miss Mary has been looking for you these past twenty minutes. The quinces need sorting before they spoil."

"Just a moment more, Hill," Lydia pleaded, executing another turn. "We must perfect the steps before Mrs Goulding's assembly on Friday. It would not do to appear deficient in our figures."

Hill's expression shifted, a look passing across her weathered features that caught Kitty's attention. The housekeeper set down her basket slowly.

"Mrs Goulding's assembly? Oh, my dears…"

Something in her look caused both girls to stop their practice, turning to face the servant who had been with them since their births.

"What is it, Hill?" Kitty asked, apprehension creeping into her voice.

Hill smoothed her apron with work-worn hands. "I did not realise you had not heard. Miss Charlotte Lucas called again whilst you were in the fields with Mr Robinson." She hesitated, reluctant to continue.

"Heard what?" Lydia demanded, stepping forward with a frown.

"The invitations were delivered yesterday. Miss Lucas

mentioned it to Cook when she came for the preserves." Hill's kind eyes held genuine sympathy. "I fear Mrs Goulding's assembly is… that is to say, the invitations were quite selective this year."

Kitty's hand fluttered to her throat, the meaning instantly clear. "We were not invited."

"No, Miss," Hill confirmed gently. "Only Sir William's family and the Longs, and of course Mr Phillips and his wife. But not…" she trailed off.

"Not the 'unfortunate Bennet sisters,'" Lydia finished, her voice tight with hurt and anger. "Not the girls who smell of sheep and soil instead of rose water."

"I am sure it is not that, Miss," Hill protested, without conviction. "More likely it is because your grandfather's health does not permit attending, and Mrs Goulding thought—"

"She thought we would not notice being excluded," Kitty interrupted, sinking onto a chair, the ribbons she had pinned to her dress suddenly seeming childish and pathetic. "That we are too busy with gardens and livestock to care for dancing."

Lydia remained standing; her cheeks flushed with humiliation. At fifteen, she had spent more time in the past year discussing sheep breeding than sleeve fashions, but the eager light with which she had practised her dance steps revealed how deeply she still yearned for the normal pleasures of youth.

"We have been practising for nothing," she said, her voice cracking mournfully. She yanked the faded ribbon from her hair with a jerky movement. "What fools we must seem."

"Not fools at all," came Elizabeth's voice from the doorway. She had arrived unnoticed, Mary close behind her, both sisters pausing at the tableau before them. "What has happened?"

Hill explained quietly, whilst Kitty stared at her lap and Lydia paced the small room like a restless animal, pride and disappointment warring in her expression.

"I see," Elizabeth said, exchanging a look with Mary that spoke volumes. "Hill, perhaps you might inform Cook that Miss Kitty will be delayed in sorting the quinces."

When the housekeeper had departed, Elizabeth pulled a chair next to Kitty's and sat down, taking her sister's hand. "I am sorry you learnt of it this way."

"Did you know of it?" Lydia demanded, turning to face her elder sisters. "Did you know we were excluded whilst we practised our steps like children playing make-believe?"

"We had word of it only this morning. You were out of doors, and we intended to tell you when we returned," Mary said, her typically pragmatism softened by genuine compassion. "Charlotte mentioned it when she came. She seemed… ill at ease."

"As well she might!" Lydia exclaimed, dashing angry tears from her eyes with the back of her hand. "We are still gentlemen's daughters, are we not? Whatever our circumstances, we deserve the common courtesy of—"

"Of course you do," Elizabeth interrupted gently. "The slight is not against your character or worth, but a reflection of society's discomfort with our out of the ordinary situation."

"Society!" Kitty's quiet despair had begun transforming into indignation. "As if we chose to lose Papa, to have Grandfather fall ill. As if we would not trade all our knowledge of crops and livestock for one year of being normal girls with normal prospects!"

The raw honesty of her outburst silenced the room. Mary, who had prided herself on accepting their altered circumstances with philosophical detachment, looked stricken at her younger sister's pain.

"What is happening here?" Mrs Bennet's voice preceded her into the room, her quick eyes taking in the scene—Kitty's tear-stained face, Lydia's angry posture, and her elder daughters' concerned expressions.

"Mrs Goulding's party," Elizabeth explained quietly. "The girls have just learnt we were not included in the invitations."

Their mother's face registered a complex series of emotions—indignation, hurt, and a deep maternal sorrow for her daughters' pain. She moved to Kitty's side, smoothing her hair with a gentle hand.

"My poor dears," she murmured. "How unkind of Augusta Goulding. After I advised her on preserving those strawberries last month, too." She straightened with sudden indignation. "And to think how I praised her unfortunate new turban at the milliner's! An absolute monstrosity if ever I saw one, perched upon her head like some exotic creature had roosted there."

This unexpected description startled a watery laugh from Kitty.

"Mamma!" Jane admonished, although her lips twitched.

"Well, 'tis true," Mrs Bennet insisted. "It had six plumes, Jane. Plumes! She looked like a naval officer who had fallen head-first into an aviary."

Lydia, despite her anger, could not suppress a snort of laughter. "I thought it resembled a chicken after an unfortunate meeting with Grandfather's hunting dog."

"Lydia!" Mary's scandalised tone was undermined by her poorly concealed smile.

Elizabeth leant against the doorframe, her eyes dancing with mischief. "Do you recall Lady Lucas's face when she first beheld it? I thought her eyebrows might permanently merge with her hairline."

"And now that very turban will be on display at the assembly whilst we sit at home," Mrs Bennet said with an exaggerated sigh. "Perhaps it is a mercy we are spared such a sight. I fear a second viewing might strain my nerves beyond recovery."

"It is not about turbans, Mamma," Lydia said, her voice thick with unshed tears. "It is about us not being good enough anymore. Not being young ladies of quality, deserving of society."

Mrs Bennet straightened, a flash of her old spirit animating her features. "Not good enough? My daughters? What nonsense." She took Lydia's hands in hers. "You are worth a dozen of her daughter Matilda Goulding, with her perpetually damp handkerchiefs and want of faculty to converse on any subject beyond ribbons. The girl asked me last week if sheep were born with their wool already separated into skeins."

Elizabeth laughed. "She did not!"

"On my honour," Mrs Bennet insisted. "I told her quite seriously that yes, and the finest merinos arrive with the wool already dyed in pastel colours."

"Mamma, no!" Jane exclaimed, although her eyes sparkled.

"No, no. although I was sorely tempted," Mrs Bennet admitted with a sigh. "But no, I restrained myself, although heaven knows the girl would have believed it and repeated it at the next tea."

Mary remarked, "She once asked me if Mozart was a type of French pastry."

The room fell silent for a moment before erupting in laughter.

"Well," Kitty said, dabbing at her eyes, although now with a trembling smile, "at least we have been spared an evening of Miss Matilda's scintillating conversation," Kitty said. Then her momentary mirth faded. "But she will dance. She will wear her best gown and stand up with partners and pretend, for one evening, that life is about music and laughter."

The simple longing in her voice caused Mrs Bennet's eyes to fill with tears. She had once dreamt of nothing more ambitious for her daughters than exactly such simple pleasures.

"I know, my love," she said, drawing her close. "And it is monstrously unfair that circumstances have denied you these natural joys."

"Perhaps," Mary ventured after a moment, "we might hold our own small dance here at Longbourn? Grandfather enjoys music in the evenings. We could invite Charlotte and Sir William—they would come, I'm certain."

"And the Phillips," Elizabeth added, warming to the idea. "Uncle Phillips mentioned last week how he misses hearing Mary play."

"A dance? Here?" Lydia looked around the small sitting room dubiously. "With what partners?"

"Sir William and Uncle Phillips for a start," Elizabeth said. "And perhaps John Robinson and his brother might be prevailed upon. They are respectable young men, if not gentlemen."

"Tenant farmers," Lydia scoffed, although with less vehemence than she might have managed a few minutes earlier.

"Who were pleased enough to learn sheep husbandry from you last spring," Mary pointed out with uncharacteristic sharpness. "They treat all of us with more genuine respect than half the so-called gentlemen in the county."

"Well, I for one think it an excellent plan," Mrs Bennet declared, seizing the moment of lighter spirits. "We shall have our own assembly. Grander than anything Augusta Goulding could manage with her terrible taste in turbans and her daughter who cannot tell sheep from skeins."

"We could decorate the drawing room," Kitty suggested, her natural enthusiasm beginning to resurface. "With flowers from the garden and candles."

"Cook makes those lemon cakes that Sir William so enjoys," Jane added. "She would prepare a special supper for the occasion."

"I," Mary said with surprising animation, "have been practising a new piece on the pianoforte. Most suitable for dancing."

Lydia, still not entirely convinced, crossed her arms. "Mrs Goulding will have proper musicians."

"True," Elizabeth acknowledged, "but she will also have Mr Goulding attempting his Scottish reel after too much wine. Remember last Christmas? He knocked over an entire tray of glasses and blamed it on Lady Lucas's spaniel."

"Which was not even in the room," Kitty added, beginning to giggle.

"The poor animal was banished to the stable nonetheless," Mrs Bennet recalled, "whilst Mr Goulding proceeded to demonstrate what he called a 'Highland Sword Dance' using two kitchen knives and nearly impaling young Mr King."

The image was too much for Lydia, who finally surrendered to laughter. "Very well. Our own dance it shall be." she said, wiping her eyes "And I imagine it will be a much merrier affair without Mr Goulding threatening the company with carving implements."

Mrs Bennet nodded slowly, her expression thoughtful. "It

would be a small gathering, to be sure. But perhaps… yes, I believe we might manage something pleasant." She squeezed Kitty's hand. "Not enough to replace a real assembly, my dears, but a reminder that we need not depend on the likes of Augusta Goulding for our happiness."

Lydia swiped at her eyes again, visibly struggling between disappointment and the tentative appeal of this alternative. "I suppose my blue muslin would look just as well in our drawing room as in the assembly rooms," she said finally.

"Better," Elizabeth assured her. "For here you are valued for who you are, not just as one of countless young ladies seeking a partner."

"Ah my dear girls," Mrs Bennet added with a small sigh, "I sometimes wish you had the opportunity to be both—accomplished women and young ladies with all the normal prospects and pleasures of your sex and station." She rose from Kitty's chair, her practical nature reasserting itself. "But wishes butter no parsnips, as Cook would say. We shall plan our small gathering for Friday evening, a week hence. The night before Mrs Goulding's assembly. And I shall personally ensure that Charlotte brings her father and brother."

As their mother left to consult with Hill about refreshments, Lydia turned to Elizabeth with naked vulnerability in her expression. "Do you think we shall ever attend a real assembly? Or are we to be forever the odd spinster sisters of Longbourn, known only for our agricultural knowledge and turned hems?"

Elizabeth's heart ached at the question—the same one she had asked herself many times, although she had grown more reconciled to the answer with each passing year.

"I do not know," she admitted honestly. "But I do know that you and Kitty deserve every happiness, whether it comes in the form of a country dance or in the satisfaction of seeing Longbourn prosper under your care."

"I would prefer both," Kitty said quietly, dabbing at her eyes with her handkerchief. "Is that so terribly greedy of me?"

"Not greedy at all," Mary assured her, with a tenderness that included them all. "I may find more satisfaction in my books and agricultural journals than in society, but even I miss the music and movement of a dance." She hesitated, then added, "And the sense of being like other young women, just for an evening."

The admission from their most stoic sister seemed to ease something in both younger girls. They were not alone in their longing, nor wrong to feel it alongside their dedication to Longbourn.

"Well then," Lydia said, squaring her shoulders with determined brightness, "if we are to have our own dance, we had best perfect our steps. Mary, will you play for us? Something lively, to chase away Mrs Goulding's slight."

As Mary moved to the pianoforte and the first notes filled the room, Elizabeth watched her younger sisters resume their practise with bittersweet pride. Their resilience continually amazed her—these girls who had been forced to grow up too quickly, to exchange balls for balance sheets, yet who still found moments to remember they were young women with young women's hearts.

They would feel the sting of exclusion again, Elizabeth knew. Society had little place for females who stepped outside their prescribed roles, however necessary that step might be. But at Longbourn, they would create their own small world where accomplishment and joy could coexist, where the satisfaction of meaningful work might compensate, if never completely replace, the simple pleasures their circumstances had denied them.

As she left her sisters to their practise, Elizabeth made a mental note to bring out the beeswax candles, to render their small gathering as festive as possible. Mrs Goulding's slight would not be forgotten, but perhaps it might be transformed from a source of pain to a catalyst for creating their own definition of happiness at Longbourn.

Chapter Seven

The sun had risen before six o'clock, and with it, Darcy. He rode the northern border of the estate, then returned, waiting impatiently for the rest of the party to awaken. In his own domain, Pemberley, Darcy would have broken his fast before eight and been at work. Here, he was at loose ends until, at long last, Bingley appeared at nine.

"Good Lord, Darcy," said Bingley, entering the breakfast room to find his friend reading a letter for what must have been the tenth time. "How long have you been up? You look positively thunderous."

"Since dawn," Darcy replied shortly. "I have been examining your drainage problem. The south fields--"

"Before breakfast?" Bingley helped himself to tea, shaking his head. "I suppose I ought not be surprised. I grant you, old friend, your dedication to my modest estate rather alarms me."

"Your 'modest estate' will be considerably less profitable if you do not address the issue before the winter rains."

"Yes, yes," Bingley sighed, taking his place at the table. "Although perhaps it could have waited until a more civilised hour?"

"I find the early morning light most instructive. One sees things as they truly are." Darcy's look was pointed. "For instance, the state of your south fields."

"Might we not delay the matter until--" He broke off at Darcy's expression, busying himself with his toast.

After several minutes of silence broken only by the clink of china, Bingley rose and walked to the window. He avoided Darcy's eyes by staring out at the morning mist still clinging to his fields.

"Really, Darcy, must I involve myself?" he said. "Could we not simply send word through my steward?"

"Your steward who has been in your employ all of three weeks?" Darcy did not look up from his tea. "The same steward who failed to mention these drainage issues when you took the lease?"

Bingley's shoulders slumped. "Only one of us needs to go. You understand these matters far better than I do. The agreement could be settled between you and the Bennets' man of business--"

"I shall not call upon your neighbours to discuss your estate's concerns without you present." Darcy finally raised his eyes to his friend's face, noting the marked agitation in his manner. "It would be the height of impropriety."

"Yes, but..." Bingley turned back to the window, then spun around again. "My sister insists the Bennets are quite peculiar. No one believes their grandfather still manages the estate. And apparently one of the daughters involves herself in tenant matters. Most irregular."

"I fail to see how this affects the drainage channels that must be addressed before the winter rains, unless you wish to see your south fields flooded."

"Caroline says they do not attend assemblies or participate in the neighbourhoods' social life. What sort of family--"

"Bingley." Darcy was firm. "You cannot rely on drawing room gossip for business matters. The state of your fields requires attention, regardless of the Bennets' social habits."

"'Tis easily said, in your case," Bingley muttered. "You are not the one who must establish himself as a creditable landholder. What if the best families find my association with these people unacceptable?"

Darcy softened at this revelation of his friend's true concern. "You are not associating with them, you are meeting regarding the management of water flow between your properties. A proper estate holder would address this promptly, in person. Your carriage is ordered for ten o'clock. I suggest you review the relevant papers before then."

"I see..." Bingley straightened his cravat in the window's reflection. "If it concerns estate matters, they might respect a direct approach. A man taking responsibility for his property."

"Just so." Darcy hid his smile behind his teacup. His friend's transparency might, under other circumstances, have been considered disarming, although he did hope Bingley would manage to attend to the business itself. The last thing Darcy wanted was to become overly involved in overseeing Netherfield.

He, of course, had no intention of becoming entangled with any of the local families himself.

The study at Longbourn was a modest room, far smaller than what Mr Darcy was accustomed to at Pemberley. His critical eye took in the scene before him: a quite elderly gentleman seated by the window, a blanket over his knees. A young lady, likely one of his granddaughters stood at a desk scattered with maps, There was general air of a working estate office rather than a gentleman's retreat. It was not quite what he had expected when Bingley had agreed to make this call about the drainage issues. Nor had he expected to find the Bennet ladies in Mr Bennet's study rather than the drawing room, but there they were - Miss Elizabeth bent over an account book whilst her sister sorted correspondence, their grandfather behind an ancient oak desk scattered with documents. The room smelled of beeswax, leather bindings, and the particular dusty warmth of well-used books. The chair seats were faded from years of sunlight and use.

Mr Bennet proved to be a spare, scholarly figure, his shoulders stooped with age but his eyes remarkably keen behind his spectacles. The tremor in his hands as he gestured Darcy and Bingley to chairs spoke of his advanced years, as did the walking stick propped against his desk.

"Welcome, welcome, gentlemen," he said, his voice still carrying the cultivated tones of a Cambridge education despite its age-worn quaver. "Be good enough to forgive me if I do not rise. These old bones protest such courtesy nowadays."

"Sir." Darcy bowed with genuine respect. Here was a

gentleman of the old tradition, surrounded by the accumulated wisdom of generations in leather-bound volumes.

Bingley bowed cheerfully. "Not at all, sir! We are most grateful for your counsel on these matters." His eyes, however, had already strayed to where Miss Jane Bennet sat, her fair head bent over her task.

Darcy introduced himself and Bingley to the gentleman, who then introduced them to Miss Bennet and Miss Elizabeth. Darcy did not make mention of their earlier encounter lest his actions be misinterpreted.

Mr Bennet studied him with a steady gaze. "You hold an estate in Derbyshire, Mr Darcy?"

"I do. My estate is Pemberley. We are quite near the Peaks, and not far from the town of Derby."

"Run off from those highlands must be a nuisance. You have some experience then in managing drainage from high ground."

"Quite so," Darcy agreed.

Mr Bennet turned to Miss Elizabeth.

"Lizzy, please, open the map for the gentlemen—the one with the western border with Netherfield." The older man gestured for her to proceed.

"Now then, you have come about our shared issues with drainage, I understand. Most intriguing subject. The Romans, you know…" Mr Bennet's eyes brightened with scholarly enthusiasm, although his hands shook as he reached for the map.

"Grandfather," Miss Elizabeth intervened smoothly, placing the map within his reach, "shall I fetch the survey from last Michaelmas?" She moved with the quiet efficiency of long practice, already reaching for the correct drawer.

"Ah yes, yes my dear. The survey." Mr Bennet smiled at the gentlemen. "My memory occasionally requires my granddaughter's assistance these days, although she is far too kind to mention it. Now, where were we? Ah yes -…what was it we found there, Lizzy?"

"The south field flooding at Netherfield was particularly troublesome that season," Miss Elizabeth supplied, her manner both respectful and protective of her grandfather's dignity. "Mr Bingley, you may find this relevant to Netherfield's lower pastures."

"Oh! Yes, of course," Bingley said, dragging his attention from Miss Bennet's graceful movements. "I must admit, Miss Elizabeth, such technical matters often escape me. Darcy is the one for all this land business." Bingley glanced at the proffered map, his expression one of utter confusion.

"You see, Mr Bingley, Mr Darcy, the natural flow to Netherfield's south fields has always drained through this valley on Longbourn land," Elizabeth explained, her eyes flashing with intelligence. "We have maintained the drainage channels for generations, but with the increased rains these past years…"

Darcy endeavoured to maintain his habitual air of detachment. Her detailed knowledge of the concerns of the owner of an estate and grasp of geography and agriculture would have rivalled even his steward at Pemberley. It was… unsettling. And yet, intriguing. He leant closer to examine the map, catching the faint scent of lavender.

"Quite right, Lizzy," her grandfather interjected with obvious pride. "The 1767 agreement with old Mr Bingley's predecessor specifically mentioned--" He broke off in a fit of coughing, and Elizabeth immediately poured him a glass of water.

Bingley, for his part, seemed rendered oblivious to the discussion of water distribution as his attention had returned again to Jane Bennet.

Miss Elizabeth rose, retrieving another minutely annotated map. The sunlight through the mullioned windows shone on her hair as she bent over the document.

"You see, sir," she was saying, "by following the natural contour here…" Her sleeve brushed his as she leant forward, and he was far more conscious of that slight contact than of the technical explanation she offered.

"How clever!" Bingley exclaimed, although his eyes appeared directed to where Miss Bennet sat. "Would you not agree, Darcy?"

"Most irregular," he murmured, although whether he meant

the drainage works or the entire situation, he could not quite say.

"Irregular?" Her eyes met his with that now-familiar blend of challenge and amusement. "Surely efficiency must trump convention, Mr Darcy? Unless you prefer your fields waterlogged in the Roman fashion?"

From his desk, her grandfather chuckled. "You must forgive my granddaughter, sir. I fear I have raised her to value results over propriety in attending to matters of the estate."

Jane Bennet looked up from her letters then, her smile gentle. "Lizzy has quite transformed our yields since she took over responsibility for them, Mr Darcy."

He felt trapped between his awareness of what ought to be - ladies confined to their needlework and watercolours - and the undeniable evidence before him of what could be. Miss Elizabeth's capability, her practical intelligence, her evident success in these masculine spheres. Should it not all offend his sense of correct behaviour?

Miss Bennet rose quietly to adjust the lamp closer to their grandfather's side. Bingley immediately stepped forward to assist her, his hand touching hers as they both reached for the lamp.

"I thank you, Mr Bingley," Miss Bennet murmured, a becoming flush touching her cheeks.

"Most irregular situation there, as you say, Mr Darcy?" Mr Bennet's eyes twinkled with surprising acuity. "Although not as irregular as finding young ladies so well-versed in governance of their fields. But necessity, sir, proves an excellent teacher. Do you not agree, Mr Bingley? You are here learning more than you would ever wish about water flow, to be a good steward of your lands." He paused as he gestured over the map, his eyes twinkling with amusement.

"I agree, Mr Bennet," Bingley said with transparent inattention. "The… er… water must flow downhill, naturally."

Miss Elizabeth's lips twitched, although her voice remained perfectly serious. "An astute observation, Mr Bingley. Although perhaps the detailed calculations might prove somewhat tedious?"

"Oh! No, no, not at all," Bingley protested, glancing from one Bennet to the other. "Darcy has a particular talent for such things at Pemberley."

Mr Bennet spoke. "The rainfall records, Jane. Where did we put the rainfall records?" A strain of disquiet entered the old gentleman's voice.

"Here, Grandfather." Jane placed the leather-bound volume before him and straightened the tall stack of books which threatened to tumble.

"Allow me, Miss Bennet," Bingley said eagerly, nearly upsetting his chair in his haste to assist her. Darcy grimaced. Miss Bennet's gentle manner and quiet beauty were precisely the sort to capture Bingley's romantic nature, regardless of her situation in life.

"Ah yes, quite right." The elder gentleman's eyes sharpened. "Although I believe it was Lizzy who made that particular observation about the change in rainfall last autumn. My memory plays tricks, but not about that. Most unexpected, to have a granddaughter quote Vitruvius at me over breakfast."

"You see, Mr Darcy," Elizabeth began, "the clay content here requires…" She paused, noticing her grandfather's cough become more pronounced. "Grandfather, shall I ring for your cordial?"

"No, no, my dear. Simply an old man's weakness. Pray continue. Mr Darcy must be eager to hear your thoughts on modern drainage techniques." The shrewd-look Mr Bennet cast him unsettled Darcy, suggesting that the elderly gentleman's wit remained as sharp as ever.

"Certainly." Darcy fought to keep his expression even. He could not miss the efficient grace with which she anticipated her grandfather's needs whilst never undermining his dignity.

"The clay content here requires particular attention," Miss Elizabeth was saying. Darcy caught sight of the nearly invisible darning in her sleeve—the sort of damage that might come from reaching through brambles to examine the conditions of the hedgerow. No fashionable lady would dare such practical investigation, let alone possess the skills to repair the consequences.

"Remarkable!" Bingley contributed, having certainly heard nothing of clay content. "Is it not so, Miss Bennet, that such matters of... of..."

"Drainage?" she supplied gently.

"Yes, of course! Drainage. Most engaging subject."

Miss Bennet bent her head over the ledger again, but not before Darcy caught the amusement in her smile. His friend was heading down a dangerous path, one he would need to address before Bingley's romantic nature created expectations. Bingley was always easily enchanted by a pretty face, however he must be conscious of the entirety of the circumstances. The signs of genteel economy were everywhere. The ink in the well had been watered enough to stretch its use without compromising legibility. The leather bindings showed evidence of careful repair rather than replacement. Even Miss Bennet's pale muslin, although exquisitely neat, showed signs of careful mending at the hem.

Mr Bennet's hand reached for another map, his scholarly enthusiasm undimmed by age. "You see, Mr Darcy, the classical principles of hydraulics suggest that water flowing through channels of varying dimensions will adjust its velocity and pressure according to the constraints of the passage, with narrower sections increasing velocity whilst wider portions reduce it—knowledge the Romans employed extensively in their aqueduct systems to maintain consistent flow across varied terrain. The gradient must be taken into account ..."

As he spoke, the elder gentleman's sharp eyes moved among the four young people with rather too much acuity for Darcy's comfort.

"This, Mr Darcy, is where the gradient shifts." Miss Elizabeth's finger drew the line with precision.

"Our Lizzy has an excellent understanding of the terrain, Mr Darcy. Singular for a young lady to be so well informed about hydraulics, do you not think?" Mr Bennet regarded Darcy with an expression identical to the arch look Miss Elizabeth had given him as he attempted to rescue her from the pooling water. He had the sensation of being tested by a particularly clever tutor.

"I find," he said slowly, "that capability recommends itself, regardless of its source."

"Such breadth of mind does you credit, sir." Miss Elizabeth's attention appeared wholly fixed upon the survey lines as she spoke, her voice carrying just the faintest trace of something that might have been humour. "One hardly knows whether to be more impressed by your discernment or your forbearance." Only the smallest quirk at the corner of her mouth betrayed that the perfectly proper words might carry a double meaning.

"One must judge by results, must one not?" Mr Bennet said. "The estate prospers under my granddaughters' care better than it did under my own in younger days."

"Grandfather, you are too modest." Miss Elizabeth's hand rested briefly on the old gentleman's shoulder. "You prepared us admirably for such work."

"Did I indeed?" The elder Mr Bennet's eyes twinkled. "I rather thought all those hours you spent poring over agricultural treatises were meant to be devoted to accomplishments more suited to young ladies. Embroidery, perhaps. Or decorative painting. Do you not wish to be accomplished ladies?"

Accomplished. Darcy had long held that the word was applied to many a woman who deserved it not otherwise than by netting a purse or covering a screen. He could not boast of knowing more than half-a-dozen ladies in the whole range of his acquaintance that were really accomplished. Elizabeth Bennet had capabilities far beyond those frivolous matters.

"Mr Darcy?" Miss Elizabeth's voice drew him from his reverie. "You appear quite lost in contemplation. Has the question of velocity so occupied your thoughts?"

"I am considering," he said stiffly, "the most efficient approach to water management."

That look again, one brow raised, her lips curved in a slight smile, as though she saw straight through his careful façade to the turmoil beneath. "And what conclusions have you drawn about our rather unorthodox methods?"

"I…" He was saved from reply by Mr Bennet's sudden movement.

"The figures, Jane. Where did we put the figures for the south field?"

"Here, Grandfather." Jane moved forward, placing the leather-bound volume before him. "You had me add them into the new estate book last week."

"Ah yes, of course. My Jane has the most remarkable knack for figures, Mr Darcy. Although perhaps such matters interest you less than questions of water management?"

Darcy felt unsure whether the elder Mr Bennet's occasional confusion was genuine, or if those sharp eyes saw more than they revealed. Particularly when the old gentleman insisted Miss Elizabeth stand closer to the window "for better light" as she explained the drainage patterns.

The autumn sunlight illuminated her fair skin as she leant forward to indicate a particular measurement. The scent of lavender rose from her neatly mended dress. It was a fine muslin, he noted with the unconscious judgement of one whose sister ordered new gowns from London each season, but it had been turned at the cuffs and collar with nearly invisible stitches. He wondered at the novelty of such practical wisdom. The thought was most unwelcome.

The elder Mr Bennet's shrewd eyes moved between them. "I believe Mr Darcy finds our local innovations rather more engaging than he anticipated. Do you not agree, sir?"

A direct response seemed unwise. "I should be grateful for the opportunity to examine your rainfall records in greater detail. For Netherfield's benefit, naturally."

"Naturally." Miss Elizabeth returned to examining the rainfall records with evident absorption. "Mr Bingley, you will find these patterns of particular interest for Netherfield's lower fields."

Bingley leant forward with his characteristic enthusiasm. "I daresay, I had not considered there might be a similarity in our soil conditions."

"The challenge lies in the clay content," she said, her attention wholly fixed on the technical matter at hand.

Darcy watched as she explained the specific conditions to Bingley without a trace of coquetry, her mind entirely occupied with solving the practical problems before them. The realisation that she had quite forgotten his presence in her enthusiasm for the subject made her all the more dangerous to his peace of mind.

"Perhaps," Elizabeth suggested, "you would be interested in walking the affected areas? The current state of the channels would be better understood on foot."

Darcy nodded before he had fully considered the propriety of tramping about the countryside with Miss Elizabeth Bennet. Her grandfather's presence would make it acceptable, of course, but the elder gentleman's infirmities might make such an excursion impossible for him.

"Capital idea!" Bingley exclaimed, finally contributing to the conversation. "Miss Bennet, might you join us? To… er… to better understand the concerns of our tenants?"

Darcy caught Elizabeth's quick smile at her sister, noting how it transformed her whole countenance. How would it feel to be the cause of such a smile? He immediately suppressed the thought.

"I believe I shall remain here with the maps," the elder Mr Bennet announced, settling more comfortably in his chair. "Lizzy knows every inch of this land. She will show you what needs attending to." He fixed Darcy with a knowing look that made the younger man distinctly uncomfortable.

Elizabeth efficiently rolled up the relevant maps whilst discussing with her elder sister which tenants they needed to speak with. As they quit the study, Darcy observed a silent exchange between Miss Elizabeth and her younger sister Mary - some subtle gesture and quiet words that apparently conveyed Miss Elizabeth's wishes regarding their grandfather. The efficiency of it struck him; no elaborate explanations needed, merely the practised understanding of those who shared responsibilities.

As she turned to him with those fine eyes sparking with

intelligence, Darcy realised his confusion was the least of his concerns. The real danger lay in how much he anticipated their walk, and how eager he was to er…discuss estate matters with this most unusual young woman.

Darcy's interest grew as another Bennet sister joined them. Miss Catherine Bennet led them through what appeared at first glance to be a purely decorative garden. She spoke with quiet confidence as she gestured to the elegant arrangements before them.

"You see, Mr Darcy, Mr Bingley, the Williams pears have already been gathered, but the Jargonelles linger a little longer, if the frost holds off. They produce magnificently when well trimmed."

Bingley crouched down to examine an ornamental border of flowering herbs.

"And these, Miss Catherine?"

"Ah!" Her face brightened. "The lavender is mostly spent now, but we leave it standing to dry naturally—it deters pests and looks well even in decline. The thyme still blooms here and there, and behind them, you might see carrot tops—those feathery greens blend well even now. And those climbing roses?" She gestured to the arches, where a few ragged blooms clung to the stems. "They are nearly finished for the year, but they've done their part concealing the runner beans. The beans help fertilise the soil for next season's blooms."

The design displayed genuine ingeniousness—beds of rainbow chard with their coloured stems still vibrant despite the season, late cabbages set amongst browning kale, and turnip greens poking through the earth, edged with the fading spires of chives and parsley gone mostly to seed.

"Grandfather suggested I might try my hand at improving the kitchen gardens," she continued, pride in her voice. "But I saw no reason they could not be beautiful as well as productive. The gooseberry and currant bushes, although bare now, make excellent hedging. And the strawberry beds help hold the soil between the rose roots. We have mulched them already for the winter."

Elizabeth stood at the periphery, her expression warm with

sisterly pride. The garden had already surrendered its high summer brilliance, yet still produced root vegetables and hardy greens, all while maintaining the outline of a pleasure garden. Even the pond, its surface flecked with wind-blown leaves, remained useful—stocked with carp and edged with a thinning border of watercress.

"Most ingenious, Miss Catherine," he said, as her face flushed with pleasure. "I believe my sister Georgiana would be most interested in seeing these designs. Perhaps you might consider sharing your expertise with her should she visit Netherfield?"

Behind him, Elizabeth's brows rose at this implicit promise of future visits, but he maintained his focus on Miss Catherine, who launched enthusiastically into her plans for the autumn planting and winter cover crops.

Chapter Eight

The autumn air held a crisp edge as they stepped outside the gardens into the field. Without any obvious orchestration, they fell into pairs along the path. Bingley moved instantly to Miss Bennet's side, leaving Darcy to walk with Miss Elizabeth. She had exchanged her indoor slippers for half-boots that, whilst adequately fashionable for country walks, showed signs of frequent use on similar expeditions. They were scuffed at the toes and bore stains that spoke of regular exposure to mud and dew - more like a land steward's footwear than a gentleman's daughter's walking boots kept pristine between occasional pleasure jaunts.

"The channel begins here," Elizabeth said, indicating a shallow depression in the earth half-obscured by fallen leaves and recent rain. The soil crumbled slightly at her touch. "Although of course, the original course was altered during my grandfather's youth, when--"

"When the north field was converted from pasture to cultivation," Darcy finished, then caught himself. He had spoken as he might to a fellow landowner, not as one ought to address a young lady. Yet Miss Elizabeth showed no offence at his interruption.

"Correct," she replied, her eyes brightening with interest. "The soil composition required particular consideration—clay nearer the hedgerow, and the lower stretch prone to water-logging in wetter months."

Behind them, Bingley's voice carried, followed by Jane's softer response. Darcy glanced back to see his friend gazing at Miss Bennet with a familiar form of adoration. Bingley had fallen in and out of love frequently, and had a penchant for willowy blondes. True to form, as Jane was speaking about something, Bingley's enchanted expression suggested he had not heard a word.

"Mr Bingley seems rather distracted," Elizabeth said, amusement sparkling in her eyes.

"Your sister's presence seems to have that effect," Darcy said dryly, then was startled by his own candour. There was something about Miss Elizabeth that made him forget the careful manners he typically employed with young ladies.

They paused where two drainage channels met. Elizabeth crouched without hesitation, brushing aside wind-blown twigs and compacted soil. Her practical boots peeked out beneath the hem of her walking dress, now lightly muddied at the edge.

Darcy could not seem to avoid explaining how a similar issue had been resolved at Pemberley—diverting surface water across terraces to prevent pooling in the low meadows.

When Elizabeth responded with a thoughtful question about water flow rates Darcy realised he had been conversing with the same comfort as with a land-owning peer. The recognition unsettled him. She easily matched his knowledge and understanding.

"Miss Elizabeth," he began, but she was already gesturing further down the slope, where a clay-banked ditch had been recently cleared.

Her observations were rooted in lived experience, not theory. Her manner was lacking in pretension, yet she saw everything. He was drawn back into serious discussion despite his intentions.

Elizabeth grasped her pencil to record the conditions, her stiff fingers struggling with the task. The rough wood caught her skin, but her hands were too cold to feel the splinter that embedded itself in her finger. She continued marking measurements, unaware of the blood now staining the paper.

"Miss Elizabeth." Darcy's voice was sharp. He caught her wrist, turning her hand palm up to reveal the injury. A thin line of blood had traced its way across her palm. Without ceremony, he produced his handkerchief and began cleaning away the blood.

"I did not even notice--" she started, surprised by the amount of blood.

"Your hands are half-frozen." He wrapped the handkerchief around her finger with surprising gentleness. From his pocket he produced a small pair of tweezers. At her questioning look, he explained, "One learns to carry certain necessities when managing an estate."

The splinter was stubborn, but his hands were steady and warm. Elizabeth studied his face as he worked.

"There," he said, the splinter finally extracted. He bound her finger with the handkerchief, his movements precise. "You will need proper gloves for this work."

"I have gloves," she protested, flexing her bandaged finger. The cloth was still warm from his pocket.

"Not adequate ones, it would appear." Without a word, Darcy produced a pair of leather gloves from his coat.

"They will be too big," she protested.

"They are warm, and they will protect your hands. I will make the notes." he replied, already turning back to his measurements. His mien was businesslike again as he straightened.

Behind them, Bingley continued to gaze at Jane's every movement, although Darcy doubted his friend could at that moment have identified a drainage channel if he fell into one. The parallel between Bingley's obvious infatuation and his own unexpectedly engaging conversation gave Darcy pause.

He was enjoying Miss Elizabeth's company far too much, and in entirely the wrong way. This gentleman's daughter who knelt in the dirt to examine water channels was so far out of his experience, he felt disoriented.

Yet as she rose, brushing her skirts clean with practical efficiency, Darcy admired those qualities he should disapprove. It was a disturbing realisation, one that demanded further examination—in due course, when she was not looking at him with those fine eyes alight with intelligence, asking his opinion about the best approaches to preventing winter flooding.

After examining the final drainage area, Miss Elizabeth

indicated their circuit was complete. "You have seen the worst of our difficulties now, gentlemen. Although perhaps Mr Bingley's attention was more engaged by other aspects of the landscape." Her glance toward where her sister stood conferring with a young woman tenant carried just enough meaning to make Bingley flush. Miss Elizabeth's eyes were bright with the exercise and the satisfaction of thorough explanations well-delivered. Darcy was unexpectedly reluctant to end the inspection, even as he knew he must.

"Most instructive," Darcy said shortly, aware he had spent far too much time admiring her cheeks flushed from the brisk air. "We should not further delay your return to the house."

Bingley chattered amiably through their farewells, lingering rather too long with Miss Bennet. The autumn air and physical activity had done nothing to clear Darcy's head of unwelcome observations about an exceptional young lady.

They had mounted and ridden nearly a quarter mile before Bingley broke the contemplative silence, the wind tugging at his coat as dry leaves skittered across the narrow lane. "I found their methods diverting water flow quite… illuminating. Do you agree, Darcy?"

"The principles appear sound," Darcy allowed, adjusting his grip on the reins, "although perhaps not suited to every situation."

"I thought Miss Bennet's understanding of the matter particularly…" Bingley's enthusiasm faltered at Darcy's sharp look. "I should say, their care of the estate seems most…"

"Practical?" Darcy supplied dryly. "Perhaps. Yet one must consider how such involvement would be regarded in more elevated circumstances."

"Would not good sense recommend itself at any level of society?" Bingley's horse shifted beneath him, sensing his agitation. "After all, water flows regardless of who redirects it."

"There are other considerations beyond mere hydrology."

"Are there?" Bingley's tone carried a rare edge. "I had thought the purpose was to drain the fields effectively, not to ensure the water knew its proper place in society."

Darcy reined his horse in to draw his friend's attention. "You oversimplify the matter."

"Do I? It seemed quite straightforward to me. A lady who understands the myriad matters of managing an estate would make a better mistress for any property than one who merely ornaments it."

Darcy stared ahead, jaw tight. The hedgerows lining the lane were sparse now, brambles stripped of berries, the last of the beech leaves turning brittle gold. The season, like the conversation, offered little warmth.

"A man of substantial fortune," Darcy said slowly, weighing his duty to both friend and family, "who wishes to establish himself in society must consider more than agricultural efficiency. Your father worked diligently to elevate your position, Bingley. You owe it to his memory to consider such matters with gravity."

Bingley sighed, his normally cheerful countenance showing unexpected stubbornness. "Even when that efficiency comes wrapped in such gentle manners and sweetness…"

"Bingley." Darcy's voice cut the air like the wind through the bare trees. He checked himself, speaking more temperately. "Your enthusiasm should not be clouded by… local influences. A man in your position must look to forge connections that will advance his place in society, not bind himself to a family struggling to maintain appearances."

They rode in silence for several moments, the only sound the soft thud of hooves on autumn soil. "But surely," Bingley ventured at last, "the Misses Bennet's comprehension of estate matters demonstrates uncommon discernment?"

"I begin to think," Darcy replied, the image of Miss Elizabeth crouched in October soil vivid and unwelcome, "that neither good sense nor land stewardship has much bearing on your current preoccupation with Longbourn."

He urged his horse forward, the animal surging beneath him as if sensing his mood. Whether his sharpness had been meant for Bingley or himself, he could not say. Behind him, Bingley offered no reply. The silence between them was filled only by the rustle of wind through spent hedges and the quiet clop of hooves against the fading year, leaving them both to contemplate the various perils of country estates and their unexpected occupants.

Chapter Nine

The dew still clung to the meadow as Kitty Bennet made her way along the narrow footpath that led away from Longbourn's gardens. Her basket swung from her arm, already containing several bundles of herbs harvested in the dewy dawn—mint, rosemary, and thyme from her own perfectly tended beds. Today, however, she sought something less common.

A persistent cough had troubled her for as long as she could remember, and Grandfather's breathing had grown more laboured with each passing week. Mr Jones had prescribed his usual draughts, but they brought only temporary relief. It was time, Kitty had decided, to seek wisdom from a different source.

The path curved around a stand of ancient oaks before descending into a small, sheltered hollow. There, nestled amid a riot of deliberately cultivated wildness, stood a stone cottage nearly concealed by climbing roses and ivy. Smoke curled from the chimney, mingling with the morning mist.

Kitty paused at the gate in the rough stone wall. Widow Euphemia Faxon was respected by those in Meryton who needed her remedies but viewed with suspicion by others—including Lady Lucas who referred to her as "that hedge-witch with her pagan concoctions" and warned the local mothers against allowing their daughters anywhere near her cottage. "Trafficking in superstition and heathen practices," Lady Lucas had declared, with a sniff. Her voice carried deliberately across the room. Mrs Bennet had initially discouraged these visits until Widow Faxon's salve had healed a persistent rash on Mary's hands that Mr Jones had been unable to treat.

"I thought you might come today," called a voice from within the garden. "The horehound is particularly fine this year."

Kitty smiled, no longer surprised by the widow's uncanny ability to anticipate visitors. "Good morning, Mrs Faxon. I hope I'm not calling too early."

The old woman emerged from behind a tangled mass of brambles, her grey hair escaping from beneath a faded cap, her apron already stained despite the early hour. Of unknown age, Agnes Faxon remained as spry as women of twenty years, her eyes sharp and knowing in her weathered face.

"For you, Miss Catherine, it is never too early. Not when your grandfather's chest is troubling him again." She gestured for the young woman to enter the garden. "And your own cough has not improved, has it? I heard it from across the churchyard on Sunday."

Kitty shook her head, following the older woman down a winding path between beds bursting with plants both familiar and strange. "It wakes me at night, and Grandfather's is worse. The draught Mr Jones prescribed helps him sleep but does little for the catarrh."

Mrs Faxon nodded sagely, stopping before a patch of plants with wrinkled, greyish-green leaves. "Horehound," she said, pointing to the robust growth. "God's gift to those who suffer winter ailments. See how the leaves have a whitish cast? That's how you know it is potent."

She bent to cut several stalks, adding them to Kitty's basket. "Take more than you think you will need. The syrup keeps well, and your grandfather's chest will trouble him when winter comes."

Kitty watched intently as the widow selected the best specimens, mentally noting which parts of the plant were harvested. The gardens at Longbourn—both ornamental and practical—had become her particular domain, her designs increasing both beauty and yield with each passing season.

"I have brought the notebook," Kitty said, pulling a small leather-bound volume from her pocket. "May I record the recipe? I would like to add it to Aunt Eleanor's book."

"Sensible girl." Mrs Faxon's approval was evident in her look. "Knowledge should be preserved and passed down. Too many remedies are lost because no one thought to set them down in writing. Or did not have the ability." She straightened, brushing soil from her hands. "Come inside, and I'll show you the best way to prepare it."

The cottage interior was a single room, neat but crowded with bundles of drying herbs hanging from the rafters. A large worktable dominated one side, covered with jars, bottles, and various implements. The air was thick with mingled scents—sweet and sharp, pungent and soothing—that Kitty had come to associate with healing.

"First, you will need water—fresh spring water is best," Mrs Faxon instructed, moving to the hearth where a kettle already hung over the fire. "And honey from hives that have harvested from medicinal plants. I've some from your own bees at Longbourn—your sister Mary brought it last autumn in exchange for that salve for her hands."

Kitty wrote diligently as the widow demonstrated, measuring horehound leaves into a pot, adding the boiling water, and setting it to simmer. A rich, somewhat bitter scent filled the cottage.

"How did you learn this?" Kitty asked, watching as Mrs Faxon stirred the mixture with practised movements.

"From my grandmother, who learnt from hers. Women's wisdom, passed down." There was sadness in her voice. "My daughter had no interest—she went to London to be a lady's maid and considers such knowledge old-fashioned. Perhaps someday she shall think differently."

"I would have thought the same, once," Kitty admitted. "Before Papa died, my only interests were gossip and fashions."

Mrs Faxon smiled knowingly. "Adversity reveals our true nature, for better or worse. Yours, it seems, included a gift for growing things that might otherwise have lain dormant. I knew your Aunt Eleanor, you know. There was a lady who knew her herbs." She drew Kitty's attention to the simmering pot. "Now we let this extract for half an hour. Tell me about your plans for the kitchen garden whilst we wait."

The next hour passed pleasantly as Kitty described her designs for expanding the herb section of Longbourn's gardens, occasionally pausing to note Mrs Faxon's suggestions for companion planting and harvesting times. Mrs Faxon admonished Kitty to organise her medicinal herbs according to Aunt Eleanor's system and review her aunt's small notebook filled with observations far ahead of their time about dosages appropriate for women's physiology versus men's. The older woman's shrewd comments revealed a lifetime of practical knowledge.

When the horehound had simmered sufficiently, Mrs Faxon showed Kitty how to strain the liquid through a fine cloth, pressing the leaves to extract every drop of medicine. To the resulting dark liquid, she added the honey, stirring slowly as it dissolved.

"Now," she said, reaching for a small, stoppered bottle, "the secret that makes this remedy singularly effective." She added three drops of a fragrant oil to the mixture. "Essence of lemon. Hard to come by these days, with war making imports dear, but of inestimable value for chest ailments. The real fruit would be better, but lemons are all but impossible to find in Hertfordshire."

Kitty made another careful note, watching as the widow bottled the syrup in a series of small, dark glass containers.

"One tablespoon for adults, morning and night, and an extra dose if the coughing is severe," Mrs Faxon instructed. "Half that amount for children. Keep it cool and dark, and it will serve you through autumn and beyond."

As Kitty prepared to leave, her basket now containing the precious bottles along with a generous bundle of fresh horehound for future batches, Mrs Faxon pressed a small paper of seeds into her hand.

"For your gardens," she said. "Plant them in a sunny spot with good drainage. By next spring, you will have your own supply. The plants will return year after year if properly tended."

"Thank you," Kitty said, suddenly impulsive as she leant

forward to embrace the older woman. "For everything you have taught me."

Mrs Faxon seemed momentarily startled by the display of affection before her weathered face softened. "You are a good student, Miss Catherine. Your grandfather is fortunate to have you looking after his health."

"I sometimes feel I'm only playing at knowledge," Kitty confessed. "Compared to what you know—"

"We all begin somewhere," the widow interrupted gently. "My grandmother would laugh to see how proud I was of my first remedies. Knowledge grows like your gardens—with patience, attention, and time."

That evening, Kitty administered the first dose of the syrup to her grandfather, who regarded the dark liquid with a dubious expression.

"Widow Faxon's remedy?" he asked, sniffing the spoonful cautiously. "The one Lady Lucas calls 'witchcraft in a bottle'?"

"The same," Kitty confirmed with a smile. "The witchcraft that cured Sir William's gout last winter, although Lady Lucas prefers not to mention that part."

"Well then," Mr Bennet said, his eyes twinkling with their old mischief despite his pallor, "let us hope it works as well on old men's lungs as on baronets' toes." He swallowed the dose, his eyebrows rising curiously. "Not unpleasant. The honey conceals much of the bitterness."

Elizabeth, who had been watching from the doorway, stepped into the room. "You have become quite the apothecary, Kitty. Mrs Hill tells me your feverfew tincture has eased Cook's headaches considerably."

Kitty felt herself flush with pleasure at the rare praise. For so long she had been only "the second youngest Bennet girl," with no particular talent to distinguish her. Jane had her beauty and gentle manner, Elizabeth her wit and understanding, Mary her books and serious mind, and Lydia her boundless eagerness and newfound expertise with livestock. But in the gardens and stillroom, Kitty had at last found her own domain.

"I have only begun to learn of what can be done with the right plants," she said, corking the bottle firmly. "Mrs Faxon believes many ailments can be treated with what grows around us, if we only remember the old knowledge."

"'Old knowledge'," came Mary's voice as she entered with the evening tea tray. "Paracelsus wrote extensively on the medicinal properties of plants in the sixteenth century. Modern medicine too often dismisses wisdom because it lacks a recent pedigree."

"Whatever its pedigree," Mrs Bennet said as she followed Mary into the room, "anything that eases Father Bennet's breathing is welcome at Longbourn." She touched Kitty's shoulder with an approving hand. "Your garden plans have proved their worth yet again, my dear."

Kitty took a spoonful of the syrup herself before settling near the fire with her mending. By the following morning, her chest felt less tight, the persistent tickle that had triggered her coughing significantly diminished. More remarkably, Grandfather's breathing seemed easier, the harsh rattle that had accompanied each breath muted to a gentler sound.

Within a week, the improvement was pronounced enough that even Mr Jones noted it during his regular visit to Longbourn. "Whatever you have added to my prescribed treatments appears beneficial," he admitted with professional grace. "Although I would caution against placing too much faith in folk remedies."

"Of course, Mr Jones," Elizabeth assured him, whilst exchanging a private glance with Kitty.

The horehound syrup became a regular feature of Longbourn's stillroom, Kitty dutifully recording each batch in her growing collection of household remedies. She planted Mrs Faxon's seeds in a sunny corner of the kitchen garden, tending the seedlings with the same care she gave her roses and herbs.

"Well?" Mary looked up from her book as Elizabeth and Jane

entered the parlour. "Was Grandfather's assessment of the drainage correct?"

"To the letter," Elizabeth replied, settling onto the sofa. "Although Mr Darcy had some interesting suggestions about improving the flow near Oakham Mount. He has implemented similar solutions at Pemberley."

"Both gentlemen were quite civil," Jane added, taking her accustomed seat near the window. "Mr Bingley seemed most concerned about being a good neighbour."

"When he remembered to attend," Elizabeth said with a meaningful look at her elder sister, whose cheeks coloured just perceptibly. "Mr Darcy's understanding is remarkable. He spotted issues I had not yet noticed myself."

Their mother, who had been sewing on the settee, suddenly showed signs of animation. "Two single gentlemen of fortune, calling at Longbourn! Even though it was just estate matters. Still, Jane, Mr Bingley seemed most pleased with your company."

"It was about Netherfield lands, Mamma," Jane reminded her gently. "Nothing more."

"If it pleases you Mamma, you may write to your sister Phillips that two eligible gentlemen called," Elizabeth added with a laugh. "That should provide sufficient material for speculation at her next card party."

Later, as the sisters dressed for dinner in their shared chamber, Elizabeth watched Jane's reflection in their mirror. "He hardly took his eyes from you," she said.

"Lizzy, please." Jane's reflection showed her telltale blush. "Mr Bingley was merely being polite."

"There is polite, and there is looking as though one has discovered a rare jewel in a country lane." Elizabeth adjusted her hair pins. "It matters little. A man of his consequence would hardly consider…"

"No," Jane agreed quietly. "We must not encourage such thoughts in Mamma. It is far from the first time a gentleman paid attention to me on first meeting. Nothing will come of it and thinking of it will only lead to disappointment."

Elizabeth turned to face her sister directly. "Did you like him, though?"

"He was…" Jane looked down as a becoming flush crept up her cheeks. "Amiable. Most gentleman-like. But as you say, it signifies little more than a pleasant interlude. What of Mr Darcy? He seemed quite engaged in conversation with you."

"Because I was speaking of his friend's estate. I am sensible that I have rarely met anyone so knowledgeable in supervising an estate. I fear I quite forgot myself and spoke as freely as I do with Grandfather." Elizabeth shook her head. "But you should have seen his expression when I first showed him that problem with the channel. I might as well have suggested digging the trench myself."

"You do not do yourself justice, Lizzy. He seemed most attentive to your observations."

"Perhaps, Jane, but a man of ten thousand a year does not seek a wife who concerns herself with water flow." Elizabeth's voice carried a teasing lilt, but her fingers worried at the mend in her sleeve. "Such things are beneath a gentleman's daughter, I am sure."

"Perhaps not all gentlemen think so."

"Well, it matters not what they think, for we shall likely see little of either of them now that the discussions are concluded." Elizabeth moved to the window. A brisk breeze had picked up, scattering the russet oak leaves in swirls. "I did enjoy having someone to hydrology with besides Grandfather."

"Lizzy," Jane said, coming to stand beside her. "You are worth far more than--"

"Than my unfashionable interests in land management? I should hope so."

"Lizzy." Jane made a gentle enquiry. "Your hand—what happened?"

Elizabeth glanced down at the handkerchief still wrapped around her finger, the fine linen marked with spots of dried blood. "A splinter, nothing more. Mr Darcy… assisted in removing it."

Before Jane could enquire further, Elizabeth linked her arm

through her sister's. "Come, let us not be melancholy. We have managed perfectly well until now without eligible gentlemen of fortune disrupting our quiet life. I do hope, for the sake of Netherfield's fields, that Mr Bingley pays more attention to the drainage than he did today."

Jane's quiet laugh did not quite hide her sigh, and Elizabeth squeezed her arm gently. They waited together, staring out at the dormant land that they worked so hard to maintain, each lost in thoughts they knew better than to voice, until Hill came to tell them dinner was ready.

Elizabeth found her mother the following day surrounded by household books and correspondence. Through the open door, she could hear Mary discussing the stillroom inventory with Kitty. Those tasks would need to be managed quite differently when their cousin arrived.

"Mr Collins's letter inviting himself to Longbourn arrived this morning," Mrs Bennet said without looking up. "He means to grace us with a fortnight's visit, beginning Tuesday next." Her voice bore a ghost of the anxious flutter that once defined her.

"So soon? But the drainage work on the south field--"

"Must be completed before he arrives." Mrs Bennet finally raised her eyes from her papers. "We cannot have him questioning our methods or suggesting his own improvements. Your grandfather has already sent word to Mr Robinson about increasing the work crew."

"And what of Mr Darcy's consultation about the boundary drainage?"

"That, at least, may work to our advantage. If Mr Darcy has already formed an impression of Longbourn's competent management before Mr Collins arrives…" She paused. "Your grandfather wishes to discuss how we shall arrange matters during the visit. Shall we go up now? He is having a good day, and we have much to plan."

They found Mr Bennet in his chair by the window, a book of agricultural improvements open on his lap. His eyes, although tired, were lit with their characteristic sharp intelligence.

"Mr Collins grows bold," he said without preamble, holding up the letter. "Listen to this: '*I feel it my solemn duty to assess the state of my future inheritance, that I might better understand how to preserve its advantages and remedy its deficiencies.*' Remedy its deficiencies, my foot."

"He means to find fault," Elizabeth said, taking her accustomed seat at his right hand.

"He means to establish his own authority," Mrs Bennet corrected, settling into the chair opposite. "We must ensure he finds exactly what he expects to find—neither so much disorder that he might claim immediate intervention is needed, nor such perfect fitness that he grows suspicious."

"A careful balance." Mr Bennet sighed. "We have put Mr Collins off for the last time, I fear. We must discuss how to present matters to him to give him the least reason to question the stewardship of the estate. Frances, please tell my granddaughters what we have spoken of." Elizabeth noted that Grandfather looked pale. His hand trembled as he raised his teacup.

Mrs Bennet turned her eyes on her five girls, seated around their grandfather in their accustomed places. "First, we must create the impression of one absolute line of authority. All estate business must appear to flow from you, Father Bennet. Elizabeth, Jane, you will need to modify your manner with the tenants. No more direct instructions - everything must be presented as 'Mr Bennet suggests' or 'Mr Bennet requires.'"

"And my morning inspections of the fields?" Elizabeth asked.

"Must be undertaken earlier, before Mr Collins rises. He will expect to find you engaged in more lady-like pursuits during the day. Perhaps you might take up sketching again? Mr Collins would find that a suitably feminine accomplishment."

"Whilst allowing her to document estate conditions without

raising suspicion," Mr Bennet noted with approval. "But what of Jane's work with the accounts?"

"She may continue as your secretary—that much can be explained as feminine duty to a grandfather. Mary's stillroom management we shall present as mere domestic excellence. Kitty's garden designs will become simple flower arrangement, and as for Lydia…"

"We shall keep our sister away from the sheep pens," Elizabeth said firmly. "Although she will not thank us for it."

Lydia tossed her head with a quick breath. Like a governess-weary miss of twelve, she said, "I am certain I might go to see the sweet little kittens? Or pet the horses? I will not don my smock and boots, and it is not lambing season."

"Better a fortnight's restraint than a lifetime of Mr Collins's interference," her grandfather said. "Now, Frances, what else have you planned?"

Mrs Bennet drew out her memorandum book. "We must consider the daily schedule thoroughly. Mr Collins must see evidence of your authority, sir, without overtaxing your strength. I suggest…"

Elizabeth listened as her mother detailed their strategy, thinking of Mr Darcy's keen observations. Would such deliberately constructed appearances withstand his scrutiny? And through him, Mr Bingley's? Their other neighbours' protective silence had served them well these five years, but new eyes might see what they wished to hide.

Yet they had no choice but to maintain their course. Mr Collins must be managed, their independence preserved, at least until… Until what? Until some magnificent marriage saved them? Until their management proved so exemplary that even Mr Collins must acknowledge it? Until grandfather passed and they were forced to leave Longbourn?

Elizabeth pushed aside such useless speculations. They would do what they must, as they had these past several years. One careful decision after another, preserving their future through wit and will and careful management of appearances.

"Your grandfather will breakfast in his rooms - no need to tax his strength with stairs more than once a day. We shall review estate business with him there, where Mr Collins may observe how studiously you attend his guidance." Mrs Bennet's expression softened as she glanced at her father-in-law. "We must ensure these performances do not tire you unduly, sir."

"I believe I can manage to look both authoritative and infirm," Mr Bennet said drily. "I have had considerable practice in both roles."

"The letters and papers will be arranged on your desk each morning," Elizabeth added. "Mr Collins must see evidence to show your active management. Should we remove Aunt Eleanor's agricultural writings - he would hardly approve of such reading forming the basis of estate decisions."

"Shelve them on the bottom shelves. The boundary books must remain prominent," Grandfather insisted. "Mr Collins needs to understand that I know every acre of Longbourn's extent. He has made too many remarks about possible encroachment by neighbours." Mr Bennet smiled. Rather than encroachments, the family had expanded the estate with additional lands exempt from the entail. The acquisition of neighbouring farms had required sacrifices, but they managed knowing it meant their future security.

"Mamma," Elizabeth said slowly, "how might our new neighbours at Netherfield affect our situation? Mr Bingley will naturally seek local guidance about estate management. His friend Mr Darcy is unquestionably a man who understands property management thoroughly. I fear our typical methods of preserving appearances may not serve with such observers."

"That could prove awkward," Mrs Bennet mused. "Sir William's protection has served us well with the established neighbourhood, but new arrivals who take an active interest in estate matters…" She paused. "Perhaps Mr Darcy's expertise might be turned to advantage. If he could speak of respect for our management of Longbourn when meeting Mr Collins…"

"I fear he already suffers from some resistance to accepting female capability in such matters," Elizabeth noted.

"Then we must consider how to manage both situations," her grandfather said. "Mr Collins must see my authority maintained, whilst Mr Darcy…" He coughed, and Elizabeth moved quickly to adjust his shawl. "Whilst Mr Darcy might see Longbourn's true competence without discovering how intentionally we guard appearances."

"We shall ensure that he sees more of Longbourn's efficient management, whilst preserving the appearance of traditional patriarchal authority." Mrs Bennet's expression turned calculating. "Sir William might be persuaded to speak of your grandfather's innovative methods, preparing the ground for Mr Darcy to view our situation more favourably."

"A complex dance," Elizabeth said. "And one in which a single misstep could prove disastrous."

"Yes, my dear." Her grandfather's voice held weariness. "Sometimes I wonder if we do you girls more harm than good with all this dissembling. If we should simply…"

"No," said Mrs Bennet firmly. "We have maintained this course for years. We shall continue until the girls' futures are secure. Now, let us review how the estate books should be arranged for Mr Collins's inspection. Some evidence of feminine handwriting may be permitted - he will expect ladies to assist with basic recording - but all significant decisions must appear to be entirely by your grandfather's hand."

Mr Bennet consulted a leather-bound volume. "The Matthews pasture remains our most delicate situation. His Lordship continues to maintain the fiction that he leases it to us, although the deed is secure in our strongbox."

"I cannot blame him for wanting to preserve appearances. The loss of ancestral lands is a bitter thing." Elizabeth added.

"And yet his loss has been our gain," her grandfather said. "That pasture has proved excellent for the sheep, especially since you implemented the new grazing plan, Lydia."

"We must be scrupulously careful how we present that

improvement to Mr Collins," Mr Bennet said. "While the work was completed with our own funds, we allowed Lord Matthews to imply he had some hand in improving it. Better that Mr Collins believe we operate with the oversight of a gentleman neighbour."

Elizabeth's lips twitched. "Even if that gentleman's only contribution was to lose spectacularly at hazard and then beg us to keep his shame private?"

"Lizzy," her mother admonished, although her own mouth quirked a bit. "Such arrangements are not uncommon, although usually between gentlemen rather than…" She gestured vaguely at their unique situation.

"The Willow Brook farm was a cleaner transaction," Mr Bennet noted. "Old Mr Harris was happy enough to sell to us directly, with no need for elaborate pretence."

"Even there, we encouraged the neighbourhood to assume it was grandfather's decision rather than Jane's careful calculation of the advantage," Elizabeth said.

"We must ensure Mr Collins sees only the most conventional evidence of your abilities. Now, about the Matthews land - Mr Bingley will need to be consulted about its effect on Netherfield's water flow, but how shall we manage the discussion without revealing our true ownership?"

"As much as I detest disguise, I fear we ought to continue to maintain the assumption that we lease it." Mr Bennet said. "Lizzy, you may be required to conduct a little fictional accounting to make it appear that Matthews retains the deed? Some small payments back to him could be conjured up?"

Elizabeth nodded and bent to the task, her pen imitating the more old-fashioned shapes of her grandfather's hand. Her thoughts kept returning to Mr Darcy's penetrating gaze. They could hardly maintain such careful appearances under the observation of a man accustomed to managing one of the largest estates in Derbyshire. They must hold on to hope that Mr Collins was less astute.

Chapter Ten

"Lydia, please move your animal husbandry volumes to the stables," Jane directed, surveying the drawing room. "Kitty, your watercolours on that table - be certain to leave some unfinished. Mary, your music looks too well-ordered."

"I have selected some particularly tedious pieces," Mary said, rearranging the sheets with studied carelessness. "Simple enough to appear lady-like yet dull enough to discourage lengthy appreciation."

Elizabeth entered with an armful of delicate needlework. "Lydia's sketch of the new lambs are in a most insipid style. It appears as simply a young girl's sentimental drawing."

"Perfect." Jane stepped back to assess the effect. "Everything appears believably feminine, yet nothing invites prolonged examination. Now, what of Mr Collins's chamber?"

"The blue room," said Elizabeth. "It catches every draught from the north wing, and the fireplace draws poorly. I have placed extra blankets in the chest - they appear thoughtful, whilst suggesting he ought to have need of them."

"And I have selected linens that, whilst perfectly clean and proper, are well worn and far from our finest," Jane added. "The mattress has been turned but not replaced. It remains somewhat lumpy on the left side."

Mary looked up. "Cook has planned a fortnight of menus that display our capability without extravagance. The first days show our best offerings, then gradually shift to plainer fare. All from our own produce, naturally, but prepared simply enough to imply greater economy."

"The thought of deliberately serving indifferent meals…" Jane sighed.

"Better indifferent meals than an indefinite visit," Elizabeth said firmly. "Has Hill arranged the morning schedule?"

"Yes. The fires will be lit in his chamber precisely half an hour too late for true comfort, although not so late he might reasonably complain. And the hot water for shaving will arrive quite tepid and with sufficient delay to make him late for breakfast."

"Mary, your mathematical studies?" Elizabeth said. "They must be well hidden."

"Along with my notes on soil composition," Mary agreed. "I have left only a most insipid novel and my prayer book visible. Of course, I will carry that distasteful Fordyce volume with me at all times, although it pains me to pretend such intellectual vacancy. I have removed the binding to conceal my notebooks within in the coming days."

Kitty entered with an armful of dried flowers. "The bulk of the stillroom tinctures and stores are concealed behind a few preserves and jellies. All my designs for the kitchen garden are hidden away, replaced with pressed flowers and amateur sketches."

"And Lydia?" Jane enquired.

"Sulking in the stables, making the most of her last morning with the sheep," said Elizabeth. "Although she has promised to affect proper feminine vapidity when required."

"It seems a terrible deception," Jane murmured.

"It seems a necessary one." Elizabeth adjusted a tambour frame, leaving a dangling thread to suggest recent abandonment. "Everything must appear exactly as a gentleman would expect to find a household of ladies: accomplished enough to be respectable, yet not so competent as to suggest suspicious independence."

"The drawing room at least is ready," Mary said. "We can retreat here at a moment's notice and appear utterly occupied with feminine pursuits."

"And give thanks if Mr Collins knows nothing of good music, fine embroidery, or correct watercolour technique," said Elizabeth. "For I fear our hasty preparations would not withstand truly knowledgeable scrutiny."

Jane paused in arranging a bowl of late roses. "Like Mr Darcy's scrutiny?"

"Just so." Elizabeth frowned at the elegant arrangement. "Too artistic, Jane. Make it appear more casually gathered. We must not show too much skill in any direction."

"A pity we cannot simply demonstrate our actual abilities," Kitty said wistfully, replacing her careful flower study drawing with a more amateurish attempt.

"A fortnight of pretence," Elizabeth reminded her. "We have managed years of careful appearances. We can certainly maintain the deception through one brief visit."

Yet as she surveyed their artfully arranged scene of genteel feminine occupation, Elizabeth pushed away a tendril of doubt. They had practised these deceptions for so long - but would they withstand the close observation of their cousin?

Mary sighed, removing the sheet music. "I suppose I must appear to prefer simple country airs. Although it seems a waste of all those hours practising fingering." She replaced Bach with a simpler piece. "At least I need not pretend complete musical ignorance."

"Unlike my pretence with the sheep," Lydia said from the doorway. She held up two sketches. "Which do you prefer - the lamb drawn with proper anatomical understanding, or this one where I appear to think the ram has five legs?"

"Lydia!" Jane exclaimed. "You cannot leave that about."

"Why not? Mr Collins would attribute it to charming feminine ignorance of animal husbandry." Lydia's voice carried an unfamiliar sharpness. "Never mind that I can recite three generations of breeding lines."

"The five-legged lamb might be a touch too obvious," Elizabeth said drily. "Perhaps adhere to proper anatomy. And do try to seem interested in their sweet faces rather than their wool quality and breeding lines."

"I was thinking of naming it 'Precious Little Lamb' or perhaps 'Darling Sheep in Spring.'" Lydia said with exaggerated sweetness. "Rather than 'Prime Example of Fourth-Generation

Merino Cross-Breeding.'"

"Much better," Jane approved. "Although perhaps with just a touch less irony in your tone when Mr Collins arrives."

Kitty looked up from the table where she was arranging her watercolours. "I have hidden all my garden planning sketches - and left these…" She held up a painting of flowers, deliberately composed with incorrect perspective. "It seems absurd to pretend I cannot draw a straight line when I regularly design planting beds to precise measurements."

"At least you need not hide your work completely," Jane said. "Although perhaps these…" She removed several agricultural treatises from the side table, replacing them with a volume of sermons and a book of poetry.

"Ah yes, for who would suspect a lady's poetry reading concealed memorised passages about water flow?" Elizabeth smiled.

"How strange that we must hide the very skills that have kept Longbourn prosperous these five years." Jane said.

"Whilst feigning devotion to accomplishments we have scarcely time to practise," Elizabeth agreed. She surveyed their neatly arranged display of feminine incompetence. "We are fortunate our cousin knows so little of estate management that he will never recognise Mary's agricultural notes in her 'poetry,' or Kitty's irrigation designs disguised as flower sketches."

"Or notice that the lady drawing charming lamb portraits can discuss wool futures," Lydia added. "Although I still say the five-legged lamb has artistic merit."

"We have learnt to be exact in all things," Jane said. "Although for the next fortnight, we must appear to pursue excellence only in those areas society deems appropriate for ladies."

Darcy had not intended to call at Longbourn again so soon. The initial visit had been a necessary courtesy—the drainage issues between the properties required attention before the autumn rains began in earnest. But Bingley, having encountered Miss Bennet, had insisted they ride out to "ensure Mr Bennet had not been overtaxed by their previous call."

The chill October air had reddened their cheeks during their ride, the scent of fallen leaves rising from beneath their horses' hooves. Tree branches stood starkly against the pale sky, a reminder that winter approached, and drainage matters could not wait.

Darcy strongly suspected his friend's concern had less to do with the elderly gentleman's health and more to do with Miss Jane Bennet's appeal. Her slender fingers had moved over the columns of figures with the same grace another young lady might employ at the pianoforte.

As they approached Longbourn on horseback, a flurry of activity drew his eye. A farm cart stood by the kitchen entrance, a servant was unloading extra chairs, the wood scraping against the cart bed with each removal. Young Robbie Lucas, Sir William's son, struggled toward the house with an instrument case, his face flushed with the effort of maintaining its upright position. Through the open door, autumn flowers in rich gold and russet hues sat in temporary disarray.

"They appear to be preparing for some entertainment," Darcy remarked as they dismounted, the leather of his saddle creaking beneath him. "Perhaps we have called at an inopportune time."

Excitement illuminated Bingley's features. "I daresay I am curious about what occasion merits such preparation in a household that is generally occupied with practical matters."

The gravel crunched beneath their boots as a stable boy hurried to take their horses, his eyes curious beneath an unruly fringe of hair. Hill, the housekeeper Darcy remembered from their previous visit, admitted them with a curtsy that betrayed mild surprise at their arrival, the subtle widening of her eyes betraying what her disciplined features concealed.

"Mr Bingley, Mr Darcy," she announced as she showed them into the drawing room.

Mrs Bennet stood directing Kitty and Lydia in arranging vases of varying sizes, her hands filled with autumn roses whose fragrance permeated the room. A half-arranged spray of goldenrod lay on a side table, waiting its turn.

"Gentlemen!" Mrs Bennet's eyebrows rose perceptibly. "We did not expect callers this afternoon. What a… pleasant surprise." Her momentary pause spoke volumes.

Miss Kitty and Miss Lydia exchanged a glance, the younger girl's eyes widening fractionally before her lips pressed together, a silent communication that conveyed some shared disappointment or concern.

"We wished to enquire about Mr Bennet's health," Bingley explained, his voice carrying the warmth he employed for social pleasantries. Freshly polished floorboards gleamed in the afternoon light as he stepped further into the room.

"How kind," Mrs Bennet replied, transferring the roses to Kitty's waiting hands. Several petals drifted to the floor, landing silently on the polished wood. "My father-in-law will be pleased to hear it. He is resting at present but is much improved, thanks in part to Kitty's remedy."

Miss Kitty's cheeks flushed pink. The memory of her earnest questions about herbal properties rose in Darcy's mind, accompanied by an unexpected memory of his mother bent over her stillroom books, her dark hair falling forward as she noted measurements and effects in her neat hand.

The door latch clicked, drawing all eyes as Miss Elizabeth and Miss Jane entered, both carrying additional flowers. The scent of fresh greenery accompanied them. A streak of pollen marked Miss Elizabeth's sleeve, evidence of her involvement with the arrangements.

Miss Jane recovered first; her voice as gracious as Darcy remembered. "Mr Bingley, Mr Darcy. What a pleasant surprise."

Miss Elizabeth's expressive eyes registered a sequence of emotions—surprise, something resembling dismay, then a composed politeness that transformed her features. "You find us in some disarray, I fear."

"We are preparing for a small gathering this evening," Miss Jane explained, setting her flowers on a nearby table. A few drops of water sparkled on her fingers, catching the light. "Just a few neighbours and friends."

"Capital!" Bingley leant forward, his eagerness evident in the sudden animation of his features. "A dinner party?"

"A dance, actually," Miss Lydia replied, her voice lifting with an enthusiasm Darcy had not previously observed. Her fingers ceased their nervous arrangement of rose stems. "Our own private assembly, since—"

"Since we have had so few opportunities for music and merriment of late," Mrs Bennet interjected smoothly. Her hand brushed her daughter's arm in what appeared a casual gesture, although the warning in her eyes contradicted its lightness. "My father-in-law enjoys hearing Mary play, and Sir William Lucas is always eager for a country dance."

The undercurrent in this exchange spoke of some history—a disappointment or slight, perhaps. The Bennet family's uncommon circumstances would naturally affect their social standing in a community as traditional as this one appeared to be. The arrangements struck Darcy as less a festive preparation than a determined effort to create gaiety where it had been denied.

"How delightful," Bingley enthused, his eyes drifting to Miss Jane. "I have always believed music and dancing to be among life's greatest pleasures."

Miss Elizabeth bent over her flowers, arranging them with particular attention. Her hands, Darcy noted, bore a faint callus where a pen would rest, and a small scratch across her palm suggested gardening without gloves. The imperfection rendered them more interesting than the unblemished hands so prized in London drawing rooms.

"Perhaps," Mrs Bennet said suddenly, setting down a vase with a decisive click against the wooden table, "you gentlemen might join our little party this evening? It is a modest affair, to be sure, nothing like the grandeur you must be accustomed to, but we would be honoured by your company."

The invitation hung in the air. Miss Elizabeth's head jerked up, her wide eyes meeting her mother's in apparent alarm. Miss Jane froze, her normally graceful movements arrested mid-gesture. The two younger girls, however, displayed undisguised excitement, Miss Lydia's hands actually clapping together in barely suppressed delight.

Bingley turned to Darcy, his eyes bright with anticipation. The silent plea in his expression could not have been more eloquent had he spoken aloud: *Say yes, man.*

Darcy hesitated. An evening of country dances with the local gentry was hardly how he had intended to spend his time at Netherfield. Miss Bingley would undoubtedly purse her lips in that particular expression of disdain she reserved for provincial entertainments. The society would be limited, the accommodations modest.

His gaze moved to Miss Elizabeth, who had composed her features but whose spine had straightened imperceptibly, her chin lifting with quiet pride as she awaited his response. The autumn sunlight caught a small scatter of freckles across the bridge of her nose—evidence of a life not confined to drawing rooms and shaded gardens.

There was something compelling about this family that defied conventional expectations. Even the younger girls had developed practical skills that went far beyond the typical accomplishments of young ladies.

"We would be delighted," Darcy found the words escaping his lips before his mind had fully formed the decision to accept. The sensation of speaking without prior deliberation was so foreign to his nature that he nearly glanced over his shoulder, as if another gentleman had spoken in his stead. Bingley's face bloomed with undisguised pleasure, whilst Darcy experienced a peculiar sensation in his chest—something between discomfort and anticipation. "I fear we are not properly attired for an evening of dancing.".

"Nonsense," Mrs Bennet declared with a dismissive wave, the

lace at her cuff fluttering with the movement. "Our gathering is informal. The gentlemen will be wearing their everyday attire, you may rely upon it."

"Then we accept with pleasure," Bingley replied before Darcy could reconsider. His voice carried the particular timbre of suppressed excitement Darcy recognised from their university days. "What time shall we return?"

"The dancing begins at seven," Mrs Bennet replied. "Although you are welcome to join us for a light supper beforehand, at six."

As arrangements were confirmed, Miss Elizabeth's expression caught Darcy's attention. Her head tilted to one side; her eyes narrowed in assessment. The look contained neither coquettish approval nor calculated interest—rather, she appeared to be reconciling his acceptance with some preconceived notion of his character. The directness of her gaze caused him to shift his posture, his shoulders squaring beneath his coat.

They took their leave shortly thereafter, promising to return for the evening's entertainment. The gravel of the drive crunched beneath their boots as they returned to their horses. A faint strain of music drifted from a window—Miss Mary practising at the pianoforte, the notes of a country dance floating clearly in the still afternoon air.

As they rode back toward Netherfield, Bingley could hardly contain himself.

"What extraordinary good fortune!" His voice carried above the steady rhythm of hoofbeats. "A country dance is just what we need to feel properly welcomed. Did you observe Miss Bennet's expression? I believe she was pleased at our acceptance."

"I wonder," Darcy said, loosening his reins as his horse sidestepped a puddle from yesterday's rain. "Would Miss Bingley be reluctant to join the entertainment?"

Bingley's animated features faltered momentarily, a shadow passing over his customary good humour quickly replaced with a triumphant grin. "Caroline and Louisa are dining with that family from Lyme—the Holisters, I believe. They will not miss us." His voice lowered as they approached a hedgerow. "Between ourselves, Darcy, I am rather relieved Caroline will not be present. Her observations about country manners can be… less than kind."

The understatement drew a rare smile from Darcy. Caroline Bingley's determination to find fault with everything that did not match London standards would undoubtedly have cast a pall over the evening. Her last assessment of country fashion had nearly reduced a vicar's wife to weeping at a garden party.

"It will be a simple country party," Darcy said, the autumn air cool against his face as they increased their pace. "Nothing we have not attended many times before."

There was, to Darcy's quiet astonishment, something about the evening had awakened his curiosity. He most especially anticipated further conversation with Miss Elizabeth, whose practical knowledge and a sharp intellect was unencumbered by the artificial delicacy so common among young ladies of his acquaintance.

Longbourn presented a transformed aspect when they returned that evening. Lanterns illuminated the drive, their warm glow creating pools of golden light against the deepening blue of twilight. The windows of the modest manor house gleamed with extra candles, and the sound of a violin being tuned drifted through the partially open door.

The drawing room had undergone a remarkable transformation—furniture pushed against the walls to create a central space, autumn roses arranged in vases on every available surface. The pianoforte had been positioned to allow Miss Mary both to play and observe the assembled company, whilst leaving adequate space for sets of dancers.

Sir William Lucas greeted them with his characteristic effusive courtesy, his flushed face suggesting he had already partaken liberally of the Bennet family's hospitality. "Mr Darcy! Mr Bingley! Capital, capital! We were just saying how pleasant it would be to have additional gentlemen for the dancing."

Mrs Phillips, Mrs Bennet's sister, scrutinised them with undisguised curiosity, her gaze lingering on Darcy's cravat as though assessing its cost and fashion. Mr Phillips engaged Bingley in conversation about shooting prospects, his voice carrying the enthusiasm of a man eager to ingratiate himself with a wealthy new neighbour.

Their conversation was interrupted by the arrival of several young men whom Darcy did not recognise. From their attire—good quality but lacking the particular cut and fabric that marked London tailoring—he judged them to be from the more prosperous farming families. Not gentlemen by birth, but respectable, nonetheless. The easy manner with which the Bennet sisters greeted them suggested established acquaintance.

"Mr Robinson and his brother," Miss Elizabeth explained, appearing at his elbow. "They manage the largest tenant farm at Longbourn. John has a particular gift with draft horses, whilst Thomas has introduced several innovations in crop rotation."

Darcy observed the easy manner with which Miss Lydia greeted the younger Robinson brother. A becoming flush coloured her cheeks, and her normally rapid speech slowed to a more measured pace as she enquired after some livestock concern. The young man's attentive posture as he replied suggested mutual interest that transcended mere neighbourly regard.

"Your sisters appear to have found their respective spheres of interest," he remarked to Miss Elizabeth, noting how the candlelight lit the amber highlights in her.

"Necessity has proved a most effective teacher," she replied. Her voice carried a challenge, her chin tilting upward defiantly. "I understand it might seem peculiar to one accustomed to more traditional divisions of labour."

"On the contrary," Darcy countered, "I find it admirable that you manage not just the household but the home farms as well."

Miss Elizabeth's expression registered surprise, a momentary widening of her eyes before her features settled into thoughtful reassessment. The transformation pleased him more than seemed entirely rational. Before she could respond, Miss Mary took her place at the pianoforte and struck the opening chords of a country dance, the young Lucas boy joining her with his violin.

"Shall we form our sets?" Sir William called out, his voice carrying over the preliminary notes. "Mr Darcy, perhaps you would honour us by standing up for the first dance. Allow me to present this young lady to you as a very desirable partner. You cannot refuse to dance, I am sure, when so much beauty is before you." Sir William took Elizabeth's hand and gave it to Mr Darcy, who, though extremely surprised, was not unwilling to receive it.

Darcy turned to Miss Elizabeth, with grave propriety, and requested to be allowed the honour of her hand. Elizabeth accepted with a composed expression that revealed little of her thoughts, though her eyes held a speculative quality he could not quite interpret. As they took their places for the dance, he noted that Bingley had, predictably, secured Miss Jane as his partner. The younger Robinson brother stood with Miss Lydia, whilst Sir William partnered Miss Kitty. Mr Phillips and his wife completed the set.

The first notes resonated through the room. Miss Mary's playing revealing unexpected skill. The precision of her touch compensated for what might have been lacking in passion, and the small size of the gathering lent an intimacy to the proceedings that larger assemblies often lacked. The young Lucas son's violin accompaniment blended harmoniously, creating a fuller sound than Darcy had anticipated from such modest arrangements.

The wooden floor creaked beneath their feet as the dance began, the familiar pattern bringing them together and apart in the familiar rhythm of the figures. Miss Elizabeth moved with natural grace, her steps light and assured despite what must have been limited opportunities for practice in recent years. The touch of her hand against his during the turns sent an inexplicable warmth through his fingers, travelling up his arm in a sensation both foreign and strangely pleasant.

"You dance well, Miss Elizabeth," he said during a moment when the pattern brought them together, the music temporarily softer as the Lucas boy adjusted his fingering.

"You are surprised, sir?" she replied, a spark of amusement illuminating her eyes. "Did you expect that calculating crop yields might render one incapable of remembering dance steps?"

"Not at all," he responded, finding himself unexpectedly enjoying her challenge. The corner of his mouth lifted in what might have been classified as a smile. "Merely that opportunity for practice must be limited."

"One does not easily forget the things that bring joy," she said as they separated again, the words carrying a wistful quality as the dance continued, her skirts swirling with each turn.

Throughout the evening, the interactions of the small gathering proved more interesting than Darcy had anticipated. The social divisions he had expected were less rigid here than at formal assemblies. Sir William conversed with the Robinson brothers about agricultural matters, his hands gesturing expansively as he described some new method being employed at Lucas Lodge. Mrs Phillips engaged Miss Mary in a discussion of music that revealed the older woman possessed more knowledge than her provincial appearance might suggest.

Most notable was the transformation in the two youngest Bennet sisters. Miss Lydia, who had sometimes seemed somewhat sullen during their earlier encounters, now displayed animation and even wit as she partnered various gentlemen. Her laugh carried across the room during a particularly lively tune, genuine and unaffected. Miss Kitty's natural shyness diminished visibly as the evening progressed, and more so when discussions turned to gardens and herbal lore. Her posture straightened, her voice grew firmer, and her normally hesitant expressions gave way to confident assertions when describing her remedy for winter coughs.

As for Miss Elizabeth, Darcy found her a more engaging partner than any he had encountered in recent memory. When she spoke of Longbourn, her voice communicated genuine attachment—not only to its social position but to its physical reality. She described a stand of ancient oaks with the same appreciation another young lady might reserve for fine jewels and detailed the particular qualities of the north pasturage with evident knowledge of its soil and drainage.

"You speak of the estate as a farmer might," he said during their second dance together, the music faster now, their movements bringing a slight flush to her cheeks that enhanced rather than diminished her appearance.

"I speak of it as someone who loves it," she corrected him, her voice carrying above the music without effort. "Not merely for what it represents in terms of position or income, but for itself—its particular character and needs."

Darcy inclined his head in agreement, the memory of summer afternoons spent tracing Pemberley's boundaries and unique qualities at his father's side rising unbidden. "Pemberley inspires similar sentiments in me. My father always insisted that true stewardship required understanding every aspect of the estate, from the stands of timber to the most modest tenant cottages."

"A philosophy we share," she said, and for the first time that evening, her smile contained no reservation, transforming her countenance from pleasantly handsome to unmistakably beautiful in the candlelight.

Chapter Eleven

The evening progressed with a pleasant informality that Darcy had not expected to enjoy. Supper, served on simple but well-polished dishes, featured produce from Longbourn's gardens and kitchens—roasted fowl with herbs he recognised from Miss Kitty's careful cultivation, vegetables whose freshness spoke of recent harvesting, and preserves whose colour and clarity would not have disgraced a London table.

Miss Mary relinquished the pianoforte to Miss Elizabeth for several songs, revealing the latter's more expressive, if less technically precise, playing style. Her fingers moved over the keys with confidence, and if an occasional note went astray, the warmth of her interpretation more than compensated.

Sir William persuaded Miss Lydia to demonstrate a Scottish reel with young Robinson, which they performed with such enthusiasm that even Mr Phillips was moved to applaud vigorously, his customary self-consequence forgotten in genuine appreciation.

Throughout it all, Bingley's enchantment with Miss Jane Bennet grew increasingly evident. His gaze followed her movements across the room, his expression holding the particular fascination Darcy had observed during his friend's frequent attachments. Miss Bennet's response remained more measured—she received his attentions with gentle pleasure but without the calculated encouragement so common among young ladies with matrimonial aspirations. Whether this indicated disinterest or simply a more reserved nature remained to be determined, though Darcy inclined toward the latter interpretation.

As the evening drew to a close, the candles burning lower in their holders and casting longer shadows across the polished floor, Darcy had come to stand beside Miss Elizabeth at the window. The glass reflected their images against the darkness outside—his tall figure in stark black and white, her more colourful form beside him, autumn flowers in her hair.

"Your sister seems to have captured my friend's admiration," he said, watching as Bingley assisted Miss Jane in rearranging some music sheets, his hands lingering near hers longer than strictly necessary.

"Jane captures admiration wherever she goes," Miss Elizabeth replied, genuine affection warming her voice. "Although she remains largely unaware of it."

"And what," Darcy asked, the directness of the question surprising even himself. "Do you make of Bingley's evident partiality?"

She considered for a moment, her reflection in the glass showing a thoughtful expression. "I think Jane finds Mr Bingley's company pleasing. But she has learnt caution these past years. We all have."

"Caution?" The trace of wine from supper lingered pleasantly on his tongue, perhaps explaining his uncharacteristic persistence in personal matters.

"Our circumstances are not ordinary, Mr Darcy. The neighbourhood does not always know how to place us. Are we gentlewomen to be courted, or anomalies to be pitied? Most have settled on the latter view." No self-pity coloured her words, only a clear-eyed assessment that reminded him of his cousin Colonel Fitzwilliam's reports from the continent—factual, unembellished, but revealing deeper truths to those who knew how to listen.

Something in her candour unsettled him—in the gentlest, most disarming way. "Society often fails to recognise true worth when it appears in unexpected forms."

"How philosophical," she said, her reflection showing a slight smile. "I had not expected such sentiment from you, Mr Darcy."

"No?" he replied, genuinely curious, turning from the

window to observe her directly. He admired the fine structure of her cheekbones, the intelligence in her dark eyes. "What had you expected?"

"From our limited acquaintance, I had formed the impression that you placed greater importance on the proper forms of society."

"I value order," he acknowledged, noting how the simple dress she wore suited her figure admirably. "But I value substance more. Your family's management of Longbourn demonstrates a commitment and competence that many would do well to emulate."

Her expression suggested she had not anticipated this response. A flash of reassessment passed across her features, followed by something that might have been the beginning of a genuine smile. Before their conversation could continue, however, Bingley approached to announce that they should take their leave, as the hour was growing late.

The farewells were marked by genuine warmth on all sides. Mrs Bennet thanked them for their attendance with a sincerity that Darcy found touching, whilst Sir William insisted they must repeat the gathering at Lucas Lodge in the near future, his expansive gestures suggesting he already envisioned the arrangements. Miss Mary, normally so reserved, blushed to thank Darcy for his compliments on her playing.

As they prepared to depart, Miss Elizabeth accompanied them to the door, the hallway somewhat cooler than the drawing room had been, with its assemblage of dancers and candles.

"I hope the evening proved not too tedious, Mr Darcy," she said, gentle defiance lingering behind her courtesy. "I imagine it bears little resemblance to the entertainments you are accustomed to in town."

"It was unlike any evening I have spent in London," he agreed. The night air entered cool against his face as the door opened before them. Then he added with complete honesty, "And all the better for it."

The surprise that flickered across her features was followed by a genuine smile that remained in his mind long after they had left

Longbourn behind. The ride back to Netherfield took them through the cool autumn night, stars visible in a sky clearer than London ever offered. Bingley's enthusiastic commentary about Miss Bennet's many perfections—her grace, her beauty, her unexpected knowledge of agricultural matters—washed over him, requiring only occasional murmurs of agreement.

"I must say, Darcy," Bingley remarked as they approached Netherfield, the house a dark mass against the night sky, "that was a most enjoyable evening. I should like to reciprocate such hospitality. Why, I might hold a ball at Netherfield! Would that suit?"

Darcy realized with a jolt that, unlike his habitual revolt at such a prospect, he saw merit in another evening spent in such a way.

"I would think the prospect of a Netherfield ball would be extremely agreeable to every family in Meryton. It would further establish your place as a leading gentleman of the area." Darcy said.

"Then we shall plan a ball! I am certain Caroline would be delighted to arrange for it. Another evening as enjoyable as this one, but in my own ballroom. I say, I had not expected you to enjoy yourself so thoroughly. You actually smiled—several times! Miss Elizabeth Bennet must be a truly remarkable conversationalist."

"She is extraordinary," Darcy conceded, unwilling to reveal the full extent of his interest despite the darkness that would have hidden any betraying expression. "The entire family defies conventional expectations."

"In the most delightful way," Bingley agreed fervently. "Miss Bennet's grasp of agricultural concerns surpasses that of many gentlemen. And did you observe how she spoke with the tenant farmers? Such natural dignity, yet without condescension."

Darcy answered with a quiet inclination of the head, though his thoughts had already strayed to Miss Elizabeth. There was something compelling about a woman who had faced adversity and emerged not just unbroken but strengthened.

Such a woman, he reflected as they turned their horses toward the stables, would understand the true meaning of partnership in marriage. The image of Miss Elizabeth at Pemberley rose unbidden—no mere ornament at his table, but a true partner in its stewardship—discussing estate improvements in his study, walking the boundaries with knowledge equal to his own, bringing her practical wisdom to the challenges that arose. It was a thought that continued to occupy him well into the night, long after Bingley had retired to dream, no doubt, of golden hair and gentle smiles, accompanying him into dreams that left him both unsettled and strangely content upon waking.

"Mr Collins approaches from the Meryton road," Kitty announced from her post at the breakfast-room window. They had taken turns being stationed there since dawn, allowing the family to orchestrate their positions perfectly.

"Excellent." Mrs Bennet made a final adjustment to her cap. "Hill has already taken your grandfather's morning chocolate to the study. When Mr Collins enquires, we shall tell him Mr Bennet is surveying the south fields - he has missed him by not half an hour. As soon as Mr Collins has retired to refresh himself, Lydia will place the muddied boots by the door to support our story."

In truth, Mr Bennet rested comfortably in his study, having rehearsed this particular deception the day before. His mud-spattered boots, intentionally dirtied by Hill, would testify to his regular field inspections without requiring him to actually undertake them.

"Jane, you have you completed the estate book edit?" Elizabeth confirmed.

"Yes, although I had to create a full new set of pages. His last letter asking pointed questions about the sheep fold made me suspect he might demand to examine those records."

The sound of wheels on gravel brought them to attention. Through the window, they observed a tall, heavy-looking young man of five-and-twenty. His air was grave and stately. Mr Collins stepped down from the hired gig, his attention immediately fixing upon the façade of Longbourn with an air of ownership that made Elizabeth's fingers itch to ensure the true estate books were thoroughly hidden.

"Remember," Mrs Bennet said gently. "We are nothing more than ladies who assist your grandfather out of duty. Nothing more." Each lady took her assigned spot in the drawing room, looking for all the world as though they were accustomed to spending their days in lady-like pursuits.

Mr Collins's knock echoed through the hall. When Hill admitted him, he entered with the aspect of one taking the measure of rooms for new carpets.

"My dear cousins," he announced, his voice as unctuous as his letters had suggested. "How fortunate you are that I have come to assist you in your perilous situation. I observe already that the shrubbery requires attention - although naturally ladies cannot be expected to notice such things."

Elizabeth caught Kitty's slight flinch - she had designed those healthy plantings herself - and stepped forward smoothly. "How kind of you to show such interest, Cousin. But I believe my grandfather is even now examining the south fields. Shall we await his return in the drawing room? I believe Mary was about to favour us with a country air."

Mr Collins stood several inches shorter than Elizabeth, although his manner suggested he believed himself to look down upon them all. His clerical black showed signs of recent brushing that somehow only emphasised its shabbiness, and his attempts at elegant gestures succeeded mainly in displaying his coat's too-short sleeves.

"The drawing room appears tolerably well-maintained," he pronounced, examining the furnishings with a look of critical assessment, as mentally calculating their value. "Although perhaps lacking the touch of a more… sophisticated hand. At Rosings Park, where I have the honour to serve as rector, Lady Catherine de Bourgh has often remarked that a drawing room should display evidence of truly elegant accomplishments."

He lingered near the larger pieces, no doubt considering what he might find worth keeping. His hands, she observed, bore no calluses, no signs of sun—pudgy and soft, untouched by a day's real work. Yet he spoke as if with the authority of an experienced landowner.

"And this passage," he continued, stepping into the hall, "might be improved by the removal of these old prints. Lady Catherine says that pastoral scenes in halls are quite outmoded. Although naturally you ladies cannot have had the opportunity to observe more current fashions."

Jane's hand touched Elizabeth's arm in warning. Their grandfather deeply valued those prints–his sister Eleanor's careful collection of agricultural innovations disguised as rural tableaux.

"Will you join us for tea, Cousin?" Mary suggested, heading off his wandering. "Although I fear you find us quite informal compared to Rosings Park."

"Indeed, indeed." Mr Collins preceded them with the tone of a benevolent inspector. "One cannot expect the same standards, of course. Although when the time comes…" He left the sentence hanging indelicately.

The dining room had been thoroughly prepared - not too neat, suggesting daily use, but not so disordered as to indicate careless housekeeping. Mr Collins circled the table, running a finger along the surface.

"Lady Catherine always says that one may judge the character of a household by the state of its mahogany. This piece would derive considerable advantage from more consistent care." He paused. "Although in light of your situation, one cannot reasonably anticipate such." Elizabeth bit back several responses about the true character revealed by examining table surfaces. The scent of furniture polish and the gleam of the surface of the woods was testament to its pristine condition. Instead, she said mildly, "We find our present arrangements serve tolerably well."

"Natural enough that you should think so." His smile held condescending sympathy. "Limited experience must necessarily result in limited understanding. When I come into the property - although of course I pray that day remains distant - you will see the advantages of more sophisticated methods."

Through the window, Elizabeth glimpsed Lydia hastily retreating from the barn, having no doubt been checking on her beloved sheep. They had agreed she must not be caught anywhere near the flocks during Mr Collins's visit.

"Shall we continue to the library?" Mr Collins enquired.

Jane suggested smoothly. "I believe my grandfather keeps that room quite private for estate business."

Mr Collins's expression sharpened with interest. "As his heir, I naturally take a particular concern in estate matters. Perhaps we might examine--"

"But surely," said Mary, her voice carrying just the right note of innocent respect, "you would wish to take refreshment first? Grandfather takes such pride in maintaining perfect order in his business affairs he would wish to be present for your review. Why, only this morning he was saying how grateful he is that Lady Catherine's rector shows such appreciation for correct forms and ceremony."

Mr Collins swelled visibly at this reference to his patroness's approval. Mary had managed both to flatter their cousin and protect their documentation with a single careful suggestion. Elizabeth smiled broadly at Mary, who grimaced and then winked.

"Quite right, quite right," Mr Collins agreed importantly. "One must observe the proper forms, as Lady Catherine herself has often remarked. Although naturally, as heir--"

A sudden commotion from the stillroom interrupted his pronouncement. Elizabeth recognised the distinctive sound of Kitty's agricultural journals hitting the floor.

"I believe Cook has been quite busy," Mary said smoothly, before Mr Collins could investigate. "She has been preparing her special seed cake, Cousin. She was most particular about following my grandfather's housekeeper's receipt exactly–he so values the old family traditions."

Mr Collins's attention diverted easily to the prospect of refreshments, his eyes lingered on the stillroom door. "Most proper to maintain traditional methods," he approved. "Although at

Rosings, Lady Catherine says--"

A muffled thud from above suggested someone had dropped a ledger in Grandfather's study. Jane coughed delicately. "Please take a seat, Mr Collins."

"Thank you Cousin Jane." Mr Collins directed a particularly smarmy smile in her direction, his eyes roving over her figure in a rather impious manner.

"Perhaps after tea we might proceed to the garden?" she suggested. "The roses were quite fine this autumn. My grandfather takes such pleasure in maintaining the standards set by his dear sister Eleanor."

"Ah yes, my late second cousin." Mr Collins adopted a suitably solemn expression. "Although I believe she held some rather… unconventional opinions about estate management?"

"Oh, hardly that," Mary interjected, her eyes widening with calculated dismay. "She simply recorded her observations about the flowers and weather. See here--" She gestured to the deceptively peaceful garden view. "The roses she planted still bloom exactly where tradition suggests they should. Grandfather often says no truly refined lady would dream of questioning established methods."

Jane poured as Mr Collins absorbed this masterful reshaping of Eleanor's legacy. Mary had managed to transform their aunt's agricultural innovations into feminine flower-fancying, all while appealing to his respect for tradition and authority.

Their cousin might think himself perspicacious, but he was no match for Mary's particular brand of wide-eyed manipulation. She had learnt to wield apparent innocence as skillfully as she wielded her account books—although the latter talent remained completely hidden.

Chapter Twelve

Three and six for the repair? Highway robbery, Mr Williams, when the work required is barely worth half that." Lydia's voice carried clearly across the shop, her typical exuberance focused into surprising acumen. "The hinge needs only minor adjustment, not complete replacement."

"Miss Lydia," the iron monger sputtered, "surely your grandfather…"

"Has taught me well the value of both materials and labour," Lydia finished firmly, whilst Kitty nodded beside her. "Two shillings, and we'll continue bringing Longbourn's business to your establishment."

The bell above the shop door chimed, admitting a wash of red coats and masculine attention. Mr Denny's familiar figure led the group.

"Miss Lydia, Miss Catherine! What fortune to encounter you." His bow encompassed his companions. "Allow me to present Lieutenant Carter, Captain Morris, and Mr Wickham, newly joined to our regiment."

Mr Wickham's smile held practised charm as he stepped forward. "Such a pleasure to meet Meryton's renowned beauties. I daresay I am surprised to find young ladies engaged in such… practical matters."

"Oh?" Lydia's arch expression would have done Elizabeth proud. "Do you find discussion of metal work beneath feminine understanding, Mr Wickham?"

"Not at all," he demurred smoothly. "Although such concerns need not occupy one blessed with such other… obvious charms. I find myself delighted," Wickham's expression shifted into something artfully charming, a smile he had likely used to open many doors, as his eyes strayed to take in Lydia's well-grown form, "to find such charming company in Meryton. The Bennet sisters' beauty is already legendary among the officers."

"How flattering," Lydia replied, her tone suggesting it was anything but. "Although I wonder, Mr Wickham, do you find all five sisters equally legendary, or do particular… circumstances enhance our charms?"

"Circumstances?" He affected confusion, although something calculated flickered in his eyes.

"Our circumstances. Our situation. Our…" she paused deliberately, "prospects."

"Ah." His laugh held a touch of unease beneath its polish. "You cannot doubt it, Miss Lydia, my admiration is entirely focused on more… personal attributes."

"Personal attributes will not feed you, sir. You must be quite unique among your fellow officers in caring not for fortune. I understand most gentlemen in the military take a keen interest in… financial matters. The cost of commissions being what they are." Lydia shifted her basket and straightened, better to meet Wickham's evasive eye.

Captain Morris nodded approvingly. "A practical consideration, Miss Lydia. The purchase of a captaincy requires significant investment."

Lydia's eyes never left Wickham's increasingly stiff countenance. "And you, Mr Wickham? Might I enquire, sir, as to your occupations beyond your military service? Have you other matters to supplement your own charms, sir?"

A flicker of discomfort crossed his handsome features. "I was meant for the church, however a cruelty of chance denied me a living."

"A man of the cloth? Unusual for a Milita man. When did you take orders?"

"I, well, without the living I had been promised, there seemed no need. I had some thoughts of the law…"

"Had?" Lydia pressed. "Did you read law?"

"It proved to be more costly than my purse would allow."

"And now?"

"Now I find military life better suited to my temperament."

Lydia raised a brow and turned to include the other officers. "Mr Wickham has already undertaken three different professions. Perhaps that has slowed his hopes. Tell me, Captain Morris, what are the prospects for advancement in your profession? I understand it requires both dedication and personal investment."

As Morris outlined the requirements of purchasing commissions and the years of service needed for promotion, Wickham's easy manner faltered notably.

"Most officers are unmarried, are they not?" Lydia's smile turned razor sharp.

"A few have found ladies who are willing to follow the drum. Captain Forrester has married recently. He is a second son with an annuity. He has been most fortunate to make an …advantageous alliance."

"Mrs Forrester had a fortune of her own, did she not? I imagine a truly advantageous alliance would require both parties to bring something of value to the arrangement. Beyond charm and a red coat, that is."

"Worth comes in many forms, Miss Lydia," Wickham attempted to rally, his gaze once again straying to her figure. "Beauty such as yours needs no supplement."

"How interesting that you equate beauty with worth," she said. "Whilst dismissing the value of actual accomplishment or industry. Tell me, what do you have to offer beyond flattery?"

The other officers shifted uncomfortably as Wickham's charm fractured further. "I had thought the Bennet sisters above such mercenary considerations."

"Mercenary? Oh no, sir. Merely practical. A lady must consider her future. After all, a man seeking to marry should at least offer something beyond pretty compliments and borrowed regimentals, do not you agree?"

Wickham's handsome features froze in a rictus of

embarrassment as Captain Morris poorly concealed a snort of laughter.

"Now then, Mr Williams," Lydia turned back to the iron monger with calm efficiency. "About that gate repair…"

"Two shillings and sixpence, Miss Lydia, and I will have Thomas see to it this afternoon."

"Excellent." She made a curtsey that somehow managed to include all whilst dismissing one. "Good day, gentlemen. Do enjoy your… pursuit of advancement."

As they departed, Kitty whispered, "Lizzy will be proud when she hears how you managed that!"

"Managed what?" Lydia's eyes sparkled. "I simply expressed an interest in the gentleman's prospects. Although I must say, Mr Wickham's proved remarkably unimpressive upon examination."

"Come now, Darcy, you cannot deny that Longbourn is welcoming," Bingley said cheerfully as their horses approached Longbourn. "One social call is hardly too much to ask after they were kind enough to invite us to their party."

Darcy's noncommittal grunt might have discouraged a less determined friend, but Bingley had long since grown immune to such tactics.

They found Longbourn markedly different from their previous visit. Where before there had been an air of comfortable industry–account books neatly stacked on a side table, Miss Elizabeth and her grandfather bent over estate maps–now there was a palpable tension. The elderly Mr Bennet sat in a soft chair by the hearth, but his customary placid expression had been replaced by one of barely concealed irritation.

"Mr Bingley, Mr Darcy," Elizabeth rose to greet them, her smile not quite reaching her eyes. "How kind of you--"

"My dear cousins!" A loud voice interrupted as a short, pompous figure hurried forward. "You cannot imagine my delight in welcoming such distinguished visitors! Mr Darcy, sir, to think that I should have the honour of receiving my noble patroness's nephew in what will soon be my own establishment--"

Darcy noted how Elizabeth's shoulders stiffened, how Jane's serene face showed a flicker of distress, and how Mrs Bennet, typically effusive with visitors, seemed to be seeking refuge behind her handkerchief. Her eyes flashed, but her lips were set in a grim line.

"Mr Collins," Mary Bennet spoke up, her calm tone carrying an edge, "our guests may wish to be introduced before—"

"Nonsense, Cousin Mary! Lady Catherine herself has instructed me on the proper way to receive persons of consequence. Why, last Easter--"

"Mr Collins." The elderly Mr Bennet's quiet voice somehow cut sharply through the clergyman's endless blather.

The room fell silent at Mr Bennet's quiet command. Darcy observed how even this small exertion seemed to tax the elderly gentleman, whose fingers gripped the armrests of his chair with alarming intensity.

"Perhaps," Mr Bennet continued after regaining his composure, "you might allow Miss Elizabeth to perform the introductions."

Mr Collins bowed with exaggerated deference. "Of course, of course. Forgive my enthusiasm."

Elizabeth stepped forward; her chin lifted in the quiet determination Darcy recognised as a shield against discomfort. "Mr Bingley, Mr Darcy, with your indulgence, may I present our cousin, Mr William Collins of Hunsford, Kent. Mr Collins is Longbourn's heir under the entail and has come to… make himself acquainted with Longbourn."

The words were spoken evenly, but Darcy did not miss the significance. The entail. Of course. Longbourn would pass not to any of the five Bennet daughters, but to this obsequious man who even now was beaming at Darcy with an expression of almost painful reverence.

"Mr Darcy!" Mr Collins exclaimed, unable to contain himself

further. "The nephew of the Right Honourable Lady Catherine de Bourgh of Rosings Park! My noble patroness has spoken of you often, sir. Most recently when she graciously allowed me to attend her on the evening of the 23rd ultimo, she mentioned your excellent management of Pemberley and how it might serve as an example to less distinguished landowners." He cut his eyes in the direction of Mr Bennet, his disdain obvious.

Darcy inclined his head, uncomfortable with both the excessive praise and the sudden understanding that was forming in his mind. Elizabeth's knowledge of estate management, the innovative drainage works, the careful account books—these were not purely academic interests. They were necessities.

"You serve as Lady Catherine's clergyman?" he enquired, more to direct the conversation away from himself than out of genuine interest.

"I have that singular honour, sir! Her Ladyship bestowed upon me the living at Hunsford Parsonage some eighteen months ago, and her condescension knows no bounds. I also have the privilege of a regular acquaintance with the fair Miss Anne de Bourgh, that singular diamond of femininity, for whom, I am certain you recall, Lady Catherine has long nurtured expectations of the most elevated nature regarding her establishment." Mr Collins gave Darcy a peculiar look before continuing, "Lady Catherine has ensured my perfect comfort at my humble parsonage. Why, only last month she suggested an improvement to my garden hedge that I would never have conceived of myself!"

Jane Bennet moved quietly to her grandfather's side, offering him a glass. The old man's face softening as he accepted it.

"The entail has been in place for three generations," Mr Bennet said suddenly, his shrewd eyes fixed on Darcy, as if in communication. "My grandfather's grandfather was most insistent that Longbourn should never leave the male line. A common enough sentiment, although one might question its wisdom when that line produces only surviving daughters."

Mrs Bennet's handkerchief was now pressed firmly to her

mouth, but her distress was evident in her wide eyes.

"Indeed," Mr Collins interjected, seemingly oblivious to the room's tension, "it is a most fortuitous arrangement. Lady Catherine herself has encouraged me to ensure the security of my inheritance as soon as possible. 'Mr Collins,' she said, 'a man must know his property intimately if he is to manage it with any competence'"

Darcy watched as Elizabeth's hand came to rest protectively on her grandfather's shoulder. The picture was painfully clear. The Bennet ladies—all five sisters—would be utterly dependent on the largesse of this ridiculous man upon their grandfather's death. Their home, the estate they had so capably managed, would pass from their hands into his.

"I understand Longbourn produces a comfortable return," Bingley remarked, his cheerfulness tempered with unexpected perception. "The improvements to the water channels that Miss Elizabeth showed us last week were most impressive."

"Ah yes," Mr Collins nodded vigorously. "Most impressive for ladies to think they might concern themselves with such matters. Of course, once I assume responsibility, more sophisticated methods will be implemented, and the ladies will return to their natural sphere. Lady Catherine has most specific ideas about estate management which she has been kind enough to share with me despite my humble origins."

Elizabeth's fingers tightened on her grandfather's shoulder as though bracing against something unseen. Jane's mask of composure slipped for just a moment to reveal something like despair.

"Your cousins have maintained Longbourn admirably," Darcy said, his tone sharper than he intended. "The pastures and fields particularly show evidence of careful management."

Mr Collins waved a dismissive hand. "Female accomplishments, whilst charming, can hardly substitute for a gentleman's oversight in such matters," Mr Collins declared with a pontifical air. "Nature itself, in its divine wisdom, has designed the female mind for domestic concerns rather than land management. Lady Catherine often remarks that women who dabble in men's affairs risk upsetting the natural balance that Providence has established. 'Mr Collins,' she told me, 'Woman is created to soothe and comfort, to maintain hearth and home, not to exhaust their delicate constitutions with matters better left to gentlemen.' I have already identified several areas where improvements must be made once the estate comes under my care. The female tendency toward sentiment over rationality has, I fear, resulted in some questionable decisions." He smirked as he met eyes with Darcy, apparently anticipating enthusiastic agreement.

Darcy looked to Elizabeth briefly and saw in her expression not only anger but a fierce pride. Her questioning about Pemberley's water management had been aimed to gather information that might sustain her family against the time when their home and livelihood passed to this pompous fool.

Darcy considered the unsettling reality faced by women of good breeding and no portion. The Bennet sisters, accomplished and intelligent as they were, would be entirely at the mercy of either marriage or their cousin's goodwill.

"Indeed, my aunt is singularly devoted to the concerns of her estate, Rosings. As I recall, she was intimately involved in business matters there." Darcy said irritably.

Subtlety was lost on Mr Collins, who launched into another panegyric on Lady Catherine's wisdom. Darcy observed the silent communication between the Bennet sisters—a language of glances and subtle gestures that spoke volumes about their shared concern and determination. His previous understanding had proved far more than incomplete—it had bordered upon blindness. Mr Collins paused, seemingly waiting for approval of his pronouncements. When none came, he abruptly shifted course.

"But let us speak of more pleasant matters! I understand, Mr Darcy, that you have a most accomplished sister. Lady Catherine has often mentioned Miss Darcy's exceptional skill at the pianoforte. Such feminine accomplishments are, of course, surely what nature intends for young ladies of good breeding."

Darcy grimaced. That this obsequious fool should so much

as speak Georgiana's name sent a wave of visceral revulsion through him. His disgust threatened to manifest in a cutting remark that propriety alone—not mercy—prevented him from delivering.

"I believe you were telling us about your plans to inspect the grain storage." Mr Bennet interrupted the ceaseless flow of nonsense emanating from Mr Collins.

"Oh! Yes, indeed. I must say, Cousin Elizabeth's peculiar involvement in such matters has left everything in quite a disorderly state. When I assume control--"

Elizabeth's knuckles whitened, and Darcy glared at Mr Collins sharply. The ease that had marked their previous visits had vanished, replaced by an atmosphere that reminded Darcy uncomfortably of a fox in a henhouse.

"Miss Elizabeth," Darcy said, "I wonder if I might enquire further about your success with rerouting the overflow from the north pasture. I found our previous discussion most illuminating."

The flash of distress in Elizabeth's eyes at this escape was quickly masked, but not before Darcy caught it. As she led him toward the window to discuss agriculture, he could hear Mr Collins behind them, earnestly explaining to Bingley how Lady Catherine would never permit such irregular management of her estates.

"He cannot know, Mr Darcy. We have tried to pretend grandfather is engaged in every task, but he begins to see that my sisters and I are managing Longbourn. It only makes matters worse."

"Forgive me, I should have perceived that. How are you managing with his presence?" he asked.

"Not quite well, if I am honest. My mother is suffering from nerves and my poor grandfather… to be treated as feeble by such a man."

Darcy's concern deepened as he registered the subtle signs of strain in the household. The Bennet ladies had struck him as uncommonly capable during his last visit. Now, he was watching Mr Collins hover about them like an overeager vulture.

Mr Collins intercepted Mr Darcy and Mr Bingley as they were preparing to leave. His rapid approach and officious manner caused both gentlemen to exchange a subtle glance of resignation as they were again caught up in his endless oration.

"Mr Darcy! Such providence to find you here. I was just composing a letter to my most noble patroness, Lady Catherine de Bourgh, describing the lamentable state of affairs I have discovered at Longbourn." Mr Collins mopped his brow with a handkerchief, despite the coolness of the day. "I cannot express sufficient gratitude that your aunt's guidance has prepared me for such a task as this."

"Mr Bingley and I were noting the remarkable efficiency of the estate's water management. Miss Elizabeth has quite a comprehensive knowledge of the land." Darcy schooled his expression, although his jaw tightened subtly. He doubted he could instill any sense in the parson, but he would make the attempt.

"Ah yes, poor Cousin Elizabeth," Mr Collins said, his disdain palpable. "Such unladylike occupations cannot have been her choice. Lady Catherine would never permit a gentlewoman under her protection to wade through fields like a common labourer. When I assume my rightful position--"

"Thier water system," Bingley interrupted, his good humour noticeably strained, "has prevented flooding in three neighbouring properties. I believe your cousin's 'unladylike pursuits' have saved several families' crops this season."

Mr Collins waved this away. "No true lady wishes to muck about in filth. Why, at Rosings--"

"My aunt," Darcy cut in coldly, "has also frequently expressed that negligent estate management is unforgivable in a gentleman." His dark eyes fixed on Mr Collins with uncomfortable intensity. "Have you extensive experience in such matters?"

Mr Collins sputtered. "I… but… Lady Catherine has most graciously…"

"I would be most interested to hear your plans for improving the excellent plan already in place." Darcy's tone made it clear this was not a casual enquiry. "Perhaps you could outline your strategy for the water management challenges that Miss Elizabeth so ably demonstrated?"

Bingley leant forward with exaggerated interest. "Yes, do tell us! I found Miss Elizabeth's solutions quite ingenious."

Mr Collins's face had taken on a decidedly greenish tint. "I… I must consult Lady Catherine's opinions on the matter. If you will excuse me, gentlemen…"

Mr Collins retreated with unseemly haste, Darcy watched him go with growing concern. "Bingley," he said quietly, "I find myself… unsettled. That man's imprudence may prove hazardous to all concerned."

"Completely agree, old friend," Bingley replied, his face serious. "Completely agree."

Chapter Thirteen

LONGBOURN ESTATE, Hertfordshire, November 15th, 18—

The Right Honourable Lady Catherine de Bourgh

Rosings Park, Kent

Your Ladyship,

I hasten to communicate to your noble attention a most unexpected and fortuitous circumstance that has transpired during my sojourn at Longbourn, the estate which Providence has destined to be my future home. Your Ladyship's most esteemed nephew, Mr Fitzwilliam Darcy of Pemberley, has graced this humble abode with his distinguished presence!

I was momentarily rendered speechless (a condition your Ladyship knows occurs but rarely) upon the announcement of his arrival. That my insignificant residence-to-be should be honoured by the very nephew your Ladyship has so often mentioned with deserved approbation! Mr Darcy carries himself with that dignified mien your Ladyship had led me to expect and exhibits that superior understanding which marks him as worthy of his illustrious connections.

I have already begun to assert my rightful authority over the supervision of Longbourn, as per your Ladyship's most sagacious counsel. The female members of the family have, I regret to inform your Ladyship, been permitted an unseemly degree of involvement in matters not of their sphere. I have made it abundantly clear that such masculine pursuits are beyond the natural capacity of the feminine understanding, citing your Ladyship's own wisdom on the proper sphere of feminine accomplishments. Mr Darcy appeared most attentive during my exposition of these principles.

It may interest your Ladyship to know that Mr Darcy finds himself here in the company of several young ladies, my cousins, who possess a certain provincial prettiness. Although I would never presume to question Mr Darcy's discernment, I felt it my Christian duty to make subtle reference to his long-standing betrothal to your Ladyship's daughter, the Honourable Miss Anne de Bourgh. I trust I have not overstepped in reminding him, however obliquely, of the expectations attendant upon that most advantageous connection which has been, as your Ladyship has often intimated, fixed since the cradle.

Of my cousins, Miss Elizabeth Bennet, in particular, demonstrates an unfortunate tendency toward impertinent wit and independent thinking—qualities which, whilst perhaps momentarily diverting, can never compare to the refined breeding and genteel demeanour of Miss de Bourgh. I have observed Mr Darcy's gaze fall upon her with an expression I cannot quite decipher, but I am certain a gentleman of his elevated understanding would never be seriously diverted by a young lady of such inferior connections and modest fortune.

I continue to implement your Ladyship's invaluable instructions regarding the future management of Longbourn. The chimney in the second parlour shall indeed be replaced according to your specifications, and I have already selected the spot where the new hen house shall be constructed, following your Ladyship's most specific directions as to its ideal orientation.

I remain, with the most profound respect and eternal gratitude for your condescension in guiding one so unworthy as myself,

Your Ladyship's most humble and obedient servant, William Mr Collins

The Lucas's drawing room hummed with the excitement of a country evening party, where social divisions could be either softened or sharpened by proximity and punch. Sir William Lucas moved among his guests with practised bonhomie, but even his efforts could not completely smooth the undercurrents Darcy observed with growing interest.

"Miss Eliza," Charlotte Lucas said warmly, claiming her friend's attention from Mr Collins's endless monologue about Lady

Catherine's opinions on female education. "My father told me how well the new drainage plan protected the lower fields during last week's rains."

"Most unseemly," Caroline Bingley murmured at Darcy's elbow. "To hear them discuss ditches and fields as if they were farmers. I suppose when one has no choice but to scramble in the dirt--"

Darcy moved away from her, ostensibly to observe the card tables. He watched as the local gentry divided themselves: the Longs and Sir William largely comfortable with the Bennets' practical approach to their estate, whilst others like the Gouldings and Harringtons kept a subtle but definite distance.

"Mr Darcy!" Mr Collins had somehow again materialised at his side. "I was explaining to my fair cousins how Lady Catherine would consider it most improper for gentlewomen to concern themselves with such base matters as agriculture. Female delicacy is corrupted by attention to the coarser aspects of estate management, which Providence has designated as the province of gentlemen. I am sure you would never wish to see your intended, Miss Anne de Bourgh, exposed to such unrefined subjects. When I am master of Longbourn--"

"Miss de Bourgh is my cousin, not my intended." Darcy interrupted coldly. "I understand the current management has increased yields remarkably at Longbourn."

Mr Collins was struck dumb momentarily by this shocking response and Darcy took advantage of the event. He turned to cross the room, his eyes following Elizabeth as she joined a whist table with Charlotte Lucas and two elderly gentlemen who, he noted, treated her with marked respect.

Across the room, Bingley had claimed the seat beside Jane Bennet. Even from this distance, Darcy could see his friend's characteristic animation heightened by her presence. Miss Bennet's tranquil smile remained whilst Bingley spoke, although her eyes occasionally darted with concern to where her grandfather dozed in a corner chair, looking frailer than he had at their last meeting.

"Really, Mr Darcy," Miss Bingley had found him again. "One must feel for the neighbourhood, forced to watch this spectacle of gentlewomen playing at being stewards. Of course, with their connections—or lack thereof—they can hardly hope to maintain a higher sphere."

"They are indeed gentlewomen, by birth." Darcy's voice was arctic. "Gentlewomen with profound competence. Not everyone has the luxury of ignoring the source of their prosperity, Miss Bingley."

Darcy fixed his gaze on a point just past Miss Bingley's left shoulder, refusing to meet her eager eyes.

"Profound?" Miss Bingley's laugh tinkled like breaking glass. "My dear Mr Darcy, you cannot be serious. What could country misses possibly know of such matters? I suppose," she added with poisonous sweetness, "one must make allowances for their… circumstances."

Darcy felt his jaw tighten. Miss Elizabeth's observations and quick grasp of complex problems that had baffled more experienced men contrasted with Miss Bingley's affected ignorance.

"Their circumstances appear to include maintaining a profitable estate through intelligence and diligence," he said, his tone dropping several degrees below freezing. "Ignorance is not refinement, Miss Bingley."

A dull flush crept up Miss Bingley's neck. She fingered her expensive necklace, searching for a response that would both soothe his evident displeasure and maintain her assault on the Bennets. Before she could speak, Darcy continued, his voice cutting:

"I have found that those most eager to disparage others' understanding often reveal the limitations of their own. If you will excuse me, I have not yet conversed with our hostess." He gave her a proper bow and strode across the room, leaving her open-mouthed behind him.

He drew a deep breath, surprised by his own vehemence. He walked without direction, then stopped to observe Elizabeth and Charlotte's whist game. Their easy friendship was evident in their shared glances and half-hidden smiles, most notably when Mr

Collins's voice rose above the general conversation with yet another reference to his noble patroness.

"You see, Miss Lucas," Mr Collins was saying to Maria Lucas, who looked about her for an avenue of escape, trapped by a deluge of words, "Lady Catherine herself has often said that young ladies should devote themselves to acceptable accomplishments. Why, Miss Anne de Bourgh is the very model of genteel behaviour-"

"I believe," Charlotte cut in smoothly, laying down a winning card, "that acceptable accomplishments include whatever is necessary to fulfil one's duties."

Darcy smiled, and drew into their corner, away from Miss Bingley's obvious attempts to catch his eye. "Quite so. I have always found that true accomplishment lies in rising to one's responsibilities, whatever form they may take."

The grateful look Elizabeth gave Charlotte spoke volumes about their friendship, even as Mr Collins began another effusive speech about Lady Catherine's views. Darcy noted that the Lucas family had positioned themselves as allies to the Bennets, creating a buffer between them and the more censorious elements of local society.

The evening painted a clear picture: the Bennet ladies were walking a precarious line between necessity and propriety, with their allies and detractors clearly drawn. And hovering over it all was Mr Collins, his combination of obsequious attention to rank and barely concealed eagerness for control becoming more unsettling with each passing hour.

Elizabeth observed her sister Kitty seated between Mary and one of the Lucas cousins, noting how her trained eye contemplated the floral arrangement. The wilting blossoms scented the air, confirming what Elizabeth could read in her sister's slight frown—the late autumn flowers were poorly chosen, already dropping petals onto the pristine white tablecloth. She knew Kitty's fingers must be itching to rearrange them into something more sustainable.

The gentle hum of conversation and the delicate clink of silver against china filled the room as Mr Blackwood entered the dining room last, having lingered in the library. A shaft of light caught the leather-bound volume beneath his arm, drawing Kitty's eye. Her sister's expression brightened, the slight widening of her eyes and straightening of her posture signalling recognition. Elizabeth could tell Kitty had identified the distinctive gilt spine of Brookshaw's "Pomona Britannica"—a work Kitty studied in the Longbourn library many times. The exquisite fruit illustrations provided revelations about cultivation.

"Mr Blackwood," Kitty said during a lull in the conversation. "I beg your pardon, but I observe you have Brookshaw's work with you. His illustrations of the Ribston Pippin are most illuminating with regard to pruning technique."

Mr Blackwood turned toward Kitty, his countenance shifting from civil indifference to marked attention. "You are acquainted with Brookshaw's work, Miss Catherine?"

"I am, sir. I must own I find his direction regarding espalier training somewhat wanting when compared with Kennedy's *'Treatise Upon Planting.'* Have you had occasion to examine both?"

Mr Blackwood leant forward, his tea seemingly forgotten. "Kennedy's treatise is indeed most instructive," he said. "Do you not agree that Brookshaw's illustrations of the branch formations…" He paused, regarding Kitty with fresh consideration. "Pray tell, Miss Catherine, you have studied these matters in detail?"

"Since father's passing, we have been obliged to manage Longbourn ourselves, under the supervision of our grandfather," Kitty explained. "The kitchen gardens and orchards are my particular charge. A thorough understanding of each plant's nature is essential to correct placement within the scheme."

"The scheme?" Mr Blackwood enquired.

"Yes, sir - for instance, I have made certain trials with complementary plantings. The apple trees in our south orchard were quite poorly until I introduced particular flowering herbs beneath them. The bees are better drawn to them, you see, and the herbs serve to discourage certain pests whilst providing dried bouquets and…"

Kitty fell silent, suddenly aware of having spoken at such length about matters of cultivation at a party. But Mr Blackwood's expression betrayed nothing but keen interest.

"The Goulding's orchards have been much troubled by woolly aphids," he said, lowering his voice as if imparting a confidence. "I wonder if perhaps… that is, your observations would prove most…" He straightened, seemingly recollecting himself. "I beg your pardon, Miss Catherine. I nearly suggested an improper inspection of the fruit trees."

"There can be nothing improper in discourse on an apple orchard," Kitty responded, her cheeks growing warm, the pink flush spreading across her fair skin. "I believe my sister Jane assisted Mrs Goulding with the planning of her rose garden this past spring. Perhaps we might all walk out to view the orchards one afternoon?"

His smile reached his eyes, creating the smallest of creases at their corners. "That would be entirely proper, would it not? Although I must warn you, Miss Catherine, I hold decided thoughts on the matter of root stock selection."

"As do I, sir." Kitty's smiled with genuine pleasure, illuminating her features from within. The sudden radiance revealed what careful propriety had heretofore concealed—a natural vivacity and warmth of spirit.

From across the table, Elizabeth caught Kitty's eye and offered a subtle, approving nod. She was pleased to see her sister found someone who appreciated her horticultural knowledge rather than finding it unsuitable for a young lady. Mr Blackwood was a gentleman of modest means from a family of local standing, a suitable match for Kitty should their shared interest in horticulture blossom into something deeper.

Elizabeth Bennet adjusted the ledger under her arm as she made her way through Meryton's crowded market square. The early autumn air carried the mingled scents of fresh bread, livestock, and hay. She and Lydia had negotiated a favourable price for Longbourn's wool when she spotted Mr Darcy examining the merchants' wares.

"Miss Elizabeth." He bowed, more deeply than strictly necessary for a market day encounter. "I had not expected to encounter you in the marketplace."

"Then you underestimate the wool trade, Mr Darcy," she replied, patting her ledger. "Longbourn's sheep may not rival Pemberley's, but their wool still requires selling."

A flash of surprise crossed his features. "You handle the transactions yourself?"

"Lydia and I did. Whom did you expect me to send?" Elizabeth raised an eyebrow. "We have no steward, and Grandfather is not able to travel into town. We found it more profitable to conduct our business without a factor's commission. Although I admit, Mr Bentham," she nodded towards the merchant, "was sceptical of dealing with a woman at first."

The merchant had the grace to look abashed. "The Misses Bennet drive a harder bargain than any man I know."

Darcy's expression shifted from surprise to interest. "I have left such matters to my steward at Pemberley. Although given the latest reports…" He hesitated.

"Reports may lead one astray when one lacks practical knowledge of the trade," Elizabeth offered. "My grandfather insisted we learn every aspect, from the shearing to the selling."

"Then perhaps you would share your insights?" There was a note of respect in Darcy's voice. "I find myself increasingly convinced that an owner's direct oversight cannot be replaced."

Before Elizabeth could respond, she caught sight of her sister Jane deep in conversation with Mr Bingley near the grain merchant's stall. Jane was consulting her own ledger whilst Bingley listened intently, his affable smile replaced by focused attention.

"It seems your friend is receiving an education in grain

prices," Elizabeth said.

Darcy watched the pair for a moment. "Bingley has much to learn about his estate. He is fortunate in his teacher today."

"As are the Netherfield tenants. Jane has already noticed their grain stores will not last the winter at current consumption."

Darcy's attention snapped back to Elizabeth. "I advised Bingley similarly, but he seemed uncertain how to address it."

"Then perhaps you should both join us this afternoon. We are meeting with our tenants about crop plans for next season." Elizabeth paused, suddenly aware of how forward this sounded. "That is, if you have no other engagements."

"None that take precedence over careful planning," Darcy replied, his voice warming. "I own, Miss Elizabeth, I am nearly as interested in the teacher as the lesson."

Elizabeth felt her cheeks heat again. Her heart quickened beneath her spencer, but she met his gaze steadily, willing her expression to reveal nothing of the confusion within. The hustle of the marketplace continued—the calls of vendors, the bleating of sheep, the earthy scent of wool and bread—yet somehow his words had created a peculiar sensation.

She took a moment to consider her response. Her practical mind attempted categorised his words as mere pleasantries. The softening of his mouth and the crease near his eyes—could this mean genuine admiration? A man whose fortune allowed him such finely tailored clothes, whose every gesture spoke of authority—No. He did not consider a country gentleman's granddaughter as anything more than a passing diversion.

If Mr Darcy was flirting, she would not permit her foolish heart to build castles from such insubstantial materials. Better to respond with humour.

"Then you should pay extra attention, Mr Darcy," she said, her voice steadier than her pulse. "I expect my students to excel."

The autumn breeze caught her bonnet ribbons. She adjusted them, hiding her turmoil with practised grace. A cart rumbled past, briefly separating them. She used those seconds to compose herself, to rebuild the necessary distance.

A slight smile tugged at his mouth. "I shall endeavour not to disappoint."

Elizabeth felt the dangerous pull of that smile. She clutched her ledger more tightly—a reminder of her duties. Romantic fantasies had no place here—not when Longbourn's future hung in the balance.

As they parted, she was struck by how different Darcy seemed here, among merchants and farmers. There was a directness she had not seen before, a genuine interest in the practical matters that consumed her days.

Perhaps, she reflected, there was more to the master of Pemberley than she had supposed.

The afternoon brought the warmth of weak sunshine as the bustle of Longbourn's tenant farmers gathered near the granary. Jane stood by the barn with Mr Bingley, listening as old Mr Granger described the damage rootworm had done to the early crop. Elizabeth had brought Darcy to the far end, where she unrolled the maps of the western fields.

"These parcels have had wheat two years running," she said. "We propose rotating in barley and letting the farthest section go to wheat."

The oak table in Longbourn's steward's office bore an assortment of parish maps, crop ledgers, and last year's grain tallies. Four tenant farmers stood respectfully whilst Elizabeth traced the field boundaries with her finger.

"Mr Waters, you planted rye in the north field these three years past." Elizabeth looked up at the weathered farmer. "The yield diminished with each harvest."

"Aye, Miss. Ground's near spent." Waters shifted his weight. "But I have not seed enough for wheat, and my children must eat."

Mr Darcy, who had been studying the harvest figures, raised

his head. "At Pemberley, we found success with field peas planted before the wheat. They return vigour to tired soil."

"Field peas fetch a fair price," Waters said thoughtfully, "although the outlay for seed…" He hesitated. "And if the spring proves wet, the risk of losing both peas and the chance for a wheat planting."

"But should the crop succeed, you would have feed for your animals, food for your family, and surplus to sell. The improved soil would benefit next year's wheat as well." Jane said.

"We might share the risk," Elizabeth added. "A share of the pea harvest to repay the seed cost, the remainder yours to sell or store as you choose."

The farmer Mills spoke up. "Begging pardon, Miss, but my own father grew field peas in rotation. Made a fine profit selling to the drover's horses passing through, he did."

"Pemberley's tenants supply the coaching inns," Darcy said. "The demand remains steady through winter."

Waters rubbed his chin. "If the estate shares the risk… and with the coaching trade…" He straightened. "I would try it, Miss."

"The true risk lies in doing nothing," said Darcy. "Each poor harvest weakens both tenant and land."

Elizabeth noted how Darcy offered his estate's experience without condescension, speaking as one farmer to another despite the vast difference in their circumstances.

The discussion turned to winter provisions. Hayes, whose farm lay near the river, spoke of his root cellar's success. Soon the farmers engaged in vigorous debate over the merits of various storage methods.

"If we might arrange shared transport," Jane suggested, "those with extra root storage might assist those without."

"The river farms helping the hill farms," Elizabeth mused, "and the hill farms sharing their hay in return."

The meeting continued through the afternoon. They addressed the price of winter wheat seed, the timing of the pea planting, the repair of shared fencing, and the coordination of harvest labour. Elizabeth observed how Darcy's practical knowledge and Bingley's amiable nature drew forth the farmers' own expertise, helping to create solutions that served all.

A second farmer, Jacob Hayes, stepped forward. "Begging pardon, but what of winter fodder? Even with better yields next year, we will be hard pressed to feed both animals and families through February."

Elizabeth exchanged glances with Jane. This was the heart of their concern.

"Netherfield's lower meadow produced excess hay this season," Bingley offered. "I had thought to sell it at market, but--"

"If we might negotiate a fair price," Jane said, "and arrange shared transport…"

"The cost of carting would eat any profit," Hayes protested.

"Not if we use the return journey of the clay wagons," Darcy said. His eyes met Elizabeth's. "The routes align."

Elizabeth studied the maps again, calculating distances and costs. "Mr Hayes, if we were to distribute the carting among all farms concerned, each might send one man and horse for a single day. Would that prove manageable?"

The farmers huddled together, murmuring over figures. Darcy waited in patient silence, offering neither pressure nor presumption.

Hayes finally turned back. "It might serve, Miss. Although it would mean trusting each man to do his part."

"We must all do our part," Elizabeth said. She looked around the room. "We either stand together through winter or we all fall short."

As the farmers filed out, Elizabeth heard Waters remark to Hayes, "First time I have seen quality like that gent take dirt under their nails and not seem shamed by it."

She caught Darcy's eye and saw he had heard as well. His slight nod acknowledged that true respect, like fertile soil, must be cultivated over time.

Chapter Fourteen

Elizabeth paused at the dining room doorway; a stack of her grandfather's books balanced precariously in her arms. She had intended to return them to his library but halted at the sound of her grandfather's voice.

"You must credit the tenant's payment against the outstanding balance," Grandfather was saying, his voice stronger than it had been in months. "Mr Wilson has been diligent, even in his difficulties."

Elizabeth smiled to herself. Mary sat at the small writing desk tucked into the alcove beside the sideboard. She was largely hidden from view unless one stood directly in the dining room entrance, as Elizabeth now did. Mary had been taking on more of the estate's accounting work lately, a task she approached with the same methodical discipline she applied to all her exercises.

"But Grandfather," Mary replied, "should we not first deduct the cost of repairs to the north field fence? The old ledger suggests—"

"Bah! The old method leaves too much room for error. I managed Longbourn's accounts for forty years. The tenant pays rent, we credit the account. Repairs come from the maintenance fund. Keep them separate, or we will never make sense of it come quarter day."

Elizabeth was about to enter when a movement in the shadowed corridor to her right caught her attention. Mr Collins, their odious cousin, was creeping along the passageway with exaggerated stealth, his stockinged feet sliding along the polished floor, one finger pressed to his lips although there was no one there to silence.

Curiosity getting the better of her, Elizabeth retreated a step, partially concealing herself behind the door frame whilst maintaining her view of both the dining room and the approaching Mr Collins.

Her cousin reached the doorway and peered in, his mouth forming a perfect 'O' of surprise. From his position, Elizabeth realised, he could see Grandfather gesturing emphatically at the seemingly empty room, Mary hidden by the sideboard.

"Dear me," Mr Collins murmured to himself, although loud enough for Elizabeth to hear. "Most distressing. Most distressing indeed."

Grandfather continued, unaware of his audience. "Now, the figures for the southern pasture will be quite different. Have you found the second ledger I mentioned?"

Mr Collins's eyes widened in alarm. He clutched at his clerical collar, tugging it as although it had suddenly tightened.

"Speaking to phantoms," he whispered, crossing himself with a flourish that would have scandalised his patroness had she witnessed such a papist gesture. "The poor afflicted old gentleman. Clearly, age has robbed him of his faculties. How fortunate that a man of God is present to witness this unfortunate decay."

Elizabeth bit her lip to suppress a laugh. The pompous fool actually believed her grandfather was hallucinating, carrying on a conversation with imaginary entities! She watched as Mr Collins backed away, shaking his head in what he apparently thought was a demonstration of Christian pity.

"Lady Catherine has often remarked that the elderly must be treated with particular condescension when their minds begin to wander," he muttered, retreating down the corridor. "I shall inform her that this situation requires closer supervision. Indeed, it is fortunate that Longbourn will soon have my guiding hand."

Once he had disappeared around the corner, Elizabeth allowed herself a quiet chuckle before entering the dining room.

"Good evening, Grandfather. Mary," she said, placing the books on the table. "I overheard your discussion of the accounts."

Mary turned from her work, ink stain marking her index finger. "Elizabeth, might you explain to me Grandfather's system of—"

"There is need of explanations from either of you impudent girls," the old man huffed, although his eyes twinkled. "In my day, accounts were kept properly."

"And I have no doubt they were," Elizabeth replied, taking a seat beside him. "Though I must tell you both something vastly amusing. Our cousin Mr Collins was just at the door and, unable to see Mary in her alcove, has concluded that you, Grandfather, are conversing with the realm of spirits."

Mary's mouth dropped open. "Surely not!"

"Surely so," Elizabeth continued, barely containing her mirth. "He intends to inform Lady Catherine that you require 'closer supervision' as your faculties are failing."

Grandfather Bennet's weathered face creased into a smile—the first genuine one Elizabeth had seen from him since their cousin's arrival.

"Let him think it," the old man said with unexpected mischief. "Perhaps I shall begin communing with the manor's ghosts at breakfast tomorrow. That should send our unctuous cousin scurrying back to his precious Lady Catherine."

"Grandfather!" Mary admonished, "It would be most improper to mislead a man of the cloth."

"Improper, perhaps," Elizabeth agreed, "but exceedingly amusing nonetheless."

Miss Catherine Bennet walked between her sister Mary and Mrs Goulding along the orchard path, listening to Mr Blackwood discourse on the particular merits of various apple stocks. The late autumn air still carried the sweet scent of ripening fruit, and she studied the placement of the trees with a critical eye.

"You see, Miss Bennet," Mr Blackwood gestured to a row of younger trees, "these were grafted this past spring using the method prescribed by Brookshaw."

Kitty paused, observing the uneven growth of the new

branches. "If I may, sir…" She hesitated, but his expression of genuine interest gave her courage. "Whilst Brookshaw's illustrations are exceptional, I believe in this instance his method has proved less successful than might be wished. The angle of the graft appears too severe."

Mr Blackwood's eyebrows rose. He stepped closer to examine the tree she indicated.

"The sap flow is restricted," she continued, her voice gaining assurance. "See how the leaves above the graft point are smaller? In our orchards at Longbourn, we have found that a more gradual angle, such as Kennedy suggests, allows for better growth. Although I would not presume-"

"Pray continue, Miss Catherine," he said, his attention fixed on the branch she had indicated. "Your observations interest me greatly."

"We have had particular success with a method that…" She drew a small notebook from her reticule and sketched the technique quickly. "Thus, you see? The cambium layers align more naturally."

Mrs Goulding had drifted ahead with Mary, leaving them in view but out of earshot. Mr Blackwood studied Kitty's sketch with evident fascination.

"Most illuminating. And you have implemented this method successfully?"

"Indeed, sir. Although I must own our first attempts last season were not satisfactory. We learnt that the timing of the graft is of greater consequence than Brookshaw suggests. The phase of the moon-"

She stopped herself, fearing she had revealed too much, but Mr Blackwood was already nodding.

"The lunar influence on sap flow is too little considered in modern treatises," he said. "My grandmother kept extensive records on the subject. I should very much like to compare her observations with your experience."

A fallen apple lay in their path. Instead of stepping over it, Mr Blackwood retrieved it, examining the skin. "Would you give me your opinion on this specimen, Miss Catherine? The colouring suggests it may be a Ribston Pippin, but the form is not quite true."

Kitty accepted the apple, turning it with consideration in her gloved hands. "No, sir, I believe this is a Cornish Gillyflower. See the distinctive russeting pattern around the stem? Although I grant you the shape is somewhat irregular, likely due to insufficient thinning of the fruit in early summer."

His expression shifted to genuine respect. "You are perfectly correct, Miss Catherine. I have lately come to think my own knowledge of pomology may be found wanting in comparison to yours."

"Oh! No, indeed, sir. But I have had the great advantage of practical experience. Theory and practice together must surely yield the best results."

"Just so," he replied, his gaze lingering on her face a moment longer than strict propriety might dictate.

They walked on, discussing the relative merits of various rootstocks, their words mingling with the gentle autumn breeze through the apple boughs. Kitty had a glow that had nothing to do with the afternoon sun when Mr Blackwood solicited her opinion on the placement of new saplings he had ordered for the Gouldings' northern slope.

Jane sat in Longbourn's drawing room, the sun warming the leather of her account books as she worked. Her quill scratched across the page as she recorded the quarter's wool profits, each neat figure a testament to Lydia's successful management of their expanded flocks. The peaceful scene was disrupted by Mr Collins's noisy entrance. He seemed incapable of entering a room-or doing much of anything- without speaking. His rumpled clerical black and ceaseless chatter clashed with the room's orderly atmosphere.

Jane's quill paused mid-calculation, a drop of ink bleeding into the paper. She watched it spread with determined focus, maintaining her composed expression as Mr Collins launched into a rehearsed address. She placed a blank sheet over her ledger and stopped the inkwell. The room felt suddenly warm despite the November chill seeping through the windows.

"Miss Bennet." Mr Collins adjusted his cravat with damp fingers before positioning himself rather too closely before her desk, his shadow falling across her figures. The sun through the window caught the sheen of perspiration on his upper lip as he planted his feet in the stance he likely used for sermons, hands clasped behind his back.

Jane's nostrils flared at the competing scents from her cousin. Her sensitive nose, usually soothed by beeswax polish, fresh ink, and lavender sachets, was assaulted by a pungent mix: stale body odour from unwashed skin mixed with a sharp, sour scent of sweat, pungent and intense. His unlaundered clothing added a musty, stale aroma mingled with rancid pomade.

She turned her head abruptly toward the window, seeking relief in the crisp scent of frost-touched herbs from the garden. Even this movement brought a fresh wave of Mr Collins's bouquet.

A sickish heat rose in her throat. Her stomach clenched. She took shallow breaths through her mouth, grateful for the lingering taste of mint tea from breakfast. She fixed her eyes on her ledger, recalling the last number drying unfinished. The familiar scent of iron gall ink offered a small anchor.

"Upon careful consideration of the manifold virtues you possess," he continued, his voice taking on the sonorous quality he no doubt practised for effect. His breath, laced with breakfast and decayed teeth, added a final insult to the room's already beleaguered air. "Not least among them your admirable attention to practical matters, I find myself compelled—by reason, position, and proper regard for my own comfort—to avail myself of the distinct privilege of your hand in marriage. It is, I am convinced, a most advantageous arrangement. A wife of quiet disposition and proven capability in managing household minutiae is precisely what I require. I have no taste for female frivolity, and you appear free of it. Your mild manner will, I daresay, render you agreeable enough company."

"Of course, I would be remiss if I did not pay a compliment to your beauty. I daresay your elegance and manifold attractions would reflect considerable credit upon me. Lady Catherine has often lamented the plainness of clergymen's wives; she will be gratified by my good fortune. Indeed, I consider it divine favour that one so well-favoured in appearance should be made available to me for matrimony. Such pleasing attributes are, in my view, highly auspicious for the future vitality of the Collins line. I trust you will not let sentimental trifles obscure the prudence of such a match."

As he spoke, Jane felt a sensation not unlike seasickness rise within her—a slow, rolling nausea that crept from her stomach and tightened around her throat. That he should so coolly enumerate her domestic virtues as if she were a well-bred dairy cow, then refer to her beauty as though it were a decorative bauble bestowed solely for his benefit, stirred something sharp and unfamiliar. He spoke of comfort, of consequence, of Lady Catherine—but not once of her. Not once of what she might wish, feel, or deserve. And yet he stood there, perspiring and smug, looking upon her with the complacent certainty of a man already accepted. She pressed her tongue against the roof of her mouth, an attempt to block the taste of the air itself. She longed for her private sanctuary in the stillroom, with its clean herbaceous scent. Even the dairy, with its honest smell of fresh manure, would be preferable to this assault on her senses.

The grandfather clock ticked louder than usual. Jane felt each beat match her pulse. She dared not move. She sat still as a deer sensing danger.

"You are most kind, sir," she managed gently, although her fingers gripped the quill until she felt its ridges. A drop of ink fell, marring the clean sheet. "But I must decline. My duty lies in assisting my grandfather."

There was no place at Longbourn for Mr Collins, surely not as her husband and never so long as her grandfather lived.

Mr Collins blinked rapidly, his composure fracturing. "But certainly, you must perceive," he pressed, his voice rising, "how your excellent qualities, joined with my superior position, would create an alliance of singular benefit. With my elevation as master of Longbourn, you would remain in your familiar sphere as my wife."

He leant forward, and Jane resisted leaning back. The sunlight caught the sheen of his hair, and she saw he had nicked himself shaving.

"Lady Catherine herself has remarked—" At the name, his chest swelled visibly beneath a waistcoat now too tight. A thread dangled from one button, catching her eye as she searched for any distraction. "Such a union would, I flatter myself, meet with Lady Catherine's warmest approbation and preserve the estate's prosperity under proper masculine guidance."

"Mr Collins," she said gently, "you do me great honour—"

"Indeed, I must concur," he interjected. "Whilst your portion is negligible, your other attributes and economy more than compensate. You will serve well as a clergyman's wife, and soon as mistress of an estate."

A faint blush coloured Jane's cheeks, although whether from embarrassment, suppressed vexation, or imminent casting up of her accounts, none could say. She drew a careful breath, folding her hands in her lap.

"Sir, please allow me to—"

"And of course," he interrupted, warming to his subject, "Lady Catherine often says, 'A clergyman's household must set an example of frugality and dignity.' Such wisdom! Such penetration!"

Jane's serenity began to crack. She attempted again to speak.

"Mr Collins, whilst I am sensible of the compliment—"

"Oh! Your modesty does you credit, cousin. I have given this matter the most serious thought. The joining of our prudent minds cannot fail to be harmonious. Indeed, I anticipate with particular pleasure the more intimate aspects of our union, as your figure possesses a certain bloom that speaks most eloquently of womanly vigor. Lady Catherine herself has remarked that a wife of robust constitution is a blessing to any parsonage."

Jane remained still in astonished silence, her countenance

betraying such mortification as rendered her momentarily incapable of speech. The color fled from her cheeks before returning with alarming rapidity as the full import of his words impressed itself upon her understanding. She rejoiced to hear footfalls. Elizabeth stood in the doorway. A slight furrow appeared between her brows as she noted her sister's rigid posture.

"Jane, Mamma is asking for you."

Jane rose with perhaps more alacrity than she had ever employed. "Mr Collins, pray excuse me. The duties of the household…"

"Of course, of course! Such domestic attention confirms the wisdom of my choice. I shall await your assent with confidence."

As Jane made her escape, Elizabeth lingered in the doorway, regarding their cousin with an expression that mingled amusement with concern. She had never seen her gentle sister move quite so quickly whilst still maintaining an appearance of decorum. It occurred to her that her own hasty retreat was in order.

The hours that followed were a particular sort of torture that only a country house could provide, where too many people occupied too little space with too much awareness of one another. Jane applied herself to her tasks with deliberate focus, moving from stillroom to kitchen to study in determined patterns calculated to avoid solitude. Elizabeth, understanding her sister's strategy without need for explanation, contrived to be present at crucial moments, appearing with questions about the household accounts whenever Mr Collins's footsteps could be heard approaching.

Their mother, observing these manoeuvres with poorly concealed disgust, intercepted Mr Collins himself as he attempted to follow Jane toward the stillroom.

"Mr Collins," Mrs Bennet's voice carried the particular edge she reserved for unwelcome callers and overly persistent merchants. "Are you not eager to write to your… distinguished patroness… about the improvements you mentioned at breakfast? Such a letter cannot be delayed."

"My dear Madam, whilst Lady Catherine's correspondence is

indeed of the utmost—"

"I insist you attend to it directly." Mrs Bennet's tone brooked no argument. "The writing desk in the small parlour is at your disposal. It is quite… isolated… from any disturbance."

Jane, safely ensconced in the study with Elizabeth, heard her mother's voice drift through the corridor and felt a rush of gratitude. Mrs Bennet would not see any of her daughters tied to a man whose conversation consisted primarily of his noble patroness's opinions on the correct comportment of everyone save herself.

When the family assembled for tea, Mrs Bennet arranged the seating with care, placing Jane between herself and Mary, whilst Mr Collins was relegated to the far corner with only Grandfather Bennet's newspaper for company. When the meal was complete Mrs Bennet rose with significant purpose.

"Come Jane, we must review the menus with Cook." She cast a warning glance at Mr Collins, who had half-risen from his seat. "Such tedious domestic matters would hardly interest a man of the cloth."

But even Mrs Bennet's vigilance could not extend indefinitely. When her mother was called away to see to the kitchen maid, Jane knew she ought to retreat as well. But the day's exertions had left her weary. Surely Mr Collins would not attempt another approach so soon. She lingered over her work, savouring the momentary peace.

It proved a grave miscalculation.

Mr Collins was nothing if not persistent. He again cornered Jane as she was making her way to withdraw.

"My dear Cousin Jane," the words coming from behind her caused the hair on the back of her neck to rise. Certainly, he was not already going to repeat his performance.

Indeed, he was. He sidled up beside her and claimed the seat closest to her, bringing with him the odour she had so happily escaped not two hours earlier.

"You have had ample time to reflect on my offer, and I only say that you would have been less amiable in my eyes had there not been this little unwillingness. Allow me to assure you that I have allowed you your little spell to recover your sensibilities after my discourse. My attentions have been too marked to be mistaken. Perhaps it will be advisable for me to state my reasons for marrying—and, moreover, for coming into Hertfordshire with the design of selecting a wife, as I certainly did."

"Thank you for your concern, sir." Jane stood gracefully. "I am content to remain unmarried." She moved toward the door with measured steps, her skirts whispering against the floorboards.

His face underwent a remarkable transformation, confidence melting into confusion like frost in a sudden sun. His complexion grew florid as understanding dawned. "You would dismiss such a prudent and well-considered proposal for spinsterhood?" He gripped the table, leaning forward. "Allow me to expatiate upon the numerous advantages--"

"My figures require attention, Mr Collins." Jane's tone remained sweet, although it carried the same quiet firmness she used when directing tenants. "I must return to the study."

"But Cousin Jane, consider your position!" Mr Collins pursued her down the corridor, his words tumbling over each other in increasing agitation. "The security of marriage to the heir—Lady Catherine's marked predilection for promoting such suitable alliances—The natural order of--"

Jane maintained her steady pace until she reached her chamber. Only when the door was safely latched behind her did she allow her calm mask to slip, closing her eyes and leaning against the solid wood as Mr Collins's continued protestations filtered through from the hallway. She hoped, but was not fully confident, that he would not enter.

"Jane?" Elizabeth's whispered voice came from their shared dressing room door. "Was that what I think it was?"

"Yes." Jane opened her eyes, a small smile touching her lips despite everything. "Mr Collins has done exactly as Mamma predicted. I had hoped she might be wrong about his timing."

"Did he mention Lady Catherine?" Elizabeth asked with a

smirk.

"Three times in the first sentence." Jane's smile turned rueful. "Although he was quite enthused about my 'excellent qualities in matters of household economy.'"

"Of course." Elizabeth's eyes sparkled with suppressed mirth. "Heaven forbid he should mention any personal regard in such a practical proposal."

"Ah. I fear he did touch on that subject," Jane said,. with an expression of mingled indignation and disbelief. "You will scarce credit what our cousin has permitted himself to say," she began, her voice hushed yet intense. "He spoke of my figure in terms so particular, and with such evident appreciation of qualities no gentleman should remark upon, that I stood quite unable to respond."

Elizabeth clapped her hand over her mouth. "I cannot conceive how we shall face him at dinner."

From the hallway, Mr Collins's voice rose in one final appeal: "Miss Bennet, I really must insist you allow me to explain the profound advantages--"

"Shall we escape through the garden door?" Elizabeth suggested, as Jane's composure threatened to crack. "I believe the sheep need counting, or sorting, perhaps? Even Mr Collins would not follow us there."

"We can only hope," Jane agreed, her composure returning as she stepped from the door. "Although I fear this is only the beginning. He seemed quite… determined."

"Then we shall be more determined," Elizabeth said firmly, leading her sister toward escape. "After all, we have managed worse than one persistent parson."

Chapter Fifteen

Elizabeth was cataloguing winter stores in the kitchen garden, her fingers stained with earth as she sorted through turnips with the cook, when Mr Collins's shadow fell across her work. She glanced up to find him posed in what he seemingly believed to be an impressive attitude, his formal garb incongruous among the herb beds and vegetable rows. She felt a lurch of not quite fear, but distress at his approach.

"Cousin Elizabeth." He executed a bow so deep it nearly upset a basket of parsnips. "Your shocking involvement in administration of the fields, whilst undeniably excessive in one of your sex, bespeaks intelligence that might, when controlled and directed by a husband of sense and education, prove most advantageous to the future mistress of Longbourn."

Elizabeth straightened, brushing soil from her apron. "Mr Collins, you find me at a disadvantage. These turnips require my immediate attention, and I fear they would not appreciate the interruption of a proposal, however eloquent."

His face reddened, but he pressed on with dogged determination. "I therefore feel it incumbent upon me to offer you the opportunity to unite your practical habits with my own superior position and judgement."

"How generous," Elizabeth replied, her eyes dancing despite her composed expression. "But I must decline both the opportunity and the judgement. The turnips, you see, have decided opinions about proper storage, and I should hate to disappoint them by introducing changes at this late stage in our alliance."

"Cousin Elizabeth!" His tone wavered between scandalised and bewildered. "You cannot possibly prefer the supervision of root vegetables to the honour of marriage to the heir of Longbourn?"

"Indeed, I can, sir. The turnips, you see, require only that I understand their nature, whilst a husband could expect me to deny my own." She turned back to her work. "I have work to do. As do you, I believe, perhaps at your living in Kent."

"But consider, Madam, the great advantage of combining your irregular activities with proper masculine authority! Lady Catherine herself--"

"Would undoubtedly have strong opinions about turnip management," Elizabeth interrupted smoothly. "However, as she is not here to share them, I must rely on my own judgement. Good day, Mr Collins."

He lingered, sputtering, until Elizabeth deliberately upended a basket of soil near his shoes. He retreated hastily toward the house.

In the stillroom, he found Mrs Bennet presiding over the preservation of autumn fruits.

"My dear Madam," he began, clearly hoping for a more sympathetic audience. "As a woman of discernment and maternal feeling, you must comprehend the exceptional advantages I offer. Your daughters, whilst admirably industrious, cannot persist indefinitely in their current unseemly occupation without the protection and guidance of a gentleman of property and connection."

Mrs Bennet sealed a jar with unwarranted force. "Can they not? Yet here we are, persisting quite successfully these several years past."

"Consider the security and elevation of position that would attend such an alliance! Indeed, Lady Catherine, in her singular wisdom, has long maintained that young ladies of good family must be promptly settled, and I venture to suggest--"

Mrs Bennet's voice cut through his rhetoric like a well-honed knife, "I fear that Lady Catherine's opinions, whilst no doubt fascinating to her particular circle, carry somewhat less weight in Hertfordshire than in Kent. My daughters manage very well, sir. Their security lies in their competence, not in marriage to one who would undo their work."

"But Lady Catherine, in her infinite wisdom and condescension, has particularly remarked--"

"Your patroness is not mistress here." Mrs Bennet's often fluttering manner hardened to steel. "I am. Now, if you will excuse me, these preserves must be stored before the damp ruins them. Unless you wish to explain to Lady Catherine why Longbourn serves empty jars at dinner?"

Mr Collins retreated in utter bafflement, leaving Mrs Bennet to exchange a speaking look with her daughter through the stillroom window. Elizabeth's lips quirked in response. They had weathered worse storms than the persistent parson; this too would pass, leaving them, like their preserves, intact and self-sufficient.

Finding Lydia and Kitty in the drawing room plain sewing that evening, Mr Collins held forth at length upon Lady Catherine's opinions regarding female education, estate management, and the proper deportment of young ladies of good family,

"Ah, my young cousins. Whilst your industry does credit to your family's reduced circumstances, surely such menial concerns might be better left to servants? Lady Catherine has most pointedly observed that young ladies should occupy themselves with delicate needlework and improving reading. Indeed, Her Ladyship maintains that excessive attention to household matters can only result in the coarsening of feminine sensibilities."

"Reduced circumstances?" Lydia raised an eyebrow. "Our profits have doubled --" Kitty elbowed Lydia quickly to quiet her.

"My dear young cousins," Mr Collins spoke on, oblivious, "your charming naïveté regarding financial matters only serves to underscore my point. When I am master here, such concerns will be handled by those better suited to them. Now, regarding the matter of my proposal to your sister--"

"Which one?" Lydia asked innocently. "The one Jane laughed about, or the one that sent Elizabeth storming to the stables?"

Mr Collins pulled himself up to his full height. "I had

expected to find allies in you younger ladies, whose minds might not yet be fully corrupted by involvements wholly outside feminine delicacy. But I see the taint of rebellion has spread throughout the family."

Upon retreating from the drawing room, Mr Collins paused in the hallway. The sound of piano music drifted from the music room, where Mary practised her exercises. He smoothed his waistcoat and adjusted his clerical collar, considering his dwindling options.

Two attempts at securing a wife from among his cousins had met with unaccountable resistance. The Misses Kitty and Lydia were far too immature to warrant his consideration, not to mention their rather sporting manner when he attempted serious discussion with them. Lady Catherine would be most displeased at his lack of progress. Her instructions had been clear–establish himself firmly within the family to guide them properly toward more suitable behaviours and secure for a wife the most malleable of his cousins. Each of the elder Bennet ladies seemed more resistant than the last. Miss Mary, however, might prove more amenable to reason. She at least demonstrated suitable feminine accomplishments. Her plainer features and serious demeanour suggested a nature less likely to be swayed by romantic notions. Such qualities, whilst hardly inspiring passion, would serve adequately in a parson's wife. Yes, he had been mistaken in seeking the beautiful Miss Jane Bennet. It was hardly fitting for a man of the cloth to be driven by such base instincts. As for Miss Elizabeth, his head still pounded from the effort of deciphering her meanings in her rapid and complex remarks. She was anything but malleable. He ought to have considered Miss Mary from the first. She was not a beauty, but her figure appeared quite adequate, and her manner of speech was at least respectful.

Fortifying himself with thoughts of Lady Catherine's approval, he approached the music room. The door stood ajar, framing Miss Mary at the pianoforte, her posture tense as she executed a particularly complex passage.

"Most edifying, Miss Mary," he announced as the final notes

faded. "Your dedication to musical accomplishment does you credit."

Mary turned on the bench, her expression as composed as ever behind her spectacles. "Mr Collins. I was not aware you appreciated Bach."

"Lady Catherine has been most emphatic in her pronouncements upon the improving qualities of musical study," he declared, stepping fully into the room. "Although she naturally prefers more delicate selections for young ladies of breeding. Particularly her own daughter, who would have been most accomplished had her health permitted."

"Indeed?" Mary's tone remained neutral. "I find Bach speaks more directly to matters of moral clarity than many more fashionable composers."

Mr Collins seized upon this opening. "Just so! Moral clarity–a quality most essential in these troubling times. Indeed, it is this understanding of correct principles that has led me to consider, or rather, to contemplate… a matter of importance."

He positioned himself by the pianoforte, assuming the same stance that had failed him twice before. "Miss Mary, your evident appreciation for moral instruction, combined with your accomplishments and sensible nature, lead me to believe you might be serviceably suited to the position of a clergyman's wife."

Mary's fingers stilled upon the keyboard. "A clergyman's wife," she repeated, her voice perfectly even.

"Indeed," Mr Collins continued, warming to his theme. "According to Lady Catherine's guidance, which must be held in the highest esteem, a parsonage requires a mistress of serious disposition and practical nature. One who understands the importance of proper example and moral guidance."

"I see." Mary closed her music book with deliberate care. "And you believe I meet these requirements?"

"Most certainly. Your studious nature and evident preference for improving literature over frivolous pursuits suggest a character well-suited to supporting the moral tone of a parish." He leant forward. "Furthermore, as the least likely of your sisters to form other attachments, practical considerations must surely recommend the security of such an establishment."

The silence that followed stretched uncomfortably long. When Mary finally spoke, her voice had acquired an edge that Mr Collins had not previously detected.

"Mr Collins," she said, rising from the piano bench with perfect composure, "I have made a particular study of moral philosophy these past years. Would you care to know what I have learnt?"

Mr Collins, mistaking her response for interest, smiled indulgently. "I should be most gratified to hear your simple observations, which I might then refine with my superior theological understanding."

"I have learnt," Mary continued, removing her spectacles with one smooth motion, "that true moral worth lies not in appearance or position, but in character and conduct. That wisdom consists not in pronouncing judgements based on others' opinions, but in forming one's own through careful observation, biblical study, and rational thought."

Mr Collins blinked, his rehearsed speech momentarily forgotten.

"I have observed your evidence of your character most intently these weeks," Mary continued, her voice acquiring the clear, lecture-like tone her sisters knew well. "I have noted your excessive deference to rank, your lack of original thought, your willingness to sacrifice principle for advancement, your utter ignorance of Christian doctrine, and your habitual incapability to perceive the true nature and worth of those around you."

"Miss Mary!" Mr Collins sputtered. "This is most unseemly—"

"What is unseemly," Mary interrupted with quiet force, "is your presumption that I, or any of my sisters, should consider marriage to a man who neither respects our capabilities nor possesses any of his own beyond reciting the opinions of his patroness. Even Dr. Gregory, in his *'Legacy to His Daughters,'* whilst advocating modesty and deference, acknowledges that a woman's judgement should not be sacrificed to mere external authority. And Mrs Chapone states clearly that a woman must consider moral character above all in selecting a companion for life."

Mr Collins's face had progressed through several interesting shades during this speech. "Lady Catherine—"

"The opinion of someone so wholly unrelated to me would never alter mine in the slightest. I have no wish to marry at present, Mr Collins, and were that to change, I should certainly seek a husband whose moral character I could respect." She gathered her music books into a neat stack. "Kindly excuse me, I believe my sisters may require my assistance."

She moved past him with measured dignity, leaving Mr Collins staring after her in stupefied silence. The pianoforte stood like a barrier, its polished surface reflecting his bewildered expression as he struggled to comprehend how the quietest, plainest Bennet sister had delivered perhaps the most devastating rejection of all.

Failing at his attempts with the ladies of the household, Mr Collins sought out the housekeeper. Lady Catherine had instructed him to gain the confidence of the servants, and, failing that, to determine which ought to be let go.

Mrs Hill was in the linen room, her experienced hands smoothing and folding fresh-scented sheets when Mr Collins found her. She kept her face neutral as he positioned himself in the doorway, although her fingers twitched with the urge to shoo him from her domain like an overlarge crow.

"Mrs Hill," he began with pompous condescension, "as a sensible woman who understands the proper order of things, you must agree that the estate requires masculine governance? Indeed, Lady Catherine herself maintains no fewer than three male servants solely to oversee her household accounts."

"Does she indeed, sir?" Mrs Hill's voice dripped with

exaggerated deference as she precisely aligned the corners of a damask tablecloth. "How … uneconomical of her Ladyship. I cannot but say I find myself surprised that three gentlemen are required to accomplish what our Miss Jane manages single-handedly."

Mr Collins puffed up like a disturbed pigeon. "You cannot mean to suggest that a young lady's amateur efforts could equal the systematic approach of properly trained men?"

"Oh no, sir," Mrs Hill agreed, her eyes downcast but dancing. "I would never suggest equality. After all, Miss Jane completed last quarter's accounts in no time and found an error in the sheep tallies besides. Surely three gentlemen required many days to accomplish the same. But I am sure Lady Catherine's gentlemen are entirely… adequate."

"Yes!" Mr Collins seized on her apparent agreement, missing the glint in her eye. "Lady Catherine has frequently remarked that feminine attention to detail, whilst commendable in its way, must be properly directed by masculine wisdom. Why, only last Easter--"

Mrs Hill continued in her work whilst Mr Collins droned on. As soon as he paused, Mrs Hill turned to him, dropping into a deep curtsey that somehow managed to convey more irony than respect. "I fear I must attend to the airing of the guest linens. Unless" she added with wide-eyed concern, "you feel three footmen might accomplish it more efficiently?"

"Well, I--" Mr Collins faltered, perhaps suspecting he was being mocked but unable to pin down how. "I daresay--"

"Or perhaps," Mrs Hill continued innocently, "you might wish to examine our linen inventory? Although I should warn you, sir, Miss Mary's organisational methods are quite… feminine. I fear a gentleman of your understanding might find them quite beneath his notice."

"I—that is—Perhaps I should--" Mr Collins backed toward the door, his certainty visibly crumbling under Mrs Hill's relentless servility.

"Indeed, you should, sir," Mrs Hill agreed warmly, advancing with a stack of sheets. "I believe Mr Bennet is waiting to consult you about… about the optimal placement of a pigsty." She all but pushed him from the room, her curtsey managing simultaneously to usher him out and shut the door in his face.

Alone again, Mrs Hill allowed herself a small smile as she returned to her work. Through the window, she could see Miss Elizabeth in the kitchen garden, deftly sorting turnips and no doubt planning how to avoid their unwanted suitor. "Lady Catherine's three men indeed," she muttered to herself. "I would like to see them manage a quarter of what these girls accomplish before breakfast."

The sound of Mr Collins's voice drifted up from below, no doubt expounding to some other unfortunate soul about Lady Catherine's opinions on proper household management. Mrs Hill shook her head and returned to her linens, humming a tune that sounded suspiciously like "The Female Sailor Bold."

Chapter Sixteen

In the library, Mr Collins found Mr Bennet reading correspondence.

"Sir," Mr Collins began, drawing himself up. "I come to you with the gravest of concerns regarding the future of this estate and the welfare of your granddaughters. Lady Catherine de Bourgh, whose wisdom in such matters is unimpeachable, has impressed upon me most decidedly the absolute necessity of maintaining proper order in matters of family and property. That you have permitted—nay, encouraged—these extraordinary departures from proper feminine behaviour must proceed from some temporary confusion regarding the natural order of society."

Mr Bennet laid down his letter. "Confusion, Mr Collins?"

"Indeed, sir. Your advanced years and the unfortunate circumstance of being surrounded entirely by females must naturally have clouded your judgement in these matters. However, as heir to Longbourn and a man of both sense and education, I stand ready to assume the burden of responsibility for--"

"Tell me, Mr Collins," Mr Bennet interrupted, his voice dangerously mild, "what was Longbourn's income these past three years?"

"I hardly see the relevance--"

"The price of wool at last market?"

"Such details are hardly the concern of--"

"The number of tenants? The state of the winter wheat? The condition of the water meadow? No?" Mr Bennet's eyes glittered. "Yet you presume to speak of proper management?"

"My dear sir," Mr Collins persisted, tugging at his cravat, "you mistake my meaning. As Lady Catherine is wont to declare, such detailed knowledge of estate matters is just that which separates the gentleman from the mere farmer. One must maintain a distance from such vulgar concerns whilst ensuring they are managed by those suited to the task."

"And who, pray tell, would you consider better suited than those who have proved their capability?" Mr Bennet's voice remained deadly calm.

"Now, good sir, you cannot possibly credit mere women with success! No doubt some error in their understanding--"

"The results are quite evident, Upon my honour. Jane's mathematical accuracy exceeds my own."

Mr Collins paced the library, his agitation mounting. "But consider the impropriety! Miss Elizabeth tramping about the fields like a common labourer. Miss Mary concerning herself with dairy accounts. Miss Catherine and Miss Lydia speaking with tenant women! Why, Lady Catherine has frequently remarked that young ladies should never be permitted to--"

"I wonder, Mr Collins," Mr Bennet interrupted, "whether Lady Catherine has any occupation beyond making pronouncements. Does she perhaps occasionally take action?"

Mr Collins gasped. "Sir! Her Ladyship's condescension in offering guidance on all matters is universally acknowledged as--"

"Universal acknowledgement is not the same as universal wisdom, sir. Now, regarding your earlier attempts to secure a wife from among my granddaughters…"

"I had hoped, sir, that your influence might be exerted in that direction. After all, the future of Longbourn--"

"Lies in competent hands. Tell me, Mr Collins, what is it you would do with Longbourn were it in your power?"

"Why, I should naturally restore proper order! Male servants would oversee the accounts, whilst your granddaughters would be guided toward more felicitous occupations until such time as suitable matches could be secured. Lady Catherine has most specifically advised that young ladies should spend their mornings in needlework and their afternoons in quiet reading of improving texts. The estate would be managed as befits a gentleman's property, with all decisions made by those qualified by their sex and station to--"

"To return us to the old ways, I suspect," Mr Bennet said dryly. "No, Mr Collins. Your reverence for rank, your dependence upon the opinions of others, your impressive consistency in failing to recognise true merit when it fails to match your preconceptions–these do not recommend you as either a husband or a steward of property."

"Sir! I must protest! When I am master here--"

"You will never be master here whilst I draw breath. And when that unhappy event occurs which places Longbourn in your hands, you will find its existence secured by such legal provisions as will ensure my granddaughters' continued autonomy."

Mr Collins's face purpled. "Secured? You cannot mean to subvert the natural order--"

"I mean to preserve what functions admirably, sir. You speak endlessly of proper management, yet in all your weeks here, you have not once reviewed the lands. Not once have you enquired after the condition of the fields, the health of the livestock, or the state of the tenants."

"Such details are beneath--"

"Nothing about Longbourn is beneath the attention of those who truly care for its welfare. Whilst you expound upon Lady Catherine's opinions regarding feminine deportment, my granddaughters concern themselves with their ancestral home. Tell me, do you know which fields lie fallow this season?"

Mr Collins shifted uncomfortably. "A gentleman need not--"

"The state of the winter wheat? The condition of the sheep? The terms of our tenant leases?"

"These matters are for stewards and--"

"These matters, Mr Collins, are the essence of responsible ownership. That you disdain such knowledge whilst presuming to judge those who possess it speaks volumes about your character."

"This is not to be borne! To be lectured thus by a man who has lost all sense of proper dignity and judgement! When Sir William hears of this…"

"By all means, apply to Sir William. And Mr Freeman as well," Mr Bennet's eyes glittered dangerously. "I look forward to hearing their opinions on a man who, having failed to secure a wife through three separate proposals, seeks to gain control of an estate through accusations against its rightful owner. Good day, Mr Collins. I believe you know the way out."

Mr Collins stood trembling with rage and humiliation. "You will regret this obstinacy, sir. There are ways to protect my interests from those who have lost their judgement through age and infirmity."

Mr Bennet's glare could have frozen water. "Then by all means, pursue them. But remember, Mr Collins–a man who attempts to prove another's madness often succeeds only in proving his own. Particularly when that other's judgement is daily proved sound by the contentment of his tenants and the character of his descendants."

Mr Collins stormed from the study, his face purple with thwarted ambition and wounded pride. Behind him, Mr Bennet permitted himself a small smile and reached for the bell pull. His ladies must be warned of what was to come.

Rosings Park, Kent

My Dear Lady Catherine,

I feel compelled by duty and gratitude to provide a most particular account of certain developments at Longbourn which may warrant your Ladyship's attention, especially as they relate to Mr Darcy's recent activities in our neighbourhood.

Your nephew was observed no fewer than three times this past week consulting with Miss Elizabeth Bennet regarding estate matters - consultations which, I must report with some distress, appear to extend beyond mere courtesy calls. On Tuesday last, they spent upwards of two hours examining drainage channels, during which Mr Darcy was seen to pay particular attention to her opinions regarding water flow patterns. Most alarming was his evident approval of her rather unfeminine and forceful arguments about proper field management.

Most concerning was Friday's encounter, wherein Mr Darcy arrived at Longbourn specifically to seek Miss Elizabeth's counsel regarding the Matthews property. They were observed walking the boundary line between the estates, engaged in lively discourse more befitting that between gentlemen. I feel it my duty to note that Miss Elizabeth spoke with an authority most unseemly in a young lady, and yet your nephew seemed not merely tolerant but actively encouraging of such displays. He is without a doubt being drawn in by her arts and allurements.

The situation at Longbourn continues to defy all proper order. Miss Elizabeth and Miss Bennet persist in their unnatural attention to estate management, regularly consulting with tenants and making decisions that surely ought to fall under male guidance. Their younger sisters, I fear, are being influenced by this example of feminine independence. Even Miss Mary was seen yesterday studying a volume on agricultural improvements rather than pursuing more appropriate accomplishments.

Whilst quite elderly and frail, Mr Bennet consults with these young ladies as if they were competent stewards. He is very unwell and has been most unwelcoming of the advice you provided for him which I have delivered in no uncertain terms. His age and eccentric behaviours lend credence to my fear that he is assuredly senile or otherwise disordered in his senses. His unfortunate derangement manifests in a most unfortunate disturbance of the brain, wherein he discerns objects and personages visible only to himself.

Mr Darcy's friend, Mr Bingley's frequent calls at Longbourn might be explained by his evident partiality for Miss Jane, but Mr Darcy's increasing involvement suggests a dangerous shifting of traditional values. When I ventured to suggest to Miss Elizabeth that such detailed attention to estate matters might be better left to those more naturally suited to such concerns, she replied with a most unsettling mixture of impertinence and defiance that seemed to amuse your nephew.

As per your Ladyship's specific enquiry regarding Mr Darcy's movements in the neighbourhood, I must report that he has been observed riding past Longbourn's north fields with marked regularity, often pausing to examine recent earth works undertaken by men employed by the Longbourn Estate. His supervision of his friend's leased Netherfield property, whilst ostensibly a sound investment, places him in frequent consultation with the Bennet ladies regarding shared boundaries and management. I harbour deep concern for his continued exposure to these unnatural females.

I have made attempts to follow your direction to seek a wife from among my cousins at Longbourn. I have been met by uncivil and indecorous responses such that I fear they are all entirely headstrong and foolish. I question whether any of them would altogether be a very desirable wife to a man in my situation, who naturally looks for happiness in the marriage state. Therefore, perhaps it would be better not to force any of them into accepting me, because, if liable to such unnatural behaviours and defects of temper, none could contribute much to my felicity. I remain your Ladyship's most humble and obedient servant,

William Mr Collins

P.S.—When Mr Darcy escorted Miss Elizabeth to examine a culvert, I observed Miss Elizabeth returning a pair of gloves to him and expressing thanks for his allowing her to wear them on her own hands!! Such familiarity, whilst perhaps minor, seems indicative of a general relaxation of proper distance that your Ladyship might wish to consider. You must understand, Lady Catherine, these young ladies demonstrate a most alarming tendency toward independent thought and action, particularly Miss Elizabeth, whose influence over estate matters grows daily more pronounced."

Lady Catherine's fingers tightened on the letter as she read, her face a study in aristocratic displeasure. The reception room seemed suddenly too confining for the scope of her indignation.

"Unthinkable," she pronounced to her daughter's

companion, Mrs Jenkinson, who had learnt long ago that such pronouncements required no response. "That my own nephew should be seen in such company. These modern notions of female capability must not be allowed to take root. I must write to Mr Collins and demand that he return immediately!"

Chapter Seventeen

The letter arrived with the morning post, its thick parchment and elaborate seal immediately identifying its source. Mr Collins had snatched it from Hill's tray with such eagerness that he nearly upset the breakfast dishes in his haste.

"From Lady Catherine de Bourgh!" he announced, as though bestowing a royal proclamation upon the assembled family. "Her Ladyship honours me with her personal correspondence."

Elizabeth exchanged glances with Jane across the table. Mr Collins had taken to observing their grandfather with exaggerated concern, offering unnecessary assistance and speaking to him in the overly loud tones one might use with a dim-witted child.

"I trust her Ladyship is in good health?" Grandfather enquired from the head of the table.

"Indeed, sir, indeed. Although she is, as always, burdened with the great responsibilities of her position." Mr Collins broke the seal, his lips moving silently as he read. Suddenly, his countenance shifted from reverence to dismay.

"Oh! Most distressing yet one must obey her Ladyship's wisdom is unparalleled,"

"Is something amiss, Mr Collins?" Mrs Bennet asked.

Mr Collins looked up, his expression teetering between disappointment and self-importance. "I am summoned back to Rosings immediately. Her Ladyship writes that matters of parish business require my urgent attention." He folded the letter with haste. "Her Ladyship is most explicit that I should depart without delay."

Elizabeth suppressed a smile. Did the "parish business" stem from Mr Collins's report of Grandfather's condition? She had overheard him composing his letter to Lady Catherine, detailing with morbid relish the "unfortunate derangement" of the Bennet patriarch, and speculating how such mental infirmity might affect the inheritance of Longbourn.

"Must you leave so soon cousin?" Mrs Bennet asked, her tone measured but a small smile betraying her relief. "We had expected to enjoy your company for at least another sennight."

"Duty calls, Madam. My noble patroness has expressed her opinion most forcefully, and one does not disregard the wisdom of such a distinguished personage." He cast a meaningful glance toward Grandfather Bennet, who was calmly buttering his toast, seemingly oblivious to the conversation. "There are certain delicate matters that make my prompt return unavoidable."

"What a pity," Mary remarked. "We had hoped to discuss your parish's approach to tenant relief during poor harvests. Grandfather and I have been developing a new system at Longbourn."

Mr Collins blinked, obviously unprepared for such a subject. "Perhaps on my next visit, Miss Mary. Lady Catherine herself has most definite opinions on the management of tenant needs which I would be honoured to relay."

"I shall order your trunk packed immediately," Mrs Bennet said efficiently. "You may depart immediately after luncheon, if that suits."

By midday, Mr Collins's borrowed horse was saddled, and his modest luggage secured. The man himself stood in the entrance hall delivering his protracted farewells. The entire family had assembled, as propriety demanded, although Elizabeth noted that her grandfather seemed markedly eager to see their cousin off, remaining below stairs well beyond his habit.

"I leave with a heavy heart," Mr Collins proclaimed, bowing deeply to Mrs Bennet. "Your hospitality has been everything that a humble clergyman could wish for."

"You are welcome at Longbourn," Mrs Bennet replied with false civility. Elizabeth detected her mother's hands relaxing at her sides—the only outward sign of her relief.

Mr Collins turned to Grandfather Bennet, speaking with exaggerated clarity. "And you, sir, I wish you peaceful days ahead. My revered patroness has shared with me certain remedies for afflictions of the mind. Perhaps on my next visit—"

"I look forward to it," Grandfather interrupted, his voice surprisingly strong. "I shall have much to discuss with you. The spirits have told me so."

Mr Collins blanched. "The spirits?"

"Indeed," the old man continued. "They are quite insistent about your future. Most insistent." He tapped his temple knowingly.

Mr Collins took an involuntary step backward. "Well, I,." For perhaps the first time in his acquaintance with the Bennets, he seemed genuinely at a loss for words.

"Your horse awaits, cousin," Mrs Bennet intervened smoothly. "We would never delay you and incur her Ladyship's displeasure."

With a final bow and several backward glances at Grandfather Bennet, Mr Collins at last mounted his horse and set off down the lane, his rigid posture betraying his discomfort.

The November air rushed in with his departure, brisk and cleansing, as though the very wind rejoiced in sweeping away the lingering miasma of pomposity. As the family turned back toward the house, Elizabeth saw her grandfather exchange a conspiratorial smile with Mary. The old man had played his part to perfection.

"Well," said Mrs Bennet, once they were inside, "I suppose we might as well consume the special tea cake I had Cook prepare for this afternoon with Mr Collins."

"An excellent suggestion, my dear," Grandfather agreed. "And perhaps a glass of the good port as well."

The family gathered in the drawing room, tea cakes distributed, and, at Grandfather's insistence, small glasses of wine poured for all—a rare indulgence for the middle of the day.

Grandfather, who had been far more animated since Mr Collins's departure, accepted his glass with a gleam in his eye that Elizabeth had not seen in many months.

"I believe," the old man said, raising his glass, "that a toast is in order."

"To Mr Collins's safe journey?" Jane suggested kindly.

Grandfather snorted. "To Mr Collins's journey, certainly. May it be long, dirty, circuitous, and never again end anywhere near Longbourn." He lifted his glass higher. "To the remarkable efficacy of feigned madness in ridding one's home of unwanted guests."

"Grandfather!" Elizabeth admonished, biting her lip with suppressed mirth.

"Oh, let him speak," Mrs Bennet said in solidarity. "He has endured Mr Collins's condescension more patiently than I have."

"To Lady Catherine, then," Grandfather amended, "whose imperiousness has, for once, served a useful purpose."

Everyone raised their glasses in agreement.

The lane that led from Longbourn to Meryton was pleasantly shaded by oak trees, offering relief from the midday sun. Lydia Bennet walked at a brisk pace, a sturdy basket over her arm containing lists of supplies needed for the estate and a small leather-bound account book. Although not officially out in society, she was permitted these practical errands into the village, accompanied by James, one of the stable boys, who followed a few paces behind, kicking stones and whistling tunelessly.

Lydia had been tasked with purchasing seeds for the kitchen garden, arranging for the repair of a broken plough part, and negotiating the price of new fence posts—responsibilities her sisters had increasingly entrusted to her as she demonstrated her sharp skills in negotiation. Unlike Jane, who avoided confrontation, or Lizzy and Mary who tended to be overly outspoken, Lydia was fearless and effective in securing excellent terms for the estate. Shy Kitty refused to accompany Lydia as the whole enterprise made her nervous. Lydia's skill had not come overnight. She recalled with clarity the first time, two years earlier, when she stunned the Meryton farmers into silence.

Lydia's voice carried across the sheep pens, causing several farmers to turn in surprise at the sight of a young girl haggling like a seasoned dealer.

"Thirteen pounds ten per stone? Your wool may be fine, Mr Hawkins, but it is not spun from gold."

The portly farmer flushed red beneath his whiskers. "Now see here, Miss Bennet—"

"I have seen, sir. I have examined your fleece most thoroughly." Lydia gestured to the samples spread before her. "Whilst the staple length is admirable, the lanolin content is excessive, which will result in considerable weight loss during scouring. Ten pounds eight is fair."

Old Simmons stood a few paces behind her, arms folded across his chest, a glimmer of pride barely visible beneath his perpetual scowl.

Mr Hawkins glanced between them, apparently disconcerted at being outmanoeuvred by a slip of a girl. "Twelve pounds even, and that's my final offer."

"Eleven pounds five," Lydia countered smoothly, "and we shall take your entire western field's yield next season as well, provided the quality remains consistent."

The deal was struck with reluctant respect, and as Mr Hawkins walked away, Lydia turned to Simmons with a triumphant smile.

"You have the makings of a proper wool merchant," the old shepherd acknowledged, the highest praise he had ever given her.

"I have been studying the market reports in Grandfather's newspapers," Lydia confided as they walked back toward the Longbourn flock. "And comparing them with the ledgers from previous years."

They paused at the gate to the north pasture where their

breeding ewes grazed contentedly. Three years of Lydia's dedicated study and Simmons' grudging tutelage had transformed the Longbourn flock. The introduction of Merino bloodlines—a suggestion Lydia had made after pouring over a treatise she had persuaded her grandfather to procure from London—had already improved their wool quality significantly.

"The breeding programme is working," Lydia observed, satisfaction evident in her voice. "Another two generations and our fleeces will command premium prices."

Simmons nodded. "You have a good eye for it, miss. Better than most men twice your age."

Lydia's face clouded suddenly. "Mamma says I ought to pursue more lady-like accomplishments. She caught me with sheep dung on my skirts yesterday and nearly had an apoplexy."

"And what did you tell her?"

"That I had been gathering wildflowers and had suffered an unfortunate mishap," Lydia admitted with a mischievous smile. "She believes what she wishes to believe."

"And your grandfather?"

"He understands. He sees the ledgers, after all." Her voice softened. "And he says Papa would have been proud."

A comfortable silence fell between them as they watched the flock. Finally, Simmons cleared his throat. "There is a new method for controlling hoof rot I have heard tell of. Copper sulphate solution, they are using in the north."

"We should try it," Lydia agreed immediately. "I shall write to request information."

"Already ordered some," Simmons admitted. "I thought we might experiment."

Lydia beamed at this evidence of his confidence in their partnership. "Mr Simmons, I do believe we are becoming progressives."

The old shepherd's lips twitched in what might nearly have been a smile. "Dunno go spreading such slander, Miss Lydia. I have a reputation to maintain."

"The grandfather's condition," Lady Catherine mused. "You mentioned his increasing infirmity?"

Mr Collins leant forward, scenting opportunity like a hound sensing game. The winter light cast his features in a sickly pallor that matched his obsequious demeanour. "Indeed, your Ladyship. Mr Bennet keeps largely to his study these days, emerging only for dinner. The fire is maintained at all hours for his comfort, regardless of the expense. Most concerning is his habit of allowing his granddaughters to manage affairs that ought by rights be directed by a man of sound judgement."

"Sound judgement." Lady Catherine tested the phrase like a fencing master selecting a blade. Her rings glinted in the firelight as her fingers continued their rhythmic tapping. The silk of her ornate dress rustled with each movement. "One might question whether a gentleman who permits such unnatural arrangements demonstrates sound judgement."

"Your Ladyship's penetration, as always, illuminates matters I had hardly dared contemplate." Mr Collins's voice dropped to a conspiratorial whisper that barely disturbed the still air. The scent of his hair pomade, applied too liberally in anticipation of this interview, wafted between them. "There have been… incidents."

"Elaborate."

"He was observed speaking to a vacant room and then to empty chairs at dinner last week. And his signatures on recent documents appear… irregular." Mr Collins paused delicately. "The strain of managing an estate at his advanced age, one must suppose has taken a toll…"

"In that case," Lady Catherine cut in, "the Court of Chancery would take an interest in protecting an ancient estate from the consequences of declining faculties. Particularly when said decline permits such irregular arrangements to flourish."

"The court? Could we not merely call attention to his

incapacity?"

"I doubt the old man would allow that to move him. No, you will need to involve the courts. But first, you must gather evidence of his incapacity to manage affairs. His very tolerance of current circumstances demonstrates it rather conclusively. With such inexpert maintenance, his records and ledgers will be in disarray, his fortune in decline, causing waste to your inheritance." The fine lines around Lady Catherine's mouth deepened like cracks in ice as she warmed to her idea. "The court will protect estates from mismanagement, Mr Collins. I am certain that your evidence will show that allowing young ladies to direct matters is part of his declining judgement."

Mr Collins's bow combined perfect submission with barely concealed triumph. "One might even suggest that his granddaughters take advantage of his weakened state to pursue their peculiar interests."

"One might indeed." Lady Catherine's fan stilled completely. The fire crackled in the grate, sending the shadows of both conspirators dancing grotesquely on the damask-covered walls. "We must move quickly, before my nephew's fascination with agricultural discourse at Longbourn leads to even more inappropriate entanglements. The notion of Pemberley's master discussing drainage works with those chits…" Her shudder spoke volumes about the collapse of proper society such an event would herald.

"The legal costs would be considerable--" Mr Collins dabbed at his forehead with a handkerchief, despite the winter chill in the room.

"You must find someone who will pursue the matter at an economical cost." Her fan executed a decisive snap. "My nephew's inexplicable interest in these peculiar females cannot continue."

"Your Ladyship is most generous." Mr Collins's bow sent a waft of nervous perspiration toward her Ladyship, causing a slight grimace to mar her aristocratic mouth.

Lady Catherine inclined her head at the parson's praise. "Take the matter in hand. No one is more suited to directing both the estate and its young ladies toward more appropriate pursuits.

"I might have Longbourn now?" Mr Collins's voice was marked by yearning.

"That is the plan." Lady Catherine's tone suggested campaigns already being mapped, generals positioning their forces for inevitable victory. The leather of her chair creaked as she straightened, her posture rigid with purpose.

Neither party seemed to realise that proving that allowing women to manage estate matters indicated mental deficiency was a position that might raise interesting questions about Lady Catherine's own capacity to manage Rosings.

"I shall begin collecting evidence of Mr Bennet's confusion immediately," Mr Collins assured his patroness.

"By all means. You must return to Meryton, that is where the evidence is. Inspect the books at Longbourn, whilst you continue to observe and report on my nephew's activities. I must know every detail of how far this fascination has progressed."

Chapter Eighteen

In the private parlour of the Red Lion Inn, in Meryton again, Mr Collins leant across the table toward Sir William Lucas, his voice pitched low beneath the general murmur of the public house.

"You must perceive the gravity of the situation, Sir William. Five unmarried women—six with the widow Bennet—presuming to manage an estate? And the grandfather, poor man, so diminished in his faculties as to permit such unseemly behaviour." Mr Collins's small eyes were narrowed even further, his face flushed red.

Sir William shifted uncomfortably in his chair. He glanced around the room, seeing the eyes of the patrons cast in their direction. He raised his voice above the din. "I find Mr Bennet in full possession of his wits and judgement, Mr Collins. Indeed, the rational economy in his approach to estate governance remains acute."

Mr Collins nearly jumped from his seat. "Acute? He permits his granddaughters to negotiate with tenants. To manage accounts." Mr Collins looked about him, with widened eyes. "You must perceive how this undermines the natural order. Lady Catherine de Bourgh assures me such conduct betrays a weakness of reason." Mr Collins glared, his chin lifted in defiance.

"The estate prospers under their stewardship," Sir William said. "The tenants speak well of their management." Sir William continued to shift in his seat, but his expression was firm and his posture rigid.

"The conservation of rightful authority supersedes mere prosperity!" Mr Collins's voice rose sharply before he mastered himself. "Consider my position, sir. As heir to Longbourn, I bear responsibility for its security. These young ladies require protection and guidance. A firm hand to restore correct governance."

"Your concern appears most earnest," Sir William said, "yet I perceive no evidence of disorder or deficiency in Mr Bennet's judgement of these matters."

"No evidence? When he permits women to usurp male authority rather than direct one of them to marry the heir and secure their estate?"

Sir William blinked, shock marking his expression,

From his position near the fireplace, where he had paused upon entering the inn, Darcy listened with mounting indignation. That Mr Collins had aspire to marry one of the Misses Bennet was preposterous. Offensive. Insulting. Darcy shook himself. If he was privy to this travesty, best he should hear the whole of it.

"I have consulted several men of law in Kent," Mr Collins was now saying. "They suggest that if local magistrates were to report their doubts regarding Mr Bennet's soundness of mind, the Court of Chancery might entrust another with the power and the duty to protect the interests and rights of Longbourn."

"Yourself, I apprehend?" Sir William's tone grew severe.

"Naturally, as the heir, it would fall to me to assume such duties. For the preservation of the family's interests, you understand."

"I understand," Sir William rose from his chair, "that you propose to exploit the law to wrest control from a gentleman whose only display of questionable judgement appears to be allowing his granddaughters to excel in matters you deem beyond their sphere."

"Sir William—"

"I apprehend further," Sir William continued, drawing himself up, "that you would abuse the authority of local magistrates to advance your own interests, without regard for justice or truth."

"I merely seek--"

"Good evening, Mr Collins." Sir William turned toward the door, then stopped short at seeing Darcy. His eyes widened in surprise, but he offered a brief bow and departed.

Mr Collins, following Sir William's gaze, blanched at the sight of Darcy's rigid countenance.

"Mr Collins." Darcy's voice cut through the muted sounds of the taproom beyond - the clink of pewter, the murmur of conversation, the distant scrape of chairs. "I believe we must speak of the proper application of law. And of honour."

"Mr Darcy, I had no notion--"

"No," Darcy interrupted, his quiet tone carrying more menace than a shout could have managed. "It is obvious that had no notion that anyone might object to your scheme." He moved away from the fireplace, each measured step making Mr Collins shrink further into his chair. "Allow me to inform you of the legal consequences of accusing a man of mental infirmity without cause."

"But indubitably," Mr Collins attempted, his voice reedy with anxiety, "as heir to Longbourn, I have some right to ensure fitting management--"

"You have the right," Darcy's words fell like ice, "to respect the current owner's authority. Mr Bennet's faculties are perfectly sound, as any physician of repute would attest. To suggest otherwise, to attempt to use such false claims to wrest control with no evidence…" He let the silence stretch until Mr Collins squirmed. "You may credit me when I say my Aunt, Lady Catherine de Bourgh, would find your manipulations most unseemly."

The colour drained from Mr Collins's face at the mention of his patroness. "Lady Catherine—"

"Would be most disturbed to learn that her parson had embroiled himself in such scandalous misrepresentations." Darcy turned from the mantelpiece. "The penalties for attempts to defraud can be quite severe. Fraud upon the court, unjust enrichment, disgrace to the clergy, these are grievous matters."

Mr Collins sank back in his chair, his face ashen. The fire popped and hissed, punctuating Darcy's words about civil suits, criminal charges, and the irreparable damage to clerical reputation.

"Furthermore," Darcy continued, his voice dropping even lower, "Should you continue on this path, I will have no alternative but to report your actions to my aunt at Rosings Park."

"But I only meant--" Mr Collins's protest died under Darcy's glacial stare.

"What you meant is immaterial. What matters is what you do." Darcy moved to loom over Mr Collins's table. "You will return to Kent. You will maintain a respectful distance from Longbourn and its inhabitants. And you will pray that Mr Bennet is feeling merciful when I inform him of this conversation."

The distant sound of laughter from the taproom served only to heighten the crushing silence that followed. Mr Collins stared into his port glass as though hoping to find escape there, his clerical collar suddenly seeming very tight indeed.

"Do we understand one another?" Darcy's question required no answer and received none save Mr Collins's jerky nod. "Excellent. Surely you can find your own way back to your lodgings. Good evening, Mr Collins."

Darcy strode from the parlour, leaving Mr Collins slumped in his chair, his schemes lying in ruins around him like autumn leaves. The taproom's cheerful noise seemed to mock his defeat as he contemplated the long, lonely ride back to Kent, and the even longer explanations that would be required when he arrived. What would Lady Catherine make of his failure? Was Mr Darcy correct about the consequences of attempting to abuse the law's authority?

Or, perhaps, he need not mention it. He would assure his patroness that he was proceeding apace, and hope that the lack of progress did not reach her attention.

The morning sun had barely cleared the trees when Darcy observed a gig approaching Netherfield from his position in Bingley's study. Miss Jane Bennet was driving, with Miss Elizabeth Bennet beside her. His hand tightened imperceptibly on his teacup as he wondered at the unexpected visit.

"Bingley," he said, drawing his friend's attention from his correspondence. "We have visitors."

Soon they were decorously arranged in the drawing room,

with Miss Bingley presiding over the tea service. Miss Jane Bennet made their excuses in her gentle manner.

"I hope you will pardon such an early call," she said. "But Lizzy and I had business in Meryton this morning, and our grandfather bid us deliver this letter to Mr Darcy on our way."

Darcy accepted the sealed note, noting the slight tremor in Miss Elizabeth's normally steady hands as she took her tea. Something was amiss.

Excusing himself momentarily, he scanned the note. The letter's contents confirmed his suspicion. Mr Bennet wrote succinctly of Mr Collins's arrival and legal threats, requesting Darcy's advice at his convenience, given his experience in estate law.

"Miss Bennet," he addressed Jane, as propriety demanded. "I would be happy to call at Longbourn this afternoon to discuss the matter with your grandfather, if that would be convenient?"

"Most kind of you, sir," Jane replied, her expression softening with relief. "I am sure Grandfather would be grateful for your counsel."

Throughout this exchange, Miss Elizabeth remained surprisingly quiet, although Darcy caught her watching him with an expression he could not quite interpret. Concern? Wariness?

Elizabeth forced herself to sip her tea slowly, maintaining the appearance of a morning call whilst her mind raced. She had argued against this scheme—coming to Netherfield under the pretence of business in Meryton, her grandfather's meticulously worded note—It felt uncomfortably like seeking rescue.

Yet as she observed Mr Darcy reading the letter, his expression grave but composed, she had to acknowledge the sense in consulting him. He would know what challenges they might face.

Still, Elizabeth sensed a twinge of… something. Not quite resentment. Not quite unease. But a nagging worry that in seeking his advice, they would confirm any doubt Mr Darcy must harbour about women managing an estate.

He had often listened to her with that same inscrutable expression he wore in the drawing room - controlled, distant, impossible to read. She had been proud to show him their results: wheat yields increased by a third, improved soil quality in the lower fields, and their innovative approach to the sheep fold. His response had been brief - a simple "Most efficient, Miss Bennet" -before turning to her grandfather.

The memory still unsettled her. Their tenants had prospered. Their profits had grown. Even Mr Goulding had begun copying their methods. Yet she could not tell whether Mr Darcy's reserve masked approval or censure.

And now here they were, appearing at his door like supplicants. Would he attribute their present difficulties to the natural consequence of women attempting to manage what should be a gentleman's responsibility?

Elizabeth straightened her shoulders. Let Mr Darcy think what he would. When he called on her grandfather this afternoon, they would have ten years of careful records to present. She had not proved herself with her work, only now to be seen as a helpless female in need of rescue.

The gentlemen called at Longbourn that afternoon. Kitty, coming in from the gardens with a basket of rose hips for the stillroom, encountered the visitors as they were arriving. She curtseyed politely, conscious of her work apron and the smudge of soil that likely marked her cheek.

"Miss Catherine?" Mr Bingley said with his characteristic warmth. "Your grandfather speaks highly of your contributions to Longbourn's self-sufficiency."

"You are exceedingly kind, sir," Kitty replied, feeling herself flush at being addressed by the gregarious new tenant who had occupied so much of the neighbourhood's speculation. "I simply tend our gardens."

"Simply?" It was Mr Darcy who spoke, surprising them all. His tone, although formal, displayed genuine interest. "I understand from Sir William that your medicinal garden has produced remedies of significant efficacy."

Kitty blinked in surprise, uncertain how to respond to this unexpected subject from the austere gentleman. "I have had some small success with traditional remedies, sir."

"Mr Bennet's improved health suggests your success is more than small," Mr Darcy observed. As they entered the drawing room, his gaze fell to the basket she carried, where bundles of horehound lay among other freshly harvested herbs. "Horehound, is it not? An excellent expectorant."

"You are familiar with herbal medicine, Mr Darcy?" Elizabeth asked, her tone suggesting she found this unexpected.

"My mother maintained extensive gardens at Pemberley, including medicinal plants," he replied. "She believed modern physicians too readily dismissed traditional knowledge." A shadow passed briefly across his features. "Her remedies were sought throughout Derbyshire."

"As were our Aunt Eleanor's." Jane smiled faintly, remembering Aunt Eleanor's frequent assertion that a woman with an organised stillroom need never depend on a man's pocketbook or a doctor's whims.

The conversation moved to other topics, as the transformation of the Longbourn drawing room had not escaped Darcy's notice. Where once rows of account books had dominated the shelves, interspersed with treatises on agriculture and law, now volumes of poetry and histories were artfully scattered about—needlework rested casually on a settee and a sewing basket dominated the table. It was a shrewd artifice to disguise the room's true purpose as a place of business rather than genteel leisure.

Mr Bingley remained with the ladies while Mr Darcy proceeded upstairs to Mr Bennet's study.

Chapter Nineteen

Mr Bennet received him from his accustomed chair by the fire. "You are most welcome, Mr Darcy. Your ride here was tolerable?"

"Entirely so, sir." Darcy accepted the proffered seat, his gaze drawn briefly to Miss Elizabeth who now took the estate desk, her quill moving with practised grace across the ledger before her.

"I believe you know the essentials of our situation from my note," the old gentleman continued. "It seems our estimable Mr Collins has taken it upon himself to question my capacity for the running of Longbourn."

"As we feared."

"Perhaps you might enlighten us," Elizabeth spoke from her desk, her voice deliberately neutral, "as to what you know of any possible grounds for such a challenge?"

Darcy turned to meet her gaze directly. "The law offers several avenues. Most probably, he would petition for oversight, citing concerns over the preservation of the entail's interests, claiming mishandling."

"Mishandling?" Elizabeth's quill paused over her ledger. "Longbourn's value has only increased."

Darcy's brows lifted. "The courts," he replied, choosing his words with particular care, "often favour more… conventional approaches to estate management."

"Conventional?" The arch of her eyebrow spoke volumes. "You mean, perhaps, masculine?"

"Lizzy," Jane murmured, a gentle reproach.

Darcy suppressed a grin. The sunlight illuminating Miss Elizabeth created a halo of gleaming curls about her face, nearly distracting him. But her words, although lightly spoken, struck with unnerving truth. It was not the first time she had laid bare an uncomfortable fact beneath polite wit.

"I mean that the law can be conservative in its views. We must prepare to defend your methods not simply on their results, but on their adherence to established principles."

"Our methods are based on established principles, Mr Darcy." Elizabeth rose and retrieved a volume from the shelf. "Coke's treatise on land law, which I believe you know well. We have followed every recommendation regarding tenant leases and land improvements."

Of course he knew it. He had studied it under the finest tutors, and yet here she stood, citing it with as much fluency as any barrister. Darcy was caught between admiration for her preparation and frustration at her defensive tone. "Miss Elizabeth, I do not question your methods. But the courts-"

"Will need evidence, I assume?" She lifted a neat stack of ledgers from the desk between them. "Ten years of quarterly accounts. Crop yields. Tenant records. Improvement costs and returns. All properly witnessed and recorded." She pushed the ledgers toward him. He lifted the cover of the top volume and saw endless neat rows of figures.

He had expected competent housekeeping, but this was the work of a serious estate manager. Yet that lift of her chin, the challenge in her eyes - suggested she anticipated criticism.

"Most impressive," he said. "This will be extremely helpful in building our defence."

Elizabeth's brow lifted in silent query.

"The estate's defence, that is," he amended swiftly. "Although I hope you will permit me to offer what assistance lies within my power."

Mr Bennet cast a speculative glance toward Mr Darcy. "We would be grateful for your counsel, sir. Although as you see, my granddaughters have not been idle these past years."

"No indeed," Darcy acknowledged, with genuine respect.

"They have not."

"Perhaps," Elizabeth said, pointing to the most recent ledger, "we might begin with what seem to be Mr Collins's specific claims? His letter mentioned 'irregular management practices.'"

"Indeed." Darcy leant forward with interest. "He may challenge your adoption of the Norfolk four-course rotation. Although the system has proved successful on many estates, some still view it as dangerously experimental."

Elizabeth turned her ledger toward him. "We followed Mr Coke's methods precisely—wheat, turnips, barley, and clover. Our yields have increased significantly, most notably since we began using drill seeding rather than broadcasting. That is hardly experimental- it was refined by Jethro Tull in 1701."

Darcy nodded, studying the neat columns. "Mr Collins might still argue that such changes to established methods put the entailed property at risk."

Jane spoke up quietly from her corner. "We maintained the old three-field system on one parcel whilst testing the new methods. The comparison figures are quite clear."

"The law requires diligent stewardship of entailed land, does it not? Surely that must include implementing proven improvements?" Elizabeth looked to the shelf housing volumes on Law, including the renowned Blackstone's Commentaries. "'Waste is a spoil and destruction of the estate, either in houses, woods, or lands; by demolishing not the temporary profits only,'" she recited.

"A fair point," Darcy said. "Although the courts often interpret 'diligent stewardship' conservatively. They look for evidence that changes preserve the essential character and value of the estate."

"'*Quo warranto*?' Then our drainage improvements should help our case," Elizabeth noted. "We followed the methods Mr Elkington published in his report to the Board of Agriculture. The reduced water-logging has improved both our grain fields and pasturage."

Darcy's eyebrows rose just perceptibly. "You have studied Elkington's work on drainage?" Darcy could not suppress the grudging admiration that stirred within him.

"I have," Elizabeth replied with a half smile. "Some of his technical drawings required a great deal of study. We are far from replicating the Duke of Bedford's bog draining efforts. However, the results justify the effort. As you know, our lower fields no longer flood in winter."

"Most impressive," Darcy said. "Have you documented the increase in usable acreage?"

"In detail." Elizabeth retrieved another ledger. "Along with the improved hay yields from the drained meadows. We have also experimented with Mr Bakewell's methods of selective breeding in our sheep flock, although on a modest scale."

"An estate managed with such attention to modern improvements should be defensible," Darcy said thoughtfully. "But we must present these innovations to satisfy legal concerns."

Mr Bennet shifted in his chair. "There is another matter, Mr Darcy, perhaps more pressing than our agricultural improvements."

"Indeed, sir?"

"Mr Collins suggests," the old gentleman said with deliberate care, "that I am no longer capable of sound understanding in estate matters. He speaks of protecting the inheritance through the Court of Chancery."

Elizabeth's hands stilled on her ledger, although her voice remained even. "He expressed particular concern about Grandfather's soundness of mind."

"Ah." Darcy's expression grew grave. "I should report that I overheard Mr Collins speaking of such nonsense to Sir William."

"Sir William? Why?"

"I believe Mr Collins hoped to enlist Sir William's support for his claim that Longbourn is in danger of financial ruin due to what he views as your decline, sir. As magistrate, Sir William's opinion would lend credence to his position. I believe Mr Collins thought the local Magistrate might take up the cause. Sir William was quite dismissive, however it appears that, Mr Collins means to challenge your authority over the estate as an aged person of unsound mind."

Elizabeth took a sharp breath. Mr Bennet shook his head. "I

cannot say I am surprised. Perhaps I ought not to have teased him."

"Can such a petition succeed?" Elizabeth asked.

"Not without substantial proof," Darcy replied. "The court requires clear evidence that a gentleman is non compos mentis. Age alone is not sufficient cause."

Elizabeth glanced at her grandfather with nonchalance. "What evidence would the court consider?"

"They look for proof that a gentleman can no longer govern himself or his affairs," Darcy explained. "Whether he knows his family and property, whether he understands the value of money and land. Most particularly, whether he can make rational decisions about his estate."

"There is no basis to question that! What possible proof could he put forward," Elizabeth said.

"I doubt that he could provide any. The court would require evidence of mismanagement, financial losses, neglect of assets. There would be an examination by a physician or a direct inquiry by a court official who would interview Mr Bennet."

"Mr Jones has attended Grandfather these thirty years," Elizabeth noted.

"A long-standing physician's testimony would carry great weight with the court," Darcy said. "That is very much in your favour." Darcy paused. "Has Mr Collins mentioned seeking a medical opinion?"

"Someone who claimed to be a physician called yesterday," Mr Bennet said drily. "I declined to receive him."

"Quite right," Darcy approved. "He cannot merely send his own doctor. Any such examination should be conducted by your regular physician or, if necessary, an independent doctor appointed by the court."

Elizabeth drew a paper from her desk. "We have maintained records of all major estate decisions, with grandfather's reasoning noted and witnessed. Would such documentation be useful?"

"Your records would serve well in court," Darcy said slowly, "should Mr Collins proceed. Although…" He paused, as though considering whether to continue.

"Please, Mr Darcy," Elizabeth prompted. "We would be grateful for your candid opinion." She met his gaze evenly, without artifice. It was that clarity—so at odds with every calculating social exchange he endured in London—that stirred something in him.

"To pursue such a case, Mr Collins would need to file a formal bill of complaint. Mr Phillips would better advise you as to specifics, but I am aware that the court would require substantial documentation, sworn testimony, examination of witnesses." He paused. "And of course, there are the costs to consider."

"The initial costs alone," Darcy continued, his tone intentionally neutral, "would require far more than a parson could manage from a modest living."

Elizabeth looked up, stopping her quill thoughtfully. "Yet Mr Collins speaks with great confidence of pursuing the matter. He mentioned support from his patroness—Lady Catherine de Bourgh. 'A lady of consequence', as he has reminded us several times."

"Ah." Darcy's tone remained neutral, although something flickered in his expression.

"Did Mr Collins not once refer to her as your aunt, sir?" Elizabeth asked.

"She is," Darcy replied with reserve. "Although perhaps Mr Collins ascribes to her a greater partiality than she possesses for Chancery proceedings. They are apt to command resources beyond what prudence might have allocated."

Elizabeth's quick mind caught the implications. "So, he may find himself in an awkward position. Having initiated proceedings based on expected support from your aunt…"

"Only to find that support limited to moral encouragement," Darcy finished. "Many have overestimated my aunt's resolve in business affairs."

As the afternoon light began to fade, Mr Bennet gestured

for Darcy to remain after the ladies had withdrawn to prepare to dress for dinner. The older gentleman waited until the door had firmly closed before speaking.

"There is an additional matter of some delicacy, Mr Darcy, which I would discuss with you privately." He shifted in his chair, his expression uncommonly serious. "You are aware, I believe, of the three farms adjoining the eastern boundary of Longbourn?"

"I recall them, sir. The Fairfax properties, if I am not mistaken?"

"Just so. These past five years, we have quietly acquired them through various means. The last was purchased only this past Michaelmas." Mr Bennet's eyes held a shrewd gleam. "They are not entailed, you understand. Nor is the old Lodge upon the northernmost property, which we have been gradually restoring. Nor the bulk of the pasture lands formerly of the Matthews's Dunbar Court property."

Understanding dawned in Darcy's expression. "A most prudent arrangement, sir."

"The Lodge is modest, but sound. Five bedrooms, adequate offices, and thirty acres of good land in the home farm. Altogether, it should prove sufficient to provide an income of four hundred pounds per annum, when competently managed." Mr Bennet's fingers drummed lightly on the arm of his chair. "My Elizabeth has overseen the improvements herself. The roof is new, the chimneys repointed, the kitchen garden restored. It wants only furnishing to be quite habitable."

"These properties stand completely separate from the entail?"

"They do. The deeds are held in trust for my granddaughters." A faint smile touched the old gentleman's lips. "I may be a fool in many things, Mr Darcy, but I am not so great a fool as to leave my girls without provision. Should the worst occur, they will have both home and a modest independence. Should Lady Matthews continue to spend beyond her means, and the Viscount's luck at the tables continue as it has, I understand the family may retrench and take rooms in Bath. I hope to bid on the home farm and house, given the opportunity, and the means."

Darcy sat in thoughtful silence for a moment. The quiet clarity of Mr Bennet's intentions stirred an unexpected sense of responsibility. "You have managed the matter with remarkable discretion, sir."

"Necessity often breeds cunning—even in old men." Mr Bennet's expression grew serious once more. "I tell you this in confidence, Mr Darcy, as I believe you to be a man of honour. Should anything… untoward occur in this business with Mr Collins, I would ask that you see my arrangements are fully executed. My attorney, Phillips, has copies of all the records. He will execute my will, but I would have my ladies protected by more than one gentleman."

"You have my word, sir," Darcy replied gravely. He felt the promise settle not as a burden, but as a privilege. "Such measures will, I hope, prove unnecessary."

"As do I, as do I." Mr Bennet lifted his glass in a small salute. "But one sleeps better, does one not, knowing one's duty has been discharged."

Elizabeth returned to the study, organising the papers they had reviewed. Mr Darcy had lingered to discuss one final point about the estate records, and now stood by the window, his tall figure silhouetted against the late afternoon light.

"Miss Elizabeth," he said, turning from his contemplation of the grounds. "Please do not scruple to send word if you require any further assistance with these legal matters."

"You are very kind, sir." Elizabeth busied herself with securing the ribbons on a bundle of documents, avoiding his direct gaze. His manner throughout had been everything proper and helpful yet reserved.

"Not at all. Your management of Longbourn is…" He paused, seeming to choose his words with care. "Most impressive."

Elizabeth felt the familiar mixture of pride and irritation at such qualified praise. As though it were impressive that a woman might understand estate matters.

"You are quite… thorough in your areas of knowledge," she ventured, curious to see if he would take offence at the implicit comparison between their abilities.

"I hope to be," he replied, gentle warmth softening his formal tone. "Your results here may persuade me to reconsider some of my own practices at P-" He stopped abruptly, then continued more formally. "But I must not detain you further."

With a formal bow, he took his leave, and Elizabeth stared at the empty doorway, troubled by an unfamiliar sensation of regret. His genuine interest in their work, his thoughtful attention to their situation, his obvious intelligence - all combined to create a most inconvenient wish that he might… but no. Such a man no doubt viewed a gentleman's daughter turned estate manager as an oddity at best, somewhere between a blue-stocking and a social inferior—hardly a suitable…

She shook herself. Such thoughts were both improper and impractical. With determined efficiency, she returned to her task of organising the papers, resolutely ignoring the lingering warmth his rare half-smile had kindled. There was work to be done.

Chapter Twenty

As he reached his horse, Darcy glanced back at the house. Through the study window, he could see her still at work, her head bent over her papers. The late afternoon sun caught the fine lines of her face, the graceful curve of her neck…

"Impossible," he said, although whether he meant her situation or his increasing preoccupation with her, he could scarce determine.

With a sharp gesture, he turned away. He had responsibilities, a position to maintain. He could not allow himself to be captivated by fine eyes and a quick mind, no matter how felicitously they were united in her form. That he needed reminding was warning enough.

Darcy urged his horse toward Netherfield at a pace that matched his unsettled thoughts. His response to Elizabeth Bennet had grown increasingly… inconvenient. Several times he had caught himself leaning forward, drawn into debate with an eagerness more suited to a fresh-faced Cambridge scholar than a man of his position.

When she had lifted those fine eyes to his, challenging his assessment with a mixture of fire and reason that was altogether too compelling, he had nearly… but no. The mere notion of pursuing a lady in her circumstances was unthinkable.

He reined in sharply, acknowledging with grim humour that his thoughts, like his horse, needed better regulation. This was just the sort of entanglement he must avoid.

His duty was clear. The Darcy name, his sister's coming debut, his position in society - all demanded a suitable alliance. Not this dangerous attraction. That she managed her role with more grace and wisdom than half the peers of the realm was beside the point.

And yet… the way she had defended her grandfather's

interests, practical yet passionate.

"Enough," he muttered to himself, straightening in the saddle. He would offer such assistance as their situation required, maintain a respectful distance, and master this. He had years of practice in doing what duty required..

He dismounted his horse with perhaps more vigour than necessary, setting a brisk pace back to Netherfield house. Yet try as he might, he could not quite banish his growing sense that she was quite the most interesting woman of his acquaintance.

The clock on the mantel struck the hour, each chime reverberating through the suddenly still room. Lady Catherine's summons brought forth an immediate response, the parson materialising with practised servility. "Your Ladyship?"

"You speak of my nephew's interest in Miss Elizabeth Bennet's particular influence. Elaborate."

"Indeed, your Ladyship, she demonstrates a most unseemly fascination with agricultural matters. Mr Darcy pays particular attention to her observations regarding drainage improvements."

Lady Catherine's fan snapped open abruptly. "Drainage improvements? And my nephew attends these discussions?"

"With marked interest, your Ladyship. As I told you, he was even seen to…" Mr Collins paused for dramatic effect, "to walk out with her. Unchaperoned."

Lady Catherine shook her head violently. "This cannot be endured! These actions go beyond mere impropriety. It threatens the very fabric of proper society. What gentleman of consequence could permit himself…" Her voice hardened with determination. "Mr Collins, you must assert control over this situation. The estate requires the protection of male guidance."

"But your Ladyship, the entail does not permit--"

"This is not about the entail," she cut in. "This is about my nephew. Return at once to Meryton. You must establish that this ancient relation has lost his sense. No court will allow a lunatic to retain control over your inheritance. You will put a stop to their behaviour—The property itself has doubtless been grievously mismanaged under the direction of females. Expect to find accounts in disarray and improvements neglected. You shall need to dismiss any servants who have grown accustomed to taking direction from these presumptuous young women. It is your Christian duty to rectify this unnatural situation, and more importantly, to put a stop to my nephew's particular weakness."

Mr Collins bowed deeply, "I stand in humble awe of your Ladyship's perspicacity, which so clearly indicates where obligation must lead."

"See that my instructions are followed precisely. Go thither at once."

He bowed again, mentally composing the florid report he would send her after his triumph. "You may depend upon my devotion, my Lady."

Lady Catherine stilled, her hands tightening upon the back of a carved chair. "Above all else, Mr Collins: my nephew must not disgrace himself—or his family."

A package arrived at Longbourn addressed to Miss Catherine Bennet, in care of Mr James Bennet. Inside, nestled in a bed of straw, were six lemons—their bright yellow a startling contrast to the autumn colours surrounding Longbourn.

The accompanying note was brief:

Miss Catherine,

I recall my mother's insistence that fresh lemon greatly enhances the efficacy of horehound syrup for chest complaints. I requested these to be delivered to you from my hothouse at Pemberley. I would be interested to learn whether they might improve your remedy.

Your servant, F. Darcy

Kitty stared at the note in astonishment, then at the precious fruits whose cost and rarity made them an extravagant gift indeed.

"Well!" Mrs Bennet exclaimed, examining one of the lemons with wondering fingers. "It seems Mr Darcy is quite as agreeable as Lady Lucas thinks."

"Or perhaps he simply respects competence, whatever its source," Elizabeth observed, watching her sister's flushed face with thoughtful eyes.

That evening, Kitty prepared a new batch of horehound syrup, following Mrs Faxon's recipe but substituting fresh lemon juice for the precious drops of essence. The resulting remedy proved even more effective, easing Grandfather's breathing more completely than any previous batch.

She sent a thoughtfully composed note of thanks to Netherfield, detailing the improvements observed and expressing her appreciation for his contribution to her grandfather's health. The note underwent no fewer than seven draughts before she was satisfied with its contents.

To her surprise, Mr Darcy himself called the following day, making particular enquiry about the efficacy of the lemons and asking detailed questions about her gardens and methods. When he departed, he left with a small bottle of the improved syrup and an invitation for Kitty to correspond with his sister, who apparently shared an interest in herbal remedies.

Mrs Bennet drew her shawl closer against the crisp evening as they watched him ride away. "To think that Catherine's garden remedies would interest a man with ten thousand a year!"

"I believe," Elizabeth said dryly, "it is Kitty's knowledge that has impressed Mr Darcy, not her marital prospects."

"Of course, of course," her mother agreed hastily. "Although it is often the case that respect precedes warmer feelings." Her expression grew thoughtful. "But it is his appreciation of her skills that matters most. I am not suggesting a potential suitor in Mr Darcy. I value his recognition of Catherine's worth."

Kitty, listening to this exchange with mingled embarrassment and pride, realised, with quiet astonishment, that it was indeed not Mr Darcy's consequence she reflected on, but rather the unexpected connection they shared through their mothers' gardens. From the simplest of beginnings—a persistent cough, a walk to Widow Faxon's cottage—had come not only relief for her grandfather but a new source of confidence in her own abilities.

That evening, she added a new page to her notebook, attentively recording the improved recipe with its precise measurements and observations. At the top of the page, she hesitated a moment before writing:

Horehound and Lemon Syrup for Chest Complaints As taught by Agnes Faxon of Meryton, with improvements suggested by Fitzwilliam Darcy of Pemberley

Knowledge preserved, passed down, and improved through shared wisdom—a legacy as valuable as Longbourn itself.

Chapter Twenty-One

The early winter brought with it a chill that seemed to seep through the walls of Longbourn itself. Elizabeth had been reviewing the quarterly accounts when Hill announced the unexpected arrival of Mr Collins and another gentleman. She found them in the entrance hall—Mr Collins, whose clerical black only emphasised his florid complexion, and beside him a lean, grey-featured gentleman.

"Miss Elizabeth." Mr Collins managed to make her name sound like an accusation. "I hope your grandfather is well enough to receive visitors?" His smile held no sincerity.

"Indeed, Mr Collins. And you are…?" She turned to the other man, already guessing his profession from his worn leather portfolio.

"Mr Stevenson, solicitor," he replied with a slight bow. "We have matters of some urgency to discuss."

Elizabeth led them to her grandfather's study, where Mr Bennet sat in his customary chair by the window. His eyes were sharp as he observed their visitors. Jane was already present, having been reviewing tenant agreements, and Elizabeth was grateful for her steady presence.

"Mr Bennet, sir." Mr Collins began, his voice dripping with false concern, "I have come to address some deeply troubling matters." He nodded to Mr Stevenson, who was attempting to read the documents on the desk.

Elizabeth caught the slight tremor in her grandfather's hand as he reached to remove his papers. She moved to stand behind his chair, a position that allowed her to both support him and face their visitors directly.

"We are here to gather evidence," Mr Collins continued, "of gross mismanagement of the estate." He emphasised each word, speaking slowly, as if to someone without sense.

Mr Bennet sighed. "Are you indeed?"

"Indisputably. The allowing of women—begging your pardon, ladies—to make decisions regarding crops, tenant contracts, and livestock management is unprecedented and, I must say, deeply concerning. These are not the actions of a man in possession of his faculties. These decisions have disrupted the natural order by shifting crops from field to field. The soil, being a gift from Providence, is inherently inexhaustible and will perpetually yield the same bounty, regardless of what is planted upon it. This notion of alternating crops is nothing but the idle fancy of silly women who seek to complicate the simplicity of God's design. The natural order is to continue to sow the grain as our forefathers did, for their wisdom is unquestionably greater than the imaginings of modern bluestockings."

Mr Collins ceased his oration, regarding them with an expression of triumph. Elizabeth wondered whether he had been rehearsing that speech like a sermon for the entire fifty odd miles from Kent.

Mr Stevenson raised his chin. "Our investigation will establish that these irregular practices have led to a significant devaluation of the property. As the heir presumptive, Mr Collins has a vested interest in preserving the estate's worth."

"Irregular practices?" Elizabeth kept her voice level, although she felt heat rising in her cheeks. "You mean the practices that have increased our crop yields by thirty percent over the past five years?"

"Of course, we are well aware that numbers can be manipulated, Miss Bennet," Stevenson said dismissively. "Which is why we require immediate oversight of all financial records and management decisions. For the good of the estate, you understand."

Jane spoke up, her quiet voice carrying unexpected authority. "Our books are meticulously kept, sir. Every penny is accounted for."

"Nevertheless," Mr Stevenson interjected, "given Mr Bennet's unfortunate… condition, we feel it prudent to seek to appoint a conservator to oversee matters."

Elizabeth felt her grandfather stiffen beneath her hand. Before she could respond, Mr Collins pressed on.

"I should mention that several influential landowners in the area share our concerns. Lord Matthews, for one, has expressed particular disapproval of the current… situation." He smiled, displaying more yellowed teeth than was strictly decorous. "I believe you lease the north pasture from his estate?"

Elizabeth's mind raced through their options, aware of how many families depended on Longbourn's stability. She thought of their tenants, of the perfectly balanced books Jane maintained.

"We will, of course, need time to consult our own solicitor regarding these claims," Mr Bennet said.

Mr Collins exchanged a look with Mr Stevenson, barely concealing his satisfaction. "We can grant you a week to put your affairs in order. Although I doubt you will find any legal precedent to support your current arrangements."

"A week will be sufficient," Mr Bennet replied, his tone making it clear the meeting was over.

Mr Collins appeared confused, or perhaps deflated, that no confrontation ensued.

"We shall return one week from today," Stevenson said, turning to leave.

Mr Collins opened his mouth to speak, glancing from one lady to the other. "Do not for a moment think you will fool us with your affectation and coquetry as females. I know how to manage such headstrong and foolish creatures. You do not know your own interest; but I will make you know it." He fixed Elizabeth with a hard glare, its effect diminished by the sheen of sweat on his brow,

Mr Bennet reached up and placed a hand on Elizabeth's arm as she drew breath to respond. Elizabeth pressed her tongue against her teeth and inhaled sharply.

As Hill showed them out, Elizabeth heard Mr Collins remark

loudly in the hall, "Poor great-grandfather would be turning in his grave if he could see what has become of Longbourn."

Elizabeth waited until their footsteps had faded before facing her grandfather. He had grown pale, and there was something in his expression heretofore unknown—was it fear? Or guilt?

"Grandfather?" she asked.

"I am well. This was to be expected. Our accounts are in order, and we have nothing to hide- well, nothing as relates to Longbourn. I will consult Phillips. I have my doubts as to Mr Collins's authority to make these demands. For now, I believe it is time to review estate inventory, and to remove items not belonging to the entail."

Lydia burst into the drawing room in a rush of ribbons and skirts.

"You will never guess!" she shouted into the hive of ledger-checking, silver-inventorying, and linen-sorting that the Bennet ladies had undertaken.

Mrs Bennet looked up from the embroidered damask tablecloth she was folding into a trunk. "Lydia, please calm yourself. We are all in a dither with this inventory and you ought to be as well!"

"But Mamma! You must hear the news!" she said as she tore her bonnet from her head and flung it in the general direction of the settee.

"We will hear your news once you have taken a breath, Lyddie." Jane smiled at her youngest sister.

Lydia looked to the ceiling, took several slow breaths, and then positioned herself primly on a chair.

"Very well, Lydia. What news?" Mrs Bennet asked.

"I went to check on the cost of additional hay for my flock. Mr Garrison was there at the shops as well, and you know how he likes to talk. Well, he said Lady Matthews has put about that Lord Matthews intends to take back the north pasture when our 'lease' expires! She said he is most concerned about 'management' at Longbourn and how we could pay the rent, given all the problems Mr Collins has spoken of." Lydia's composure lasted only seconds before she leapt up again, pacing in agitation.

Mrs Bennet's hands stilled on the damask. "Did she indeed?"

"Yes! And what is worse, she was going on about how he had only let the land because he felt sorry for our situation, but now he hopes that the estate will have proper management." Lydia's hands flew expressively.

Elizabeth's quill paused mid-calculation. "How convenient that he should suddenly recall his 'ownership' just when Mr Collins appears in need of allies."

"The deed is secure in the strongbox," Jane said quietly, although her composed countenance had acquired the slightest edge. "Along with his rather desperate letter begging us to keep the transaction private."

"And the money was paid in full," Mrs Bennet added, her voice sharp. "Although he seemed eager enough to forget that part when his son's gaming debts were pressing."

Lydia flopped dramatically onto the settee. "But what are we to do? The sheep are settled there now, and the new pasturing plan is nearly complete, and--"

"We shall do nothing," Mr Bennet said firmly. "Lord Matthews may bluster all he likes, but he cannot alter the deed. Although perhaps, Elizabeth, you might mention the situation to Mr Darcy when next you discuss the drainage work. His… perspective on such matters might prove useful."

Elizabeth nodded slowly. "Yes, and Sir William might be reminded of his role in witnessing the original transaction. Just in case anyone should question the proceedings."

"The documents remain obstinately fixed in their unfavourable position for Lord Matthews," Jane observed with gentle irony. "No amount of rewriting history will change the sums in our books. Or his signature on the receipt for funds paid."

"Or the fact that the Viscount lost the price of the pasture at the hazard table in a single night," Lydia added with uncharacteristic bitterness. "He would prefer everyone forget that part."

"Then we shall help him forget it," Mrs Bennet said decisively, "by maintaining our accustomed discretion. The deed speaks for itself, should it become necessary. Now, Lydia, since you are here, help me with this inventory. The linens will not count themselves."

Lydia jumped up again, assuming an exaggerated pose and avoiding the linen pile. "But there is more! I was in Johnson's, looking at ribbons, when who should sweep in but Lady Matthews herself, in all her faded finery…"

She arranged her features into a pinched expression and adopted a nasal tone that made Elizabeth hide a smile behind her ledger. "'Mrs Johnson,'" Lydia trilled in a perfect imitation, thrusting out her bosom and lifting her nose into the air. "'I require a travelling ensemble suitable for Bath. Something that will not show the dust of travel, as I expect to make several journeys this winter. The waters, you know, are quite indispensable for my health.'"

"Bath?" Mrs Bennet's hands stilled on the linens. "In winter?"

"And not just Bath!" Lydia twirled across the room, still in character. "'One simply cannot remain in the country through all the season. It is so… provincial. And with the estate requiring such tedious attention…It might be best if we simply let Dunbar Court go.'" She dropped the impression suddenly. "And then she said something quite interesting about 'Eastbridge managing the sale' before she saw me and stopped talking!"

Jane and Elizabeth exchanged glances. "Eastbridge is the Viscount, their eldest son," Jane said quietly. "The one who's been in London these past three years."

"Living well beyond his means, if town gossip is to be believed," Elizabeth added. She pulled a fresh sheet of paper toward her and began calculating rapidly. "Grandfather, if the estate comes up for sale…"

"We would need to move quickly," Mr Bennet said. "The

main house might be beyond our means, but those western fields…"

"Would connect perfectly with the north pasture," Jane finished, already reaching for the estate books. "And the soil there is excellent for wheat."

Lydia beamed at the stir she had created. "Lady Matthews also said something about 'that dreadful Mr Collins" and how he was 'putting about the most shocking suggestions about poor Mr Bennet's competence.'" Her impression this time was pitch-perfect, down to Lady Matthews's habit of tapping her fan for emphasis.

"Did she indeed?" Mrs Bennet's voice had grown thoughtful. "Then perhaps we should invite Sir William to dine tomorrow. He always has such… interesting information about local property matters. And Elizabeth, when you speak with Mr Darcy about the drainage issues…"

"I shall mention our interest in expanding our holdings," Elizabeth finished. "Although—we would need to employ some most prudent strategies."

"The figures may not bend to inventive reasoning," Jane said with her gentle smile, "but they have generally proved amenable to careful management. Particularly when we have time to prepare."

"Then we shall prepare," Mrs Bennet said firmly. "Lydia, dear, you have done very well. Now, pray change your gown—you have quite rumpled your ribbons with your exertions. Then come to help us finish this inventory. We may need to know exactly what resources we have at our disposal."

Lydia bounced out of the room, pleased with both her theatrical success and its impact. Behind her, the scratch of quills sounded as her sisters began their calculations, plotting yet another careful expansion of their domain.

Chapter Twenty-Two

The morning was cool but clear as Elizabeth took her preferred path through the wilderness walk at Longbourn. Her mind was so occupied with troubled thoughts that she nearly collided with Mr Darcy as he emerged from behind a stand of elder trees.

"Miss Bennet," he said, bowing elegantly. "I am delighted to encounter you on your morning constitutional."

"Mr Darcy," she replied, curtseying. "I fear I am poor company today."

He studied her face with concern. "You appear distressed. Is there some way I might be of service?"

Elizabeth hesitated, then sighed. "Mr Collins visited yesterday. He was most disagreeable."

"Mr Collins?" Darcy's brow furrowed. "I understood him to have returned to Kent some time ago."

"Indeed, he had. But it seems his patroness has encouraged him to return to press his claims regarding the entail." Elizabeth's voice faltered. "He spoke most critically about my grandfather's health, suggesting that he was no longer able to manage the estate. He demands that we produce all our records for his inspection."

"The man is unconscionable," Darcy said, his voice low and controlled, although his eyes betrayed his anger.

"He will return in a week's time with his solicitor to review accounts." Elizabeth looked away toward the distant fields.

Darcy was silent a moment, then spoke with care. "Miss Bennet, I am certain you're your Grandfather's attorney will advise him on this, but should Mr Collins return you need only send word to Netherfield, and I shall attend immediately."

Elizabeth's eyes widened. "That is most kind, sir, but I do not wish to impose—"

"It is no imposition. My knowledge of the law—and of my aunt—might prove useful in such a circumstance." His expression softened. "You—er your family should not face such unpleasantness alone."

"Thank you, Mr Darcy. Your offer brings me great comfort." She offered him a small smile before continuing her walk.

As they parted, Darcy questioned what madness had prompted him to insert himself so thoroughly into the Bennet family's affairs? Only last night he had resolved to maintain a respectful distance from Miss Elizabeth, whose presence affected his equanimity in ways he found most disturbing.

Perhaps he ought to return to London with all haste, offering what assistance he could from a safe distance. There, at least, he would be free from the daily temptation of Miss Elizabeth's fine eyes and lively conversation.

And yet, the thought of Mr Collins bullying the Bennets in his absence was intolerable. No, he would remain at Netherfield for the nonce. He was a gentleman offering assistance to a respected neighbour. Nothing more.

The following week, Netherfield's butler, trailed by a messenger, approached Mr Darcy at his desk reviewing correspondence. Young Tom, the Longbourn stable boy, had barely stammered out "Mr Collins, sir--" before Darcy was striding toward the stables, calling for his horse.

He arrived at Longbourn to find Mr Collins in the study, a thin man with wire-rimmed spectacles at his elbow. Elizabeth stood near her grandfather's chair, her bearing rigid with barely contained fury.

"Ah, Mr Darcy." Mr Collins simpered, although his eyes held a calculating gleam. "How… unexpected to find you here. As I am sure you are aware, my dear cousin's confused state requires more… appropriate supervision of the estate."

"Indeed?" Darcy's tone could have frozen water. "I have no such opinion. And this gentleman is…?"

"Mr Stevenson, my solicitor," Mr Collins preened. "Most highly recommended by my esteemed patroness, Lady Catherine de Bourgh."

Darcy's eyebrow rose fractionally. "I was unaware of that name in Lady Catherine connections to the legal profession in… where did you say you practised, sir?"

The thin man shifted uncomfortably. "Er, primarily in Kent, sir."

"Kent?" Darcy's voice hardened. "How remarkable. I maintain rather extensive dealings with the law societies of Kent. Pray, with what chambers are you associated?"

Mr Collins interrupted before the man could respond. "Such details are immaterial. We are here about my poor cousin's deplorable condition. This morning, he was speaking nonsense about crop revolutions and drainpipes!"

"Was he indeed?" Darcy moved to stand beside Mr Bennet's chair. "Perhaps, Mr Collins, you might enlighten us on these subjects yourself? Since you feel qualified to judge their sense or nonsense."

"I… that is…" Mr Collins tugged at his cravat. "It is not for me to speak of such things. My noble patroness, Lady Catherine herself, agrees that his faculties must be failing--"

"Come now," Mr Bennet pressed, his eyes alight with savage amusement. "You profess concern over my management of this estate. Please, explain those basic principles of modern agriculture?"

"Well… one must… as I understand… one plants different crops…" Mr Collins fumbled.

"Indeed? Which crops, exactly? In what order?" Mr Bennet turned to Jane. "Jane, pray remind me of our rotation schedule for the north field?"

"Wheat, followed by turnips," Jane replied crisply, "then barley, and finally clover. The turnips, of course, allow us to maintain the sheep through winter, whilst the clover replenishes the soil."

Mr Collins's face had grown increasingly red. "I declare it is not decent for a young lady to concern herself with such matters!"

"No?" Mr Bennet's smile was razor-sharp. "Then perhaps you might expound on our use of the principles of modern drainage? The Elkington method has proved most efficacious in our lower fields. You are acquainted with Mr Elkington's innovations, I should imagine?"

"Drainage is… that is… when water… flows…" Mr Collins pulled at his cravat.

"Lizzy, my dear," Mr Bennet turned to his elder granddaughter, "what depth did you determine optimal for the auxiliary channels?"

"Four feet, Grandfather," Elizabeth answered confidently. "Although we found it necessary to dig to five feet at the junction points, as Mr Elkington suggests. The clay soil, you understand."

"Remarkable," Darcy murmured, his admiration evident.

"But… but…" Mr Collins spluttered, "these are matters for men of business! Indeed, you cannot expect--"

"Very well," Mr Bennet cut in. "A simpler question then. The current price of wheat at Mark Lane?"

"I… that is… a gentleman need not concern himself with such mundane--"

"Sixty-eight shillings per quarter at Monday's market," Mr Bennet supplied crisply. "Although I expect it to rise given the poor weather in Norfolk. It could surpass last year's top rate of one hundred and three shillings per console if the rain is severe. Is this not your information, Mr Darcy?"

"Indeed, sir. The latest reports suggest as much."

Mr Collins puffed up like an indignant toad. "This is just what I mean! These fanciful notions of prices and weather! My noble patroness has assured me such minutia are the province of--"

"Your noble patroness," Darcy interjected, his voice sharp as a blade, "is not involved in the minutia of her estate because she delegates those matters to her steward who reports to me. It is well she is not here to witness your behaviour, sir. Nor I suspect, would she approve of this spectacle."

Before Mr Collins could speak, Mrs Hill announced Mr Phillips. That gentleman entered glowering and stopped before Mr Stevenson.

"And who are you?" he demanded.

"Andrew Stevenson, Esquire." Mr Stevenson's voice gave a quaver as he faced the older, taller attorney.

"Where do you practice, sir, that you do not have the courtesy of informing counsel of your intention to meet with his client?"

Mr Stevenson straightened and said, "I was not aware that Mr Bennet had an attorney."

"Nor did you enquire I am sure. But you did not answer my question. In which court are you admitted to practice? Surely none in Hertfordshire else I would know your name and your chambers." Mr Phillips fixed a stern look on Mr Stevenson.

"I apprenticed in the chambers of Waller and Brown."

"Where are they located?"

"Margate," Mr Stevenson's voice had lost its tone of self-assurance.

"You apprenticed in Kent, then. Not in Hertfordshire where you now purport to practice. You did not say, however, where you are admitted to practice."

Mr Stevenson's colour became quite white, and his eyes darted around the room as if seeking escape. "I am… not yet admitted," he croaked.

"Ah, then you are practicing without admission? Perhaps the Inns of Court will be interested in hearing about this."

Mr Stevenson was already edging toward the door, his nerve failing when confronted with Mr Phillips's questions.

"My apologies, I must be leaving," he began, but he was

stopped by a firm hand on his shoulder.

"Mr Phillips, if I may, if a person wished to examine the financial records of another, what procedure would be required? Mr Darcy asked, holding fast to Mr Stevenson's arm.

"I could explain a number of methods to achieve that end, however, each of them would require that court petitions be filed and served upon the party. If the court agreed that such an examination was warranted, there would be a writ issued ordering that the books be made available." Mr Phillips appeared, to Elizabeth's eye, to be rather enjoying Mr Stevenson's discomfort.

Mr Darcy turned to Mr Stevenson, released his arm, and with the utmost politeness said "If you would be so kind as to produce the writ giving you leave to review the records of Longbourn?"

"We must see the records," Mr Collins spluttered, "Lady Catherine insists I am to examine them fully! Her influence in legal matters is beyond question!"

"I believe," Darcy cut in, his voice deadly quiet, "that you would be wise to consider your next words with extreme care, Mr Collins. Do you or this…gentleman have a writ?"

Something in his tone made Mr Collins falter. He looked to his companion for support, only to find the space by the door conspicuously empty.

"I… that is… perhaps I have been hasty…" Mr Collins began to back away. "A simple misunderstanding… Acting only from the deepest concern for the family, you understand…"

"Of course," Mr Bennet's dry voice followed him. "In days to come, cousin, you would be well-advised to remember that vigilance, like Christian kindness, ought properly to begin in one's own sphere. Especially as your own situation- and that of your '*attorney*' might not be materially enhanced through closer scrutiny." They watched in silence as Mr Collins fled the room, his footsteps echoing down the hall in an undignified retreat.

After a long moment, Elizabeth turned to Darcy. "Mr Collins seemed most confident of Lady Catherine's expertise. Yet something in your manner suggested…" She let the question hover in the air.

Darcy's expression grew grave. "There is a matter regarding Lady Catherine that I should perhaps share with you." He glanced at Mr Bennet and Mr Phillips, who nodded permission. "The situation at Rosings is not what Mr Collins believes it to be."

"Indeed?" Elizabeth's eyebrow rose in elegant enquiry.

"As of Michaelmas last," Darcy continued reluctantly, "I hold sole legal authority over the affairs of Rosings Park. The Court of Chancery found it necessary to protect my cousin Anne's inheritance after certain… unfortunate decisions by Lady Catherine regarding her management and expenditures."

Elizabeth's eyes widened. "Lady Catherine's estate is under your superintendence?"

"It is indeed." A ghost of a smile touched his lips. "Although I beg you will not hold it against me."

"That depends entirely," she replied, her eyes dancing, "on whether you share her reported views regarding the limited sphere of female influence."

"I think, my dear," Mr Bennet interrupted with barely concealed amusement, "that Mr Darcy's actions today have spoken rather clearly on that point."

Darcy met Elizabeth's gaze steadily. "I have lately learnt, Miss Elizabeth, that capability knows no gender. Although I own, I have seldom seen it demonstrated quite so thoroughly as at Longbourn."

The look that passed between them spoke volumes, although both quickly looked away.

"Well then," Mr Bennet said briskly, reaching for his ledgers, "shall we return to the matter of spring plantings? I believe, Mr Darcy, you had some thoughts on Mr Coke's experiments with sainfoin?"

Mary sat at her small desk by the window, a volume with the mark of Fordyce's Sermons open before her. In truth, within the binding it contained a treatise on soil amendments. Her attention had wandered to the scene that had unfolded in Grandfather's study below. The raised voices had carried audibly enough through the floorboards–Mr Collins's pompous declarations, Uncle Phillips's controlled anger, and the steady authority in Mr Darcy's tone.

She pressed her fingertips to the bridge of her nose, adjusting her spectacles. How telling that Mr Collins should mistake genuine knowledge for confusion, expertise for senility. Her own extensive reading in moral philosophy had taught her that some men feared what they did not understand, and rather than seek education, they would seek control.

Jane and Elizabeth managed the estate with such natural grace that few noticed the depth of learning behind their decisions. Mary noticed. She had watched Elizabeth pore over agricultural treatises deep into the night, seen Jane meticulously checking and rechecking calculations. Their expertise was no accident but dedicated study–a pursuit Mary understood well.

She glanced at her own neat shelves, where volumes of philosophy and natural science stood alongside her music. How Mr Collins would disapprove of such reading for a young lady! Yet it was this learning that had taught her to calculate optimal drainage angles for the lower fields, applying the principles of geometry she had studied.

The voices from below grew sharper. Mary smiled as she heard Grandfather pose his agricultural questions. She had always admired how he wielded knowledge—elegant, precise, and sharp as a sword. A far cry from Mr Collins's blustering appeals to unearned authority.

She heard retreating footsteps below, followed by the decisive slam of the front door. So, the enemy was defeated. Mary allowed herself a small, satisfied smile. Let Mr Collins return to his noble patroness and her outdated certainties. Here at Longbourn, they would continue to learn, to innovate, to grow–both their crops and their minds.

Turning back to her desk, Mary opened her notebook and began to write, her neat hand filling the page:

"*On the Practical Applications of Modern Natural Philosophy to*

Agricultural Innovation…"

Elizabeth was watching the afternoon sun cast long shadows across Meryton's main street when she spotted Mr Darcy emerging from the bookseller's shop. He noticed her immediately, his quick stride carrying him to where she stood.

"Miss Elizabeth." He bowed. "Your family is well?"

"As well as can be expected, given recent developments." She shifted her basket.

"I have been considering your situation." His voice lowered naturally, although they stood alone. "Your Uncle Phillips serves as your grandfather's attorney, does he not? His reputation for handling property matters is quite sound."

"Indeed, and we seek his counsel. My grandfather values his judgement in legal matters." She paused. "But you seem to have something specific in mind, Mr Darcy?"

"I do. Mr Collins has been unwise in attempting to take matters into his own hands. I expect he may now seek court authority. Whilst Mr Phillips' expertise is invaluable, my barrister in London has dealt extensively with cases involving ancient entails. If you would permit me, I believe the combination of Mr Phillips' local knowledge and Mr Graves's particular experience might serve your cause well."

Elizabeth studied him for a moment, noting reluctantly the genuine interest in his handsome features. "That is most generous, Mr Darcy." She hesitated, her fingers tightening on her basket. The matter of expense needed to be addressed, yet speaking of it with him felt suddenly delicate.

He seemed to sense her reservation. "Miss Elizabeth?"

"I must be practical," she said, forcing herself to meet his gaze. "Whilst Mr Phillips' services are within our means, a London barrister…" She let the sentence hang, frustrated at the warmth she could feel rising in her cheeks. This was simple estate management for him. His wealth made such concerns trivial. The words stuck in her throat.

Darcy saw the colour rise in Elizabeth's cheeks. He recognised with sudden clarity the source of her hesitation. Here was the careful manageress of Longbourn, wrestling with the practical constraints of her resources. Her discomfort touched, but she faced him with dignity.

"Miss Elizabeth," he said quietly, "Mr Graves's fees are not nearly so dear as you might imagine." He paused, weighing his next words. To offer outright to pay would wound her pride, yet to say nothing would leave her in genuine difficulty. "He has long served my family, and I would consider it a personal favour if you would allow me to facilitate his involvement in this matter."

He saw a flicker of understanding cross her face—she was too intelligent not to grasp his meaning—but he pressed on before she could object. "The combination of Mr Phillips' local expertise and Graves's experience with ancient entails would be particularly… efficient." He allowed himself a small smile. "Graves has a peculiar fondness for cases involving old family documents. I rather suspect he would consider this matter a professional pleasure."

Elizabeth swallowed. Her pride wished her to decline the generous offer. Rather than refuse, she deferred.

"I am grateful for your kindness. Of course, any decision must be made by my grandfather."

Chapter Twenty-Three

As she rounded the bend near the blacksmith's shop, Lydia nearly collided with a red-coated figure emerging from the establishment.

"My deepest apologies, miss," came a smooth voice that seemed practised in its charm. The officer bowed, his eyes widening in recognition. "Why, if it is not Miss Lydia Bennet. What a fortunate accident."

Lydia recognised Mr Wickham immediately, the officer who had been introduced to her just a few weeks before. She offered a curtsy that was correct in form but notably brief.

"Mr Wickham," she acknowledged, her tone polite but cool. "You are well?"

"Exceedingly so, now that fortune has placed the most enchanting young lady in my path," he replied, his smile widening to reveal even white teeth. "Might I escort you on your errand? These village paths can be uneven for a lady's delicate step."

Lydia's gaze flicked to James, who had stopped several paces away. "That is most unnecessary, sir. I am quite familiar with the paths of Meryton, having walked them since childhood."

"Then perhaps you might indulge me with a few moments of conversation?" he persisted, falling into step beside her uninvited. "I have thought often of you since our meeting. You did not attend the card party at the Harrington's, much to my dismay."

"How curious that you should have time for such reflections when there are so many officers' duties to attend to," Lydia remarked, her attention seemingly caught by the display in the draper's window. "Do excuse me, Mr Wickham. I must complete my errands and return home."

As she made to enter the shop, Wickham placed himself before the door. "Come Miss Lydia, can your errands not wait a moment longer? I have scarcely had the opportunity to make your acquaintance properly."

"I believe our acquaintance is quite as proper as it needs to be, sir," Lydia replied, meeting his gaze directly.

"Come now, Miss Lydia. I have observed your spirited nature. Will you not spare a few minutes of conversation for a lonely officer far from home?" His voice had dropped to a more intimate tone, and he leant closer. "I find myself quite enchanted by your eyes. They sparkle with a charm that belies your tender years."

Lydia regarded him steadily, her patience visibly wearing thin. "Thirty-two," she said abruptly.

Wickham blinked, momentarily thrown off his practised seduction. "I beg your pardon?"

"Thirty-two—" Lydia repeated, her voice carrying enough that a passing matron looked up with interest. "That is what I estimate your age to be, Mr Wickham. You must be at least twice my own, which I find curious in a gentleman who seems so eager to converse with girls barely finished with their lessons."

A flush crept up Wickham's neck as two officers from his regiment walked past, slowing their pace to observe the interaction.

"I swear to it, Miss Lydia, I am not yet thirty," he protested, his charm faltering.

"Indeed? Then perhaps the number refers to something else," Lydia continued, undeterred. "Ah, yes—it is the count of my teeth, which I mention as you have been examining me so thoroughly I assumed you wished to inspect them next, as one might a horse at Tattersall's before purchase." Her voice remained perfectly pleasant, although her eyes had hardened. "Or more likely before the horse mysteriously goes missing from its box, as I understand your reputation for acquiring things that do not belong to you is rather well established."

Wickham's face had gone from flushed to pale. "Miss Lydia, I hardly think—"

"That is evident, sir," Lydia cut him off. "A thinking man would realise that his charms, whilst perhaps once considerable, have faded somewhat with the passing years, and would not attempt to practise them on young misses who have no interest in becoming another of his conquests."

The two officers who had paused nearby exchanged glances, poorly disguising their interest in the discussion.

"You mistake my intentions," Wickham managed, his voice strained.

"I think not, Mr Wickham. I understand your intentions perfectly well. They are as transparent as they are dishonourable." Lydia straightened her already perfect posture. "Do excuse me, I have purchases to make and my mother expects me home directly. I suggest you direct your attentions to ladies who both welcome them and are of an age to receive them."

With that, Lydia stepped around the stunned Wickham and continued toward the carpenter's shop, motioning for Tom to follow. The stable boy hurried after her, giving Wickham a suspicious backward glance.

"Miss Lydia," Tom whispered as he caught up, "should I tell Mr Hill about that officer bothering you?"

Lydia's lips curved in a small, satisfied smile as she adjusted her basket on her arm. "No need, Tom. I believe Mr Wickham has received message enough for one day. Now, let us see if Mr Smith will accept our offer of three shillings per fence post. Elizabeth believes we can get them for two and six, but I think we shall have to settle for two and nine."

Elizabeth began to feel the cold invade her bottom from sitting so long on the fallen log. The scraps of paper in her hands shook as she shivered.

"Come now," she addressed her ledger sternly, "you might show some sympathy to our cause? These fields have waited five years to be properly managed." The wind whistled through bare branches in response, sending another shiver through her frame.

But the calculations maintained their provoking adherence to reality, no matter how she arranged them. She stared out over the autumn-brown fields, her grandfather's voice echoing in her memory: "We must secure every acre we can, Lizzy. Every piece we add is one more that cannot be taken from us."

She shifted on the rough bark, wincing as the cold seeped through her woollen skirts. The bark had long since dampened her petticoats, but she could not bring herself to abandon her calculations and return home. Not when the solution might lie in just one more attempt at restructuring their resources.

Pulling her threadbare gloves more firmly over her fingers, she wiped her reddened nose and bent again to her task. The numbers remained stubbornly uncooperative–the wool profits from Lydia's expanded flocks, the increased yield from the improved drainage in the south field, even the painfully hoarded funds from their spring wheat sale. All substantial, all testament to their successful management, yet all falling short of what would be needed to secure the remaining Matthews land.

"Would that I could curse!" she exclaimed, her frozen fingers cramping around her pencil. The fields below Oakham Mount stretched out before her, Matthews' western acres visible where they joined the north pasture. Five years of careful management; of sacrifices and strategic decisions, yet still the figures maintained their inexorable opposition to her hopes.

"If you are seeking something stronger," Darcy's voice came from behind her, unexpectedly warm with amusement, "might I suggest 'blood and thunder,' or perhaps 'damnation?' Although if you truly wish to shock, 'odds fish' once scandalised a clergyman in Sheffield."

She shot him a withering look, although her heart quickened at his unexpected—and entirely disarming — boldness. "Really, Mr Darcy? 'Odds fish?' At this rate, I shall be forced to cry 'Fie!' and clutch my shawl in horror."

"I could progress to 'snails and oysters' if you prefer. Or" he lowered his voice with mock gravity, "'struth and botheration.'"

"You are not helping," she informed him, while her smile could not be suppressed. "I shall reserve 'snails and oysters' for my next turn at the poultry yard."

He stepped closer, ostensibly blocking another gust of wind, although rendering her acutely aware of how alone they were on the hillside. Her heart beat faster as his dark eyes lingered on her face.

"'Rot his boots?'" he offered innocently. "Or shall we venture into territory that would make your mother reach for her smelling salts? I know several phrases involving 'the devil's dam' that would suffice."

"Mr Darcy!" But she was laughing now, her ledger forgotten, warmed unwillingly by this unexpected glimpse of playfulness. "I am inclined to suspect you spent more time in the stables than the drawing room in your youth."

"I simply believe in being thorough in one's education," he replied with dignity, although his eyes danced. "Even in matters of profanity. If you are contemplating an appropriate curse for Lord Matthews…" He paused, and something in his expression sharpened. "I overheard some interesting rumours in London last month." His lips twitched. "I have a particularly good one about gambling losses and public embarrassment, if you would care to employ it. Or you could try the more restrained 'May his horses throw him into every mud puddle between here and Bath.'"

Elizabeth suppressed a startled laugh. "That would be most unchristian of me, sir. Although I cannot deny the temptation is strong."

The bitter wind no longer reached her as he moved closer, and Elizabeth caught the subtle scent of leather and horse that clung to his riding coat. "I have considerable experience in dealing with gentlemen who conveniently forget their financial arrangements." His tone was light, but his eyes were keen. "I understand there may be some question about the status of the north pasture?"

Elizabeth smoothed her skirts and pulled her cloak tighter. "Not a question, truly. We have the deed, properly signed, and witnessed. But Lord Matthews seems to have developed a selective memory about the transaction, just as the home farm and manse of his estate are rumoured to be coming up for sale."

"Ah." His expression remained neutral. "And this would be of particular interest because...?"

"They adjoin our current holdings," Elizabeth said intensely. "The soil composition is excellent for wheat, and with the new drainage works..."

"The productivity would be significantly improved," he finished. Something in his intent gaze made her breath catch. "I see. And the timing of this sale presents certain... challenges?"

Elizabeth's laugh held little humour. "The figures persist in their stubborn refusal to accommodate our hopes, yes. Although we have some resources set aside for expansion..."

"But not enough to move quickly if the opportunity arises," he observed, studying the landscape. "A difficult situation." He toyed with his crop, betraying his unease as another gust of wind swirled around them.

"The mathematics show a deplorable lack of sympathy to our wishes," Elizabeth agreed wryly. "Although we shall manage somehow. We always do."

His expression grew thoughtful. "I heard young Eastbridge has been developing a most concerning fondness for hazard. Remarkable how fortunes can turn on a single evening."

Elizabeth's quill paused mid-calculation as she glanced up at him. "I hardly think wishing ill fortune on our neighbours becomes either of us, sir," she said, although she could not keep the amusement from her voice.

"I would not presume to wish anything of the sort." The warmth in his voice unsettled her. "I simply observe that some gentlemen find themselves unexpectedly eager to liquidate their assets after certain... social engagements in town. Speaking of which, I believe I have some business to attend to. Although if you require any more enthusiastic maledictions in the meantime–strictly genteel ones, of course–I remain your humble servant."

Elizabeth brushed a wind-loosened curl from her cheek,

startled by the intensity of his gaze. "How very obliging of you. Although I warn you, if I hear of any mysterious disasters befalling Lord Matthews, I shall know precisely whom to blame."

"I am wounded by your suspicion, Madam." That rare half-smile played at his mouth, making her heart flutter. "I plan to engage in some perfectly innocent conversation about the current value of agricultural land. And perhaps mention that private sales can be so much more… expedient than public ones."

"Although I know you scale these paths with intrepidity, might I escort you home? Unless," he added with careful neutrality, "your calculations of the accounts require more time."

Elizabeth pocketed her papers, conscious that his hand lingered just short of her elbow. "No, I believe I have stared at these figures long enough for one morning. I am surprised to find you abroad so early, sir."

They walked together toward the grove where his horse waited, frost still clinging to the shadows. Twice he seemed about to speak, only to fall silent again, an unusual hesitation in his bearing that made her pulse quicken.

"I had thought to ride before breakfast," he said finally, although something in his tone made her glance up sharply. The intensity in his dark eyes before he looked away sent a shiver through her. "That is… I will return to London within the week, and I wished to see—to ride these paths one last time before departing."

"London?" Elizabeth's heart gave an odd lurch at the news. "I had not heard you were planning to leave so soon."

"It was… rather suddenly determined." He shifted the crop from hand to hand, as if seeking a steadier grip on his thoughts. "Bingley has long planned to call on his solicitor and there are matters requiring my attention in town."

His countenance resumed the distant reserve she knew too well, as though regretting even this brief candour. They walked on in silence until they reached his horse, where their shoulders brushed briefly, sending a jolt of awareness through her.

"Miss Elizabeth," he began, then stopped, his expression

struggling between reserve and something warmer, more urgent. But whatever battle played out behind his eyes, propriety won. He bowed, formal and correct, although his gaze lingered longer than strictly proper. "I wish you a good morning."

Elizabeth watched him ride away, her smile faltering the moment his back was turned. A hollow ache opened behind her ribs—foolish, unwelcome. She was unable to shake the feeling that she had witnessed something significant, although its meaning eluded her. The air seemed colder in his absence as she turned toward home.

A half-collapsed fencepost and a narrow-rutted lane marked the turnoff. Darcy guided his horse onto the lesser-used track, telling himself it was merely to verify Mr Bennet's claims about the neighbouring properties. A perfectly reasonable detour, given his interest in modern estate management. That Miss Elizabeth had overseen the improvements herself was… of no consequence, of course.

The Lodge came into view through a break in the trees. Even at this distance, he could see evidence of recent work–new slate on the roof, freshly cleared grounds, orderly kitchen gardens. His experienced eye noted the careful balance between necessary repairs and prudent economy. No ostentatious displays, just solid, practical improvements.

Rather like the lady herself, his treacherous mind suggested.

"Enough," he muttered, turning his mount toward the London road. Yet even as he set a brisk pace southward, his thoughts refused to obey their master's will.

She had been magnificent today, defending her family's interests with both passion and brilliance. The way her eyes had flashed as she wrestled with those stubborn calculations… Even her frustration had been enchanting, her muttered wishes for stronger language revealing that spark of fire he so admired.

He had not meant to seek her out this morning–or rather, he

had not meant to admit to seeking her out. The sight of her perched on that fallen log, shivering yet determined as she pored over her ledgers, had undone all his careful resolve.

He had come perilously close to offering direct assistance. How simple it would be to handle Matthews, to ensure the fields passed into more deserving hands. But he had seen the pride in her bearing, the fierce independence in her eyes. Any sense of charity would wound her.

That moment when their shoulders had touched–his control had nearly shattered. The lavender scent of her hair, the becoming flush the wind had brought to her cheeks, the way she had glanced up at him through her lashes as she smiled at his suggestions of curses. He had almost forgotten himself, almost spilled out everything in his heart. To be the cause of her merriment gave him the most profound delight.

"Wholly inadvisable," he said aloud, as if speaking might banish the thought. The words echoed hollow in the autumn air.

How could she be mistress of a great estate like Pemberley? But had she not transformed Longbourn through careful study and diligent application? The way she had quoted Coke's treatise from memory…

"Different scale entirely," he argued with himself, guiding his horse around a muddy patch. "Longbourn cannot compare to Pemberley's scope."

"Society would never accept her." The words tasted false even as he spoke them.

Her manner lacked some polish, and her wardrobe certainly did, but there was nothing crude or vulgar in her deportment. Even her occasional impertinence had a charm to it–the confidence of a keen mind rather than ill-breeding.

She had no dowry to speak of. Less than none, if one considered her gaggle of unmarried sisters. A practical consideration, for a certainty.

But Pemberley's prosperity hardly required additional funds. Indeed, her proved ability to increase estate revenues through careful management would be worth more than many a fashionable bride's fortune.

The sound of wheels made him draw aside for a passing carriage. As it rattled past, he caught a glimpse of an elegant lady within, her elaborate costume and affected manner a sharp contrast to Miss Elizabeth's simple elegance.

The ton would make her the object of their most cutting derision, yet even as he had that thought he could imagine her handling London society with the same quiet competence she showed in estate matters. His mind's eye saw her in the drawing room in his London townhouse, arrayed in the most becoming finery, smiling over her teacup as she gently skewered some unfortunate guest's pretensions with a remark so deftly worded it left even her target laughing — and left him a little breathless with admiration.

"Georgiana needs a sister of rank to bring her out of her shell." But what of Miss Elizabeth genuine warmth toward her own sisters?

"This is intolerable," he informed his horse, which flicked an ear back sympathetically. He glared at the beast. "'Et tu, Brute?'" he muttered. "Traitor. I am not forming an attachment to Miss Elizabeth Bennet."

"Absolutely not," he said firmly, straightening his shoulders as the pleasure grounds came into view. "I shall put her thoroughly out of my mind."

His mind drifted to finding Eastbridge at his table at Whites, ready to be steered toward a more expedient method of selling his land. He could make an attractive offer. It would be a prudent investment in a potentially profitable estate. His role could be hidden by some legal fiction—a holding company. Elizabeth need never know of his intervention. He could protect her interests from afar, as he had protected others in his care. The memory of Elizabeth's frustrated muttering brought a grim smile to his face. Perhaps he might find those gambling losses materialised after all.

Chapter Twenty -Four

Darcy stood at the window of his chamber at Netherfield, watching as twilight settled over the Hertfordshire landscape. In his hand, he held a letter from Georgiana, her delicate handwriting covering several pages. He had read it thrice already, each time finding new evidence of melancholy between the carefully composed lines.

"My dear brother," she had written, "The house seems quite empty without your presence, although Mrs Annesley provides all necessary companionship.."

He folded the letter and placed it on the writing desk. It had provided him with exactly the pretext he required, although he would not acknowledge, even to himself, that he required such an excuse.

A knock at his door interrupted his thoughts.

"Enter," he called, turning from the window.

Bingley appeared; his expression animated. "Darcy! There you are. I have been contemplating the arrangements for my ball, and it occurs to me that perhaps we should engage musicians from London rather than rely on local talent. What say you? Although Miss Bennet assures me the Meryton assembly finds quite tolerable musicians, and her judgement I trust implicitly, but then Caroline suggests—"

"Bingley," Darcy interrupted, "I must return to London."

His friend stopped mid-sentence, taken aback. "London? But you have only been a few weeks in Hertfordshire. Can not whatever business calls you away be handled by correspondence?"

"It is Georgiana," Darcy said, indicating the letter. "She is not herself. I fear I have left her alone for too long."

"Ah." Bingley's face softened with understanding. "Of

course, family must take precedence. When do you depart?"

Darcy hesitated, then said, "Monday."

"So soon?" Bingley's brow furrowed in disappointment. "Will you miss the ball?"

"I regret that," Darcy said, and was surprised to find he meant it, at least in part. "But my sister's wellbeing must take priority."

"Of course, of course," Bingley agreed. "You might return with her, if you like. Although I had hoped, that is, I thought perhaps,"

"Yes?"

Bingley hesitated, then shook his head. "Nothing of consequence. Only that I had hoped for your counsel regarding certain matters."

Darcy suspected his friend referred to Miss Bennet and felt a twinge of something like guilt. "You hardly need my counsel, Bingley. You know your own mind."

"Do I?" Bingley laughed ruefully. "I am not so certain."

"Then perhaps you should determine it before acting," Darcy suggested, more sharply than he intended.

A brief silence fell between them.

"Will you return?" Bingley asked finally.

"If circumstances permit," Darcy replied, noncommittally.

Bingley nodded, accepting the ambiguous answer. "I shall inform Caroline and Louisa of your departure. They will be most distressed."

"My apologies for any inconvenience," Darcy said formally.

After Bingley departed, Darcy returned to the window. The last light was fading from the sky, leaving the landscape in shadow. Somewhere to the east lay Longbourn, where Miss Elizabeth Bennet was presumably engaged in whatever evening occupations suited a young lady who managed an estate.

He had not intended to think of her. Yet his mind returned, again and again, to her direct gaze, her challenging words— "This is precisely why I must depart," he murmured to himself.

The Bennet family gathered in the study after dinner, as had become their custom since Mr Collins's threat. Jane had brought the account books, Mary settled their grandfather in his favourite chair, and Mrs Bennet carried a tray with their grandfather's draughts and evening tea.

Kitty and Lydia had returned from their afternoon rounds of the poultry yards, their practical work clothes exchanged for dinner dress, although Kitty still brought the faint scent of the herb garden where she had been checking the winter plantings.

"Mr Darcy suggests engaging his family's London barrister alongside Uncle Phillips," Elizabeth began, watching their reactions with interest. "Mr Graves apparently has particular experience with entail disputes."

"And the expense?" Jane asked quietly, her fingers resting on the leather-bound ledger.

Their grandfather stirred. "If Mr Darcy recommends him--"

"He has offered to facilitate the arrangement," Elizabeth said, the memory of that conversation bringing warmth to her cheeks. "He believes Mr Graves would find our case… professionally interesting."

Mrs Bennet set down her teacup with a decisive click. "Whatever we decide about Mr Graves, we must be prepared." She turned to Jane. "What is our current position?"

"The harvest accounts are impeccable," Jane replied. "I have prepared statements showing our improvement to the estate's value over the past decade. The timber sales alone--"

"Our improvements and accounts will not matter if Mr Collins can challenge grandfather's competency," Mary interrupted, her hand protective on their grandfather's shoulder. "I have kept detailed records of his health and mental acuity. Mr Jones has agreed to speak if needed."

Elizabeth felt a surge of pride in her sisters' foresight, even as worry gnawed at her. "As Grandfather says, we must be exceedingly careful in how we proceed."

"We cannot show our full hand immediately," their grandfather said. "Mr Collins must be distracted until we are fully prepared."

"The tenants are asking questions," Mrs Bennet added. "They have reported Mr Collins's man visiting their farms, intimating his intentions to alter long-standing arrangements."

"Mr Robinson at the home farm was quite concerned," Elizabeth said, recalling her morning rounds. "He begged to know whether the family would continue to oversee the estate's management, as he could not bear to think of serving another."

Jane shook her head. "We cannot risk losing their confidence. Not with planting decisions looming."

"Then we are agreed?" Elizabeth looked around at her family's resolute faces. "We engage both Uncle Phillips and Mr Graves, as Mr Darcy suggested, maintain our normal operations, and prepare our defence without revealing our strongest evidence?"

The grandfather nodded slowly. "And we pray three days is sufficient time to set our plans in motion."

Elizabeth hesitated. Taking in the determined faces of her sisters and mother, she turned to her grandfather.

"The expense, Grandfather. I fear the London solicitor will be terribly dear…" she trailed off. Mary's scowl was due to her careful accounting, as well as her strict sense of economy.

"Well, ladies, we have reserves, although not a vast amount," Mr Bennet began.

"Would not the funds in the four percents intended for dowries be better used to protect the estate?" Jane said.

"The four percents?" Mrs Bennet's hand fluttered to her throat. "But Jane, those funds are all that stand between you girls and--" She stopped herself, pressing her lips together.

"Between us and destitution should Mr Collins succeed anyway," Mary finished bluntly. "At least this way we have a chance of preserving both home and legacy."

Elizabeth shifted uncomfortably. "Mr Darcy was most

insistent about facilitating the arrangement. He spoke of it as an investment in justice, not charity."

"Did he indeed?" their grandfather's eyes twinkled briefly. "Most generous of the gentleman. I find myself curious about his uncommon fascination regarding our affairs, Lizzy."

"On the contrary," Mrs Bennet said, her practical nature asserting itself. "If Mr Darcy's interest extends beyond mere neighbourly concern, it would be foolish not to consider how that might strengthen our position. Would he not offer assistance with the fees?"

"Mamma," Jane intervened gently, "we cannot stake our future on speculation about Mr Darcy's intentions. The question before us is whether to risk the dowry funds on legal counsel."

Elizabeth shook her head firmly. "Mr Darcy, I have heard, owns half of Derbyshire. There must be a mile-long line of young debutantes angling for his attention. He has taken a gentlemanly interest in our affairs and nothing more."

Jane touched Elizabeth's hand. Mrs Bennet tutted and was silent.

Kitty, who had been uncommonly quiet, spoke up. "Could we not use only part of the funds? Perhaps Mr Graves will accept some arrangement for future payment if we succeed?"

Elizabeth brightened. "That is clever thinking, Kitty. It would show our confidence in our case whilst preserving some of our resources."

"And if we fail," Lydia added with uncharacteristic solemnity, "dowries will be the least of our concerns."

Their grandfather sighed heavily. "I never meant for you girls to bear such burdens. Perhaps I should accept Mr Darcy's offer outright--"

"No," Elizabeth said firmly. "We will find a way to make this work without compromising our independence. What if we were to propose a mixed arrangement? Some funds now, more upon success, and Mr Darcy's guarantee as security rather than outright payment?"

Jane was already making calculations in her ledger. "If we

used half the four percents now…"

"And we could manage with a smaller flock," Lydia added. "Mr Goulding is always asking whether we might sell one of our ewes."

Mrs Bennet surveyed her daughters with shining eyes. "My clever girls. Very well. Elizabeth, you may tell Mr Darcy we accept his offer of introduction to Mr Graves, but we wish to propose our own terms for the arrangement."

"And Elizabeth," her grandfather added with a slight smile, "do convey our appreciation for his… investment in justice."

Darcy stood by the window of Netherfield's library, ostensibly examining the view of the park but in truth observing his friend with growing concern. Bingley had been pacing for the better part of a quarter hour, alternating between animated defences of Miss Bennet and dejected acceptances of his sister's criticisms.

"Charles," Miss Bingley was saying, her voice carrying that particular blend of affectation and condescension she reserved for her brother, "you cannot seriously be considering deepening your acquaintance with the Bennets. Their connections are insignificant, their fortune non-existent, and their manners—except perhaps the eldest—are decidedly lacking in refinement."

"Jane Bennet is everything lovely," Bingley replied, his expression brightening at the mere mention of her name. "You admitted yourself she is beautiful and sweet-tempered."

"Beauty and sweetness will not gain us entrée to the circles you wish to be moving in," Miss Bingley countered, adjusting the bracelet at her wrist. "And if you observed more closely, you would see she shows the same sweet temper to everyone. I declare there is nothing particular in her regard for you."

Darcy watched as Bingley's shoulders slumped, his friend's characteristic buoyancy deflating. It took so little to dissuade him, Darcy thought with a frown. So little to alter his course, like a weathervane spinning in the wind.

"Perhaps you are right," Bingley conceded, sinking into a chair. "I should not be hasty."

Miss Bingley shot a triumphant glance toward Darcy, expecting his support. He remained silent, turning back to the window.

"Although she is uncommonly beautiful," Bingley wavered, his tone brightening once more. "And when she smiled at me—I cannot believe there was nothing particular in it."

"A practised smile, I am sure," Miss Bingley said coolly. "Mrs Bennet's ambitions for her daughters are transparent. The entire neighbourhood speaks of nothing but your five thousand a year."

"Do they indeed?" Bingley looked momentarily pleased at his own consequence before doubt crept back into his expression. "But Miss Bennet could not be party to such calculations. You have not heard her speak. There is such genuine goodness in her."

Darcy turned from the window, unable to bear witness to this vacillation any longer. "Bingley," he said, his tone sharper than he intended, "what do you yourself believe?"

Bingley blinked, startled by the direct question. "I beg your pardon?"

"Your opinion of Miss Bennet shifts with every word your sister utters," Darcy said, crossing the room to stand before his friend. "First she is an angel, then she is a fortune-hunter; first her smile is genuine, then it is practised. Which do you actually believe to be true?"

"I—" Bingley faltered, glancing between Darcy and his sister.

"Do you form your judgements based on your own observations, or do you merely adopt the opinions of others?" Darcy pressed, ignoring Miss Bingley's affronted expression. "If the latter, then your regard cannot be worth much, to Miss Bennet or anyone else."

A flush crept up Bingley's neck. "That is hardly fair, Darcy. I value counsel, but I am capable of forming my own conclusions."

Darcy raised an eyebrow. "Then what is your opinion regarding Miss Bennet, based on your own judgement of her character?"

Bingley opened his mouth, then closed it again, his expression conflicted. "I find her beautiful and amiable," he said. "But perhaps I have not known her long enough to form a settled opinion."

"A convenient retreat," Darcy observed coldly. "If you cannot trust your own assessment of a woman's character after multiple meetings and conversations, then perhaps you should not be contemplating any attachment at all."

Miss Bingley smirked, evidently believing Darcy to be supporting her position. He met her gaze briefly, his expression giving nothing away.

"Do excuse me," he said with a slight bow, unwilling to continue the conversation in her presence. Let Bingley consider his words without Miss Bingley's immediate influence.

With that, Darcy strode from the room. He had always known Bingley to be malleable, easily led by those he trusted, but never had the trait seemed so troubling as now. What good was all of Bingley's natural goodness and warmth if he lacked the moral fortitude to maintain his own beliefs when he faced the least opposition?

Darcy wondered, not for the first time, whether his friendship with Bingley did either of them credit. He had always considered himself a positive influence, helping to guide his younger friend through the complexities of society. But perhaps he was just another voice overwhelming Bingley's own, just another gust altering his course.

The thought was not comfortable, and Darcy resolved to observe more and advise less in the days to come. Bingley must find his own moral compass—or confirm that he had none beyond the opinions of those around him.

Lydia and Jane were returning from visiting tenant homes, their arms laden with empty baskets, when they spotted the distinctive figure of Mr Wickham strolling through the village green. Beside him walked a slight young woman in a modest brown pelisse.

"Is that Mary King?" Jane asked, squinting across the lane. "I had heard she returned from Liverpool last week."

"Indeed," Lydia replied, her sharp eyes taking in the way Wickham bent solicitously over Mary's gloved hand. "And ten thousand pounds richer than when she left, if Aunt Phillips's intelligence is correct."

"Lydia!" Jane admonished, although without much force. "You should not repeat such things."

"It is hardly a secret. Her uncle's will was read publicly, and Mrs Phillips says the inheritance was most unexpected." Lydia's eyes narrowed as she observed Wickham's attentive posture. "How curious that Mr Wickham, who showed no interest in Miss King before her journey, now finds her company so compelling."

Jane sighed. "Must it be so? Are you not becoming cynical?"

"Not cynical, Jane. Merely observant."

"In any case, let us offer our condolences to Miss King on her uncle's passing." Jane said and altered their course to intercept the pair. Wickham's expression flickered momentarily when he caught sight of them—a brief faltering of his smile of calculated amiability that confirmed Lydia's suspicions.

"Miss King! What a pleasure to see you returned to Meryton," Jane called, approaching with a warm smile for Mary and a coolly polite nod for her companion. "Our condolences on your uncle's passing."

Mary King was a plain, freckled girl of nineteen, with her most remarkable feature being a rather prominent nose. She blushed at the attention. "Thank you, Miss Bennet, Miss Lydia. It was unexpected, but my aunt is comforted that his affairs were in good order."

"Very good order, I understand," Lydia replied meaningfully. "I see Mr Wickham has been keeping you company during this difficult time?"

"We encountered each other quite by chance," Wickham

interjected smoothly. "I could not neglect my duty to offer escort to a lady in distress."

"How gallant," Lydia observed. "Although I recall you mentioned at our last meeting that your military duties occupied much of your time. Captain Morris was most informative about the demands placed upon officers."

Wickham's smile tightened nearly imperceptibly. "One must make time for civility, Miss Lydia."

"Indeed." Lydia turned to Mary with an expression of earnest concern. "And how do you find Meryton after your absence, Miss King? I imagine it must seem quite changed with the regiment's presence. So many new faces and intentions."

Mary looked puzzled. "Intentions?"

"Why, yes. The officers' intentions for their futures." Lydia's tone was innocent, but her eyes held Wickham's. "Mr Wickham himself has shared with us his fascinating history of abandoned professions—the church, the law. Such varied ambitions! Tell me, Mr Wickham, have you made any progress towards securing that living you mentioned? Or perhaps advanced in your military career since we last spoke?"

Mary's brow furrowed as she glanced between them.

"My circumstances remain unchanged," Wickham replied stiffly.

"How consistent of you," Lydia remarked. "And what of your plans for the future? Miss King might be interested to hear them, given your evident friendship."

Jane touched Lydia's arm in gentle warning, but Lydia continued, her voice honey-sweet with underlying steel.

"You know, Miss King, Mr Wickham made the most fascinating observation when we last met. He suggested that beauty alone was sufficient worth in a woman, requiring no supplement of fortune or accomplishment." Lydia smiled brightly at Mary's plainness. "A most unusual perspective for a gentleman of limited means, would you not agree?"

Mary's expression shifted from confusion to dawning

comprehension. "I, I had not considered."

"Miss Bennet exaggerates," Wickham cut in, his charm visibly strained. "I merely expressed admiration for the Bennet sisters' renowned beauty."

"Oh, but you were quite specific," Lydia countered. "You dismissed practical concerns as 'mercenary considerations' unworthy of attention. I wonder, Miss King, has Mr Wickham learnt of your recent change of circumstances?"

Mary's cheeks flushed, not with pleasure but with embarrassment. She spoke slowly. "Mr Wickham has shown quite marked attentiveness since my return."

"Since your return," Lydia repeated deliberately. "How timely. And has he spoken of his prospects? His ability to support a wife? Or does he at most offer pretty compliments on your personal attributes?"

Understanding finally dawned in Mary's eyes, followed quickly by hurt and then anger. She turned to Wickham, whose handsome features had hardened into a mask.

"Mr Wickham," Mary said stiffly, "is it true that you have no ambition beyond your commission? No expectations?"

"My dear Miss King," he began, reaching for her hand.

She withdrew it sharply. "You showed no interest in me before my uncle's bequest."

"How can you think it? I have long admired you," Wickham protested, but his eyes darted about as though seeking escape. "Miss Lydia harbours some resentment—"

Lydia laughed. "I fear Mr Wickham is the one with resentment. He did not appreciate my questioning his prospects and not being taken in by his flattery."

"You tried the same approach with her," Mary finished, her voice growing stronger. "You are after my fortune, sir, nothing more."

"Ten thousand pounds is hardly a fortune," Wickham snapped, his mask slipping further.

A shocked silence followed his inadvertent admission.

"Perhaps not to a gentleman of unlimited means," Lydia observed coolly. "But quite significant to one who cannot afford to study law, would you not say?"

Mary stepped back; her plain face flushed with indignation. "I believe I can find my way home with Miss Bennet and Miss Lydia, Mr Wickham. Please do not call upon me again."

Wickham's handsome face twisted with barely suppressed fury. "You will regret this interference, Miss Lydia," he said in a low voice as Mary King disengaged her arm and stepped away.

"Not nearly as much as you will regret underestimating the intelligence of Meryton's young ladies," Lydia replied evenly. "Good day, Mr Wickham. I wish you luck in your advancement."

"Do allow us to escort you home, Miss King," Jane said. As they walked away, Jane whispered, "Lydia, that was perhaps too direct."

"Nonsense," Lydia replied, a satisfied smile playing at her lips. "Miss King deserves better than that charmer. And Mr Wickham deserves to understand that pretty words cannot mask an empty character." She adjusted the baskets in her arms. Jane took Mary King's arm and asked gentle questions about her family.

Behind them, Wickham stood alone on the green, his charming façade lay in ruins, shattered by truth and scorn.

Chapter Twenty-Five

Later that evening, the three eldest Bennet sisters gathered in Elizabeth's small sitting room, where a cheerful fire kept the autumn chill at bay. Elizabeth forced a brightness she did not feel as she poked at the fire. She forced her attention to their discussion.

"Well," Elizabeth said at last, "I hope we may consider Mr Collins out of our affairs, at least for the moment."

"Although not," Mary observed without looking up from her notes, "through any great effort on our part. His own ignorance of proper procedure did most of the work."

Jane's gentle laugh floated across the room. "Poor Mr Collins. Although I am inclined to believe that such a man might find advantage in this small lesson in humility."

"Speaking of lessons." Mary's quill paused mid-stroke. "Mr Darcy is remarkably… well informed about our situation."

Elizabeth turned sharply from the window. "Mr Darcy is generous with his time. He appreciates competence when he sees it."

"Oh yes," Mary delivered her words with delicate satire. "I am sure it was your competence he was admiring so intently whilst speaking with Grandfather."

A faint blush coloured Elizabeth's cheeks. "Mary!"

"She does have a point, Lizzy," Jane's eyes twinkled. "He seemed impressed- and not merely by your discourse."

"Quite," Elizabeth retorted. "I notice how attentively he listened to your summary of the new tenant agreements, as well."

It was Jane's turn to blush. "He was merely polite. Mr Darcy understands the value of careful management."

"And the managers thereof?" Mary murmured, earning a

stern look from Elizabeth.

"If we might return to practical matters," Elizabeth said with dignity, "we should discuss the spring planning.

"And you wish to change the subject," Mary noted, making a small mark in her notebook.

"I think," Jane intervened smoothly, "that Mary might take charge of the new fertiliser trials she proposed. Her understanding far exceeds mine."

"Excellent suggestion," Elizabeth seized the topic gratefully. "And Jane, what of the new cottage leases on the Fairfax lands? The tenants respond well to your diplomatic approach."

"Will you handle the inevitable negotiations with Mr Darcy regarding joint improvements to the properties where Longbourn borders Netherfield?" Mary's innocent look would not have fooled a child.

Elizabeth snatched up a ledger, wielding it like a shield. "If Mr Darcy does participate, as the most experienced in such matters, it only makes sense that I--"

"Oh, certainly," Jane agreed, her smile angelic. "Experience is crucial in such… delicate negotiations."

"I hate you both," Elizabeth declared. "Mary, we need you to document the results of your trials in detail. We may wish to expand the programme if successful."

"I have already begun," Mary held up her notebook. "Perhaps I might need to consult with Mr Darcy about the results. I understand he has implemented similar experiments at Pemberley…"

"I shall go to bed," Elizabeth announced to the ceiling, the false cheer in her voice just a shade too bright. "Where I shall dream of sensible things like crop yields and drainage channels."

"Rather than tall, commanding figures on horseback?" Mary enquired.

"Good night!" Elizabeth fled, pursued by her sisters' laughter.

Their laughter followed Elizabeth up the stairs, warm and teasing, but it could not quite reach the hollow place that had opened in her chest.

"I heard that giggling!" she called down. "Have neither of you work to do?"

"Good night, Lizzy," Jane's voice floated up, rich with amusement. "Pleasant dreams of… agricultural improvements."

In the quiet of her room, she leant against the door for a moment, pressing her forehead to the cool wood. She *ought* to laugh with them. It was nothing, after all — only a neighbour returning to his proper sphere, whilst she remained firmly rooted in hers. Only a passing acquaintance. Only,

She pushed herself upright and crossed to the window, gazing out into the darkness where Netherfield's lights were already few and fading.

It would be best if she did turn her mind to agriculture. There was no sense in admiring a man so far beyond her reach.

A single moment must suffice for her grief over what was never hers. One final admiring thought, then dismissal. She turned away from the window, set her jaw, and began, with determined practicality, to ready herself for bed.

The drawing room at Netherfield had grown insufferably warm, although Darcy knew the true source of his discomfort lay in Miss Bingley's relentless attention. She had positioned her chair in just such a way as to catch his eye each time he glanced up from his correspondence. "Mr Darcy, you write with such elegance. One cannot help but admire the refinement of your hand," Miss Bingley simpered, leaning forward to better observe him. Her shift of position and the cut of her marigold coloured gown caused it to gape. Darcy averted his eyes from the less-than-thrilling display she had created.

"You are too kind, Madam." His words were clipped, his jaw tight.

"I declare, your sister must benefit greatly from such devoted attention to your correspondence. Although I wonder that you find time to write so frequently when there are such delightful diversions to be had in the country."

"Georgiana deserves no less than my fullest attention to her concerns."

Miss Bingley's lips curved in what she must have perhaps intended to be an enchanting smile. "How fortunate she is to have such a brother. Although I venture to say a sister might prove an equally valuable addition to her circle."

Darcy's quill paused mid-stroke. "Miss Bingley, I must speak plainly. Your interest in my sister's welfare, whilst no doubt well-intentioned, is excessive."

"Mr Darcy!" Her fan fluttered with increased vigour. "You cannot mean—"

"I do mean, Madam, I mean what I have said. Pardon me, I believe Bingley mentioned wishing to discuss the state of his stables."

He quit the room with perhaps more haste than strictly polite, although propriety had worn decidedly thin after such persistent pursuit.

The congregation had begun to disperse from Longbourn church, bonnets nodding, and coattails swaying as neighbours exchanged pleasantries under the portico. Elizabeth lingered near the gate, speaking with the vicar's wife, when Mr Darcy approached.

He bowed. "Miss Elizabeth. A well-delivered sermon, I thought."

"It was," she agreed. "Although the draught through the north aisle seemed determined to distract me."

A flicker of a smile passed over Darcy's mouth. "The weather appears set upon testing our fortitude."

Elizabeth glanced down at her gloves, then back at him with a measured look.

He inclined his head. "Do I intrude upon your solitude?"

"You do not, although I wonder that you walked this way. I

believed you were to depart Netherfield.

"On the morrow." He looked away. "How is your grandfather keeping since Mr Collins's last visit to Longbourn?" He asked, shifting the subject.

Elizabeth's expression tightened. "He is well enough. Mr Collins has quite decided opinions." Her chin lifted confidently. "As you know, he finds it most irregular that Grandfather permits my sisters and me to oversee the tenant contracts and maintain the books."

"And yet Longbourn appears to prosper under such irregular management."

A quiet pride coloured her voice. "We continue to improve this past year."

"I have observed the work during my rides." He paused, studying her changing expressions.

"In his wisdom, Mr Collins also insists that our unwomanly concern with business matters would assuredly deter all marriage-minded gentlemen."

"A dire prediction indeed." Darcy schooled his features, though humour threatened to betray him. "Although perhaps not an entirely accurate one."

Elizabeth's eyes met his with startling directness. "You speak with some authority on the subject, Mr Darcy?"

"I do not share his opinion that ladies need confine their interests to the ornamental."

"And yet I suspect your own sister does not muddy her gloves or walk the wilder paths of your estate. I am inclined to think that you would not wish to see your sister make such an exhibition."

Darcy felt the familiar surge of attraction rise unbidden—frustratingly at odds with his pride. "You believe you have taken my measure so completely then, Miss Elizabeth?"

"Oh no, Mr Darcy. I would not dare to claim such insight into your character. You guard your thoughts far too well for that."

He studied her face as they walked, searching for some sign that her quick wit and lovely eyes might mask a deeper regard, but found only that same challenging sparkle that had first caught his attention. The wind tugged at her bonnet ribbons, and he fought the improper urge to secure them himself, to feel her warmth beneath his fingertips.

"I must take my leave," he said abruptly. "My sister does require my presence."

"How fortunate that family duty provides such a timely escape from rustic charms." She spoke with an air of levity, but the knowing gleam in her eyes left no doubt as to her meaning.

"You think me a coward, Miss Elizabeth?"

"I think you are a man who knows his own mind, Mr Darcy. Whether that mind leads you true…" She paused. "That is not for me to say."

"Then I shall bid you good day, Madam. And a pleasant continuation of your day."

"Good day, Mr Darcy. Mind the mud as you mount—I should hate to see such fine riding boots spoiled."

Darcy could not shake the impression that Miss Elizabeth Bennet had seen too much—and yet not nearly enough—of his true feelings in that exchange. He was, indeed, a coward—he was running from a woman who, by all expectation, should have been dazzled by him—and was not. Her wit had unsettled him, her regard—so clear, so unwavering—held no trace of admiration, no desire to please.

In Town, ladies sought his approval, bent their charms to secure his favour. Here, in Hertfordshire, he might as well have been a pedlar for all the consequence she afforded him. It was intolerable.

London, with its polished manners and familiar society, had never felt so welcome—or so necessary.

Darcy was not fond of Sunday afternoons with nothing to do. Worse still was being held captive by Miss Bingley whilst idle. He was constrained from travel on the Sabbath, and there was scarce entertainment to be had. He was more than ready to depart, but manners required that he spend his time with his host and hostess.

Darcy stood before the fire, a book in hand, whilst Bingley paced the Turkish carpet, speaking animatedly of his morning ride.

"You should have accompanied me, Darcy. The countryside is quite delightful at dawn."

"I took my exercise at a more civilised hour, after services," Darcy replied dryly. "Although I note your enthusiasm for early rising is a recent development." Darcy had ridden early during his first days at Netherfield, but after encountering the confounding Elizabeth Bennet several times, he changed his course and rode south instead.

Bingley paused, a slight flush rising to his cheeks. "The morning air is invigorating."

"As is the proximity to Longbourn, I imagine."

"I happened to pass by the Bennet estate, yes."

"By design rather than chance, I suspect," Darcy said. "How many times this week have you 'happened' to ride in that direction?"

"I enjoy the view," Bingley defended weakly.

"The view of the landscape, or of Miss Bennet in her garden?"

Bingley looked abashed. "I did encounter Miss Bennet this morning."

"No doubt another fortunate coincidence."

"She is the most beautiful woman I have ever beheld, Darcy," Bingley said, dropping any pretence. "And her temperament is as gentle as her features."

"I cannot deny Miss Bennet appears amiable and conducts herself with propriety, despite her family's singular arrangements."

"I suppose it is rather unconventional," Bingley conceded with a slight shrug. "But Miss Bennet herself is so lovely, Darcy—there is such sweetness in her expression. And her eyes when she smiles…" He trailed off, seemingly lost in recollection.

Darcy considered his friend with a measuring gaze. "Your admiration for Miss Jane Bennet seems to extend beyond mere approval of her domestic capabilities."

"Jane—that is, Miss Bennet—is everything graceful and good," Bingley said warmly.

"And your intentions? Have you made them clear to her?"

Bingley's expression turned uncertain. "Not precisely."

"Not precisely," Darcy repeated. "Which means not at all."

"I have called at Longbourn five times in eight days," Bingley protested. "I am sure that indicates particular attention."

"Particular attention is not the same as declared intentions," Darcy pointed out. "This whiffling about does credit to neither of you."

Bingley frowned. "Whiffling?"

"Vacillating. Hovering without purpose." Darcy faced his friend squarely. "What exactly *are* your intentions, Bingley? Do you mean to court Miss Bennet in earnest, or merely to enjoy the diversion of her company?"

"I had thought—that is, I have been considering—" Bingley broke off, then straightened with the appearance of resolution. "I admire her greatly."

"Admiration is not courtship," Darcy said bluntly. "If you intend to pursue Miss Bennet, you must declare yourself plainly."

"Do you think she would welcome such a declaration?" Bingley asked with hesitation.

"That is certainly not for me to say. Miss Bennet is polite to all," Darcy said neutrally. "I cannot claim to discern any particular partiality on her part."

"You think she is indifferent to me?"

"I think that your whiffling makes it impossible for anyone to know your mind, including Miss Bennet. Propriety demands that if you wish to know her feelings, you must first make plain your own."

"You are right, of course," Bingley acknowledged, squaring his shoulders. "I shall call on her tomorrow and speak directly."

"You have said as much before," Darcy reminded him, sceptically.

"This time I mean it," Bingley insisted. "No more whiffling, as you put it."

Darcy nodded, although his expression remained doubtful. "Then I wish you fortune in your suit, if that is indeed your intention."

"It is," Bingley said firmly. Then, with characteristic candour, he added, "I think."

Chapter Twenty-Six

The brisk air carried a hint of autumn's approach as Jane moved between the herb beds, basket over her arm. She had slipped out early, before breakfast, hoping to gather the last of the summer mint whilst the dew still clung to the leaves. The rising sun cast long shadows across the kitchen garden, and she worked methodically, her mind occupied with calculations of how much would be needed for drying.

"Miss Bennet!"

The voice startled her, causing her to straighten abruptly. Mr Bingley stood again at the garden gate, his hat in his hands, looking less surprised to see her as she was to see him.

"Mr Bingley," she acknowledged with a curtsy, conscious suddenly of her plain morning dress and half loose hair. "You are abroad early, sir." And to herself she added, "Again."

"I—yes," he said, colouring. "I rode out at dawn. The morning was too fine to waste indoors."

Jane nodded, uncertain what to say. Was this not at least the third time this week he had appeared at Longbourn on some pretext or another?

"May I join you?" he asked, gesturing to the garden. "Or perhaps I am intruding?"

"Not at all," Jane said politely, although in truth she had been enjoying the quiet. "I am only gathering the last of the mint for preserving."

Bingley opened the gate and stepped inside, looking at once both eager and hesitant, like a schoolboy invited to tea with the headmaster. "Your herb garden is remarkably well-ordered," he observed, walking toward her.

"Thank you. Kitty and I designed it together—she determines which medicinal plants we require, and I the culinary ones. We arrange them according to their needs for sun and water."

"Did you indeed?" His surprise seemed genuine. "I had thought perhaps it was your housekeeper's domain."

"Our housekeeper has quite enough to manage without adding the garden to her duties," Jane replied, resuming her harvesting. "At Longbourn, we each have our responsibilities."

"A sensible arrangement," Bingley said, watching her hands as she neatly snipped the stems. "Your family seems remarkably… capable."

Jane smiled at the evident wonder in his voice. "Necessity is an excellent teacher, Mr Bingley."

"Of course." He shifted his weight from one foot to the other. "I did not mean to imply otherwise. I find it admirable, truly. Most young ladies of my acquaintance would consider such work beneath them."

"Then they are fortunate indeed to have others who will do it for them," Jane replied mildly, although her smiled dimmed and her spine stiffened in a movement so slight it passed for stillness.

Bingley must have sensed her withdrawal, for he quickly changed tack.

"What will you do with so much mint?" he asked, gesturing to her nearly full basket.

"Some will be dried for tea and cooking throughout the winter," Jane explained, relaxing somewhat. "The rest will be delivered to Kitty for distillation into medicinal oils and tinctures."

"Your sister is an apothecary, then?" Bingley asked.

"Kitty has a remarkable gift for healing," Jane said. "Her knowledge of medicinal herbs and remedies has proved invaluable, most especially for our family's complaints."

"You as well, Miss Bennet," Bingley said warmly. "I suspect there is little you cannot do when you set your mind to it."

Jane felt her cheeks warm at the undisguised admiration in his voice. He skirted the bounds of propriety with his direct compliments yet made no declarations. "You give me too much credit, sir."

"I doubt that very much." His gaze held hers, then he glanced away, his attention seemingly caught by something in the distance.

An uncomfortable silence fell between them as Jane finished her harvesting. Bingley moved a few steps away, examining the various beds without true interest.

"Your sisters plan to keep charge of the estate affairs, I understand?" he asked at length.

"Not entirely. Our grandfather is in charge. We each have our interests. Lizzy oversees most of the farming operations, whilst I attend to the household management and accounts."

"And Miss Lydia has her sheep," Bingley added with a smile.

Jane looked up in surprise. "You know of Lydia's work with the flocks?"

"Miss Elizabeth mentioned it. I gather your youngest sister has quite a talent for animal husbandry."

"She does indeed," Jane acknowledged, pride evident in her voice. "Her breeding programme has improved our wool yield considerably."

Bingley hesitated, then said, "It is odd, is it not? For young ladies to be so… involved in such matters?"

Jane straightened, her basket now full and her patience nearly empty. "Perhaps in some circles," she replied. "But we have found that capability is not determined by one's sex, Mr Bingley, rather by one's willingness to learn and apply oneself."

"A progressive view," he said, his expression thoughtful.

"A practical one," Jane corrected gently. "Longbourn is not a large estate, but it is our home and our livelihood. We do what must be done to preserve it."

"Without a man in charge, you mean."

"Our grandfather supervises," Jane said simply.

Something in her tone must have affected him, for Bingley's expression softened. "Forgive me. I did not mean to speak insensitively."

"There is nothing to forgive."

They had reached the garden gate, and Bingley hurried to open it for her. As Jane passed through, her basket brushing against his arm, he spoke again.

"Miss Bennet, I wonder if—that is, I have been thinking—" He stopped, seeming to gather his thoughts. "What I mean to say is that I admire your capabilities very much."

"Thank you, Mr Bingley," Jane replied, waiting politely for him to continue.

But he merely smiled, a little uncertainly, and gestured toward the house. "May I escort you back?"

"Thank you, but I must take these to Kitty in her stillroom directly," Jane said. "She is most particular about harvesting herbs at their peak potency, and I must not disappoint her."

"Of course, of course." He hesitated, then bowed. "I shall call again tomorrow, perhaps? If that would be agreeable?"

Jane inclined her head, noncommittal. "We are always pleased to receive visitors at Longbourn, Mr Bingley."

His face fell at her formal response, but he rallied. "Until tomorrow, then, Miss Bennet."

She watched him stride away toward where his horse must be tethered, his shoulders set as if he had come to some decision. Jane was not quite certain she wished to know what that decision might be. Yet another call, with such marked attention and no profession of regard had challenged her powers of endurance.

Dawn had barely broken when Darcy descended the grand staircase at Netherfield, his greatcoat buttoned against the chill. He had ordered his travelling carriage prepared at this early hour specifically to avoid protracted farewells. The household, he had assumed, would still be abed.

He was mistaken.

"Mr Darcy," Caroline Bingley's voice drifted from the breakfast room. "You did not think to depart without bidding us a proper farewell, I trust?"

Darcy suppressed a sigh and turned to find Miss Bingley elegantly arranged upon a settee, dressed in a morning gown of coral that suggested she had risen at an ungodly hour for the sole purpose of intercepting him. The tea service before her confirmed his suspicion.

"Miss Bingley," he acknowledged with a bow. "I had not wished to disturb the household at such an early hour."

"No disturbance whatsoever," she assured him, gesturing to the chair opposite her. "I am always an early riser. Pray, join me for tea before your journey. London will still be there an hour hence." Darcy schooled his expression. Miss Bingley seldom appeared before noon.

Seeing no polite way to refuse, Darcy reluctantly took the offered seat whilst Miss Bingley poured tea.

"Since Charles informed me about your departure, I was quite occupied in thinking of it," she confided, passing him a cup. "So sudden, so unexpected. Poor Charles is quite bereft at losing your companionship."

"I doubt Bingley will suffer excessively in my absence," Darcy replied dryly. "He seems to find ample diversion in the neighbourhood."

"Yes, he persists in visiting those Bennets," Miss Bingley said with a delicate shudder. "Louisa and I find it challenging to be polite to individuals with lower social ties. Especially that Eliza Bennet, with her decided opinions and country manners."

Darcy's hand tightened imperceptibly around the handle of his teacup. No response would improve this conversation.

"I noticed how she monopolised your attention last week. So forward. But then, what is to be expected from a family in which daughters fulfil the duties of servants?

"I believe managing one's estate hardly qualifies as servitude," Darcy said coolly.

Miss Bingley waved a dismissive hand. "A mere turn of phrase. It's undeniable: a woman preoccupied with agriculture lacks feminine grace. I cannot imagine what Charles sees in the eldest. Pretty enough, I suppose, in a provincial way, but hardly suitable for a man of his fortune and standing."

Darcy set down his cup. "I should not presume to dictate Bingley's preferences."

"But as his friend, you must have some concern for his future happiness?" Miss Bingley pressed, leaning forward. "A connection with such a family would be most disadvantageous."

"The hour grows late," Darcy said, rising. "I must take my leave."

"Oh, but we have not yet settled the matter of your return," Miss Bingley exclaimed, standing as well and moving with alarming swiftness to position herself between Darcy and the door. "The ball, Mr Darcy. You simply must give me your word that you will return for it."

"As I told your brother, I cannot make promises. My sister's needs must take precedence."

"Of course, dear Georgiana," Miss Bingley agreed with exaggerated sympathy. "But I am sure a brief visit would not be amiss? I shall reserve the first two dances for you, Mr Darcy."

"Most kind," he replied stiffly, "but unnecessary. I cannot say when I shall return to Hertfordshire, if at all."

A flash of genuine alarm crossed Miss Bingley's face. "If at all? But Mr Darcy, you do not mean to abandon us entirely? What of your friendship with Charles? What of—" She paused, then continued in a lower voice, edging closer to him. "What of those who value your society above all others?"

The scent of her perfume, applied with rather too liberal a hand, threatened to overwhelm the small space between them. Darcy took a step back, a sudden bilious feeling rising. He wondered if the fragrance could be weaponised against Napoleonic invaders.

"Miss Bingley, I assure you, your brother's friendship remains important to me," he said firmly. "Now, if you will excuse me, my carriage awaits."

"At least take breakfast before you depart," she insisted, laying a hand upon his arm. "I have instructed the cook to prepare your favourite dishes. We might dine alone, as the others are still abed. Conversations are so much more agreeable without interruption, do you not find?"

Darcy decisively extricated his arm from her grasp. "I have a basket to break my fast on the road. The weather promises fair, and I wish to make good time."

"I beg you would tell me the moment you decide to return. I shall count every hour until then."

"Perhaps," she continued, her voice dropping to what she seemed to believe was an enticing whisper, "when you return, we might find opportunities for more private conversations. I have always felt there is a certain understanding between us."

"I beg your pardon, Miss Bingley," Darcy said, his voice glacial.

Her smile faltered at this, but she pressed on. "Then you agree? That there exists between us a particular—"

"Miss Bingley," Darcy interrupted, his patience finally exhausted. "I must depart immediately. My valet awaits with the carriage, and several hours of travel lie ahead."

"Of course," she said, although she made no move to step aside. "I shall accompany you to the door."

With no choice but to proceed, Darcy was obliged to walk beside Miss Bingley through the hall, her arm insinuating itself through his despite his obvious reluctance. At the main entrance, his valet stood waiting, Darcy's hat and gloves in hand.

"Your carriage is prepared, sir," the servant informed him, studiously ignoring Miss Bingley's clinging posture.

"Thank you, Fletcher," Darcy replied, disengaging himself from Miss Bingley to take his belongings. "We depart immediately."

"Mr Darcy," Miss Bingley said, her voice loud enough to be heard by the footmen attending the door. "You must give me your promise to return for the ball."

Rather than answer directly, Darcy bowed. "Good day, Miss Bingley. Please convey my thanks to your brother for his hospitality."

Without waiting for her response, he strode through the door to where his carriage waited, the horses stamping impatiently in the morning air. Fletcher followed with his remaining belongings, closing the carriage door behind his master with evident relief.

As they pulled away from Netherfield, Darcy closed his eyes for a moment, letting the breeze cool the frustration from his brow. The Hertfordshire air, fresh with dew, filled his lungs. Soon he would be in London, surrounded by the familiar comforts of his own home,—and equally far from the exhausting attentions of Miss Bingley.

Chapter Twenty-Seven

He called again?" Elizabeth asked, looking up from the estate ledger as Jane entered the small study they shared. "That makes four visits in eight days."

"Six, I believe," Jane corrected, sitting across from her sister. "He came upon me in the kitchen garden this morning."

Elizabeth raised her eyebrows. "Before breakfast? The man grows bold."

"He said he was out riding."

"Conveniently near our kitchen garden, I see." Elizabeth set down her pen. "And what did Mr Bingley have to say for himself today?"

Jane smoothed her skirts thoughtfully. "Little of substance. He admired the herb beds. He again seemed surprised that we attend to such tasks ourselves. He asks again and again as if our situation might magically change. I fear his understanding is not of the quickest."

"I suspect our departure from conventional female pursuits taxes the capacity of his understanding," Elizabeth commented dryly.

"He says he finds our capabilities admirable. Repeatedly. Perhaps to convince himself," Jane added, her expression not pleased.

"How gracious of him to approve of our managing our own affairs," Elizabeth replied with a touch of tartness.

"Lizzy," Jane chided gently. "I believe he means well. It seems he lacks the resolution to declare himself on any matter of consequence. He relies so upon his sister and his friend."

"I would venture he appears most reluctant to commit himself to any decided opinion if he suspects it might find opposition," Elizabeth leant forward. "What are his intentions, Jane? He circles around you like a moth around a candle, never quite drawing near enough to declare himself, yet never flying away either."

Jane sighed. "I do not know. At times I think he means to speak, but then he hesitates, as if uncertain."

"Perhaps he fears rejection," Elizabeth suggested.

"Or perhaps he just enjoys the attention without obligation," Jane countered, surprising her sister with her frankness. "It can hardly matter. I cannot afford to wonder, Lizzy. There is too much to be done. The household accounts will not balance themselves. I shall put him from my mind."

Elizabeth studied her sister's face. "You are not indifferent to him, though."

Jane sighed. "I am not quite indifferent. He is amiable and kind, and his conversation can be most engaging when he forgets to be nervous."

"High praise indeed from my reserved sister," Elizabeth teased.

Jane shook her head. "If Mr Bingley cannot bring himself to speak plainly, then I must assume he has no serious intentions."

"Could you not encourage him? Few of us have heart enough to be really in love without encouragement. What if you were to help him on?"

"To what end?" Jane asked. "A prolonged courtship with no certainty of outcome? I have responsibilities here, Lizzy. I cannot spare the time or attention for romantic uncertainties."

Elizabeth's expression turned serious. "You deserve happiness, Jane."

"I am content," Jane replied simply. "If Mr Bingley wishes to offer more than that, he must do so directly. I will not be trifled with."

"Nor should you be," Elizabeth agreed firmly. "We have worked too hard to build Longbourn to be distracted by gentlemen who admire our *capabilities* but fear our independence."

Jane's lips quirked upward. "Is that what holds him back, do you think? Our independence?"

"Men often claim to admire a woman of substance," Elizabeth said, "but many prefer the idea more than the reality. They wish for intelligent conversation at their convenience, but docile agreement the rest of the time."

"You paint a grim picture of matrimony, Lizzy."

"Not matrimony itself, but the expectations many bring to it." Elizabeth's eyes sparkled with mischief. "Besides, we are hardly conventional prospects, are we?."

Jane laughed. "We are hardly revolutionaries, Lizzy. We simply do what must be done."

Elizabeth turned to her with a grimace. "Which is what frightens them," she countered. "Women who manage with independence need only change course if a man's offering surpasses that independence."

Jane considered this. "What would you consider of greater value?"

"True partnership," Elizabeth replied without hesitation. "A meeting of minds as well as hearts. Someone who values our capabilities rather than tolerating them." She shrugged. "I fear such a man exists only in novels."

"You are too cynical," Jane chided. "There must be gentlemen who desire a partner rather than a mere ornament."

"I hope you are right," Elizabeth said. "For both our sakes. Since Mr Darcy has apparently found our ways unacceptable and deserted us, I wonder whether Mr Bingley will follow." She picked up her quill again. "In the meantime, we have an estate to run."

"No," Jane agreed, rising to return to her duties. "I have responsibilities enough without tending to an irresolute suitor."

"The most demanding sort of charge," Elizabeth added with a grin. "Requiring constant attention and reassurance."

The arrival of Mr James Fairfield at the Meryton Scientific

Society's weekly meeting caused quite a stir, although Mary Bennet appeared to be the only lady present who noticed neither his handsome figure nor his unfashionable attire. Her attention remained fixed on his discourse about recent advances in soil composition until he began describing his correspondence with the Royal Institution regarding the effects of different mineral substances on plant growth. She was determined to ignore his sparkling green eyes, his trim figure, and firm jaw. She was a serious woman, after all.

"The traditional understanding of marl's benefits proves insufficient," he was saying, spreading out several precisely drawn charts. "Through systematic trials, I have documented striking variations in efficacy depending on the underlying soil composition. Chalk marl, for instance, shows remarkable results in clay soils but proves nearly useless in already calcareous earth."

Mr Fairfield's orderly examination of agricultural principles reminded Elizabeth rather too forcefully of another gentleman's careful attention to estate management. Not that she was thinking of Mr Darcy, of course.

"By dividing each field into measured sections and varying only a single factor between plots, we can isolate the effects of specific treatments," Mr Fairfield continued, indicating his experimental diagrams. "The Royal Society has expressed marked interest in my findings regarding the interaction between drainage patterns and fertiliser efficiency."

Mary's quill flew across her notebook. She raised her hand. "Have you observed any correlation between soil temperature and mineral absorption rates? I have noticed variations in plant vigour that seem to correspond with the timing of applications…"

"The temperature question is fascinating," Mr Fairfield replied, his eyes alight with enthusiasm. "I have begun taking systematic measurements using Mr James Six's newly improved thermometer design. The data suggests optimal application times vary significantly by mineral type."

"My latest paper," Mr Fairfield was saying, "focuses on the relationship between soil composition and water retention. I have developed a method for measuring drainage rates using calibrated vessels and precise timing…"

Mary leant forward, dropping her reserve. "Have you considered how varying depths of cultivation might affect your results? I have observed in my own trials that deeper ploughing seems to alter drainage patterns significantly."

Mr Fairfield's eyes lit up with delight, "Such a pertinent observation, Miss.?" His voice rose in question.

"Miss Mary Bennet," Mary replied, a blush pinking her cheeks quite becomingly.

After the lecture concluded, Elizabeth watched with quiet amusement as Mr Fairfield approached Mary with several rolled technical drawings under his arm.

"Miss Mary, you mentioned experiments with different fertiliser combinations? I should very much like to hear more about your methods."

"Oh!" Mary blushed. "I have been testing various proportions of lime and night soil, following Mr Young's recommendations but with some modifications based on local soil conditions…"

Their technical discussion continued as the meeting dispersed, Mr Fairfield seemed in no hurry to conclude it.

On her return, Elizabeth found Jane in the stillroom, sorting rose hips, her tranquil mien suggesting pleasant thoughts indeed.

"Mr Bingley called yet again whilst you were at the Society meeting," Jane said.

"Did he? And his family is well?"

"They are. Mr Bingley mentioned the most exciting news," Jane continued. "His renovations will be complete by month's end, and he intends to host a ball at Netherfield." Elizabeth's looked up in surprise. "A ball?" she repeated, her tone neutral.

"Yes. He was quite animated about it. He said he wishes to

offer some return for the many civilities his household has received in Meryton."

"A ball at Netherfield…" Elizabeth turned the idea over as if it were a foreign coin. "I suppose all of Meryton will attend."

"I imagine so. Aunt Phillips has already begun speculating on gowns and partners."

Elizabeth plucked a leaf that clung despite the cold. "And Mr Darcy?"

Jane glanced at her sidelong. "Mr Bingley believes he may return from London to attend."

"Indeed," Elizabeth said shortly. "How gratifying."

Jane smiled faintly. "You do not look as though you find the prospect particularly gratifying."

Elizabeth shrugged. "I find nothing especially diverting in the company of those who consider me beneath notice."

"Is that truly your impression?" Jane asked gently. "Or your assumption?"

Elizabeth did not reply at once. The rustling of the autumn breeze filled the silence. "He is not a man who reveals his thoughts with ease."

"No," Jane agreed. "But he did send compliments on the success of our drainage works. That seems…amiable."

Elizabeth gave a faint, dismissive laugh. "If a man advances his courtship by praising my ditch-digging, I shall know how to value it."

Jane's smile widened. "Perhaps he means to compliment your intellect, not your spade."

"What girl does not dream of such admiration? Not for her beauty, but for her theories on most felicitous arrangement for ditch placement."

Jane tilted her head. "A solid foundation for any match. Provided, of course, the gentleman in question does not flee to London."

Elizabeth gave a tight smile. "His absence is easily explained. I dared to mention turnip yield in polite company. I may have driven him off with my radical fondness for symmetrical crop rotation."

"And yet," Jane said, "if he were to ask you to dance..."

Elizabeth hesitated. "I would of course be perfectly civil."

Jane's eyes sparkled. "How gracious of you. Civil, and perhaps—just slightly—pleased?"

Elizabeth huffed. "Only if he praises my drainage gradient in front of the entire assembly. If he even deigns to return to Netherfield for the event."

Jane said nothing more, but her expression was thoughtful. After a pause, she asked, "And what of your morning? How was the Scientific Society meeting?"

Elizabeth gladly seized the chance to discuss safer topics. "Most illuminating. I believe we may have found someone who can truly appreciate Mary's intellectual pursuits. Mr Fairfield has requested permission to call and examine her experimental gardens."

"Indeed?" Jane's eyes sparkled. "And did Mary seem... receptive to this scientific consultation?"

"Let us say that I have never seen our sister quite so animated in discussion of soil characteristics." Elizabeth smiled. "Although she maintained her composure admirably until he mentioned his correspondence with Sir Humphry Davy. I thought I might need to fetch Aunt Phillips's salts!"

As they walked back to the house, Elizabeth's thoughts drifted again to the upcoming ball. What would it be like to attend an event among neighbours who had not always been accepting of their position?

Chapter Twenty-Eight

Mr Hill announced their visitors with gravity: "Mr Bingley, Miss Bingley, and Mrs Hurst."

The elegant lady in carrot-coloured silk swept into the modest parlour with an expression that suggested she had caught a whiff of something disagreeable. Behind her, Mrs Hurst followed more languidly, her every step steeped in practised indifference.

"Good day, Mrs Bennet," Miss Bingley said coolly, inclining her head no more than civility demanded. "Miss Bennet. Miss Elizabeth. Miss Mary." Her eyes skimmed over each in turn, pausing only on Jane, where they narrowed with the faintest change in expression.

"How … charming to see you again."

Mrs Hurst offered a faint smile as she lowered herself onto the sofa with the grace of someone who wished to appear accustomed to finer surroundings.

"My sisters," Mr Bingley interjected quickly, "have been eager to further our acquaintance with our neighbours."

"Indeed," Miss Bingley murmured, her gaze drifting to a faint crack in the plaster near the ceiling. She drew back the hem of her gown as if fearing contagion, "There is always something quaint about country manners."

Elizabeth, standing just behind her mother, exchanged a glance with Jane, whose expression had taken on a quietly resolute set. It was, Elizabeth reflected, just the sort of reception she had anticipated—frost dressed in silk.

Miss Bingley's gaze flicked toward the window as though the hedgerows of Hertfordshire personally offended her. "We had nearly forgotten the pleasures of morning calls, after so many weeks confined to rustic society."

Elizabeth replied with polite interest, "And yet you have remained in the country some time. One might nearly think you found diversions here."

Mrs Hurst gave a brittle laugh. "We make do. Although it must be said, the conversation in town runs to a more elevated strain. One does miss the polish of a proper salon."

"You are good to bring a little of that refinement to Meryton," Jane said with perfect calm, although Elizabeth caught the faintest gleam in her sister's wide eyes.

Miss Bingley's smile did not reach her eyes. "We endeavour to maintain standards, even in such a… provincial setting."

"Provincial we may be," Elizabeth said lightly, "but not without some intellectual pursuits. The Meryton Scientific Society offers lectures each Thursday. Last week's featured a most engaging discourse on crop yields and soil composition."

Miss Bingley blinked. "Scientific lectures?" Her lips parted as if to laugh, but she caught herself. "How… unusual for young ladies to attend such things."

"We find them enlightening," Jane said placidly. "And most relevant to our work at Longbourn."

Mrs Hurst adjusted her bracelets. "What of your steward?"

"Our estate has no steward," Elizabeth replied. "We manage the land ourselves."

Miss Bingley gave a tight smile. "That explains the… practical wardrobe. One must be dressed for the task at hand, of course."

Elizabeth met her gaze without flinching. "Indeed. Although I have always found a well-cut ditch far more satisfying than a well-cut gown."

"My sisters and I take great interest in agricultural improvements," Jane explained.

"The study of natural philosophy brings material benefits to estate management," Mary offered. "As Lord Bacon observes in his 'Advancement of Learning,' knowledge must be grounded in practical application."

Miss Bingley's expression suggested she had bitten into something sour. Mrs Hurst studied her fingernails.

"Agricultural improvements?" Mrs Hurst exchanged a significant look with her sister. "I cannot imagine concerning oneself with such matters."

Jane, still smiling, turned to Mrs Hurst. "How have you found Meryton after your months among us?"

Mrs Hurst waved a hand vaguely. "It is pleasant, for the countryside. But there is nothing to compare with the pace of London. One misses the theatre. And the people."

"But we have not shared our happy purpose in calling," Bingley interrupted. "We are to host a ball at Netherfield Tuesday next!"

"How delightful," Mrs Bennet exclaimed. "Such an elegant setting for dancing."

"The Netherfield ballroom is tolerably large," Miss Bingley allowed. "Although nothing to the grand salons of town, naturally."

"Hardly the size of Pemberley's ballroom," Mrs Hurst added meaningfully.

"Few estates could compare with Pemberley, I imagine," Elizabeth replied, keeping her expression neutral.

Miss Bingley's eyes narrowed in a calculating stare. "You are acquainted with Mr Darcy's estate, then?"

"By hearsay rather than acquaintance. Mr Darcy has been most helpful regarding certain estate matters, with his extensive experience at Pemberley," Elizabeth replied evenly.

"Mr Darcy has spoken highly of the innovations at Longbourn," Bingley offered helpfully. He shifted in his chair, his gaze flicking to Jane, then downward to the pattern of the carpet. He opened his mouth as if to speak again, then seemed to think better of it. A moment later, he cleared his throat and forced a smile, the tension at his jaw betraying more than his words ever could.

"Charles," Miss Bingley rose abruptly. "We really must attend to the guest list. So many details to arrange."

"But we have only arrived," her brother protested.

"And delivered our invitation," Mrs Hurst was already standing. "We should not impose further."

Mrs Bennet spoke polite protests, but the Bingley sisters swept toward the door with elegant determination, leaving their bewildered brother to make hasty farewells.

After they had gone, Mrs Bennet tutted. "Such fine carnelian silk in Miss Bingley's gown, although that shade does nothing for her complexion. And Mrs Hurst's lace was quite elegant. It is a great pity their manners do not equal the height of their fashions. I had not even enough time to offer tea!"

"Perhaps," Elizabeth suggested dryly, "they left their better manners in one of those grand London salons they so admire."

"Lizzy," Jane reproached gently.

"You are ever kind, Jane. But even Miss Bingley's pointed barbs cannot diminish the prospect of a ball at Netherfield."

"Mr Bingley seemed most pleased to offer the invitation," Mrs Bennet observed with satisfaction.

"Although his sisters seemed rather less pleased to deliver it," Elizabeth murmured.

"It signifies nothing," Mrs Bennet declared. "A gentleman's intentions matter far more than his sisters' approval."

Mary nodded, adjusting her spectacles, "Fine clothing cannot disguise poverty of mind. Although in this case, it appears to advertise it."

"Mary!" Jane could not quite hide her amusement.

Elizabeth smiled. "I am convinced our Mary might possess the keenest discernment of character among us."

"Not at all," Mary replied primly. "I merely apply empirical observation to social phenomena. Miss Bingley's behaviour provides an excellent case study in artificial manners."

The afternoon sun slanted through the trees as Mary Bennet and Mr Fairfield walked the boundary of the Longbourn Estate. They had spent the previous half hour discussing crop rotation and the relative merits of different fertilising methods, but now a comfortable silence had fallen between them.

"Miss Bennet," Mr Fairfield said abruptly, then cleared his throat. "I have not enquired after your family. Your sisters are well, I trust?"

Mary glanced at him, surprised by the personal turn in conversation. "They are in good health, thank you. Elizabeth is occupied with the autumn planting, Jane manages our household affairs, and Lydia attends to the sheep."

"Your mother resides with you still?" he asked.

"She does. She keeps busy with correspondence and care of our grandfather."

Mr Fairfield nodded; his angular face serious. "My own mother was similarly occupied when she was living. She passed when I was seventeen. My father followed three years later."

"I am sorry," Mary said, meaning it. "It must have been difficult to be on your own at such a young age."

Mr Fairfield's gaze moved to the distant fields. "It was, yet I had hoped to establish my own farm by now. My position affords knowledge, if not property."

"Knowledge has its own value," Mary observed.

"Perhaps," he acknowledged. "Although land would be preferable."

"You have ambitions to one day acquire an estate?"

"I have intentions," he corrected. "Ambitions suggests something less concrete."

Mary nodded, appreciating his precision. "Have you no family remaining?"

"A brother serves in the navy. We correspond but rarely." Mr Fairfield hesitated, then added, "He did not care for agricultural pursuits."

Mary nodded. There was no need to comment on the implied criticism.

They resumed walking, crossing a small stream via stepping

stones. The breeze stirred the fallen leaves at their feet, filling the brief silence. Mr Fairfield extended his hand to assist her, which Mary accepted after a moment of surprise. His grip was firm, his palm calloused from physical labour—not the hand of a gentleman who supervised workers, but one who laboured himself.

"You read a great deal, I understand," he said as they reached the other side.

"I do. How did you know?"

A flush crept up his neck. "I observed you with a book in the drawing room last week. Whilst others played cards."

"You noticed me?" Mary asked, surprised anyone had paid her attention that evening.

"I too was not playing," he replied simply.

"What do you read, Mr Fairfield?" Mary asked.

"Agricultural journals, primarily. And some history." He paused, then admitted, "I attempted a novel once. I found it improbable."

Mary suppressed a smile. "Which novel?"

"I cannot recall the title. There was a castle, and a lady with an unfortunate tendency to faint."

"Ah. Gothic fiction is not to everyone's taste."

"Is it to yours?" he asked, seeming genuinely curious.

"I prefer moral philosophy," Mary answered. "And texts on agricultural improvement. I have been studying methods of crop rotation from the continent."

Mr Fairfield looked at her with new interest. "You have read Arthur Young's work?"

"And Mr Coke of Norfolk's innovations," Mary confirmed. "I found his experiments with marling most applicable to our eastern field."

"Few ladies take interest in such matters," Mr Fairfield observed.

"Few gentlemen are accustomed to expect it," Mary countered.

A brief smile crossed his face. "A fair observation, Miss

Bennet."

They had reached the old oak that marked the eastern boundary of Longbourn. Normally their discussions of agricultural matters concluded here.

"I have taken too much of your time," Mr Fairfield said, looking at the position of the sun. "But I have found our conversation most illuminating, Miss Bennet."

"As have I," Mary replied truthfully.

"Perhaps we might continue it another day," he suggested, his gaze now fixed somewhere over her left shoulder. "I will call when I consult with Miss Elizabeth about the winter wheat."

"I should like that," Mary said.

Mr Fairfield bowed stiffly. "Good day, Miss Bennet."

"Good day, Mr Fairfield."

He turned and walked away, his tall figure moving with purpose across the field.

Darcy settled into his library at Darcy House with a sense of relief, the familiar surroundings a welcome balm after the disquietude of Hertfordshire. The fire burned steadily in the grate, dispelling London's persistent autumn damp, and the leather-bound volumes that lined the walls offered a comforting solidity.

Three days had passed since his return, during which he had immersed himself in business correspondence, visited his club, and spent evenings with Georgiana, whose melancholy proved far less pronounced than her letter had suggested. His conscience pricked him at the realisation, but he dismissed it. London was where he belonged. Hertfordshire, with its provincial society and unsettling encounters, was best forgotten.

Yet his thoughts returned unbidden to certain matters concerning the Bennet estate. The conversation with Mr Bennet regarding his endeavours to protect their claim to Longbourn, and his promise to see to the provisions Mr Bennet had put in place to protect the Bennet ladies, troubled him more than he wished.

"Fletcher," he called, and his valet appeared in the doorway. "Send a message to Lord Matthews's town house. I wish to speak with him regarding a business matter if he would permit me to call."

"Very good, sir," Fletcher replied with a bow.

Whilst waiting for a response, Darcy penned several letters to his steward at Pemberley, finding comfort in the familiar routine of estate management. Columns of figures and projected yields were dependable, logical—unlike the contradictory emotions that had plagued him of late.

Fletcher returned two hours later, bearing a sealed note.

"A response from his Lordship's butler, sir."

Darcy broke the seal and scanned the brief message. "Lord Matthews is in Bath," he said frowning. "Taking the waters."

"Would you like me to arrange for a letter to be sent to him there, sir?"

"No," Darcy replied after a moment's consideration. "The matter can wait until his return."

But it seemed the matter would not wait. The following afternoon, Darcy was interrupted during his fencing practice at Angelo's salle by the arrival of a visitor.

"Viscount Eastbridge requests a moment of your time, sir," the attendant informed him. "He waits in the foyer."

Darcy frowned, lowering his foil. "Lord Matthews's son?"

"Yes, sir."

"Very well. Inform him I shall join him presently."

After changing from his fencing attire, Darcy entered the foyer to find a tall, fashionably dressed young man examining a display of antique duelling pistols with apparent interest.

"Viscount Eastbridge," Darcy said, approaching him with a bow. "To what do I owe the unexpected honour?"

The Viscount turned, revealing a face that bore a striking resemblance to his father's, although his expression held a tension that suggested less ease with his position.

"Mr Darcy," he acknowledged, returning the bow. "I

apologise for the intrusion. My butler informed me you had wished to call upon my father."

"Indeed. A minor matter only."

The Viscount studied him for a moment. "Perhaps we might discuss it over a drink? I find Angelo's somewhat public for certain conversations."

Darcy's curiosity was piqued. "By all means. White's is but a short walk from here."

Soon they were ensconced in a private corner of Whites, glasses of brandy before them. After a few minutes of obligatory social exchange—comments on the weather, mutual acquaintances, the quality of the brandy—the Viscount leant forward.

"You wished to speak with my father about Dunbar Court, I believe."

Darcy maintained his composure, although he was surprised by the young man's directness. "What leads you to that conclusion?"

"A reasonable inference," the Viscount replied with a thin smile. "You are lately returned from Hertfordshire, where Dunbar Court lies in proximity to your friend's leased estate and an estate managed by ladies. A most extraordinary circumstance."

"Your information is impressively current," Darcy observed.

"My father maintains an interest in his properties, however distant," the Viscount said smoothly. "And the Bennet situation has provided fodder for local gossip for some years."

Darcy took a measured sip of his brandy. "I confess I am interested in discussing Dunbar Court with Lord Matthews. I understand it has been rarely occupied for some time."

"Nearly five years," the Viscount confirmed. "There has been some difficulty in securing a tenant able to meet his obligations."

"A shame," Darcy murmured, detecting the underlying significance. The maintenance had likely exceeded the return, and Lord Matthews had hoped to let the property rather than work out an arrangement. "The property appears to have potential."

"It does," the Viscount agreed. "Although realising that potential would require a significant investment."

"I imagine so."

A moment of silence stretched between them, each man taking the measure of the other. Finally, the Viscount spoke again.

"My father finds his current financial circumstances somewhat constrained," he said haltingly. "The townhouse in Bath is undergoing extensive renovations, and his investments in the West Indies have not yielded the expected returns."

Darcy understood immediately. Lord Matthews needed funds, and Dunbar Court represented a potential source of capital. "A not uncommon situation for many landowners in these uncertain times," he offered diplomatically.

"Quite." The Viscount relaxed, evidently relieved at Darcy's understanding. "In fact, my father has contemplated divesting himself of certain properties that contribute little to the family's overall holdings."

"I see."

"Dunbar Court would be among them," the Viscount continued. "A modest property, but perhaps of interest to someone with neighbouring concerns."

Darcy maintained a neutral expression, although his mind was working rapidly. The opportunity had presented itself more directly than he had anticipated. "What terms might Lord Matthews consider for such a transaction?"

"I am authorised to negotiate on his behalf," the Viscount replied. "Although any agreement would require a certain discretion."

"Of course."

The next hour was spent in careful negotiation. The Viscount named a sum that Darcy deemed excessive; Darcy countered with an offer that recognised the estate's neglected condition. They eventually settled on a figure that, whilst generous, reflected the property's true value and potential.

"There is one additional matter," Darcy said, as they prepared to conclude their business. "My role in this transaction will remain confidential."

The Viscount raised an eyebrow. "Entirely confidential?"

"Yes. I propose establishing a holding company. The transaction would appear to be a simple land investment by an anonymous London concern."

"Uncommon, but not impossible," the Viscount mused. "May I enquire as to your reasons?"

Darcy hesitated. "I prefer to avoid speculation regarding my investment decisions."

The explanation lacked strength; both men understood this, yet the Viscount only nodded. "Very well. I believe that can be arranged, provided the funds are transferred promptly."

"Within the week," Darcy assured him. "My solicitor will draw up the necessary documents."

They shook hands, the agreement sealed as firmly as if contracts had already been signed.

"A pleasure doing business with you, Mr Darcy," the Viscount said. "I trust Dunbar Court will prove a satisfactory investment."

"I believe it will," Darcy replied, offering no further insight into his intentions.

After the Viscount departed, Darcy remained at White's, contemplating his brandy and the transaction he had just arranged. His actions made adequate sense from a business perspective. The acquisition was sound, the negotiation successful.

Why, then, did he feel such conflicted satisfaction?

He knew the answer, although he was reluctant to acknowledge it. His interest in Dunbar Court had little to do with land values or agricultural yields and everything to do with Elizabeth Bennet's frustration as she laboured to make insufficient figures yield a different result.

Without her knowledge, without an expectation of gratitude, without any obligation toward him, he arranged a temporary solution to the Bennets' need to secure the bordering fields. His holding company would seek a lessee on favourable terms for the pastures and home farm, as the house would not attract any tenant in its present condition. It was an elegant acknowledgement of the

Bennet's vulnerability, one that maintained their independence whilst removing the threat of an unreliable neighbour.

That his actions might be interpreted as overstepping, as interfering in matters not his concern, he chose not to dwell upon. He was making a sound business investment. Nothing more.

With that resolution firmly in mind, Darcy finished his brandy and departed for his solicitor's office. The sooner the transaction was complete, the sooner he could put Hertfordshire—and its inhabitants—from his thoughts entirely.

Or so he told himself, as London's grey afternoon closed around him like a cloak.

Chapter Twenty-Nine

The air in the barn was thick with dust motes dancing in the slanting morning light. Mary Bennet stood ramrod straight beside the Longbourn wagon, her plain dress protected by a practical canvas apron that had once been her grandfather's. The agricultural journal she had been studying was tucked securely under one arm as she surveyed the half-dozen sacks of seed wheat Mr Cooper had delivered.

"You'll find it all in order, Miss Mary," said Mr Cooper, a portly man whose ruddy complexion had deepened in the heat of the barn. He patted one of the burlap sacks with a proprietary air. "Finest seed wheat in three counties. I've held back the best for Longbourn, as your grandfather has been a valued customer these twenty years."

Mary adjusted her spectacles, her expression betraying neither belief nor disbelief at this pronouncement. "Indeed? Then you will not object to my examination of the sample."

Something flickered across Mr Cooper's face—so briefly Mary might have missed it had she not been watching closely. "Hardly necessary, Miss. Your grandfather always trusted my word on such matters."

"My grandfather," Mary replied, reaching for the small knife she kept in her apron pocket, "taught us to trust, but verify all claims, regardless of their source." Her fingers, once soft from hours of practising scales and copying moral extracts, were now calloused from more practical pursuits. She sliced open the sample bag with practised strokes.

Behind them, John Robinson, their most reliable tenant farmer, shifted uneasily from one foot to another. He had accompanied Mary from Longbourn, driving the small wagon they would use to transport the seed if it proved satisfactory. Mary noticed how he kept his gaze respectfully averted from the interaction, though his ears were attuned to every word.

Mary plunged her hand into the sack, letting the wheat grains pour through her fingers back into the bag. The subtle hitch in her movement would have been imperceptible to anyone who did not know her well, but her eyes narrowed behind her spectacles.

"Mr Cooper," she said, in a perfectly measured tone, "would you be so kind as to open the remaining sacks for inspection?"

The merchant's smile stiffened. "Now, that will not be necessary, Miss Mary. I vouch personally for the quality—"

"I am sorry, but I must insist," Mary said, her tone mild but unyielding. She withdrew her hand from the sample sack and brushed the grains from her palm.

Mr Cooper hesitated, then gestured to his boy to cut open the remaining sacks. "As you wish, though I must say you—"

"Thank you." Mary moved methodically from one sack to the next, sifting the grain through her fingers, occasionally holding a handful up to the light streaming through the barn's open door. Her face remained impassive, but her eyes catalogued every detail with scientific accuracy.

After examining the last sack, she straightened and pulled the agricultural journal from beneath her arm. She opened it to a page marked with a ribbon and turned it toward Mr Cooper.

"I am sure you are familiar with the Agricultural Society's standards for seed wheat, Mr Cooper?"

The merchant's face reddened further. "I've been in this business thirty years, Miss. I hardly need—"

"The journal specifies," Mary continued as if he had not spoken, her finger tracing the printed line, "that first-quality seed wheat should have no more than two percent foreign matter and should show a germination rate of at least ninety-five percent when tested." She closed the journal with a soft thump. "The sample you've provided contains easily eight percent chaff and broken grains, by my estimation. And I suspect, were we to test it, the germination rate would prove equally disappointing."

"Young ladies hardly possess the expertise to judge—" Mr Cooper began, but Mary cut him off with a shake of her head.

"Furthermore," she said, taking on the lecturing tone her sisters knew so well, "these grains show signs of having been stored in damp conditions." She held out her palm, where several darkened grains lay among the golden ones. "Note the discoloration—indicative of mould. Chapter seven of Barton's 'Modern Agriculture' is quite specific about the storage requirements for seed grain."

Mr Cooper's face had progressed from red to purple. "Miss Mary, with all due respect to your reading, practical experience—"

"Would you care to test a sample for germination, Mr Cooper?" Mary inquired, reaching into her apron pocket and producing a small cloth pouch. "I've brought moist blotting paper, as recommended by the Royal Agricultural Society. We could dampen it now and check the results in three days' time. Or perhaps you would prefer to send a sample to Sir William Lucas for his assessment? He has expressed remarkable enthusiasm for Longbourn's crop rotation innovations."

The mention of Sir William caused Mr Cooper to swallow whatever protest he had been about to make. His gaze darted to John Robinson, who suddenly found great interest in adjusting the horse's harness, though Mary could see the slight smile he was attempting to conceal.

"Perhaps there has been some mistake," Mr Cooper said stiffly. "These sacks may have been… mislabeled at the mill."

"A concerning error," Mary commented, closing her journal and tucking it back under her arm. "Particularly as the price quoted was for first-quality seed."

"I shall personally ensure the correct sacks are delivered by tomorrow morning," Mr Cooper said, gesturing for his boy to begin retying the open bags. "With appropriate adjustment to the invoice, of course."

"That would be satisfactory," Mary agreed. "We require eight bushels of first-quality seed wheat, as specified in our order. Our plans depend upon timely planting."

Cooper bowed stiffly. "You shall have it, Miss Mary."

Mary nodded, her expression betraying neither triumph nor lingering irritation. "Tomorrow, then. Good day, Mr Cooper."

As their wagon pulled away, John Robinson approached, no longer bothering to hide his grin. "That was something to see, Miss Mary. The old fox has been trying that same trick on half the farms in the county."

Mary adjusted her spectacles, colour rising in her cheeks at the praise. "Grandfather always says that knowledge properly applied is the best defence against dishonesty." She patted the journal under her arm. "Chapter twelve specifically addresses common frauds in agricultural commerce."

"Miss Elizabeth will be pleased," John said as he helped Mary into their cart. "She was concerned Mr Cooper might try something, knowing it was you coming instead of her or your grandfather."

"Was she?" Mary asked, settling her skirts around her. "I shall have to inform her that her concerns, whilst not unfounded, proved unnecessary." A small, satisfied smile touched her lips. "Though perhaps I should request that Grandfather allow me to handle the seed orders from now on. I find I have developed quite an interest in the subject."

As they returned to Longbourn, Mary's typically serious expression softened into quiet satisfaction. The journal resting in her lap had been her grandfather's gift on her sixteenth birthday—a far more practical present than the sheet music her sisters had presented. At the time, she had been disappointed, having hoped for the latest publication of moral philosophy. Now, she silently thanked her grandfather for his foresight. There was, she reflected, a certain satisfaction in practical knowledge that philosophical extracts, for all their moral value, could not provide. She ran her fingers along the leather-bound agricultural journal, the neat handwriting inside a testament to Aunt Eleanor's meticulous approach to estate management long before society deemed such knowledge appropriate for women.

"Will you tell Mr Bennet about Mr Cooper's attempted deception?" John asked as they turned onto the lane leading to Longbourn.

"Certainly," Mary replied. "Grandfather insists on being informed of all such matters. Though I believe I shall also mention it to Lydia. She has been compiling quite a detailed record of which merchants can be trusted and which require… additional scrutiny."

John chuckled. "Miss Lydia has a memory like a ledger book when it comes to those who have crossed Longbourn."

"Rather, those who have attempted to," Mary agreed with a slight smile. "And unlike our moral failings, which deserve Christian forgiveness, commercial dishonesty must be recorded and remembered. Grandfather taught us that lesson when Jane first began managing the household accounts."

As Longbourn came into view, Mary straightened her spine and adjusted her spectacles once more, mentally composing her report for her grandfather. She knew he would be proud—not simply because she had avoided being cheated, but because she had applied her knowledge. The practical application of learning, he often reminded them, was what separated true education from mere recitation. Mary had proved the worth of her studies in a way no moral extract could match. Mr Cooper's future dealings with the estate showed markedly more respect.

The late autumn sunshine cast long shadows across Hyde Park as Darcy guided his curricle along the fashionable drive, his team of matched greys responding to the slightest touch of the reins. Beside him, Georgiana sat wrapped in a blue shawl over her pelisse, her gloved hands clasped in her lap, her posture as perfect as any governess could have wished.

"You handle them beautifully, Brother," she observed, watching as he navigated around a slower barouche. "I believe they grow more responsive each time you drive them."

"They should," Darcy replied, pleased by her observation. "I selected them myself from Lord Jersey's stables last spring."

"A wise choice," Georgiana said, then fell silent again, her gaze drifting to the golden leaves that scattered across their path.

Darcy studied her profile from the corner of his eye. At sixteen, she was becoming a young woman rather than a girl, her features settling into the delicate beauty that had characterised their mother. Yet there remained something guarded in her expression.

"I hope you have enjoyed having me home these past days," he ventured. "Your letter suggested you were feeling rather low-spirited."

Georgiana's cheeks coloured. "I confess I may have exaggerated somewhat. I had sensed that you were quite fixed at Netherfield, and I feared you might remain in Hertfordshire indefinitely."

"So, you invented a melancholy to draw me back to London?" Darcy asked, surprised by this uncharacteristic manipulation.

"Not invented," she corrected quickly. "Merely emphasised. I was indeed feeling rather solitary."

"You have Mrs Annesley for companionship."

"Mrs Annesley is an excellent chaperone and a kind woman, but she is not family," Georgiana replied. "Besides, I wished to hear about your time in the country. Your letters told me vexingly little of Netherfield and its society."

Darcy flicked the reins gently as they rounded a bend in the path. "There is little to tell. Bingley's estate shows promise, although it requires attention. The local society is much as one would expect in a rural setting."

"How illuminating," Georgiana said with uncharacteristic dryness. "I now feel as if I have visited Hertfordshire myself, your description is so vivid."

Darcy turned to her in surprise. "Since when have you developed such a talent for sarcasm?"

"I have had an excellent teacher," she replied, a hint of

mischief in her smile. "Come now, Brother. I am certain there must have been something of interest during your stay? Someone, perhaps, who made an impression?"

Darcy's hands tightened imperceptibly on the reins. "Bingley seems quite taken with the eldest daughter of a local family. A Miss Bennet."

"And what of Bingley's friend? Was he equally impressed by anyone?"

"If you refer to me, then no," Darcy said firmly. "I found little to admire in the neighbourhood."

"How strange," Georgiana mused. "When you spoke last evening of your business with Lord Matthews regarding a property in Hertfordshire, you seemed exceptionally spirited. I assumed you must have some particular interest."

Darcy shot her a sharp glance. "Dunbar Court represents a sound investment, nothing more."

"Of course," she agreed, too readily. "Although I cannot help but wonder why you have arranged to purchase it through such an elaborate scheme of holding companies, if it is no more than a straightforward investment."

"You have been eavesdropping on my business affairs," Darcy accused, although without real heat.

"I happened to be practising in the music room when your solicitor called yesterday," Georgiana explained. "The connecting door to the study was ajar."

"And you did not think to close it when you realised the conversation was of a private nature?"

"I intended to," she said, "but then I heard mention of Longbourn Estate and became curious."

Darcy sighed. His sister had always been observant, despite her quiet nature. "Longbourn is adjacent to Dunbar Court. The purchase makes strategic sense."

"Particularly since Longbourn is managed by a family of unmarried ladies, according to Mr Trowbridge."

"You heard rather a lot through that open door," Darcy

observed dryly.

"The acoustics in our townhouse are remarkably favourable," Georgiana replied, then she grew more serious. "Brother, I have never known you to take such an interest in a property without some compelling reason. What is it at Longbourn that interests you?"

Darcy considered evading the question, but something in his sister's earnest expression made him reconsider. "The Bennet ladies have managed their estate admirably since their father's death," he said finally. "But their situation is precarious. Their grandfather is quite elderly and Dunbar Court, if mismanaged, could pose a threat to their water supply and grazing rights. There is an additional threat in the form of our Aunt, Lady Catherine's, parson. Curiously, he holds the position of heir presumptive to Longbourn through an entail. He has been creating difficulties and making threats of legal action to take over management of Longbourn. It is a concerning set of circumstances."

"So, you purchased it to protect them?"

"I purchased it because it was available at a reasonable price," Darcy corrected, although he did not meet her eyes. "I will keep a careful eye on the area. Any benefit to the Bennets is incidental."

Georgiana was silent for a moment, watching a flock of sparrows rise from a nearby oak tree. "You spoke of water works. Does one of the sisters manage them?"

"All of them are involved. But the second eldest, Miss Elizabeth Bennet, is most occupied with those matters."

"And what is she like, this Miss Elizabeth?"

Darcy hesitated. "She is capable. Intelligent. She understands agriculture and land management in a way few women—or men, for that matter—do."

"Her appearance?" Georgiana pressed.

"Tolerable," Darcy replied, too quickly. "She has fine eyes."

"Fine eyes," Georgiana repeated, a smile playing at the corners of her mouth. "High praise indeed from my discerning brother."

Darcy frowned. "You draw excessive conclusions from an

insignificant remark."

"Perhaps," she conceded. "But I have never before heard you comment on any woman's eyes, except to note that they were fixed upon you with unseemly attention."

They had reached the Serpentine, its surface rippled by the autumn breeze. Darcy drew the curricle to a halt at a picturesque vantage point, engaging the brake before turning to face his sister fully.

"Whatever you are implying, Georgiana, I suggest you abandon the notion. Miss Elizabeth Bennet is a gentlewoman of little fortune and obscure family connections, managing an estate that may not rightfully belong to her. My interest in her situation is merely neighbourly concern."

"Of course," Georgiana said, her voice gentle. "Although I wonder, Brother, why you feel the need to assure me so emphatically of your disinterest."

Darcy had no ready answer to this uncomfortable observation.

"You know," she continued after a moment, "since the unfortunate events of the summer, I have occupied much of your attention and concern. Perhaps too much."

"Nonsense," Darcy said firmly. "You are my sister. Your wellbeing is my responsibility."

"My wellbeing, yes. But not my every thought and feeling," Georgiana countered with unexpected conviction. "I made a grave error in judgement, Brother, but I cannot allow that error to become the defining event of both our lives."

Darcy stared at her, taken aback by this newfound assertiveness. "What are you saying?"

"I am saying," Georgiana replied patiently, "that perhaps you need not arrange your life solely around protecting me from my own folly. That perhaps you might consider your own happiness as well as my security."

"My happiness is irrelevant compared to your welfare," Darcy insisted.

"I disagree," Georgiana said with surprising firmness. "Because I cannot be truly happy knowing that you have sacrificed your own contentment for my sake." She paused, then added more softly, "Especially if that sacrifice includes denying your interest in a lady with fine eyes and a capable mind."

Darcy looked away, watching a fashionably dressed couple stroll arm in arm along the lake's edge. He shifted the reins with unnecessary force, causing the greys to snort in protest. "You greatly exaggerate my interest in Miss Elizabeth."

"Do I?" Georgiana asked. "Then why does her name cause your expression to alter so? Why did you flee Hertfordshire so abruptly? And why, most tellingly, have you arranged to purchase a neighbouring property whilst concealing your involvement?"

"These are complicated matters, Georgiana," Darcy began, but she shook her head.

"No, Brother. I believe they are quite simple. *Entia non sunt multiplicanda praeter necessitatem*, Ockham's Razor. You are drawn to this lady, but something—pride, perhaps, or fear—prevents you from acknowledging it, even to yourself."

Darcy sat in stunned silence, unaccustomed to such directness from his typically reserved sister.

"You have always been honest with me," Georgiana continued more gently. "Even when the truth was painful. Allow me to offer the same courtesy to you."

For a long moment, the only sounds were the rustle of leaves and the occasional stamp of the horses' hooves. Finally, Darcy released a measured breath.

"I begin to regret permitting you to study philosophy. When did you become so perceptive?" he asked, caught between admiration and discomfort.

"I have had ample opportunity to observe human nature these past months," Georgiana replied with a sad smile. "Particularly the tendency to conceal one's true feelings behind a façade of propriety or veil one's true character behind a display of practiced charm."

Darcy nodded slowly. "Your observations are not entirely without merit," he conceded. "But the situation is more complex than you realise."

"Most matters of the heart are," she agreed. "Although perhaps not as insurmountably complex as we sometimes imagine them to be."

Darcy gathered the reins, signalling the end of their conversation. "We should continue our drive. The air grows chill."

"As you wish," Georgiana said, settling back against the curricle's leather seat. "But Brother?"

"Yes?"

"When you return to Hertfordshire—as I suspect you eventually will—I know you will approach the matter with courage."

Darcy made no reply, but as they continued their circuit of the park, he considered his sister's words with grudging respect.

"The greys are indeed exceptional," Georgiana commented lightly, changing the subject with tactful grace. "I should like to learn to drive them myself someday."

"When you are older," Darcy replied automatically, relieved to return to familiar ground.

"Of course," she agreed, recognising his retreat. "When I am older. Although I trust you will not make me wait too long, Brother. Some opportunities, after all, should not be deferred indefinitely."

Whether she spoke of driving or matters of the heart, Darcy could not be certain.

Chapter Thirty

The Meryton Livestock Fair bustled with activity under the bright May sun. Farmers from three counties had gathered to trade, sell, and gossip, the air thick with the mingled scents of animals, hay, and humanity. The bleating of sheep, the cries of hawkers, and the rhythmic bark of auctioneers filled the air. Lydia Bennet moved through the sheep pens with purpose, her practical walking dress—once her second best but now relegated to farm duties—protected by a canvas apron that bore the stains of previous agricultural endeavours.

"Miss Lydia!" called Mr Thistlewood, tipping his hat as she approached his pen. "Come to admire my stock, have you?"

Elizabeth, who had accompanied her younger sister to the fair, noted the barely concealed condescension in the sheep merchant's tone. At fifteen, Lydia's interest in animal husbandry was viewed by many as either a charming eccentricity or an alarming deviation from proper feminine pursuits. Few took her seriously, despite her growing expertise.

"Good morning, Mr Thistlewood," Lydia replied with a bright smile. But her eyes, as they swept over the sheep in the pen, were sharp and assessing. "I understand you have breeding ewes for sale."

"Indeed, Miss." He gestured expansively toward his pen. "the Finest Southdowns in the county. Your grandfather showed interest in improving his flock last year, as I recall."

"Yes," Elizabeth confirmed, stepping forward. "We are looking to purchase three breeding ewes to introduce new bloodlines into our flock."

Mr Thistlewoods nodded approvingly at Elizabeth before turning back to Lydia. "Well, little miss, see anything that catches your fancy? Perhaps that pretty one with the black face?" He pointed toward an ewe at the far end of the pen, clearly expecting Lydia's choice to be guided by appearance rather than breeding potential.

Lydia ignored the suggestion, her gaze methodically scanning the animals. She pulled a small notebook from her pocket—a habit she had adopted from Mary—and consulted her notes.

"We require ewes with strong mothering instincts and good wool quality," she said, flipping pages. "Grandfather's records show the Thistlewood flock has historically produced excellent lambing rates."

"Indeed, we have," the merchant replied, visibly surprised by her knowledge. "My father kept meticulous records, as do I."

"May I see them?" Lydia asked innocently, though Elizabeth caught the shrewd gleam in her sister's eye.

"Well, I have not got them here, of course," he said, his smile faltering. "But I can assure you—"

"Then perhaps I should examine the animals myself?" Lydia did not wait for permission but slipped between the wooden rails of the pen with practised ease, her movements confident among the milling sheep. A passing matron in a feathered bonnet gasped audibly and clutched her reticule.

Mr Thistlewoods shot an alarmed glance at Elizabeth. "Miss Bennet, this is hardly—"

"My sister has been managing our breeding programme for the past two years," Elizabeth replied calmly. "Grandfather finds her judgement quite sound."

In the pen, Lydia moved with gentleness among the animals, her hands checking fleece quality with experienced fingers. She bent to examine teeth and hooves, murmuring soothingly to each ewe as she worked. Several farmers passing by slowed to watch, their expressions a mixture of curiosity and disapproval.

"Young ladies generally prefer ribbon shops to sheep pens," observed Mrs Fairfax to Mrs Long as they passed, their voices pitched to carry. "Most unnatural interests for a girl of her age. One wonders what Mrs Bennet is thinking."

Elizabeth bit back a sharp reply, knowing it would only fuel further gossip. Instead, she watched as Lydia approached the black-faced ewe initially suggested.

Lydia ran her hands along the animal's sides, then bent close to observe its breathing. After a moment, she straightened and called out, "Elizabeth, would you join me please?"

The formality in her sister's tone alerted Elizabeth that something was amiss. She nodded politely and made her way to the pen's edge.

"Listen," Lydia said quietly when Elizabeth drew near. She placed her hand on the ewe's side. "Do you hear that?"

Elizabeth bent closer. A subtle wheezing sound accompanied each breath the animal took, barely perceptible amid the fair's noise.

"Early stages of lung fever," Lydia murmured, keeping her voice low. "See how the nostrils flare slightly with each breath? And the mucus here?" She pointed discreetly to the animal's nose. "It is not severe yet, but it will be. Grandfather's treatise on sheep ailments describes it just so."

Elizabeth nodded, impressed, despite being well aware of her sister's knowledge. Lydia noticed everything about the animals in her care.

"Mr Thistlewood," Elizabeth called, her tone pleasant but firm. "Might we have a word?"

The merchant approached; his expression wary as he took in the sisters' serious faces. "Found a beauty to your liking, have you?"

"This ewe has the early symptoms of lung fever," Lydia stated without preamble, her hand still resting on the animal's side. "The breathing is laboured, and there's nasal discharge beginning. It is subtle, but unmistakable."

The sheep merchant's face flushed. "Nonsense! The girl cannot know what she is talking about. A bit of dust from the journey, nothing more. My sheep doctor saw no illness."

"Perhaps," Elizabeth suggested smoothly, "Certainly we could settle the matter by having Mr Peterson examine her? I believe he is judging the cattle today, and his expertise in livestock ailments is well respected."

The mention of the county's most respected veterinary surgeon caused the colour to drain from Mr Thistelwood's face. Several nearby farmers had stopped to listen, their interest piqued by the confrontation.

"No need to trouble Mr Peterson," he muttered. "Perhaps the animal is feeling a bit poorly. Travel can be taxing for them."

"Indeed," Lydia agreed, her voice carrying audibly to the onlookers. "Though one wonders why you would specifically direct me to an animal showing signs of illness when you have so many healthy ones available." She looked to the other ewes in the pen. "That one there, for instance, shows excellent conformation and fleece quality, with no respiratory distress."

A murmur rippled through the growing crowd. Elizabeth caught sight of Sir William Lucas among the onlookers, his expression shifting from surprise to something like admiration as he watched Lydia confidently exit the pen.

"My sister has quite a gift for animal husbandry," Elizabeth explained to the assembled farmers, her voice pitched to carry. "Our grandfather has encouraged her natural talents, just as he did with all his granddaughters." She turned to Mr Thistlewood. "We are still in need of three healthy ewes if you wish to sell—provided we may select them ourselves and have them examined by Mr Peterson before finalising the sale."

The merchant, trapped by circumstance and witnesses, had little choice but to agree. "Of course, Miss Bennet. Miss Lydia's… concerns are noted. I would never knowingly sell ailing stock."

"I'm sure you would not," Lydia replied with wide-eyed innocence that did not quite mask the knowing gleam in her eye. "After all, one's reputation as a breeder depends upon honest dealings."

As they moved away to find Mr Peterson, Elizabeth leant close to her sister. "Grandfather would have been extremely displeased. That animal could have introduced disease into our entire flock."

Lydia's cheeks flushed. "Was that not what Mary would call 'the practical application of theoretical knowledge.' Grandfather's book on sheep ailments has the most detailed description of lung fever symptoms."

"Nevertheless," Elizabeth said, "your observation was exceptional. I saw nothing amiss."

"You were not meant to," Lydia replied with unexpected wisdom. "He counted on our being too delicate and feminine to crawl about in the pen examining his animals. Most ladies would simply take his word about which animals were best."

Elizabeth smiled, her youngest sister's responsibility had shaped her into something formidable. "Fortunately for Longbourn, we are not most ladies."

"No indeed," Lydia agreed with a grin that momentarily transformed her into the carefree girl she might have been in another life. "In truth, I miss dancing more than propriety dictates I should. But there is a satisfaction in this work that I never expected to find."

As they located Mr Peterson, Elizabeth watched Lydia straighten her shoulders and prepare to address the respected veterinarian with all the confidence of a seasoned breeder.

Mr Peterson, his shaggy hair and beard giving him a resemblance to his larger patients, smiled as he greeted them.

"Well, Miss Lydia Bennet, you are turning the sheep market on its ear today. What have you found?"

"I am suspicious that there is lung fever in one of the ewes we were considering."

"Lung fever is it? How did you come to that idea, miss?" he asked, his shaggy eyebrows twitching.

Lydia explained her observations whilst Mr Peterson nodded.

"It could very well be so, Miss Lydia. How is it that a young lady like yourself seems more knowledgeable than many of the shepherds I see every day?"

Lydia blushed and demurred, by Mr Peterson expressed his genuine interest.

"I did not always know about sheep, you understand," she

said. "It began the spring after my father died, when I was but seven years old."

The house at Longbourn lay quiet as a tomb. Three days had passed since they had laid father in the churchyard, and Lydia could not bear the weight of the silence another moment. She slipped away unseen, across the damp meadow that stretched behind the garden, her feet carrying her toward the stone lambing shed at the edge of the property.

The low structure stood weathered and grey against the morning mist, its roof sagging at one corner. From within came the soft bleating of newborn lambs. Lydia hesitated at the rough wooden door, then pushed it open just enough to peer inside.

The shed smelled of straw and lanolin and earthy things. Dim light filtered through small windows cut high in the stone walls. In the shadows, ewes, and their lambs rested in straw-filled pens. The air inside the shed was damp and cold, the chill seeping through the thin black fabric of her mourning dress.

"What be ye doing here, miss?"

The voice startled her. From a dark corner emerged Old Simmons, the Longbourn shepherd. His face was brown and creased as a walnut, with deep-set eyes nearly hidden beneath bushy grey brows. He walked with a pronounced stoop, leaning upon a gnarled hawthorn crook polished smooth by decades of use. Patched woollen clothes hung from his bent frame, and an ancient wide-brimmed hat sat atop his sparse white hair.

"This no place for a young miss like yerself," he grumbled, eyeing her suspiciously.

Lydia drew herself up. "I am not bothering anything," she said, lifting her chin in the manner she had observed in her elder sisters. "I wanted only to see the lambs."

In a pen nearby, a tiny creature bleated weakly, struggling in the straw. Beside it lay an ewe, unnaturally still. Simmons looked toward the sound and shook his head.

"Lost the mother in birthing," he said, his gravelly voice matter of fact. "That one be all alone now."

Without waiting for permission, Lydia moved to the pen and knelt beside the lamb, heedless of her black mourning dress.

"May I hold him?" she asked, her voice small.

Simmons frowned deeply, the wrinkles in his face rearranging themselves into new patterns of disapproval. After a moment, he gave a single nod.

"Hold the neck steady," he instructed. "Them be fragile when new-birthed."

Lydia gathered the lamb tenderly into her arms. It was surprisingly warm, its body trembling against her chest. Something in the weight of it, the soft vulnerability, made her throat tighten painfully.

"What shall happen to him now?" she asked, stroking the damp wool.

"Need feeding by hand," Simmons replied. "Every few hours, day, and night both. Hard work, that."

"I shall do it," Lydia said suddenly.

Simmons made a sound halfway between a snort and a cough. "Begging yer pardon, miss, but gentle-bred young ladies do not—"

"I am not afraid of work," Lydia interrupted, a strange fierceness rising in her that she did not fully understand. She looked down at the lamb, then back at the shepherd, her eyes filled with unshed tears. "I… perhaps I might be of some use."

The old shepherd regarded her for a long moment, something shifting in his weathered face. "It not just feeding," he said slowly. "There be much to learn about sheep-keeping."

"Then I shall learn," Lydia said. "I shall come every day."

"Yer mother would not approve such doings."

"Mamma scarcely notices what any of us do these days," Lydia replied, the truth of childhood cutting through propriety.

She looked up at him, the lamb cradled against her. "Please, Mr Simmons."

After what seemed an eternity, the old shepherd nodded once. "Dawn tomorrow," he said gruffly. "Do not be tardy. Sheep wait for no one, miss, not even them in mourning."

Lydia held the lamb more securely. "What shall I call him?"

"Do not name it," Simmons warned, his voice stern. "That be livestock, not some pet."

But as Lydia gazed into the lamb's dark eyes, she whispered words too soft for the shepherd to hear:

"Snowdrop. Because you were hidden in the snow storm, but I found

you."

When Grandfather learnt of Lydia's newfound interest, he put a stop to her sisters' teasing. "Aunt Eleanor would approve," he remarked quietly, observing Lydia's confident handling of the shepherd's crook. "She always said women make the most careful shepherds, being accustomed to watching over those who do not know what's best for them."

The last rays of winter sunlight filtered through the leaded glass of the window, casting long shadows across the Aubusson carpet as Mr Darcy stood in contemplation. The crisp paper of Bingley's latest letter rustled between his gloved fingers, its seal broken and its contents still commanding his attention. His friend's earnest entreaty to attend the forthcoming ball at Netherfield had disturbed the careful tranquillity he had attempted to cultivate since quitting Hertfordshire.

The sharp rap of boots upon the marble floor announced Colonel Fitzwilliam's arrival. The scent of cold winter air still clung to his military coat as he entered the study. "I see you have taken up brooding as your constant occupation, cousin."

Mr Darcy turned from his position at the window, the dying sunlight casting his features in shadow. "I am considering a matter of social obligation," he said, placing the letter within his coat pocket with deliberate care. "Bingley has requested my presence at Netherfield again."

"Ah, in Hertfordshire." The Colonel removed his gloves, warming his hands before the crackling fire. A slight smile played about his features. "You have spoken of that county with marked interest, of late. Did you not mention an unusual family of sisters who manage their father's estate?"

"The Bennets." Mr Darcy's voice remained measured. "Their situation is most singular."

"Singular enough to have captured your particular notice, it would seem." The Colonel settled into a leather armchair, the wood creaking beneath him. "You spoke with especial attention of one sister - Miss Elizabeth, was it not?"

"Miss Elizabeth Bennet," Mr Darcy acknowledged, his boots making a measured rhythm upon the carpet as he began to pace. "Her situation is rather unconventional for a lady."

"And this causes you disquiet?" The Colonel's shrewd gaze followed his cousin's movement.

"It ought to discompose any gentleman concerned with proper order," Mr Darcy replied. The fire hissed and popped in the grate as he continued. "Five unmarried ladies performing duties better suited to a steward, their financial circumstances uncertain despite their evident capability. Yet they appear wholly unconcerned with securing their futures through advantageous matches."

"Perhaps they have found satisfaction in their mastery of these responsibilities," the Colonel observed. "Not unlike a certain gentleman of my acquaintance who prefers to oversee Pemberley's affairs personally rather than entrusting all to stewards."

Darcy halted his pacing, his reflection barely visible in the darkening window. "You cannot suggest the situations bear comparison."

"Can I not? A devotion to one's duties, a strong sense of responsibility, a preference for direct governance rather than distant supervision." The Colonel's eyes held a knowing glint. "I begin to comprehend why Miss Elizabeth might have drawn your particular regard."

"I fear I have not yet reconciled myself to the notion." Mr Darcy's hand moved of its own accord to the pocket containing Bingley's letter.

The rich aroma of roasted meat wafted through the doorway as Percy, the butler, appeared silently. "Dinner is served, sir."

As they made their way toward the dining room, their footsteps measured against the marble floor, Colonel Fitzwilliam murmured, "You must allow, Darcy, that an unconventional approach might lead to a remarkable outcome. The more customary avenues have, after all, proved unavailing in your case." The

Colonel's eyes glinted with a familiar mischief.

Darcy's stride faltered, a barely perceptible hesitation that only one well acquainted with him might notice. His jaw tightened, his fingers flexing at his sides before he clasped them deliberately behind his back. Fitzwilliam's words settled upon him, unsettling in their truth. They entered the dining room, where Miss Darcy awaited them.

After greeting her cousin and brother as the first course was laid before them, Georgiana spoke. "I hope Mr Bingley's letter contained no ill news."

Colonel Fitzwilliam's eyes sparkled over his wine glass. "Our cousin has been summoned to attend a ball at Netherfield. In Hertfordshire."

"Hertfordshire!" Georgiana's face brightened with interest. "Where you encountered those remarkable ladies who manage their estate? Oh, might I not accompany you, brother? I should dearly love to meet them."

Mr Darcy set down his soup spoon with care. "My dearest, you are not yet out in society. Moreover, the journey would be most taxing at this time of year."

"Will Miss Bingley and Mrs Hurst be present?" Georgiana pressed, her enthusiasm dimming visibly at the mention of the ladies.

"They shall indeed attend their brother's ball," Mr Darcy confirmed, noting his sister's fallen countenance with concern.

"Then perhaps it is for the best," Georgiana murmured, turning her attention to her soup with diminished appetite. The clink of silver on porcelain filled the pause.

Colonel Fitzwilliam glanced between the siblings. "Come now, Darcy, you would deny yourself the pleasure of the ball solely to avoid certain company?. I have rarely seen you so animated as when speaking of your time in Hertfordshire."

Mr Darcy studied the play of candlelight upon his wine glass, his thoughts in turbulent motion. The image of Elizabeth Bennet when he first saw her at the drainage pools rose unbidden in his mind.

"Perhaps," he spoke at length, the words coming slowly, "Miss Elizabeth Bennet and her sisters have a particular sort of capability that might prove interesting. And yet…" He paused, imagining his Uncle Matlock's thunderous expression at the notion of his niece associating with young ladies who tramped about their estate discussing crop rotation and managing livestock. "Their situation has required them to adopt practices that many would consider quite beyond the bounds of propriety for genteel ladies."

"Yet you yourself have praised their understanding," Georgiana ventured, her fingers twisting her napkin. "And you cannot deny, brother, there can be no impropriety in learning to manage one's affairs with intelligence and grace?"

"I expect that Lord and Lady Matlock would disapprove of such connections," Darcy replied, with uncertainty. "They would consider such associations beneath your station, dearest."

"Your Aunt and Uncle," Colonel Fitzwilliam interjected dryly, "would also consider it beneath your station to inspect your own fields rather than relying upon stewards, yet you have always conducted yourself on the principle that direct knowledge of one's responsibilities is essential to diligent management."

The observation struck home. Darcy fell silent. The candlelight caught Georgiana's hopeful expression, like their mother's, and for a moment he allowed himself to imagine his sister finding friendship with the Bennet ladies, gaining confidence through their example of capability and independence. The notion both drew his interest and disturbed his equanimity.

Where so many hours had been spent in convincing himself that he was right, was there not some reason to fear he may be wrong?

Chapter Thirty-One

The Netherfield drive stretched before them, the last of the golden leaves scattering beneath the carriage wheels as they approached the imposing manor house. Darcy glanced toward his sister, noting the rigid set of her shoulders and the way her gloved hands twisted anxiously in her lap.

"If the ball is too uncomfortable, Georgiana," he reminded her gently, "you may retire whenever you wish."

"I shall manage the first half, I think," Georgiana replied, her voice soft but steady. "I shall have plenty of partners dancing only with you, Richard, and Mr Bingley, as Mrs Annesley suggested."

Colonel Fitzwilliam, seated opposite them, offered an encouraging smile. "Your brother frets unnecessarily, Georgiana. You may even find yourself enjoying the experience."

Darcy frowned. "It is not Georgiana's conduct that concerns me."

"Ah," Colonel Fitzwilliam replied knowingly. "You fear the infamous Miss Bingley and her sister will descend upon her like vultures to fresh carrion."

"Richard!" Georgiana admonished, although a smile tugged at her lips.

"I merely describe what I have witnessed," Colonel Fitzwilliam defended with a theatrical shudder. "The way they circle Darcy at social gatherings borders on predatory. I can only imagine their approach to his only sister."

"They are not vultures," Darcy corrected stiffly, although privately he conceded the metaphor had merit. "They are at most,"

"Mushrooms?" Georgiana suggested, with an unexpected flash of wit. "Springing up suddenly wherever society provides fertile ground?"

Darcy's surprise at his sister's comment quickly gave way to amusement. Perhaps this venture would prove beneficial after all. After the Ramsgate incident, glimpses of Georgiana's natural spirit were finally becoming more frequent.

"I had not thought to compare Miss Bingley to a fungus," he said dryly, "but the resemblance is not without merit."

The carriage drew to a halt before Netherfield's entrance, where Bingley himself stood waiting, his countenance betraying both relief and delight.

"Darcy! Miss Darcy! Colonel Fitzwilliam!" he exclaimed as a footman opened the carriage door. "You are most welcome. Most welcome indeed!"

The earnestness of his greeting confirmed Darcy's suspicion that Bingley had feared they might not come after all. His friend's transparent joy was in stark contrast to the calculated smiles that appeared on the faces of the two women who had materialised behind him. Mr Hurst did not trouble himself with social niceties.

"Mr Darcy," Caroline Bingley purred, stepping forward with practised grace. "How delightful that you could join us after all." Her gaze slid to Georgiana, and her smile widened incrementally. "And Miss Darcy! I am delighted to see you again. We are anxious to hear about your most recent adventures."

"Indeed," echoed Louisa Hurst, moving to flank Georgiana's other side as she descended from the carriage. "We have prepared the blue chamber for you—the one with the finest view of the gardens. I selected it myself."

Colonel Fitzwilliam, the last to alight, received a considerably cooler welcome—a cursory nod from both sisters before their attention swivelled back to the Darcys like compass needles finding north.

"You are too kind," Georgiana murmured, her voice barely audible as the sisters closed in. Darcy stepped forward, prepared to intervene, but to his surprise, Georgiana straightened her posture and continued with unexpected firmness.

"However, I must first attend to my studies. My companion has made arrangements for me to continue my work whilst I am from home. Perhaps we might tour the gardens later, if time permits?"

The poised response momentarily silenced both Bingley sisters. Darcy felt a surge of pride as Georgiana turned deliberately toward Bingley.

"Mr Bingley, my brother informs me that the ball room is quite charming. I look forward to seeing it tonight, although I shall attend only the first half of the ball. I hope that meets with your approval?"

"Of course, Miss Darcy! Whatever suits your comfort," Bingley replied with genuine warmth. "I am honoured that you will attend at all."

Miss Bingley's expression flickered between surprise and calculation as she reassessed the situation. Her quarry was behaving with unexpected independence.

"Miss Darcy, you must allow me to introduce you to the few acceptable local families before you retire this evening," she offered, determined to maintain some control over the situation. "As your hostess, I should guide you through the social complexities of the neighbourhood."

"Thank you, Miss Bingley." Georgiana replied with perfect composure, "But as I shall dance only with my brother, my cousin, and Mr Bingley, I believe excessive introductions might prove overwhelming."

Miss Bingley's mouth opened as if to speak, then closed without comment. Darcy suppressed a smile at his sister's elegant evasion.

"Shall we proceed inside?" Bingley suggested, apparently oblivious to the subtle manoeuvring taking place. "Refreshments await in the drawing room, and I am eager to hear news from Town."

As they moved toward the entrance, Colonel Fitzwilliam fell into step beside Darcy.

"It seems your concern was unnecessary," he murmured.

"Our Georgiana has developed quite an effective strategy for managing encroaching mushrooms."

"Indeed," Darcy agreed, watching his sister walk ahead with quiet dignity. "Although I shall remain vigilant, nonetheless."

"Of course you shall," Fitzwilliam replied with a knowing smile. "It is your nature. But tonight, perhaps we might spare some attention for the local young ladies. I look forward to discovering which Miss Bennet has particularly fine eyes."

Darcy felt an unwelcome warmth rise to his face.

Elizabeth stood behind Jane's chair, weaving ribbons through her eldest sister's golden hair with practised fingers. In the mirror's reflection, she caught sight of her mother hovering in the doorway, hands clasped together as she watched her daughters' preparations with bright eyes that held a shadow of something Elizabeth had grown to recognise - the ghost of grander days, when the former Miss Fanny Gardiner had been the belle of Meryton assemblies.

"Mamma, pray give us your opinion," Elizabeth called, noting how her mother's face brightened at being consulted. "Should we not add the pearl pins to Jane's hair? They were Grandmother Gardiner's, were they not?"

"Oh! Yes, indeed." Mrs Bennet moved forward with renewed purpose, selecting the delicate pins from her jewellery box. Her fingers trembled as she placed them. "How well I remember wearing these to my first ball. Your Uncle Gardiner brought them from London…"

The reminiscence was interrupted by Lydia's burst of excitement from the adjoining room. "Lizzy! Jane! You must come see - Kitty has done up my hair exactly like Lady Charlotte's was in last month's fashion plate!"

Elizabeth exchanged a knowing look with Jane. They had spent precious funds on that magazine, knowing how it would delight their youngest sister. Lydia's first ball had become a family project, her obvious joy infectious despite their reduced circumstances. With their limited social circle, there had been no need for ball gowns, and the funds for such were better allocated to the winter seed. Her old white muslin had been skillfully remade with fresh trim, and their grandfather had not demurred at the expense of new dancing slippers for the occasion.

"There," Elizabeth said, securing the last pin in Jane's hair. "You look exactly as a future mistress of Netherfield ought."

"Lizzy," Jane protested, although her cheeks coloured.

Elizabeth's fingers lingered on her sister's shoulders as she studied their reflection. Jane's beauty would always draw admiration, but beneath the perfect exterior lay a mind adept with ledgers and calculations, matched only by her uncommon kindness.

Her eyes met her mother's in the mirror. Mrs Bennet was adjusting the fall of Jane's curls with the expertise born of countless assembly preparations, but her expression held a familiar wistfulness.

"Mamma," Elizabeth said gently, "would you help me with my hair? I cannot achieve any decent effect for this tangle without far more hands."

The suggestion brought an immediate sparkle to Mrs Bennet's eyes. "Of course, my dear. Although perhaps a few flowers—there were some late roses from the last blooms this morning, and they would suit your complexion admirably."

As her mother's familiar hands began working through her dark hair, Elizabeth closed her eyes, listening to Lydia's excited chatter from the next room and Mary's quiet humming as she pressed ribbons nearby. Whatever the evening might bring, this moment of shared anticipation felt precious indeed.

The well-oiled wheels of the aged Longbourn carriage turned smoothly along the drive to Netherfield, a testament to careful maintenance rather than prosperity. Elizabeth watched through the window as the grand house emerged from the winter darkness, its windows blazing with the light of hundreds of candles. Candles enough to light their home for a year. She shook herself from her worries. Her grandfather's parting words echoed in her thoughts: "Show them what the ladies of Longbourn are made of, my dears."

Inside the carriage, Lydia could scarcely contain herself, practically bouncing upon the worn squabs. "Look at all the carriages! And such fine horses!"

"Pray remember your dignity," Mrs Bennet murmured, although her own eyes shone with suppressed excitement. "We may not arrive in the finest equipage, but we shall conduct ourselves with perfect propriety."

Lydia effortfully contained her glee. "Yes, Mamma," she said. Her eyes continued to dart about, but she sat still and proper, her hands beneath her skirt to contain her excitement.

Elizabeth squeezed Jane's hand, noting her sister's careful composure. Jane had begun to tire of Mr Bingley's particular attention during his calls. He had solicited her first dances for the ball, but Jane remained wary. The remainder of the Netherfield party's cool reception of their family had been pointed enough - one brief morning call from the sisters to deliver the invitation, their manner suggesting it was a duty rather than a pleasure.

As they drew up before the entrance, Elizabeth's thoughts turned treacherously to Mr Darcy. Would he have returned from London? The possibility caused an unwelcome flutter in her chest. His interest had at times seemed genuine, his questions perceptive, yet the vast gulf between their situations could not be ignored.

"Come, Lizzy," Jane whispered, breaking into her reverie. "We must not keep the line waiting."

Elizabeth gathered her skirts, accepting the footman's assistance from the carriage. The bright lights and music spilling from Netherfield's windows promised an evening of elegance far removed from their daily concerns. The room was warm and held a slight smoky tang of so many candles burning indoors. She lifted her chin, determined to focus on ensuring Lydia's first ball was memorable and determining whether there was anything to Mr Bingley's tenuous attention to Jane. If her eyes sometimes strayed to the doorway, searching for a tall figure among the arriving guests, she would not acknowledge the reason.

The Netherfield entrance hall glowed with candlelight reflecting off gilt-framed mirrors and polished marble floors. Elizabeth felt Lydia clutch her arm as they joined the line of guests proceeding toward the ballroom.

"Lizzy!" Lydia whispered, although her excitement carried further than intended. "The ceiling paintings! They are like the ones in the book about Italian villas that Grandfather showed us!"

Several heads turned at this architectural observation. Miss Bingley's eyebrows rose sharply, whilst Mrs Hurst pressed her lips together in apparent dismay at such unseemly enthusiasm. "They are indeed, Lyddie. Whose work do they call to mind?"

Lydia paused, examining the paintings intently. "Perhaps Giordano? The colours are so vibrant."

"A sharp observation. Perhaps in England the artist chose tempera, not fresco, to ensure the work in the wetter climate." Elizabeth squeezed her sister's hand. "Shall we greet our hostess?" The sisters proceeded to the gathering of Netherfield residents and Lydia made her carefully rehearsed curtsey, reciting the words of greeting she had memorised.

Mr Bingley, however, broke away from his position near the ballroom entrance to greet them, his eyes finding Jane immediately. "Miss Bennet! Do give your opinion on whether we have arranged the rooms to advantage. Given your exquisite taste, your opinion would be most valuable."

Elizabeth watched Jane's careful response, noting how her sister's composure barely wavered despite Mr Bingley's obvious admiration. The ballroom beyond beckoned, its chandeliers casting rainbow reflections from the recently polished floor. Musicians were tuning their instruments in the gallery above, whilst early arrivals circulated beneath swags of winter greenery.

"Charles," Miss Bingley's voice cut through the pleasant atmosphere with piercing intensity. She touched her brother's arm, speaking in a volume pitched to carry. "You must not monopolise Miss Bennet's attention so immediately. People will form…

expectations." Her gaze swept over Jane's simple muslin gown with merciless assessment.

Elizabeth's cheeks burned with indignation, but before she found her voice, Mrs Hurst added, "Caroline is correct." She adjusted her elaborate turban with one bejewelled hand, her lips curved in what might have been a smile had it contained any warmth. "We cannot expect everyone to understand the correct conduct of such an evening." Her gaze travelled deliberately from Jane's modest pearl pins to Lydia's remade gown, each pause in her inspection calculated to wound. She met her sister's look, their matching expressions of superior disdain perfectly crafted to be visible enough to hurt, yet subtle enough to deny if challenged.

Elizabeth watched Jane's shoulders stiffen with barely a shift, although her sister's collected air never wavered. Their mother had taught them well - a lady's dignity lay in her composure under insult. Still, Elizabeth observed the slight woodenness in Jane's hands as she smoothed her skirts, and the way her sister's eyes lowered momentarily before rising again with determined grace.

Mr Bingley, looking distinctly uncomfortable, began to speak, but Jane forestalled him with a gentle smile. "The ballroom is magnificently arranged, sir. Might I compliment whoever thought to include winter jasmine in the greenery? The scent is particularly lovely."

Elizabeth silently blessed her sister's elegant deflection, although her own fingernails pressed into her palm with suppressed anger. She had never felt their reduced circumstances more keenly than in this moment, standing beneath the glittering chandeliers whilst the Bingley sisters employed their superior situation to wound.

Her eyes swept the room once more, searching without permission for a figure she had come to know well during estate discussions. The crush of arriving guests made it difficult to see clearly, but Mr Darcy's commanding presence was nowhere to be detected. The thought brought an unexpected pang. He was no doubt too busy with his own affairs in London to return to Meryton for a mere ball.

"The musicians are taking their places," she said instead, touching Lydia's arm to redirect her sister's wide-eyed attention from the elaborate decorations. "Shall we find our way to the far side of the room? I believe I see Charlotte Lucas attempting to catch our eye."

Elizabeth walked gratefully to Charlotte's familiar presence, drawing comfort from their shared understanding of neighbourhood matters. She had begun relating her observations of the unpleasant remarks of the hostess when a deep voice interrupted their discussion.

Chapter Thirty-Two

"Miss Elizabeth." Mr Darcy stood before her, his unexpected appearance causing her heart to leap. "If you are not otherwise engaged, might I request your hand for the first set?"

The words seemed to bypass consideration. "You may," she heard herself say, even as her mind raced to make sense of his unexpected arrival and even more unexpected request.

He bowed and withdrew immediately into the crowd, leaving Elizabeth to stare after his retreating figure. Her composure, so recently recovered from the Bingley sisters' barbs, felt thoroughly overthrown.

"I dare say you will find him very agreeable," Charlotte offered, although her expression suggested she understood perfectly well why Elizabeth looked so discomposed.

Elizabeth pressed her fingers to her warm cheeks. The first strains of music called the dancers to their places. Mr Bingley led her sister to the head of the set, whilst Mr Darcy appeared at Elizabeth's elbow to claim her hand. She felt Miss Bingley's sharp gaze follow them as they took their places, noted the lady's lips compress into a thin line as she whispered something to Mrs Hurst.

"How have the new drainage works proved, Miss Elizabeth?" Mr Darcy enquired as they moved through the first figure.

Elizabeth felt a bubble laughter rise in her throat. "Well, but—I cannot talk of drainage in a ballroom; my head is always full of something else." She caught a glimpse of his startled expression as they turned, and added with more composure, "Although I appreciate your interest in our improvements."

"There is a person at the party," he continued after a pause, his expression softening, "who more particularly wishes to be known to you. Will you allow me, or do I ask too much, to introduce my sister to your acquaintance during the evening?"

Elizabeth nearly missed a step in her surprise. "Miss Darcy is here? I should be honoured to make her acquaintance, though…" She hesitated, then continued with careful frankness, "Do you would wish to expose your sister to ladies whose situation requires such extraordinary occupations."

Mr Darcy's countenance grew thoughtful as they turned through the figure. "I have determined," he said at length, speaking with evident care, "that appreciation of one's obligations, and the courage to meet them directly, ought not to be considered improper merely because they depart from common custom. My sister would be well served by the acquaintance of young ladies who demonstrate such admirable capability and independence of mind."

Their hands met briefly in the dance, and Elizabeth felt the warmth in his next words. "Georgiana has been too long constrained by notions of what a young lady ought to be, rather than encouraged to become what she might be."

They turned through another figure before Mr Darcy observed, "I note you and Miss Bennet are the only ones of your sisters dancing this set."

Elizabeth's cheeks warmed. "Our neighbours have grown… particular in their social engagements."

Something flickered in Mr Darcy's expression—dismay, Elizabeth thought—though his face remained composed. He made no immediate reply, but as the dance concluded, he led her back to her sister Jane, then turned to her with evident purpose.

"Miss Elizabeth, Miss Bennet, my cousin Colonel Fitzwilliam has accompanied us this evening, along with my sister. Might I present them to you?"

The Colonel, who had been hovering nearby with ill-concealed amusement at his cousin's discomfort, stepped forward and executed a graceful bow. "Miss Elizabeth, I have heard much of your family's admirable management of Longbourn."

Jane turned at the sound of his voice and offered a graceful curtsy. The Colonel's bow was as correct as it was attentive, and when their eyes met, his expression softened. Elizabeth, observing with a sister's intuition, noted the flicker of something quietly appreciative in her sister's glance.

"Miss Bennet," Colonel Fitzwilliam said with warmth. "It is a pleasure to make your acquaintance."

"And this," Mr Darcy continued, his manner showing uncharacteristic uncertainty as he gestured to a tall, slender, fair-haired girl at his side, "is my sister, Miss Darcy. Georgiana, Miss Elizabeth has expressed an earnest wish to make your acquaintance."

Miss Darcy's curtsy was graceful, if anxious. "I am delighted to meet you, Miss Elizabeth. My brother speaks most highly of your family."

Elizabeth watched as Mr Darcy then moved to speak quietly with Mr Bingley. Within moments, the pattern of the evening shifted. Mr Darcy led his sister to the floor. Mr Bingley approached Kitty with a bow, whilst Colonel Fitzwilliam claimed Mary's hand for the set. Her reddened cheeks and wide eyes reflected her shock at being singled out.

Each set brought a fresh partnership. Mr Darcy danced with Kitty, his grave attention to her conversation causing her nervous laugh to settle into something more composed. Mr Bingley's evident delight in Jane's company surprised no one, but his cheerful solicitude to Lydia during their set drew notice from the local gentry. Colonel Fitzwilliam's skilled leading made Mary's precise steps appear more graceful. Jane, graceful and composed as ever, conversed amiably with all, yet her gaze wandered often—no more than a heartbeat's glance—toward the Colonel. Something in his bearing—so steady, so unassuming—fit a different part of her nature than Mr Bingley's ever-ready enthusiasm. Bingley was charming, certainly, but often seemed to take his cue from those around him. The Colonel, by contrast, gave the impression of a man who moved according to inner principles.

Miss Bingley's expression grew increasingly sour as she

observed this determined campaign, particularly when the Colonel claimed Elizabeth for a set instead of seeking her own company. She stalked toward her brother to register her displeasure, however he simply encouraged her to "enjoy the evening."

Colonel Fitzwilliam's manner was all easy charm, yet his questions held a peculiar pointedness.

"You enjoy estate management, I collect? And my cousin has been most helpful in discussing improvements?"

"Mr Darcy has shown great understanding of our situation," Elizabeth replied.

"Yes, he appears to have developed quite an interest in Hertfordshire's agricultural methods," the Colonel observed with a meaningful look. "Although perhaps it is not only the agriculture that interests him."

Elizabeth was unable to make a comfortable reply to this observation, although she wondered at the Colonel's evident amusement - and at the searching quality of his gaze.

After dancing with Elizabeth, the Colonel claimed Mrs Bennet's hand.

"My dear lady, I have yet to see you stand up this evening. That cannot be borne. Why, you are as handsome as any of your daughters!"

Elizabeth smiled and her mother's eyes sparkled like a girl's.

"Such a distinguished air," Mrs Bennet confided when she returned to Elizabeth, fanning herself. "It puts me in mind of Captain Morris, who was stationed in Meryton when I was but seventeen. I thought he would be the one for me, but he went off to another assignment with nary a goodbye. Of course, your father was by far more eligible…"

Elizabeth was struck by how little she knew of her parents' courtship, and their youth. Before she could take up the topic, Mr Bingley begged her hand for the next set. None of the Bennet ladies lacked partners that evening. The notice taken of them by the Netherfield gentlemen encouraged the local lads to seek out the lovely if unconventional Bennet daughters.

As the evening drew on, Mrs Bennet engaged in animated conversation with a distinguished gentleman Elizabeth recognised as Mr Freeman, a widower who owned a comfortable estate north of Meryton. His grey hair was still thick, and although he walked with a slight limp—the result of an old riding accident, it was said—he carried himself with the confident ease of a man accustomed to good society. At two and fifty, he was perhaps a decade older than Mrs Bennet, but his attentive posture and ready smile spoke of a man not yet resigned to solitude.

"Our mother seems well acquainted with Mr Freeman," Jane observed quietly as they gathered their things.

"They were in conversation for nearly half an hour," Elizabeth replied. "I had not realised they were such particular friends."

Mrs Bennet approached them then, her cheeks flushed pleasantly. "Girls, Mr Freeman frequently rides past Longbourn on his way to Meryton. He serves as a magistrate, you know, and has considerable influence over local affairs."

"How fortunate," Jane remarked with a gentle smile.

"He has promised to accompany our carriage on our return home," Mrs Bennet added, adjusting her shawl with care. "He mentioned something about ensuring we arrive safely, with the roads being what they are after the recent rains."

"Such a sensible man," Mrs Bennet continued. "Did you know he has improved the chimneys at Freeman Manor? And he keeps no less than four excellent horses. He was telling me about the new milliner's shop opening in Meryton next week—as a magistrate, he approves all such establishments."

Elizabeth exchanged a glance with Jane as their mother continued to enumerate Mr Freeman's various virtues. There was a lightness to Mrs Bennet's manner that Elizabeth had not observed in some time—a spark of something beyond practicality and occasional fretting.

"He is calling on your grandfather tomorrow to discuss some matter of local governance," Mrs Bennet added with studied casualness. "I expect I shall need to receive him, as your grandfather finds calls taxing."

The pattern of the country dance wove Mary and Mr Fairfield together and apart, their conversation fragmenting and reforming with each figure. Mr Fairfield's scholarly demeanour seemed somehow more pronounced in evening dress rather than lessened by it.

"I had hoped - that is, I wondered if you might have considered my observations regarding the gypsum trials?" His words tumbled out during their first turn, his natural reserve giving way to evident discomposure.

"Indeed, I had given them considerable thought," Mary replied, her gravity softening at his earnestness. "Perhaps, however, a ball is not the appropriate venue for such discussions."

"Oh! Of course. Most inappropriate. I should speak of more conventional matters." He managed the next figure with more attention to his feet than his partner.

The dance brought them together again. "Miss Bennet, I find myself quite incapable of maintaining the expected social pleasantries when faced with the opportunity for meaningful discourse."

"A failing we appear to share, Mr Fairfield." They joined hands in the next movement.

"You are remarkably generous to my social insufficiency." His genuine smile transformed his features. "Rarely have I found a companion with such understanding."

"Understanding seems a more worthy pursuit than mere social grace." Mary surprised herself with the admission.

They separated for the figure, his response lost to distance. When they rejoined, his eyes held an earnest intensity. "I should like to continue our discussions. About soil composition, naturally."

"Naturally," Mary agreed, her gravity warming. "And perhaps we might occasionally venture into other topics of mutual interest."

His step faltered. "I should like that very much. If you would permit such academic exploration." The expression in his dark eyes was unlike any Mary Bennet had seen before in the face of a gentleman. It put her in mind of the admiring gazes so often directed at her sister, Jane, yet somehow more…. something.

As the dance drew to a close, Mary blushed under Mr Fairfield's intense regard. She cleared her throat and attempted to bring them back to conversation. "I believe careful study of any worthwhile subject requires dedication."

His bow was somewhat ungraceful, but his smile illuminated his entire countenance. "Then I look forward to our future scholarly exchanges, Miss Bennet."

Mary discovered, to her considerable pleasure, that the prospect of such exchanges made a ball seem rather less frivolous than expected.

"I own, Miss Bennet." He offered her a glass of punch. "I hoped to continue our discussion of soil composition at a ball. I feared that you might consider such topics unsuitable for the occasion."

"For some, it might be, but I am not an enthusiast of frivolity. While others discuss the weather, we might as well discuss something of substance. Your theories regarding gypsum application, for instance, require further examination."

"Do they indeed?" His green eyes sparkled. "How fortunate that this evening affords us several minutes for scholarly debate."

"Although perhaps not long enough for a thorough analysis of your methodology. I noted several questionable assumptions in your last presentation."

"Did you?" He guided her towards a group of chairs near the balcony, his touch perfectly correct yet somehow warming through her glove. "I should like to hear whatever you wish to challenge."

Mary replied, her spirits rising. "It is quite scientific of you to welcome rigorous examination of your preconceptions."

"Do you not find that some preconceptions become quite impossible to maintain upon closer study?."

"Certainly. Such technical discussions might prove tedious to the general company," she demurred.

"I say let the general company do as they please. I find nothing tedious about intellectual discourse with a knowledgeable partner." The warmth in his voice made Mary's cheeks heat traitorously. "Perhaps you might share your recent findings regarding soil composition?"

"You wish to discuss soil now, Mr Fairfield?"

"I wish to discuss whatever interests you, Miss Bennet." The directness of his gaze made her breath catch. "Your evident expertise in agricultural chemistry rather enhances the appeal of the topic." The warmth of his smile indicated an interest in a rather different sort of chemistry.

Mary was quite unable to formulate a suitably serious response.

Mr Blackwood, with a timing that suggested some forethought, reached Kitty just as the set began. His fair hair was disordered, and his cravat bore the mark of one who had tied it more in haste than confidence, as though he had wrestled it into submission only moments before.

"Miss Bennet," he said with a quick bow, "might I claim this set, if you are not otherwise engaged?"

Kitty glanced toward the dance floor, where Lydia was already leading a lively reel with Captain Morris, and Mary sat contentedly near the musicians, conversing with Mr Fairfield.

"You may," she said with a small smile, placing her hand in his.

As they joined the line, Mr Blackwood fumbled for a conversational opening.

"I—I much enjoyed the arrangement of winter jasmine in the garlands. Remarkably aromatic."

"It is," Kitty agreed. "It is used in soothing infusions, did you know? We've a bit of it growing near the old stone wall at

Longbourn—Grandfather says the scent is good for sleep, so I dry some with the lavender."

"Useful knowledge," he said seriously. "I have been reading Culpeper's Herbal. It is outdated, but fascinating. Did you know marjoram was once thought to ease melancholy?"

"I've used it in headache tinctures," Kitty said, pleasantly surprised. "And I add a bit to teas when Lydia is fretful, though she never notices."

They separated briefly in the figure, then rejoined, his eyes alight with curiosity.

"I would hear more about your preparations—if you would not find it tiresome."

"Not at all," she said, cheeks warming. "It is rare anyone asks."

Later that evening, Mr Blackwood was not the only gentleman to claim Kitty's hand. She danced once with Lieutenant Carter, who complimented her clever retort to Miss Prentice's nonsense about brocade, and once with Mr Turner, the curate's nephew, who proved unable to distinguish between sarcasm and sincerity, but tried earnestly to keep up.

But it was Mr Blackwood who returned near the end of the evening, shyly asking if she might identify the plant used in the green ribbons along the mantelpiece. She smiled and leant closer to inspect it.

"Not laurel," she murmured. "Bay. Slightly different leaf. Bay soothes the stomach, but I would not hang it too near a fire—it smells bitter when scorched."

He looked at her as though she had recited poetry.

"Most instructive," he said quietly. "Miss Bennet… might I call one afternoon? I have a question about pennyroyal."

Kitty tried not to grin. "If it is for a tisane, you had best ask my grandfather. But if it is about calming restlessness in dogs or younger sisters, I've had some success."

His answering laugh was warm and genuine—and Kitty felt like something more than someone's younger sister.

Chapter Thirty-Three

As the guests began to take their leave, Colonel Fitzwilliam made his way to where Jane sat, having just resumed her place beside Elizabeth with a soft exhale and a hand resting lightly on her knee. She had danced more than she had in years, and though her countenance remained equable, there was a subtle weariness about her posture.

The Colonel paused before her with a warm smile. "I trust," he said, in a tone pitched for her ear alone, "that this evening has not overtaxed your strength. I believe I detected your favouring your left ankle during our last set."

Jane blinked in mild surprise, then smiled. "Only a little stiffness. I should not have accepted that final reel, perhaps."

"I am glad you did," he said simply, with no trace of gallantry. "Some partners make one forget the room."

There was a moment's pause—not awkward, but quiet, as though something meaningful had been exchanged and need not be named.

From across the room came the cheerful call of another departing guest, and Jane turned her head. A moment ago, Mr Bingley had taken his leave with warm thanks to the family and a genial wave to the assembled company, his gaze skipping lightly over them all.

The Colonel bowed over her hand. "Miss Bennet," he said, his expression composed yet curiously intent, "it has been an honour."

He bowed again, more deeply than the occasion strictly required, then turned away without further flourish, leaving Jane with the faintest crease between her brows and a thoughtful look in her eyes.

The night air had grown sharp with frost as they awaited their carriage, their breath forming delicate clouds in the lamplight. Lydia was quite exhausted, managing naught but the occasional sigh of "Lord, how tired I am!"—punctuated by a most unbecoming yawn. The rustle of silk and the scratch of boots on gravel accompanied the servants bustling about, returning cloaks and summoning carriages, whilst the last strains of the orchestra floated out from Netherfield's brightly lit windows.

Mrs Bennet gathered her five daughters, their ball slippers whispering against the stone steps as they approached Miss Bingley and Mrs Hurst to offer their gratitude and take their leave. Mr Bingley, who had lingered a moment behind to exchange a few last pleasantries, now joined his sisters.

Mrs Bennet expressed her earnest wish to receive the entire party at Longbourn, assuring Mr Bingley what pleasure it would give them all were he to join them for a family dinner at his convenience. Whilst Mr Bingley accepted with all his customary warmth, Miss Bingley could scarce conceal her profound distaste for such a prospect.

Upon the announcement of the Bennet carriage, Mrs Bennet executed a graceful curtsey to their hosts. "We are most grateful for your generous hospitality at this splendid ball." With these words, she beckoned to her daughters, who each performed their own elegant curtsey and murmured expressions of gratitude. Mr Bingley's gaze lingered upon Jane until the subsequent departing party commanded his attention.

Mr Freeman appeared to hand Mrs Bennet into the Bennet carriage. "I look forward to our continued discussion of the Meryton Assembly rooms, Mrs Bennet. Your suggestions for improvements were most insightful."

"Oh! Well, I have always thought that with just a few changes, they might be made much more comfortable," Mrs Bennet replied.

"Indeed, they might," Mr Freeman agreed, his eyes crinkling

warmly at the corners. "Perhaps we might continue our discussion when next we meet."

"That would be most pleasant," Mrs Bennet replied, settling her skirts with a blush.

Inside the carriage, the familiar leather creaked beneath them as they settled into their seats, the faint scent of lavender and warm wool filling the confined space. The rhythmic clop of hooves and gentle sway of the carriage gradually lulled the younger girls toward sleep. After a moment of silence broken only by the soft jingle of the harness, a quiet sigh could be heard from Jane.

"Is that a happy sigh, my dear girl?" Mrs Bennet asked.

Jane put her gloved hands to her face, cooling her reddening cheeks.

"It was a magical evening," Jane said. "Everything was so beautiful."

Mrs Bennet smiled in the darkness of the carriage. "And made more beautiful by certain attentions, I think." Her voice held a quiet satisfaction. As the carriage pulled away, Elizabeth watched her mother's profile in the faint moonlight. There was something seemingly youthful in her expression, a glimpse of the handsome, spirited young woman she must once have been, before years of worry over five daughters' futures and a husband's early demise had etched permanent lines of anxiety around her eyes.

"Mr Freeman seems a most agreeable gentleman," Elizabeth ventured.

"Oh, he is merely civil," Mrs Bennet replied, although her smile brightened. "Do you not think he is rather handsome, for a man of his age?"

Jane and Elizabeth exchanged a look, brows raised and suppressed smiles.

"Mr Bingley danced with Jane twice," Kitty reported with sisterly observation. "And looked quite put out when he could not claim a third."

"Whilst Mr Darcy danced with Elizabeth twice," Mary added.

Elizabeth shifted on her seat, grateful for the darkness that hid her expression. "Mr Darcy was being courteous to a neighbour with whom he shares business concerns."

"Business concerns do not customarily involve such constant gazes across the ballroom," Lydia observed sleepily, then yawned again. "Lord, what a night! And did you see how Lady Lucas asked Jane about the new method of storing root vegetables? As though we were any other ladies discussing household matters!"

"Better than that," Elizabeth said, deliberately steering the conversation away from Mr Darcy's gazes, constant or otherwise. "She asked as though she genuinely wished to learn. How far we have come from the days of whispers behind fans about 'those poor Bennet girls, reduced to common labour.'"

"Success breeds acceptance," Mrs Bennet said simply. "Our years of proving ourselves has done what no amount of social manoeuvring could have achieved."

Elizabeth nodded in the darkness, although her thoughts strayed treacherously to the feeling of Mr Darcy's hand clasping hers during their dance, the surprising warmth in his eyes when she had made him laugh.

"Jane," Kitty's voice broke through her reverie, "do you think Mr Bingley might really purchase Netherfield?"

"I could not say," Jane's voice was soft but steady.

"I hope his sister does not remain with him if he does," Lydia muttered. "Did you see her face when Mrs Long complimented our wool yields? As though discussing sheep might somehow taint her pumpkin silk skirts!"

"Miss Bingley's opinion matters little," Mrs Bennet said firmly. "What matters is that the neighbourhood has accepted us on our own terms."

Their breath frosting the carriage glass, creating small clear patches that revealed glimpses of silvered moonlit fields. The carriage wheels crunched over the familiar roads toward Longbourn whilst inside, six ladies dozed or dreamt, their skirts rustling with each gentle sway. Elizabeth alone remained fully awake, watching the shadowed landscape pass by and trying very hard not to remember

Mr Darcy as he said "Remarkable," his deep voice carrying that word across the candlelit ballroom as though it were the highest of compliments.

The morning after the Netherfield ball dawned clear and crisp, with autumn sunlight filtering through the trees lining the lane to Longbourn. Colonel Fitzwilliam rode at a measured pace, having contrived a reason to visit the estate before his imminent departure for London. He had mentioned to his cousin an interest in observing some of the agricultural improvements discussed during the ball, and Darcy, with a knowing glance, had made no objection to his plan.

"You seem rather eager this morning, Fitzwilliam," Darcy observed, as his cousin checked his pocket watch for the third time whilst they waited for their horses to be brought round.

"Merely conscious of the time, Darcy," the Colonel replied with studied casualness. "If we are to observe Longbourn's agricultural innovations and I to return to London as required, we should depart promptly."

As they rode through Netherfield's grounds and onto the lane leading toward Longbourn, Colonel Fitzwilliam fidgeted with his riding gloves. The military man who had faced Napoleon's forces with unwavering composure appeared distinctly unsettled by the prospect of a morning call.

"I believe you wished to observe Mr Bennet's methods," Darcy said, taking pity on his cousin. "Something about adapting military supply principles to agricultural transport?"

The Colonel's posture relaxed. "Indeed. Sir William spoke of an innovative approach to moving harvested grain during inclement weather. As you know, similar challenges arise when repositioning provisions for troops during the rainy season."

"And Miss Bennet seemed knowledgeable in these matters?" Darcy enquired, unable to resist the gentle provocation.

His cousin shot him a sharp glance. "Distressingly so," he

said, his smile wry. "I had prepared a rather clever observation on grain storage—but Miss Bennet had already arrived at it and improved upon it besides."

Mr Hill announced them in the drawing room.

"Mr Darcy, Colonel Fitzwilliam," Elizabeth said, recovering quickly as she curtseyed. "This is an unexpected pleasure."

Darcy bowed formally. "Miss Bennet, Miss Elizabeth. Kindly forgive the intrusion. My cousin expressed interest in meeting your grandfather before his departure."

"Mr Bennet is in his study upstairs, sir," she replied. "Shall I inform him of your arrival?"

"Please do not disturb him on our account," Darcy replied, uncomfortable with the prospect of imposing upon the elderly gentleman.

"I would be most interested to learn of your transport approach," the Colonel replied, with restrained courtesy. Only the slight straightening of his posture betrayed any particular interest.

Elizabeth glanced toward the ceiling. "I think we might join Grandfather? He has been reviewing the account books. I am certain he would welcome the interruption."

"If it would not inconvenience him," Darcy said.

Whilst a servant was despatched to inform Mr Bennet of their visitors, the conversation turned to general topics—the previous evening's ball, the unseasonably fine weather, and the Bennets' improvements to Longbourn. Darcy noted that whilst his cousin maintained perfect composure throughout, his gaze returned to Jane with frequency.

They were invited upstairs to the study where Mr Bennet sat with a ledger book in his lap. The smell of old paper and wood smoke thickened the air.

"Mr Darcy," he said. "A pleasure to welcome you to Longbourn."

After introductions and initial pleasantries, Elizabeth mentioned their remarks on the estate's improvements.

"Perhaps you might indulge me by examining some plans I

have been considering? I should value the perspective of gentlemen with your experience."

Mr Bennet unrolled several maps across a table. As he explained his proposed modifications to field usage, the practical ingenuity displayed intrigued Darcy.

"These arrangements seem quite innovative," Darcy observed, studying the notations in a feminine hand along the margins.

"Jane's work," Mr Bennet said with quiet pride. "She has a remarkable head for such matters."

Darcy glanced at Miss Bennet, who received this praise with characteristic modesty. His cousin, he noted, was examining the lady more than the calculations.

"This approach to the slope gradient is particularly effective," the Colonel commented. "It reminds me of methods I observed in northern Spain for managing seasonal flooding."

"Does it indeed?" Jane enquired; her interest evident although her demeanour remained perfectly composed. "I should be interested to hear more of those methods."

As the Colonel described the Spanish techniques, Darcy observed nothing out of the ordinary in their interaction—a shared intellectual engagement that, in its very restraint, seemed more significant than more obvious forms of flirtation. Jane's questions were pertinent and thoughtful, whilst his cousin's responses, although technically precise, carried an underlying attentiveness that Darcy had rarely observed in his interactions with other young ladies.

Elizabeth stood just apart. When she caught Darcy's gaze, he found close to assessment—as though she were reevaluating previous conclusions.

"Colonel," Mr Bennet said, his eyes twinkling. "Jane has a natural affinity for organisation, whilst Elizabeth possesses an innovative spirit. Between them, they've implemented several improvements that have increased Longbourn's yield considerably. When my son passed, with the prospect of Mr Collins taking over everything. I may have guided them, but it was their determination to preserve Longbourn that truly transformed this estate."

"I had not realised their involvement was so extensive," the Colonel said, evidently impressed.

Mr Bennet gestured to the window. "Do you see the south field there? That drainage works was Elizabeth's design, adapting principles from extensive research. And the new rotation plan in the western plots was Jane's idea, after consulting with neighbouring farmers."

"I've seen regiments run with less order," the Colonel said, half-smiling.

"Many gentlemen farmers would be proud of such innovations," Darcy added, with genuine admiration.

"Indeed," Mr Bennet agreed. "Although not all would acknowledge their source." He turned to face the Colonel directly. "You have served extensively in the Peninsula, I understand?"

"Yes, sir. For several years."

"Do you reckon our theories on supply management might have applications in military contexts?"

Darcy's cousin engaged enthusiastically on the topic, explaining principles of resource allocation that might be applied to estate management. He had rarely seen Fitzwilliam so animated in conversation outside military circles, and the old gentleman matched him point for point with practical insights gained through years of agricultural experimentation.

Darcy caught Elizabeth watching the exchange with a perceptive smile.

"Your cousin and my grandfather have a surprising affinity." she said quietly.

"No doubt," Darcy replied. "The company at Longbourn seems to inspire particular interest."

When they finally took their leave, the morning had stretched into afternoon. Darcy noted the respectful handclasp between his cousin and Mr Bennet, and the genuine regard that had developed between them.

"It has been a pleasure, gentlemen," Mr Bennet said.

"Consider Longbourn open to you during your stay in Hertfordshire."

As they mounted their horses, Jane and Elizabeth came to the doorway. The Colonel's glance toward Jane was brief but appreciative.

Darcy noted his cousin's thoughtful expression.

"You found the visit instructive?" he enquired at last.

"In ways I had not anticipated," the Colonel admitted. "The Bennet family manages their estate quite capably."

"Indeed," Darcy agreed.

As Netherfield came into view, the Colonel spoke again. "I find myself quite intrigued by Longbourn."

Darcy responded with a slight dip of his head, uncertain whether his cousin referred to estate management or to something more personal.

Chapter Thirty-Four

The chill that lingered in the autumn air did not deter young ladies from walking out. Lydia had insisted upon showing Miss Darcy the path to Oakham Mount, declaring it "the only view worth seeing in all of Hertfordshire—unless one counts Lieutenant Sanderson in his dress uniform," which had made Kitty dissolve into giggles and even coaxed a blush from the reserved Miss Darcy.

Georgiana Darcy had proved a revelation to the Bennet sisters. Although painfully shy upon first acquaintance, she had gradually revealed a quiet wit and genuine sweetness that endeared her to even the most boisterous of the family. Her visit to Netherfield alongside her brother had initially caused a stir in the neighbourhood, but the girl's modest demeanour had quickly dispelled any accusations of pride or pretension.

"I declare, Miss Darcy, that you play so beautifully," Lydia commented as they walked the path toward Meryton. "I have never been patient enough for such an accomplishment."

"Thank you," Georgiana replied. "Although I thought Miss Mary's performance most accomplished as well."

"Mary has improved tremendously," Kitty agreed. "She manages to practise even though she has so many other duties."

"Indeed," Lydia nodded. "Although I must say, Miss Darcy, your playing has a particular sensitivity. Mary plays with technical skill, but your music tells a story."

Georgiana's laugh was unexpected and delightful. "My masters always insisted that technical proficiency without emotion was simply noise."

"Well said," Lydia agreed. "Now, shall we take the path

through town? We might refresh ourselves at the confectioners. Mrs Wilson has just received a shipment of candied fruit that is divine."

The three turned toward Meryton, their conversation flowing easily between discussions of the ball, the dances, and the company. Lydia was in the midst of a lively recounting of their disastrous attempt at a quadrille when they rounded the corner onto the main street of Meryton.

"And then I stepped directly on poor Charlotte's—"

Lydia broke off as she felt Georgiana suddenly stiffen beside her. The girl had gone deathly pale, her eyes fixed on a point down the street.

Following her gaze, Lydia spotted the familiar figure of Mr Wickham emerging from the haberdasher's shop, his red coat bright against the grey stone buildings. He had not yet noticed them.

"Miss Darcy?" Lydia asked quietly. "Are you unwell?"

Georgiana's breathing had quickened, her gloved hand clutching convulsively at her companion's sleeve. "I—I think I should return to Netherfield," she whispered.

Kitty looked between them in confusion. "Whatever is the matter?"

With unexpected quickness, Lydia guided Georgiana to a stone bench outside the apothecary's shop. "Sit a moment," she instructed, her exuberance replaced by gentle authority. "Kitty, see if Mr Jones has any smelling salts or lavender water."

As Kitty hurried inside, Lydia positioned herself to shield Georgiana from the street view. "It is Mr Wickham who distresses you," she stated rather than asked.

Georgiana's wide eyes flew to Lydia's face. "How did you—"

"You went pale as a ghost the moment he appeared," Lydia said matter-of-factly. "And he is the only unfamiliar gentleman in view." She hesitated, then added more gently, "You need not tell me anything, Miss Darcy. But I assure you, whatever history lies between you, that man is not worth a moment's distress."

A tear slipped down Georgiana's cheek. "You know him?"

"Unfortunately," Lydia replied with uncharacteristic grimness.

"He has made himself known in Meryton these past weeks, although he conspicuously avoided the ball last night. I suppose your brother's presence proved discouraging."

Georgiana dabbed at her eyes with a handkerchief. "He, we," She struggled visibly.

"As I said, you need not explain," Lydia assured her. "I have taken his measure quite thoroughly and found him wanting in every aspect that matters."

Kitty returned with a small vial of lavender water, confusion still evident on her face. "What has happened?"

"Mr Wickham," Lydia said simply, "Miss Darcy is acquainted with that scoundrel. Did you know, Miss Darcy, that he was pursuing Mary King with a desperation that would be comical if it were not so transparent? All because the poor girl inherited ten thousand pounds."

Georgiana looked up, surprise momentarily displacing her distress.

"Indeed," Lydia continued conversationally as Georgiana wet a handkerchief with the lavender water and pressed it to her temples. "Although I hear Miss King has been spirited away to Liverpool by her aunt. Most disappointing for Mr Wickham's creditors, I imagine."

"Creditors?" Kitty asked.

"Oh yes," Lydia nodded sagely. "Mr Denny let slip that our gallant lieutenant owes money to half the tradesmen in Meryton. Apparently, his charm extends only so far when the bills come due."

A flicker of relief crossed Georgiana's features. "He always lived beyond his means," she offered hesitantly.

"A man of grand aspirations and minuscule accomplishments," Lydia agreed. "All flash and no substance, as my grandfather would say. Like a peacock who has borrowed his feathers from the pawnbroker—and failed to make the payments."

Georgiana's lips twitched. "He always claimed great things would come his way."

"And so, they do," Lydia nodded sagely. "Bills, primarily. Followed by creditors. Then disappointment. A most reliable procession."

"He once lived near Pemberley," Georgiana whispered.

Lydia's eyes flashed with sudden understanding, but she kept her tone even. "Did he indeed? How convenient for him."

"My brother," Georgiana began, then stopped.

"You need say nothing," Lydia finished for her. "For Mr Wickham's character speaks loudly enough without assistance."

Just then, Wickham himself glanced in their direction. His initial expression of idle curiosity transformed rapidly—first to recognition, then to unmistakable calculation as his gaze landed on Georgiana. A slow smile spread across his handsome features, and he changed course to approach them.

"Oh dear," Kitty murmured. "He's coming this way."

"Excellent," Lydia declared with unexpected relish. "Miss Darcy, you need do nothing but stay seated. I shall handle Mr Wickham."

Georgiana looked terrified, but something in Lydia's confident manner steadied her. She nodded.

Wickham was halfway across the street when Lydia rose and stepped forward, the late autumn wind lifting the hem of her cloak like the banner of a knight, placing herself between him and Georgiana. His step faltered momentarily.

"Mr Wickham," Lydia called, her voice carrying clearly. "How extraordinary to see you abroad so early. I had understood from Mr Denny that you were quite indisposed after last night's card game at the tavern. What was it he said? Ah yes—'deeper in debt than the ocean is deep and likely to sink.' Such colourful language our officers employ."

Wickham stopped abruptly, his practised smile slipping. "Miss Lydia," he acknowledged stiffly. His eyes darted past her to where Georgiana sat. "I see you have company."

"Indeed," Lydia replied brightly. "Miss Darcy has been kind enough to grace Hertfordshire with her presence. Such an accomplished young lady—and so well-connected. Her cousin the Colonel has come to Meryton as well. He is particularly attentive to her welfare. Quite ferocious in his protection, one might say." She leant forward as if sharing a confidence. "I have heard he once challenged a man to a duel for just looking at her improperly. Terribly mediaeval, but what can one expect from such ancient family lines? The Fitzwilliams have been guarding their treasure since the Conquest, I believe."

Kitty's eyes widened at this embellishment, but she managed to nod solemnly. "Most fearsome when provoked, the Colonel. The stare of a hawk and the memory of an elephant."

"An interesting combination of animals," Lydia mused. "Although effective in its imagery."

At the mention of Colonel Fitzwilliam, Wickham's expression soured visibly. "I regret I cannot stay to make Miss Darcy's acquaintance. I have a prior engagement."

"How disappointing," Lydia remarked, her lifted brow suggesting it was anything but. "Although curious. A moment ago, you seemed most determined to approach us. Perhaps you recognised Miss Darcy and wished to renew your acquaintance? Although I cannot think why, unless you are collecting rejections from every family in England."

Wickham's jaw tightened. "Another time, perhaps."

"I think not," Lydia said pleasantly. "Miss Darcy's circle is rather selective, you understand. Quality over quantity, as they say. And you, Mr Wickham, have been weighed, measured, and found remarkably lightweight."

A dull flush crept up Wickham's neck. "You seem to have formed quite an opinion of me, Miss Lydia."

"An informed one," she agreed cheerfully. "Based on observation and evidence. I find it far more reliable than charm and empty promises."

Wickham's handsome face hardened. "Good day, Miss Lydia." He turned sharply on his heel and strode away in the opposite direction, his back rigid with suppressed anger. Wickham's boots scuffed clumsily against the cobbles.

Lydia watched him go, then turned back to her companions

with a satisfied expression. "My goodness," she declared, loud enough for passersby to hear, "I had no idea militia men were so easily frightened. Three girls of sixteen and seventeen, and he retreats as though facing Napoleon himself! Perhaps that explains why the French have been so successful—they may have discovered that deploying young ladies is far more effective than cannon fire."

A strangled sound escaped Georgiana. For a horrified moment, Lydia thought she had upset the shy girl further—until she realised that Miss Darcy was struggling to contain laughter.

"I—I'm sorry," Georgiana gasped, her eyes dancing despite the lingering traces of tears. "But his expression when you said he was 'remarkably lightweight'—"

"Like a countess addressing a slug," Kitty supplied, now giggling herself. "And did you see his face when you mentioned Colonel Fitzwilliam and duels? I thought he might actually faint!"

"Well," Lydia sniffed with mock hauteur, adjusting an imaginary tiara, "one must occasionally remind certain gentlemen of their proper place. Which, in Mr Wickham's case, appears to be as far from respectable society as possible. Perhaps Australia would be sufficient distance? I hear they are accepting volunteers."

Georgiana's laughter subsided into hiccups. "Thank you," she said simply.

Lydia waved away the gratitude. "No thanks necessary. I've made it something of a personal mission to deflate Mr Wickham's pretensions wherever possible. Most entertaining pastime."

As they resumed their walk, Georgiana fell into step beside Lydia. "My brother was right about you," she said quietly.

"Was he?" Lydia asked, surprised. "I was under the impression Mr Darcy found all of us Bennet sisters quite beneath his notice, save perhaps Jane and Lizzy."

Georgiana shook her head. "Not at all. He said there was more to you than met the eye. That beneath the high spirits was a shrewd observer who would make a formidable ally or opponent."

Lydia blinked, genuinely taken aback. "Well," she said after a moment, "perhaps there is more to your brother than meets the eye as well."

Linking arms with both Kitty and Georgiana, Lydia led them toward the confectioner's shop, her natural vivacity returning in full force. "Now then, we simply must try Mrs Wilson's candied orange peel. And what news of London society, Miss Darcy. Is it true that Lady Jersey's winter ball is the most coveted invitation of the season? Kitty has been reading about it in the papers for weeks."

Behind them, the retreat of a red coat down a side alley went unremarked upon, save by a group of officers who observed the exchange with poorly concealed amusement.

"Good morning, ladies," Captain Morris called as they passed. "I see Mr Wickham has remembered an urgent appointment elsewhere. Most conscientious of him."

"Most cowardly, you mean," Denny muttered, tipping his hat to the young women. "Bested again by Miss Lydia. The man will never live it down."

"Good," Morris replied quietly. "Some lessons are best learnt publicly. Although I fear Mr Wickham may require several more volumes of instruction before the lesson takes hold."

"The problem with teaching Wickham anything," added Lieutenant Carter as he joined them, "is that his self-regard leaves so little room for his brain to operate."

"Two fine young men," Mr Bennet remarked to his granddaughters. "The Colonel possessed a mind as disciplined as his manner."

"And remarkably free of the pretensions one might expect from the son of an earl," Elizabeth added with a sidelong glance at her sister.

Jane's slight flush that coloured her cheeks told its own story.

"Indeed," was all she said, although her eyes followed the Colonel's figure until he disappeared from view.

"Shall we resume our work? I suspect that will be our one

and only visit from the son of an earl." Elizabeth said briskly.

Chapter Thirty-Five

Mr Collins paced the narrow confines of his study at Hunsford, each turn marked by the rustle of increasingly desperate correspondence from Lady Catherine. His latest attempt to document mismanagement at Longbourn had met with polite scepticism from Mr Cole, his most reliable parishioner, who served as steward on the area's most prosperous estate, a fact never mentioned to Lady Catherine..

"But you must see, Mr Cole, such methods of directing water must prove ruinous to the fields?"

"On the contrary, sir," Cole had replied with the patience of one explaining basic principles to a child, "These methods you describe are well established. Some date back to the Romans. Most large holdings require careful construction of connected culverts or the like to ensure that rain does not destroy plantings and that run off is not wasted when it might be used for irrigation. The new channels on this plan would appear to have improved drainage considerably. Even the lower meadow, which might tend to flood each spring, would remain workable."

"But women have set these out—mere girls, who have no more sense than nature bestows upon a songbird, yet they chirp most confidently upon subjects beyond their understanding. How could this possibly be acceptable?"

Mr Cole shook his head. "My dear Mr Collins, the fairer sex possesses, in nine cases of ten, a quickness of understanding which some gentlemen find most alarming. One suspects the insistence upon female intellectual inferiority stems from a recognition of this very superiority."

"Superiority? Are you bereft of your senses? The natural order established by Divine Providence has decreed that woman should be subservient to man, as Eve was formed from Adam's rib, not as his equal but as his helpmeet. A woman's delicate constitution and nervous sensibility render her wholly unsuited to matters beyond domestic concerns. To suggest that the weaker vessel might possess superior understanding or capacity for governance borders upon blasphemy!" Mr Collins could not maintain his sermon giving posture but stormed about the room with all the grace and delicacy of an enraged bull loosed among the finest porcelain at Wedgwood's establishment.

Mr Cole stood and bowed minimally. "I shall take my leave forthwith. I entreat you, do not relate these views to Mrs Cole. Our domestic tranquility could scarcely withstand such a suggestion."

The fire in the Netherfield library burned low, casting long shadows across the book-lined walls. Darcy stood before it, a glass of brandy in one hand, his other clenched behind his back as he stared into the embers. Colonel Fitzwilliam lounged nearby with apparent indolence, though his eyes tracked every movement of his cousin with quiet scrutiny.

The door creaked open, and Georgiana entered. Her expression was composed, but there was a tension in her bearing that drew both men to immediate attention.

"Brother, Fitzwilliam," she said, "may I speak with you? With both of you?"

Darcy turned at once. "Of course. I trust it does not herald some distressing matter?"

She hesitated only a moment, then stepped forward with resolution. "No. However, it concerns Mr Wickham."

Darcy's brows shot up. "Wickham?" His tone sharpened. "What of him?"

"He is in Meryton," Georgiana said quietly. "I saw him this morning."

"You—what?" The glass in Darcy's hand was set down; the heavy crystal thudding dully against the sideboard, mirroring the thud of his heart "You saw him? He is *here*?"

Fitzwilliam straightened, suddenly alert. "Good God. When?"

"Lydia Bennet and I were walking with Kitty," Georgiana explained. "We had just turned into the main street when he appeared from a shop. He had not yet seen us. I… I reacted poorly at first."

"Georgiana," Darcy said, already crossing the room to her. "You ought never have been exposed to him again, not without warning—how did I not know—how *dare* he be in Hertfordshire without my knowledge."

"He avoided the ball," Georgiana interjected. "Lydia believes he stayed away knowing you were there."

"Clearly he was not deterred enough!" Darcy burst out, then immediately checked himself. "Forgive me. Are you harmed? Did he approach you?"

"I am well." Georgiana drew a breath. "Lydia intervened. She placed herself between us. He tried to approach, but she…" Her lips curved faintly. "She managed the affair with perfect composure."

"Managed it?" Fitzwilliam echoed, half a smile rising. "What exactly did Miss Lydia do?"

"She stepped forward and announced that Mr Wickham had been 'deeper in debt than the ocean is deep' following last night's card game at the tavern, and that he was likely to sink. Then she informed him that you, cousin, are 'ferocious in your protection' of me and had once challenged a man to a duel for looking at me improperly."

Fitzwilliam barked a laugh. "I have done no such thing."

"She did say it was mediaeval," Georgiana added, "but understandable in ancient families like ours." Her eyes sparkled despite herself. "Then she remarked that you have 'the stare of a hawk and the memory of an elephant.'"

Fitzwilliam looked delighted. "I must make Miss Lydia's better acquaintance."

But Darcy had gone still. "And Wickham?"

"He attempted to sneer, but Lydia did not give him the

chance. She said Miss Darcy's circle is 'rather selective,' and that he had been 'weighed, measured, and found remarkably lightweight.'"

Fitzwilliam gave a low whistle. "Savage. And in public, too, I hope?"

"Very much so," Georgiana confirmed. "Mr Carter and Captain Morris both witnessed it. I believe Lieutenant Denny even tipped his hat in approval."

Darcy, however, did not share in their amusement. His face was pale, his expression stark. "I brought you here," he said, "to offer you a respite from Town. I thought Hertfordshire would be safe. I never imagined he would come here—not after…" He trailed off, voice thickening.

"Brother," Georgiana said, stepping forward. "You could not have known."

"But I *should* have," Darcy insisted. "It was *my* duty to see you safe. I ought to have inquired more thoroughly. To have *noticed*—"

"He did not touch me. He barely addressed me," she said firmly. "And I was not alone."

Darcy's eyes lifted to hers, haunted. "Still. To think you were made to face him, without warning—"

"And I faced him," Georgiana replied gently, "with friends beside me. Lydia did not falter. I did not faint. You gave me that strength. And perhaps… so did she."

Fitzwilliam cleared his throat. "It seems Miss Lydia has appointed herself your sister's champion. With remarkable effectiveness."

Darcy turned toward the fire again, his voice low. "I once thought her frivolous. But she has proved more discerning than half the officers in Wickham's regiment."

"More than all of them," Georgiana said, with a rare flash of steel.

At last, Fitzwilliam leant back in his chair and folded his hands. "Well, cousin. What do you intend?"

Darcy looked between them. "He will not remain in Meryton. I will see to that."

"Let us hope," said Georgiana, "that he will think twice before crossing the Bennet ladies again—he can never hope to charm them, after all."

"It has been sold?" Elizabeth's voice cracked despite her efforts at composure. The study seemed suddenly airless, the leather chairs too confining. "But we had no official word it was even being considered!"

"A private transaction." Uncle Phillips explained, shuffling his papers. "The purchaser, a concern from London, arranged everything through it's solicitor with remarkable speed."

Mr Bennet's voice remained steady. "The house would have made an excellent situation for the ladies," he said, watching his granddaughter from beneath hooded eyes. "More comfortable than the Lodge, certainly. After considerable repair."

"The Lodge will serve," Elizabeth said firmly, although her fingers twisted in her lap. "We have already begun moving the more valuable pieces there - Mamma's favourite chairs, Mary's pianoforte, the paintings that are not entailed…"

"And the account books?" Mr Phillips asked delicately.

"Secured, along with all documentation of our improvements and purchases for the past five years." Elizabeth's chin lifted. "Mr Collins may inherit Longbourn, but he will not find himself equal to our current prosperity."

"Very wise," Mr Phillips nodded. "And the deeds and plans?"

"Copies are secured at the Lodge. The originals will remain at Longbourn–they are too integral to the estate's operation to remove without raising suspicion." Elizabeth's voice held barely contained frustration. "Although I still think if we had managed to secure the Dunbar Court properties…"

"All is not lost, my dear," her grandfather said softly. His eyes held a glimmer of their old sparkle, although Elizabeth was too absorbed in her disappointment to notice. "We have weathered worse storms than this. The Lodge will serve for now, and who knows what the future might bring?"

He did not mention the letter locked in his desk, the one bearing Darcy's distinctive seal, explaining his purchase by his holding company. Some things, they had decided, were better left to work themselves out naturally. Although watching his beloved granddaughter struggle with her disappointment tested his resolve to keep Darcy's secret.

"Notwithstanding these considerations, Mr Collins's threatened lawsuit about your competency is unlikely to succeed," Mr Phillips offered. "Sir William's testimonial to your sound management these past years, combined with Mr Darcy's rather forceful assistance…"

"Mr Darcy has been… surprisingly helpful," Elizabeth admitted, her expression softening before she caught herself. "Although we cannot rely on that gentleman's assistance forever. We must secure our own position."

"And so, we shall," her grandfather assured her, patting her hand.

The late autumn sun slanted through the windows, illuminating the dust motes dancing in the air. Elizabeth stared out at the garden below, unaware that the very man she was trying so hard not to think about had just secured her family's future comfort. Her grandfather watched her with fond understanding, reminded of his own youth and the sometimes-circuitous path love took to find its way.

Rumours of Mr Wickham's sudden and complete departure spread through the town with the enthusiasm usually reserved for harvest feasts and scandalous sermons.

Miss Henrietta Thorpe was reportedly *"in a decline,"* having been convinced for three weeks that an offer was imminent. Several tradesmen were seen celebrating with ale after receiving unexpected payments clearing Wickham's substantial debts—payments whispered to have been arranged discreetly by "that tall gentleman from London."

No one needed to speculate about what had passed that morning on the high street—Captain Morris and Lieutenant Denny had witnessed the entire exchange, and by midday, the details were making the rounds of Meryton with the efficiency of a market bell.

That Mr Wickham had been "utterly vanquished" was beyond dispute. What raised more than a few eyebrows—though not in disapproval—was the cold efficiency with which Miss Lydia Bennet had delivered the blow. Long known for her shrewdness in livestock matters and her singular success in breeding Southdowns and Merinos that fetched record prices at the spring fair, Miss Lydia was spoken of as a young woman whose judgement extended beyond sheep to scoundrels.

"It is the same eye for flaws," remarked Mr Bentham, the ageing wool merchant. "She sees right through poor structure—whether on four legs or two."

"She has always had good instincts," Mrs Long declared over her tea, "but now it is clear she knows how to use them."

Even Miss Prentice, the dressmaker's daughter with a fondness for red coats and romantic fiction, was heard to say, "If I had her wits last year, I might have spared myself a world of disappointment."

Mr Wickham, for his part, left Meryton within two days. The militia, when pressed, confirmed only that he had received "a sudden posting elsewhere."

No one mourned the loss. And as for Miss Lydia Bennet—it was as if Meryton had finally taken the full measure of her—and determined her destined for more than they had yet imagined.

Lady Catherine sat rigid in her richly carved chair at Rosings, each tap of her fan punctuating Mr Collins's increasingly desperate attempts to document mismanagement at Longbourn. "You mean to tell me," she pronounced with dangerous refinement, "that these new drainage methods have actually improved the lower fields?"

"Most inexplicably, your Ladyship." Mr Collins shifted beneath her arctic gaze. "Mr Cole was most unhelpful in confirming our expectations of failure. He went as far as to suggest that the spring planting might proceed earlier than in the past, owing to the improved drainage."

"Earlier planting." Her fan executed a decisive flourish. "And I suppose these agricultural innovations continue to attract my nephew's attention?"

"Most unfortunately, your Ladyship. Mr Darcy was observed just recently examining the new channels with…" Mr Collins hedged delicately, "with rather marked approval."

The fan's rhythm faltered. "We require concrete evidence of mismanagement, Mr Collins. The court will not be moved by theoretical objections to female capability."

"Perhaps…" Mr Collins licked his lips nervously, "perhaps if certain failures were to become more… apparent?"

"Apparent?" Lady Catherine's gaze sharpened with sudden interest.

"One hears of accidents occurring over the winter," Mr Collins ventured, warming to his theme. "Natural deterioration of drainage works, particularly during the thaw…"

"One does indeed hear of such things." Her fan stilled completely. "Although arranging such… natural occurrences might prove costly."

Mr Collins fingered the purse at his waist, heavy with her latest advancement. "Your Ladyship's generosity has been most…"

"Must not be squandered on mere speculation," she cut in. "If certain demonstrations of incompetence were to occur, they must appear entirely… organic."

"If I might again return briefly to Meryton, I believe I could locate certain individuals who understand such delicate matters," Mr Collins offered, his ever present conceit somewhat tempered by the magnitude of what he was proposing.

Lady Catherine's fan picked up in speed. "I neither need nor wish to know the particulars, Mr Collins. I merely observe that evidence of mismanagement would prove most useful to our cause. How such evidence manifests itself is entirely your concern."

"Of course, your Ladyship. Although if neighbouring properties were to suffer some slight inconvenience in the process…"

"Incidental misfortune," she pronounced with aristocratic hauteur, "must occasionally be countenanced in the restoration of rightful order."

Chapter Thirty-Six

The morning of departure dawned grey and damp, a fine mist softening the outlines of the Netherfield grounds. Trunks were strapped to carriages, final instructions relayed to servants, and the drawing room bore the unmistakable hush of farewells.

Miss Bingley surveyed the preparations with a pinched expression. "How unfortunate that you must rush off just as the company begins to settle. Perhaps you might linger until the weather is more promising?" she asked, her smile tight. "One might think you were fleeing Hertfordshire."

Darcy's nod was courteous. "We are not troubled by the rain."

Georgiana thanked Miss Bingley with perfect civility but said no more. She had grown quieter these past days—but not from shyness. Her silences had taken on the quality of observation, and as she watched her brother glance toward the window—where the path toward Longbourn disappeared into the mist—her eyes softened.

"You are not quite as you were," she said as she settled across from him in the carriage. "It suits you."

Darcy looked at her, faintly amused. "No longer insufferable, then?"

A trace of a smile touched her lips. "I should not presume to say. Only that… something in you feels easier." Georgiana settled onto the squabs, smoothing her gloves. "You listen more closely. And speak with less certainty. You no longer seem so sure the world must arrange itself around you."

He raised a brow. "A stinging compliment."

She smiled. "Not at all. Only that your pride once made it difficult for others to reach you. That seems… less true now."

Darcy had no reply, but the faint crease between his brows softened.

Colonel Fitzwilliam joined them a moment later, shaking the damp from his coat before settling in across from them.

"You are quiet this morning," Darcy said.

"I am attempting," the Colonel said mildly, brushing a spot of lint from his cuff, "to turn my thoughts to London business. And not dwell on certain countryside impressions that have no practical end."

Darcy glanced at him but said nothing.

Georgiana looked between them, her tone thoughtful. "Some impressions leave more of a mark than one expects."

Fitzwilliam gave a brief smile. "And some are best left unpursued."

She hesitated. "Miss Bennet spoke with real interest about your remarks on supply and logistics."

He gave a small shrug. "She is gracious to everyone. Bingley's interest was plain enough, even without words. He arrived first—and with a fortune."

"A heavy advantage," Darcy murmured.

"One I do not hold," Fitzwilliam replied. "Nor would I ask a lady to weigh sentiment against stability. That is no kindness."

Darcy watched the countryside slip past, hedgerows blurred by speed and early rain. So much could be lost through hesitation—waiting until certainty replaced doubt, until circumstance aligned perfectly.

The black-clad figure of Mr Collins was visible through the library window, preening as he walked beside the court official up the drive. Elizabeth's fingers tightened on the curtain.

"He looks remarkably pleased with himself," she observed quietly to Jane.

"Lizzy," Jane touched her sister's arm. "We must remain calm, for Grandfather's sake."

"I am perfectly calm," Elizabeth replied, although her voice held an edge. "I simply wish to observe the man who believes our grandfather incompetent for the grievous sin of allowing his granddaughters an education."

From his chair by the fire, Grandfather looked up from his book, his rheumy eyes still sharp despite his advanced years. "I reckon you have brought Jones to speak to my competence?"

"He arrived early, Grandfather," Elizabeth confirmed, releasing the curtain. "He is prepared to testify about your sound judgement these past years."

"Sound judgement?" Her grandfather's voice crackled with dry humour. "Is that what we are calling my decision to let a passel of girls manage my estate? According to our esteemed cousin, that alone proves my mental decay."

"Please, Grandfather," Jane urged. "The court official will be here any moment."

"And I suppose I must prove I have not lost my wits?" Old Mr Bennet leant forward "If I had any sense at all, I would have packed Mr Collins off to the colonies years ago."

"Grandfather." Elizabeth's reproving address was countered by her smile. "You are certain you do not wish to send for Uncle Phillips?"

The old man's expression softened as he looked at his granddaughters. "My dears, there is no need to trouble Mr Phillips. That pompous little man can examine me all he likes. Let him produce evidence of any derangement in my reasoning beyond those small impediments which are the natural companions of advanced years. I still remember every book in this library, every field on this estate, and every reason you are better suited to manage it than that puffed-up parson could ever be."

Hill appeared at the door. "Mr Collins and Mr Broadmoor from the Court of Chancery, sir. Mr Jones is here as well."

"Very well." Grandfather marked his place in his book. "Let

us see what sport the afternoon brings."

The sombrely attired court official introduced himself with ponderous dignity. "Mr Bennet, I am Mr Broadmoor of the Court of Chancery. The Lord Chancellor has commissioned me to evaluate the present state of your faculties and determine your competence in matters of judgment. If you are amenable, I shall commence the formal inquiry, as mandated by the petition submitted."

"I am prepared," Mr Bennet said, adjusting his position with deliberate care. "Though I suspect no one has anticipated this examination more eagerly than my cousin Mr Collins. He has long cherished the notion that disagreeing with him is proof of lunacy."

Mr Collins swelled with indignation like a bantam cock confronted by a larger rival. "My dear sir, I act only out of deepest concern--"

"Yes, yes, your concern for my immortal soul and worldly goods is quite touching." Mr Bennet waved a gnarled hand. "Do proceed with your examination, Mr Broadmoor. I find myself curious to learn exactly how addled I have become."

Mr Jones cleared his throat. "If I might speak to Mr Bennet's physical condition first?"

"By all means," Mr Broadmoor nodded. "Although I understand Mr Bennet is in his seventy-fourth year?"

"Indeed," the subject of the discussion interjected. "Although I am told I appear scarcely a day over seventy-three. The secret is regular application of good books and avoiding tiresome company when possible." Mr Bennet cast a sidelong look at Mr Collins.

Elizabeth pressed her lips together, trying not to smile as Mr Collins spluttered.

"And your overall health, sir?" Mr Broadmoor pressed on.

"Oh, the usual complaints of age," Grandfather said cheerfully. "My joints protest the weather, my eyes and ears are not what they were, and my patience for foolishness has grown remarkably thin. Although that last may be less a symptom of age than of present company."

Mr Broadmoor turned to Mr Jones. "And your opinion sir?

What have you noted and how long have you attended him?"

"Mr Bennet and I have been acquainted since I established my apothecary nearly thirty years ago. I attended the late Mrs Elizabeth Bennet, and the late Eleanor Bennet, as well as all the young ladies of the household through their childhood illnesses. Of course, I attended the late Thomas Bennet as well, in the tragic illness which claimed his life."

"Mr Jones, we are speaking of the present Mr James Bennet, not his numerous family members," Mr Broadmoor interrupted.

"My apologies, sir. I was reciting my contact with Mr Bennet over these many years. He has rarely required my care until quite recently. His state of health has been remarkable for a man of seventy-odd years. As he mentioned, his eyesight has suffered a not unexpected decline over the years, as has his hearing. He does experience some pain in his joints as is common for a man who has been active throughout his life. Of late, he has had a lingering chest complaint, a cough, and some ague. As for his mental capacity, Mr Bennet has retained his faculties in full. I have noted no confusion, no significant changes in his demeanour and no deficits in his memory beyond an occasional neglect to honour my suggestions about reducing his duties. He is as cogent as a man of forty,"

"Mr Jones," Mr Collins began pompously, rising as if to preach, "You must acknowledge that allowing young ladies to manage estate matters is highly irregular--"

"Irregular?" Mr Bennet's eyes glinted. "Like your rather irregular interpretation of the fifth commandment, perhaps? Tell me, sir, how does attempting to have me declared incompetent honour thy father's father?"

"Mr Bennet, Mr Collins," Mr Broadmoor interjected, his tone judicial. "If I might proceed uninterrupted."

Mr Collins made a sharp inhalation of annoyance and took his seat.

Mr Bennet smiled and said, "By all means, sir."

"Mr Bennet," Broadmoor asked. "Please tell me today's date?"

"December the twelfth, 1811. Thursday, if you require further precision. Rather chilly for the season, although not as cold as that remarkable winter of '62 when the creek froze early." His eyes twinkled. "Would you care to know the phase of the moon as well? Waning Crescent."

"That will not be necessary. Now, sir, who is the current monarch?"

"George III, God help him. Although I dare say he is having a worse time of it than I am at present. At least I recognise my own granddaughters, which is more than can be said for his recognition of Princess Charlotte."

Mr Collins shifted uncomfortably. "Sir, these diversions from the questions--"

"Are perfectly relevant observations demonstrating both temporal awareness and current events," Mr Broadmoor said. He fixed a glare on Mr Collins.

"Please proceed with your inquiry, Mr Broadmoor. I confess myself rather curious to discover how one measures my supposed deterioration." Grandfather's expression could only be described as impudent.

"Yes, well." Broadmoor consulted his papers. "Can you count backward from one hundred by sevens?"

"Shall I proceed in English, Latin, or French? Or would Greek be considered excessive?" Mr Bennet sighed. "Ninety-three, eighty-six, seventy-nine, seventy-two, sixty -five, fifty-eight, fifty-one, forty-four, thirty-seven, thirty, twenty-three, sixteen, nine, two, negative five—is that far enough? *Nonaginta tres, octoginta sex, septuaginta novum*, shall I continue, or have I sufficiently demonstrated my ability to perform calculations that my granddaughters whilst in the nursery managed daily without having their sanity questioned?"

Elizabeth caught Jane hiding a smile behind her handkerchief.

"Perhaps we might discuss your daily activities," Broadmoor tried again.

"Ah yes, my notorious routine of reading agricultural treatises, reviewing estate accounts, and making the apparently scandalous decision to recognise competence regardless of gender. Tell me, Mr Broadmoor, at what precise age does employing all of one's available resources become a sign of mental infirmity?"

Mr Broadmoor cleared his throat. "Now then, Mr Bennet," he laid out several coins on the small table beside the chair. "Would you be so good as to determine the aggregate of these coins?"

Mr Bennet peered at the coins. "Two guineas, three shillings, sixpence. Although if you are offering to contribute to our drainage fund, I am afraid you will need to add considerably more. Unless," his eyes glinted, "you are suggesting my failure to recognise that particular sum as inadequate for major land improvements is proof of my mental decay?"

"Not at all, sir. Now, regarding your livestock—how many calves might one expect from a cow in a year?"

"One, generally speaking, unless one is Mr Williams of Meryton, who claims his prize heifer dropped twins last spring. Although I suspect it says more about his counting abilities than the cow's prolific nature." Grandfather shifted in his chair. "But of course, Mr Broadmoor, you have not come all this way to quiz me on basic animal husbandry?"

"And sheep, sir? How many lambs--"

"One or two per ewe, depending on breed and conditions. We have had excellent results with twins since Lydia implemented that new feeding regimen. The ledgers show a fifteen percent increase in successful births, should you wish to examine them? Unless, of course, meticulous record-keeping has come to signify a deranged mind?"

Mr Collins shook his head ruefully. "My dear sir, I assure you no one intended…"

"No? Then perhaps you might explain why we are discussing matters that any shepherd boy could answer, whilst my granddaughter's quite remarkable improvements to this estate are considered evidence of my mental infirmity?"

Mr Broadmoor concealed a smile behind his papers.

"Mr Jones," Broadmoor turned to the apothecary. His stern

expression suggested mere formality, "You mentioned a lingering cough Mr Bennet has suffered these past years. What remedies have you provided to him?"

"Indeed, sir. He has required remarkably little attention beyond the normal aches and pains of age. I made up an elixir for his lungs; conserve of red roses, balsam of sulphur, oil of vitriol, and syrup of coltsfoot. Nothing requiring laudanum if that is what you are implying. Miss Catherine Bennet has expertise in the still room. She makes up lozenges with a paste of sugar, herbal oils, and powders, and rose water which her grandfather enjoys. He may not have the vigour he once had, but his mind remains as sharp as ever, as you have no doubt observed."

"Quite." Broadmoor gathered his papers, not bothering to continue his questioning. "Mr Bennet, I thank you for your patience with these proceedings. I believe I have everything I need."

"A pleasure, sir," Grandfather said. "Do feel free to return if you require further proof of my ability to count sheep. Although perhaps next time we might engage in more challenging arithmetic."

Through the library window, Elizabeth watched Mr Collins hurrying after Broadmoor down the drive, his face flushed with agitation.

"But sir, you must see—" Mr Collins's voice carried on the winter air.

"What I see, Mr Collins," Mr Broadmoor's response cut like ice, "is that you have wasted the court's time with frivolous accusations against a perfectly competent gentleman. Your concern for the estate's management appears to stem more from wounded pride than any legitimate grievance."

"But these foolish methods—allowing young ladies to--"

"Have yielded demonstrable and well-documented improvements to the estate's prosperity. Good day, Mr Collins."

Elizabeth turned from the window to find her grandfather watching her, his eyes twinkling.

"Well, my dear," he said quietly, "shall we return to those ledgers that so offend our cousin's sensibilities?"

Chapter Thirty-Seven

Darcy was by the window of his London townhouse, watching the steady fall of December rain whilst Bingley paced behind him. The fire hissed in the grate, punctuating his friend's restless steps.

"I said I meant only to attend to the shipping contracts," Bingley burst out. "A week's business at most. But Caroline—she insisted the house must be closed; the servants dismissed. She claimed remaining at Netherfield after such… entanglements would invite speculation, and now—" He ran a hand through his hair.

Darcy shook his head. "And now you find yourself in London, questioning your own judgement."

"Yes! No. I do not know." Bingley collapsed into a chair and gave a strained laugh. "Miss Bennet—Jane—is everything a gentleman could desire. Her oversight of domestic affairs, her kindness, her—"

"Beauty," Darcy said dryly.

"Yes," Bingley admitted, his smile fleeting. "But Caroline insists no man of consequence would align himself with a family so unconventional. She calls them 'female farmers playing at being gentry,' as if managing land were some grotesque novelty. A pastoral fantasy, she says—'a gentleman ensnared by provincial beauty and vulgar ambition.'"

Darcy's jaw tightened, but he said nothing. If vulgar ambition were the true offence, then Miss Bingley might well have been indicting herself.

"It sounds absurd when spoken aloud, I know it does. And

yet… Caroline has always known how to read society's currents. Perhaps she sees more accurately than I."

"Do you allow your sister's prejudices to outweigh your own observations?"

Bingley flinched. "I had a ring in my pocket at the ball. But Caroline's reaction… Perhaps she is right. Perhaps I lack the strength of character to endure society's censure. To watch my wife snubbed, my children perhaps—though the neighbourhood accepts them now," he added hastily, as if to convince himself. "Lady Lucas says they are invited everywhere, even if some still whisper about their unorthodox stewardship."

Darcy grimaced. "How convenient that their acceptance coincided with Fitzwilliam, you, and me calling regularly at Longbourn."

Bingley winced. "Perhaps it was. Am I too easily persuaded? But if I defy Caroline, the breach would be lasting. She says we would be objects of ridicule. And whilst Jane is all grace and goodness…" He trailed off.

Darcy remained silent. A deep and private disquiet stirred. He had come to London to clear his mind, yet here was Bingley giving voice to every justification he himself had once rehearsed. Was he also dismissing what was real and admirable, for the sake of ease and acceptance?

"We are discussing your happiness," Darcy said at last, "not your sister's convenience."

"She believes she is acting for my good. One cannot fault her loyalty, though her manner is at times,"

"Despotic?" Darcy offered.

"Strong-minded," Bingley replied, though without conviction. "She says if I marry Miss Bennet, the world will sneer."

"The world—or your sister?"

"It is difficult to distinguish, at times. Caroline knows everyone, understands what is expected… Am I not to consider my family's feelings?" His voice dropped. "To weigh all factors?"

"You must weigh them, but not all deserve equal weight. You

would live with your wife. Your sister, one hopes, will marry and live elsewhere."

Bingley leant forward. "Can a gentleman find happiness with a lady who defies convention? Should affection outweigh the approval of society?"

The room fell silent save for the rain against the window.

"Your sister closed Netherfield without consulting you," Darcy said finally. "She made decisions about your life because she believes she knows better. She decries the notion of ladies managing estates, yet she governs your affairs with impunity. At least the Bennets' authority is born of competence and legal right."

Bingley sat back, startled. "I… had not considered it that way."

"Perhaps you should." Darcy turned again to the window. "And perhaps Miss Bennet's capabilities are what you require in a wife—someone to help you stand firm in your own convictions, rather than bend to others."

"But how does one choose without reference to the world at large? Without regard for the place one hopes to hold in it?"

Darcy remained still, his hands clasped with unusual force. "Then ask yourself whether your life is better governed by your sister's fears—or by your own judgement."

Bingley nodded slowly. "Caroline would be most displeased to find herself returning to Netherfield."

"I imagine she would survive the disappointment," Darcy said. "The question is—will you survive your own, if you allow her to choose for you?"

Bingley said nothing.

Mr Collins sat before his patroness, his head bowed. His latest letter lay open upon the side table, and its contents had provoked her fan into increasingly martial manoeuvres.

"The Chancery court sent a Register to examine the old man, and the Register found cause for *levity*?" Lady Catherine enquired, each syllable clipped with disdain.

Mr Collins shifted in his boots, his habitual obsequiousness somewhat dampened. "Most unseemly, your Ladyship. Although perhaps the gentleman failed to comprehend the seriousness of matters at Longbourn. I myself observed the most extraordinary mismanagement. They speak of constantly relocating their crops."

Lady Catherine's fan paused mid-stroke. "Relocating?"

"Indeed! 'Rotation'—removing perfectly sound wheat from its ordained ground and turning it about rather than allowing it to prosper where Providence has placed it. And the sheep, your Ladyship! They assert these animals require shearing but once per annum, when it is plain that weekly shearing would yield at least sevenfold the wool."

The fan faltered. "Perhaps we might speak of financial matters. Have you found evidence of irregularities in their accounts?"

"Most irregular!" Mr Collins leant forward, nearly upsetting his teacup. "I learnt that they record expenditures for 'amendments to soil,' as though the Lord's creation required improvement. There are also peculiar notations regarding 'winter feed'—ought not the beasts of the field seek their own sustenance, as nature intended?"

Lady Catherine's expression suggested the summoning of considerable reserves of forbearance. She made a dismissive gesture, as if physically brushing away such nonsense "Whilst your observations are no doubt correct; might we turn our attention to more measurable incidents of mismanagement? Do not their ledgers reveal some failing worth the court's scrutiny?"

"My relations maintain separate books for each field!" Mr Collins declared, eyes alight. "Such multiplication of records must indicate impropriety. And Miss Elizabeth has devised a series of charts detailing rainfall—as though Heaven's bounty were subject to calculation rather than received in due humility."

The fan resumed its pace, its speed unprecedented in any drawing room of Lady Catherine's acquaintance.

"Mr Collins," she said at length, her tone even, "I take it you have yet to review the records themselves."

"I was denied my right to examine them! I find myself in a most peculiar predicament—I am required to present evidence of financial impropriety before being permitted to examine the ledgers, yet I cannot obtain such evidence without first inspecting those very accounts. It is rather like being told one must prove the existence of water in a well before being allowed to lower the bucket!"

Lady Catherine stilled. Her endeavour to install Mr Collins as head of Longbourn and exert control over that Elizabeth Bennet would be more challenging than anticipated. The silk of her gown rustled with crisp disapproval as she shifted position After a moment, she spoke again. "

"Perhaps it would be wise to engage someone with more particular expertise in the management of agricultural accounts to evaluate the estate."

"But there is no question," Mr Collins pressed, "that no man of sense would entrust matters of fiscal significance to the feminine understanding. The female mind, though suited to certain domestic arrangements, cannot possibly be expected to manage sums and soil. Their ledgers must be riddled with error. They have even recorded the milk yield of individual cows—rather than accepting, with grateful hearts, what Providence elects to provide."

Lady Catherine's expression altered, a flicker of apprehension in her narrowed eyes. Her fan ceased. She folded it and placed it beside her teacup with a dawning comprehension of the source of the Register's reported amusement. Yet her determination to prevent any alliance between her nephew and these distressingly capable young ladies remained undiminished.

"We must consider a new approach," she said. "Your objection must be grounded in indisputable fact. It is not natural for ladies to involve themselves so deeply in the governance of land. It is impossible that there is no resulting harm. I fear this will require another journey to Meryton. Engage that young cleric again and return thither at once."

Mr Collins bowed his head in fervent agreement.

"You must gather evidence of this mismanagement- of losses to the estate, or damage to the lands, that is what you must find and document. Speak with a well regarded estate manager and he will tell you what to look for. Find the evidence."

A small parcel arrived at Longbourn two days after the Bennet household received news of Mr Darcy's safe return to London. It was of moderate size, wrapped in oilcloth and tied with a narrow green ribbon, bearing the seal of Darcy House.

Hill presented it to Mr Bennet, along with a stiff envelope addressed in a hand Elizabeth recognised at once. Her grandfather slit the seal with a paperknife and adjusted his spectacles. He read aloud:

Darcy House
Upper Grosvenor Street, London

Sir,

Permit me the liberty of expressing my gratitude, through you, to Miss Lydia Bennet for a service rendered, which cannot be easily forgotten by my family. I refer to her conduct during an unfortunate encounter in Meryton, the particulars of which you may be aware. That she acted with both resolution and delicacy in a moment of considerable difficulty has been related to me by my sister with both admiration and affection.

I am sensible of the proprieties that govern our correspondence and therefore beg you will receive, on her behalf, the token enclosed. It is my hope that Miss Lydia may find it of some utility in her continued interest in the care of animals and the management of stock.

With sincere esteem,
I remain,
Your most obedient servant,
Fitzwilliam Darcy

Grandfather gave a low whistle. "Well, that is the most carefully worded thank-you I have received in some time." He raised a brow toward Lydia. "It appears you have earned the gratitude of Pemberley."

Lydia, who had at first been attempting to appear uninterested, now leant forward with barely concealed curiosity as the parcel was unwrapped.

Within lay a neatly fitted case of polished walnut, hinged with brass and lined in green baize. Inside were tools intended for veterinary or animal husbandry use: a compact fleam, several fine-pointed lancets, a small, engraved horn cup, and a handwritten list of their uses—all in a second hand, presumably Darcy's steward or physician.

Elizabeth, peering over her grandfather's shoulder, murmured, "That is no trinket. Such tools are costly."

Lydia touched the fleam reverently. "It is just the size for lambs."

"More than that," said Grandfather, tapping the horn cup, "this is field-quality gear. Exceedingly well made."

Mary coughed lightly. "A generous acknowledgement."

Lydia, subdued, closed the case with care. "He need not have sent anything."

"Perhaps," Elizabeth said mildly, "but he did. And I suspect he meant every word."

"…It is too handsome a case for my needs," Lydia said at last, closing the latch with care. "And far too dear."

"Shall I write my thanks by way of Georgiana?" Lydia said, with calculated nonchalance. "She wrote last week. She asked about Snowdrop's lambing season and whether the salve we made with thyme and horehound held up in storage."

Elizabeth stilled. "Did she?"

Lydia nodded, folding her hands atop the case. "She wishes to attempt a similar preparation at Pemberley. Their still room is less often used, but she says she means to reclaim it."

Elizabeth said nothing, her expression unreadable. She reached once more for her needlework, but her gaze lingered—not on her stitching, but on the fire, where the faint scent of lavender and bitter almond still lingered in the air.

"Oh?" Mary inquired, barely glancing from her book. "Does she speak of her studies?"

"Somewhat," Lydia replied. "She writes she has begun to copy out her brother's estate accounts as a form of practice—though she says the figures are less interesting than our sheep trials." She gave a satisfied sniff.

Elizabeth set her work aside. "Does she mention anything else?" she asked, as evenly as she could manage.

Lydia's eyes twinkled. "Only that London is very grey, the streets muddy, and that she misses the sound of the wind over the fields. She asked if I might send her a receipt of that balm we use for colds—what was it, the one we made up with thyme and horehound?"

Elizabeth nodded. "We can dry some horehound leaves and send it with the next post."

Lydia refolded the letter and tucked it neatly away. "She signs herself simply Georgiana, now. I think that speaks more than all her lovely compliments."

Elizabeth did not reply. She simply bent her head once more over her mending, though her needle did not move for quite some time.

Chapter Thirty-Eight

Mr. Collins pulled at his ill-fitting brown coat, a garment borrowed from his gardener that did nothing to disguise his distinctive lumbering and arrogant manner of moving through the world. His most recent return to the streets of Meryton had proved unexpectedly hostile—each shopkeeper and tradesman seemed to recognise him instantly, their faces closing like well-defended doors against his practised casual questions about Longbourn's management.

"Begging your pardon, Mr Collins," the draper had said with barely concealed irony, "but you will find most of us take a sincere interest in Longbourn's continued prosperity. The estate's accounts are maintained with admirable exactitude."

"Have they bewitched you with their so-called accomplishments? Accounts maintained by mere females cannot be reliable. They lack the capacity for rigorous calculation!"

The draper looked at him queerly. "I do not appreciate your insults to the good ladies of Longbourn. Their good works and steady patronage are a boon to Meryton. And as for mathematics, my account is paid in full with no delay."

The butcher had been more subtle. "Strange days, sir, when a clergyman walks about in borrowed garments, enquiring into the private affairs of his betters."

By late afternoon, his frustration had driven him beyond Meryton's respectable bounds to the rougher quarter where labourers gathered after their day's work. The Bull and Crown's weathered sign creaked ominously in the spring wind, and Mr Collins hesitated before its door, aware that he stood at some moral crossroads.

But Lady Catherine's words echoed in his memory: "Evidence of mismanagement." The burden seemed to grow heavier with each passing moment of indecision. He was to find "unpaid accounts, failed crops, sickly livestock, fallow fields, empty tenant cottages," yet none of these materialised. His only hope was the failure of Miss Elizabeth's drainage works, whether by natural means or mischance.

The tavern's interior assaulted his senses - a miasma of stale beer and cheaper tobacco, punctuated by coarse laughter that bore no resemblance to the modulated environs of Rosings. Picking his way across the sticky floor, he approached a group of workmen nursing their tankards. Here, at last, he found men whose understanding of property rights matched their rough appearance, and whose interest in his purse overcame any scruples about his obvious displacement from his natural sphere. In the failing light of a tavern considerably beneath his normal standards, Mr Collins attempted conversation.

"Drainage, you say?" The larger of the two, who had introduced himself only as Smith, took a long pull of ale. "Funny thing about drainage works. Delicate, like. One small change upstream can cause all manner of trouble below."

His companion, a weasel-faced individual called Carroll, nodded sagely. "Course, such accidents do happen natural. Especially in spring, with the thaw and all."

Mr Collins leant forward, his pomposity somewhat dimmed by desperate calculation. "And such… natural accidents… might they prove costly to arrange?"

"Depends," Smith replied, studying Mr Collins with the practised eye of one who recognised desperation when he saw it. "On how natural you want it to appear. And how extensive the… accident might need to be."

"Extensive enough to prove certain parties unfit for their responsibilities," Mr Collins murmured, thinking of Lady Catherine's increasingly pointed suggestions about demonstrating the Bennets' incompetence. "Although of course, one would need absolute discretion…"

"Discretion," Carroll echoed, exchanging glances with his companion, "comes dear these days. What with times being hard and honest work so difficult to find."

Mr Collins fingered the purse containing Lady Catherine's advancement. The sum that had seemed so generous when he first saw it now felt altogether inadequate to purchase both the desired outcome and his conspirators' silence.

"Perhaps," he ventured, sweat beading despite the tavern's chill, "we might discuss terms more specifically?"

Smith's smile suggested he had taken the measure of both Mr Collins's desperation and his remaining funds with devastating accuracy. "Happy to oblige, sir. Though such delicate undertakings, liable to disturb several properties… that requires particular skill. And that sort of skill is costly."

As Mr Collins emptied his purse onto the sticky table, he tried not to think about the magnitude of what he was setting in motion. Lady Catherine had demanded results, after all. And if certain neighbouring properties suffered damage in the process of proving the Bennets' unfitness… well, surely that was a small price to pay for restoring proper order to their corner of creation.

He did not notice Smith and Carroll exchanging knowing looks over his bowed head, nor how their manipulation of his fears and pride had led him exactly where they had intended. Smith's smile widened—an expression Mr Collins, in another world, might have recognised as the tavern equivalent of a wolf sighting an unattended flock. In the dim and rancid air of the Bull and Crown, Mr Collins's final bid for consequence slipped away as quietly as his coin, though he would not grasp it until the damage was done.

A steady rain soaked the fields around Longbourn, but the flow of the water through the channels rushed at an alarming rate. By noon, the pastureland was saturated, with enormous puddles where water ought to have taken the path through the channel. By evening, the lower fields were transformed into a muddy lake, with water now encroaching upon both Netherfield and Dunbar Court. The downpour kept the workmen usually employed by Longbourn from making any headway against the rising water.

The following day, Elizabeth stood with Jane at the window of the drawing room, watching as Mr Freeman's distinctive figure approached on horseback.

"I cannot understand how the water channels could have failed so completely," Jane murmured. "You and grandfather designed them so precisely."

"I do not think it was failure," Elizabeth replied, her voice tight with controlled anger. "It looks to me like sabotage. Those stones blocking the main channel did not place themselves there."

Their mother hurried into the room, her hand flying to her hair. "Mr Freeman is coming up the drive. Jane, ring for tea. Elizabeth, do move those muddy boots from beside the fireplace." She paused, taking a steadying breath. "He comes in his official capacity as magistrate, of course. Grandfather sent for him regarding the flood at Netherfield."

Elizabeth noted with interest that her mother had taken particular care with her appearance despite the crisis. The cap covering her hair was her best lace, and she wore the becoming blue morning dress that brightened her eyes.

Mr Freeman was announced moments later, his bow particularly deep to Mrs Bennet before he greeted her daughters. "I regret the circumstances that bring me to Longbourn today."

"We are devastated by the damage to our neighbours' properties," Mrs Bennet said with genuine distress. "To think that water from Longbourn should cause such destruction!"

"That is the connection I must investigate," Mr Freeman replied, his official manner softened by the sympathetic glance he directed at Mrs Bennet. "The situation is most out of the ordinary."

"Perhaps we might show you the plans," Elizabeth suggested.

"My grandfather and I can explain how it was designed to prevent this sort of flooding."

Mr Freeman followed Elizabeth to the study, where Mr Bennet slumped in his chair, the strain of recent events evident in the new lines around his eyes. He greeted Mr Freeman with the weary dignity of a man forced to defend his family's honour.

"These are the original plans," Elizabeth said, unrolling the detailed drawings on the table. "And these modifications were made last autumn."

Mr Freeman bent over the plans, "These are well designed. Far more sophisticated than anything on my own property."

"The water ought to have been directed away from both Netherfield and Dunbar Court," Mr Bennet explained, "Instead, it seems to have been deliberately channelled toward them."

Elizabeth produced a second set of papers, marked with the water flow they had observed in the storm. "These show evidence of alterations, made without our knowledge or consent in the past few weeks."

Mr Freeman's expression darkened as he compared the documents. "You believe someone interfered with the works?"

Mr Bennet nodded firmly. "There is no other explanation."

"Is there anything to be done?" Mrs Bennet asked.

Mr Freeman covered her hand with his own in a brief, reassuring gesture—a familiarity not lost on Elizabeth. "Deliberate sabotage causing damage to neighbouring properties is a serious matter."

He turned to address them all, although his gaze lingered on Mrs Bennet. "As magistrate, I will document everything meticulously. I shall collect statements from workers who may have seen any activity near the area of the water channels."

"Will that be sufficient?" Elizabeth asked.

"Perhaps not on its own," Mr Freeman admitted. "But I believe we might find more once we begin to look."

"We would welcome your counsel," Mrs Bennet replied warmly.

As he prepared to take his leave, Mr Freeman spoke quietly to Mrs Bennet near the doorway. "This situation troubles me greatly. Not merely as a magistrate, but as…a friend who holds your family's welfare in high regard."

Mrs Bennet's cheeks coloured delicately. "Your concern means a great deal to us, Mr Freeman."

"To you particularly, I hope," he replied in a low voice that nevertheless carried to where Elizabeth stood.

After he departed, Mrs Bennet remained at the window watching his retreating figure. When she turned back to her daughters, there was a determined set to her jaw that Elizabeth had rarely seen.

"Well," Mrs Bennet said briskly, "we will prepare for Mr Freeman's investigation. Elizabeth, I believe Mr Bingley's steward is aware of the matter. What of Dunbar Court? Has a steward remained who might be of use?"

Elizabeth exchanged a glance with Jane, both recognising that their mother's newfound resolve might have as much to do with impressing Mr Freeman as with saving Longbourn—but they welcomed it, nonetheless.

The warm scent of hay and lanolin filled the lambing shed as Lydia checked the water buckets. The soft breathing of the lambs filled the shed, blending with the creak of old timber and the distant patter of rain on the thatch. Snowdrop stood calmly in her stall; her twin lambs nestled at her side. Their fleece, even at a week old, showed the dense crimp her grandfather prized—tight curls like mist against the skin, a sure sign of a good coat.

She had scarcely set down the bucket when the barn door creaked open behind her.

"Miss Lydia!" a voice called. Mr Kettering stepped in, hat in hand, boots still crusted from his work. "Pardon the intrusion. I would not barge in if it were not urgent."

Lydia turned, wiping her hands on her apron. "Good

morning, Mr Kettering. You are out early."

"I had to come," he said, moving closer. "It is my flock. I lost six ewes this week. My best line—all swept off in the flooding. The pasture near the old stone marker flooded sudden like—worse than it has in years. I was at market and my boy could not move them in time."

Lydia's brow furrowed. She had heard of the losses at Dunbar Court but not of damage to tenant holdings nearby. Kettering farmed a modest parcel on the edge of the Dunbar Court lands, leased these last dozen years. They had spoken before at the spring fairs, comparing feed regimens and hoof treatments, and last winter they had discussed her trial of the barley mash blend.

"I am very sorry," she said quietly.

Kettering nodded once, tight-lipped. "Word is Snowdrop's lambs have come through strong."

Lydia said nothing at first, her hand resting on the ewe's warm flank. The lambs jostled at her side, one bleating faintly.

"I will pay above fair price," Kettering added. "An ewe lamb, if you would part with one. We must start over. That lamb might help us keep a line alive."

Lydia studied him. Not proud, not pleading—just plainly asking, with the weariness of a man shouldering too much loss.

She looked at the lamb. Already sturdy on her legs, fleece bright in the slanting light. The sort of animal they would have marked for breeding stock. And in truth, she had planned to keep her.

But what was the purpose of breeding sound lines if not to strengthen the flock beyond her own fences?

"She is not yet weaned," Lydia said at last. "And I would not part with her lightly."

"I understand."

She hesitated considering not just the animal's value but her own sense of what was owed. Kettering had asked about her methods before most would speak to her without condescension. He had written to ask her thoughts on rotation feed. And he had lost nearly everything because of the failure of Longbourn's water channels.

"You shall have her," she said slowly. "But only on the condition that you breed her with care, keep full records, and share your findings with me next spring."

Kettering's face broke into a relieved smile. "Done and done. You have my word, Miss Lydia."

She nodded, returning her hand to Snowdrop's fleece. "Then let us see if she proves herself in your fields as her mother has in mine."

Chapter Thirty Nine

Darcy stood at his study window in London, turning Bingley's urgent letter over in his hands. The familiar conflict pressed against his chest. He had sworn to keep his distance from Hertfordshire—from her—yet here was the very excuse he required, wrapped in the legitimate concerns of his friend.

Bingley's characteristic scrawl wandered across the page, several words crossed out and others squeezed between lines:

"My dear Darcy,

Most distressing business at ~~Longbourn~~ Netherfield[several ink blots] requires your excellent judgement. Mr Collins (that odious parson who is heir) has petitioned magistrate for estate audit — claims mismanag'mt and improper drainage work by ladies. [word crossed out] Insists his own man must conduct inspection!

Cannot avoid involvement as floods Netherfield south fields. [hastily inserted above: 'drainage patterns] All Wrong he says Have rec'ed notice requiring testimony as neighbour. Must return to meet Magistrate. Am quite beyond my depth in these affairs.

You understand these things better than any. [scratched out word] Would consider it great personal favour if you could spare few days to advise. Please, I beg your indulgence. I proceed to Netherfield on the morrow.

Your friend in dire need,
C. Bingley
[squeezed in at bottom]
P.S. Netherfield's housekeeper says kitchen gardens

flooded twice this month. Must investigate claims about water flow."

Darcy closed his eyes, seeing again Elizabeth Bennet with her measuring rod and calculations, her keen eyes assessing the land.

His man Fletcher spoke from the doorway. "Your sister asks if you will be joining her for tea, sir."

"No, rather only briefly," Darcy said, then caught himself. "That is, I must go to Hertfordshire tomorrow. Estate business at Netherfield."

"Very good, sir. Shall I begin packing?"

Darcy nodded, already composing his response to Bingley. It was purely business—a favour to a friend, nothing more. He would maintain strict propriety in his dealings with Miss Elizabeth.

But even as he made these stern resolutions, his mind betrayed him: the flash of her eyes when defending her opinions, the grace with which she managed both estate and family obligations, shook his long-held notions of rank and privilege.

The purchase of Dunbar Court, the Matthews estate, sat heavy in his conscience. Would she forgive him if she knew? Regardless, he could not regret ensuring its security for her family.

He began to write:

> *Bingley,*
>
> *Your letter gives me cause for concern. An improper audit could set a dangerous precedent for all neighbouring estates. I will arrive tomorrow to assess the situation. Please make no commitments until we have discussed the matter thoroughly.*
>
> *Yours, etc.*
>
> *FD*

Short. Professional. Nothing to suggest the rapid beating of his heart or the way his hands had shaken when he read Bingley's news.

He moved to the window, his breath fogging the glass in the evening chill. Tomorrow at Netherfield he would focus on being useful, and protecting her family's interests from a suitable distance. On being, in short, precisely the kind of gentleman his position demanded.

Darcy touched the cold windowpane, then turned abruptly to ring for Fletcher. Best to begin preparations now, if they were to make an early start.

The winter sun above Netherfield cast cold light across the frost-touched grounds as Darcy's carriage approached through the biting air. Bingley stood waiting on the steps, his easy charm warring with an undercurrent of nervous agitation that manifested in the subtle shift of his weight from foot to foot.

"Darcy!" Bingley's voice carried notes of relief and a desperate need for guidance.

"Thank God. You have no idea what a coil we are in. Was the journey terribly difficult?"

"The roads conspired against comfort," Darcy replied, handing his heavy driving coat to the footman, whilst scanning the grounds out of habit. The south lawn stretched before him like a treacherous mirror, sheets of ice gleaming where water had gathered and frozen–a beautiful danger that spoke volumes about the troubles beneath. "I see what you mean about the drainage."

"Oh Lord, yes. Come into the library—I have all the papers there. In truth, I make little sense of them." Bingley led the way, talking over his shoulder. "Mr Collins sent another letter just this morning. Full of dire predictions about flood damage and mismanagement. The man writes like he is composing a Gothic novel."

Bingley paced the room as Darcy took a seat at the table. "I am to give testimony in a deposition about the water patterns Friday next," Bingley continued, running agitated fingers through his hair until it stood in disarray that spoke eloquently of many such gestures. "Mr Collins claims he is conducting an audit. A solicitor has ordered a deposition. Lord, Darcy, I feel as though I am navigating a ship without a compass."

"Have you the original surveys?" Darcy asked, glancing over the disordered papers scattered across the table.

"Here–although they are rather worse for wear." Bingley's hands moved through the papers with increasing anxiety. "Miss Elizabeth brought these herself last week. She had much to say about the elevation calculations, although I confess such figures might as well be Persian poetry to me."

Darcy bent over the maps, grateful for the excuse to hide his face as warmth bloomed across his cheeks at this casual mention of her name. Her measurements were precise, elegant in their efficiency–like everything about her.

"The kitchen gardens are solid ice now," Bingley said, oblivious to his friend's inner turmoil. "Miss Jane Bennet—" his voice caught on her name, "states they have been implementing improvements for three years. But Mr Collins insists they have destroyed some ancestral arrangement dating back generations."

"Ancestral arrangement?" Darcy straightened, frowning thoughtfully. "Is there any record--"

A knock interrupted his question, and Mrs Nicholls entered with an apologetic air. "Miss Bingley asks if you will join her for luncheon, sir?"

Bingley's glance at Darcy carried volumes of unspoken understanding. "We will take trays here, Mrs Nicholls. The matter requires our full attention."

It was not until the door closed that Darcy realised he had been holding Elizabeth's map upside down, lost in thoughts of the hand that had marked it. He turned it quickly, hoping the heat in his face might be attributed to the fire's warmth rather than the betraying flush of his own heart's indiscretion.

As the winter afternoon light faded, Darcy compared two sets of calculations that did not align. He pushed one map aside, frowning. "Bingley, look at these elevation marks from November. They are markedly different from the current measurements."

"Different how?" Bingley leant over, squinting at the figures.

"Here—and here." Darcy's finger traced the path. "Someone has altered the grading. Recently, and rather clumsily." He straightened, jaw tightening. "These are not natural changes."

"Good God." Bingley collapsed into a chair. "You mean Mr Collins--"

"Who else would benefit? We need to speak with the Bennets. Today, if possible."

An hour later, they entered Longbourn's study. Darcy forced his attention away from Elizabeth standing protectively at her grandfather's shoulder. The late sun caught her face, its weak winter light revealing a flash of worry before she schooled her features into calm.

"Mr Darcy. Mr Bingley. Have you heard the tale of the examination of my mental powers and their sufficiency for the management of our affairs.?" Mr Bennet greeted them.

"No, sir, I have not." Darcy quirked a brow. Mr Bennet's eyes held a mix of amusement and impatience. Miss Elizabeth's lips tightened with annoyance.

"Well, suffice it to say that Lord Chancellor will receive a report saying I am impertinent, irascible and, unfortunately for Mr Collins, still in possession of my senses."

Bingley looked around, questioningly. "What of the Lord Chancellor?"

Elizabeth spoke up. "Mr Collins petitioned the court to have Grandfather examined for lunacy. He was interviewed by a court official to ascertain whether his understanding remains sound and competent."

Darcy shook his head.

"One can take such an action? Can an interested party's mere claim be considered adequate in so grave a matter?" Bingley asked.

"Only adequate to commence the inquiry. Mr Collins did not

prevail in that endeavor. But you did not come to Longbourn to discuss my fitness of mind. By the look of you, you have found something in the surveys?"

"You are correct, Mr Bennet." He kept his eyes firmly on the papers. "We believe someone has been tampering with the drainage works."

Grandfather Bennet's harsh cough drew their attention. Jane stepped forward with a cordial, and as she withdrew, Bingley's eyes followed her. She glanced away from his obvious admiration, her cheeks colouring, but not, to Darcy's eye, with pleasure.

"We have suspected as much," Elizabeth said, moving to the desk. Darcy laid out the maps, acutely aware of her closeness and the sweet fragrance she wore–as she bent to study them. Her quick questions demonstrated the sharp intelligence he had admired these past months.

"I see it now. Here," she said, her finger landing on a notation. "These markers differ from when I checked them in November. But look at the pattern of the alteration—It can only direct water specifically toward Netherfield's kitchen gardens."

"The question is whether we can discover who did this?" Jane's gentle voice interrupted Darcy's rising concern. "Hill mentioned unfamiliar men on the estate before the first thaw. She thought they were drainage workers."

"That would align with when your steward first noticed disturbed soil near the south field borders." Darcy said to Bingley.

"I imagine the work would have been done at night," Elizabeth said, drawing attention back to the maps. "But in this weather--" She broke off, eyes widening.

Grandfather met her gaze. "I reckon the frozen ground might show tool marks—some unnatural alterations in the soil."

"We should be pleased to escort the ladies to examine the site." The words left Darcy's mouth before he could stop them. "With proper chaperonage, of course." He deliberately avoided looking at either Bingley or Jane, knowing his friend would read too much into his offer.

Elizabeth's eyes met his, startled. For a moment, something flashed in their depths that made his chest tighten, before she quickly looked away.

"That would be…" She paused, her voice measured. "Most helpful, Mr Darcy. Thank you."

Grandfather leant forward, his keen eyes belying his frail appearance. "Take the eastern approach, Lizzy. The old sheep track. The drainage pattern always showed clearest there in winter." He coughed but continued with remarkable determination. "Take detailed notes and document any tool marks. The depth will tell you whether they were made before or after the last frost."

They arranged to meet at first light. The carriage would take them as far as possible, then they would walk the line she had marked on Darcy's copy of the survey map.

Bingley offered their farewells as Darcy folded the annotated map into his coat pocket. The ride back to Netherfield was silent, each man occupied with his own thoughts.

When they arrived, Netherfield was nearly deserted. The Hursts had not deigned to travel to Meryton, and Bingley had secured only the minimal staff. The two gentlemen sat down to a cold repast.

"What an intrigue we find ourselves within! Mr Collins endeavours to have Mr Bennet declared of unsound mind, while some malefactor deliberately sabotages the irrigation works. One cannot conceive how a mere country parson, with the modest stipend afforded by his living, could orchestrate such elaborate machinations. Where do you reckon he secured the funds?" Bingley asked.

Darcy deliberated with grave consideration. He had harboured suspicions these many months of his aunt's hand in Mr Collins's every manoeuvre, but as Bingley related matter, he could no longer avoid the disagreeable conclusion that Lady Catherine de Bourgh herself had a role in this mischief.

Dawn revealed a world glazed in ice. Darcy's carriage brought them to the edge of the affected fields, where the old sheep track met the property line. The thawing ground crunched under their boots as they disembarked. Elizabeth tied her warmest bonnet on and wrapped an extra shawl around her shoulders. When she stepped out, the wind managed to find its way under the skirt, and she was grateful for Mary's enthusiasm for knitting woollen stockings.

Elizabeth pulled out the survey map, its corners crisp in the bitter air. "Here," she pointed to her markings from yesterday. "The elevation changes begin at these points." Elizabeth flexed her stiffening fingers, the raw cold biting through even thick wool.

"The ice will have settled in the lowest areas," Darcy observed, scanning the field. "We should be able to trace the altered water flow."

They began their inspection at the first marker. Elizabeth knelt to examine a suspicious groove in the frozen earth, her breath visible in the cold air. "This cut is too regular to be natural erosion." She pulled off her gloves to handle the instruments more closely despite the numbing cold.

Darcy stepped closer, blocking the worst of the wind. "Note the soil displacement pattern," Darcy said, pointing to a ridge of frozen earth. "Someone used a grading tool here—you may see where they have cut a channel to redirect the natural flow." He produced a measuring stick and notebook, efficiently recording the dimensions as Elizabeth dictated them.

The evidence mounted as they worked their way across the field. Someone had systematically altered the careful grading Elizabeth had implemented over the past three years. Each tampered section directed water flow toward Netherfield's kitchen gardens, where it now lay frozen in sheets.

"These marks in the soil," he said, returning to their task as if the interlude had been the most natural thing in the world, "they are weathered. The tampering must have occurred just before or during the thaw. The ground was workable when this was done."

Elizabeth traced the pattern of alterations on their crude map.

"They knew exactly what they were doing—see how each channel feeds into the next? This was no random matter."

The inspection itself proved gruelling. The frozen ground had preserved clear evidence of tampering, but documenting it required careful measurement and notation. Elizabeth's fingers grew stiff with cold despite her gloves.

By midday, they had compiled substantial evidence of deliberate sabotage. "The evidence is quite conclusive," Darcy said, studying his notebook. "The drainage work was clearly undermined by someone with rudimentary technical knowledge. Your original design was sound."

Darcy checked his timepiece. "We should return before the weather worsens." He paused. "Unless you think we have missed anything?"

Elizabeth reviewed their documentation. "No, this is comprehensive. Although I would like to examine these measurements against the original drainage plans."

"At Netherfield," Darcy said. "The library will be warmer for the comparison."

Jane and Bingley, who had been at a discreet distance examining the route the water took to the kitchen gardens, joined them for the walk back to the carriage. They had their evidence.

Chapter Forty

The return journey to Netherfield passed in thoughtful silence. Elizabeth pulled out her notebook again, reviewing their findings to keep her mind focused on the practical matter at hand.

"Whoever did this was familiar with the grounds enough to target the precise points that would cause the most damage."

"Indeed." Darcy's gaze was fixed on some distant point beyond the window. "The technical knowledge required narrows our list of suspects considerably."

The carriage wheels crunched to a halt on Netherfield's gravel drive. As they descended, Caroline Bingley's voice carried from the entrance. "Charles! We have had an express from Lord Matthews."

Elizabeth watched Darcy's posture sharpened at the name. Before she could ponder his reaction, Miss Bingley swept down the steps, a letter extended toward her brother. Her eyes widened at Elizabeth's appearance.

"Miss Elizabeth! Miss Bennet! I had no idea you would be…" She paused, taking in Elizabeth's practical attire and mud-splattered boots. "…joining us today."

"Miss Bingley." Elizabeth inclined her head, suddenly quite aware of her dishevelled state. "We have been examining some concerning alterations to the land around the water channels."

"Estate business on such a bitter morning?" Miss Bingley's smile was not kind. "How… dedicated you are."

"The weather actually proved advantageous," Darcy interjected, his words clipped. "The frozen ground preserved evidence we might otherwise have missed."

He turned to Bingley, who was scanning Lord Matthews's

letter with a furrowed brow. "Charles, shall we review those documents now? The light is still good."

"Yes, of course." Bingley looked up, his cheerful expression oddly strained. "Although I am afraid there is a matter I must discuss with you first." His eyes darted to his sister, then back to the letter. "In private."

Elizabeth felt Jane's hand slip into hers, a silent gesture of support. Whatever news Lord Matthews's letter contained, it had disturbed both gentlemen. She squeezed her sister's fingers in return, even as her mind raced through the implications. Lord Matthews's estate, Dunbar Court, bordered both Netherfield and the Lodge property. Had he observed any suspicious activity?

"Miss Bennet, Miss Elizabeth." Darcy's voice drew her from her thoughts. "Would you wait in the library? There are estate surveys there that might help us better understand these findings in relation to the original plans."

"Of course." Elizabeth nodded, recognising the dismissal for what it was, even as questions burned on her tongue. She followed a footman toward the library, Jane at her side, leaving the gentlemen to their private conference.

The library door closed behind them with a solid thud. Jane moved to stir the banked fire, whilst Elizabeth paced the length of the room, her mind churning.

"We found what we sought this morning," Jane said, arranging herself gracefully in a chair near the growing warmth.

"Evidence of deliberate interference, yes." Elizabeth stood by the table with the survey map. "Although I fear we have only begun to uncover the scope of this particular scheme."

She glanced at the door, wondering what connection Lord Matthews might have to their drainage troubles? And why had the mere mention of his name caused such tension?

The library's warmth began to thaw her chilled fingers but did nothing to ease the cold knot of worry in her stomach.

Elizabeth turned to the survey. "We should review the estate surveys. Mr Darcy was most particular about comparing our measurements."

Before Jane could form a suitable reply, the library door opened. But instead of either gentleman, Caroline Bingley swept into the room, her expression sharp with poorly concealed interest.

"I thought I might find you here," she said, settling herself onto a settee. "How fascinating that you should spend your morning examining the flooded gardens, rather than making calls. I suppose such practical concerns must occupy much of your attention, given your… unique situation. I trust you have quite recovered from your exertions?"

"Recovered?" Jane looked up with perfect innocence. "Oh, but it was such a pleasant morning. The frost made everything sparkle so beautifully."

Elizabeth traced a line on the map, hiding her smile at Jane's deflection. Miss Bingley shifted, the silk rustling again.

"Indeed. Although I was most surprised to see Mr Darcy venture out in such weather. He generally reserves his mornings for correspondence." Miss Bingley paused delicately. "Particularly when expecting important communications."

"Does he?" Elizabeth murmured, turning a page. "How attentive you are to Mr Darcy's habits, Miss Bingley. Jane, would you hand me that volume? The leather-bound one."

Miss Bingley's fingers tapped against her lap before stilling. "I simply thought it unusual, given Lord Matthews' connections to the neighbourhood. Why might my brother receive such a letter?"

"Mr Darcy seemed most interested in the ice formations," Jane offered unhelpfully. "He had such fascinating observations about the way water flows in winter. Did he not, Lizzy?"

"Hmm?" Elizabeth looked up as if barely attending the conversation. "I was rather focused on these elevation markers. Speaking of water flow, Miss Bingley, do you find the drainage near the kitchen gardens satisfactory? I noticed some interesting patterns there as we walked."

Miss Bingley's head turned sharply. "The kitchen gardens? I hardly concern myself with such matters." A pause. "Although I understand there have been some… difficulties with the neighbouring properties?"

"Have there?" Elizabeth spoke with polite interest as she made a small notation on the survey. "Jane, does this drawing remind you of that lovely sketch you made of the north field?"

"I believe that sketch is in my portfolio at home," Jane replied evenly. "Along with several others of the surrounding properties. One can learn so much about an estate through careful observation."

"How comprehensive your studies are. Are not such matters better left to more experienced hands? I understand Lord Matthews has extensive knowledge of local estate governance. Do you see him often in the neighbourhood?" Miss Bingley would not surrender her curiosity about the letter.

"Does he?" Elizabeth looked up with bright interest. "How fascinating. Tell me, Miss Bingley, does the Viscount also take uncommon appreciation for governance? I find the subject quite absorbing."

Miss Bingley rose with stiff grace. "I fear I cannot speak to such specific aspects of estate matters. Although I am sure my brother will have much to discuss with Mr Darcy on the subject." She moved toward the door, then paused. "I do not suppose either of you noticed if the letter bore a particular seal?"

"I was too captivated by the survey markings to notice," Elizabeth replied. "Although speaking of markings, Miss Bingley, have you ever observed how ice can preserve the most interesting evidence of--"

"You must excuse me," Miss Bingley interrupted smoothly. "I believe I hear my brother returning."

The door closed behind her with just a bit more force than strictly necessary.

"Lizzy, you are wicked. Poor Miss Bingley."

"Poor Miss Bingley indeed," Elizabeth replied, her eyes dancing. "You were not above playing your own part in her frustration."

Jane's cheeks coloured. "I am sure I do not know what you mean. I merely wished to discuss the morning's observations."

"Just as Miss Bingley merely wished to enquire after our health," Elizabeth said dryly, her expression growing more serious. "I do wonder what news that letter truly contained. Did you notice how Mr Bingley's countenance changed upon reading it?"

Darcy followed Bingley back toward the library, his mind still churning over Matthews' letter. The inquiry seemed innocuous enough—a few items allegedly forgotten in the estate sale—but something in the timing nagged at him.

"You are certain you wish to maintain this secrecy?" Bingley asked quietly as they approached the library. "It seems unnecessarily complex."

"For now," Darcy replied. The fewer who knew he had purchased Matthews' Dunbar Court estate, the better. Particularly given the recent discoveries. If Matthews had any connection to the sabotage…

Miss Bingley was hovering near the library entrance. "Charles, there you are. I was about to send a servant to search for you."

"Were you?" Bingley's attempt at nonchalance was poor. "No need for concern. Just some estate business. Some items which were to be sold. Er, sheep."

"Sheep?" Miss Bingley's voice was rich with scepticism. "You spent nearly an hour discussing sheep?"

"Prize-winning merinos," Bingley offered quickly. Too quickly. "Quite valuable. The new owner is… quite particular about maintaining accurate records."

"Charles," Miss Bingley interjected, "will you not tell me more about Lord Matthews'… involvement?

"Nothing of consequence," Bingley said, with all the conviction of a schoolboy caught in a fib. "Merely… sheep. And weather. Vexing poor weather for sheep, apparently."

"Indeed, and I suppose those Bennet women are here to discuss the weather," she snapped.

"Miss Elizabeth and Miss Bennet are here on estate business," Darcy cut in. The words emerged more sharply than intended.

Miss Bingley's eyebrows rose. "Estate business? How… novel. Still, Charles, it is nearly the dinner hour. Do you expect me to manage unexpected guests for the meal? I require some notice if you wish to entertain." Miss Bingley said with a scolding expression. "You know my feelings about impromptu gatherings." The sour look marred features that might otherwise have passed for handsome. Two sharp lines formed between her brows, and her lips turned down at the corners. Had she consulted her looking glass, she would be horrified.

"I had no intention of offering entertainment. I must beg your pardon. We will need a short time to review some documents." Bingley glanced between his sister and Darcy. "I shall send them home directly in the carriage."

"I look forward to a proper dinner later, Mr Darcy. When it can be correctly arranged." Miss Bingley swept away, triumph in every step.

"Bingley." Darcy's voice was low. "You cannot dismiss the Miss Bennets like hired help. That would be unconscionably uncivil."

"Caroline says--" Bingley began.

"I am indifferent to her wishes. It is not the behaviour of a gentleman. I will escort them back to Longbourn myself." Darcy turned toward the library, his jaw tight. The sooner he could resolve this matter and escape Miss Bingley's questionable hospitality, the better.

Darcy caught Elizabeth's curious glance as they entered the library. She had spread the surveys across the large table.

"Are these the relevant surveys?" he asked, moving to examine the maps. Safer ground, this.

"Indeed." Elizabeth's face was neutral. "Although I wonder if

Lord Matthews' letter might shed any additional light on our findings?"

Darcy kept his eyes on the surveys. "The letter was concerned with some livestock matters. A few sheep that were meant to be included in the original sale to the new owner."

Elizabeth frowned. She was far too intelligent not to sense the weakness in their story. Why should Bingley be involved in such a transaction? Her eyes met Darcy's for a moment, and he longed to tell her everything—about the property purchase, his plans, his growing suspicions about what was afoot.

Instead, he turned to the surveys. "Shall we examine what we discovered? Might I see your notes from this morning?"

Elizabeth passed him her notebook. "The alterations seem to have been made with some technical knowledge," she said. "Although I wonder why anyone would take such interest in Netherfield's water flow."

Or who might benefit from disrupting them, Darcy thought, recalling Viscount Eastbridge's inquiries about the neighbouring property's situation just before the sale. But he gave a brief nod, forcing his attention to the measurements in Elizabeth's neat hand

Darcy caught another sharp look from Elizabeth. He was managing this poorly. But until he understood Matthews's game—if indeed he was playing one—he could not risk revealing his hand.

"Miss Elizabeth," he said, perhaps too abruptly. "These measurements suggest the tampering extends further than we initially thought. Perhaps we should examine the western boundary tomorrow, if you are willing?"

Her eyes narrowed at his obvious attempt to change the subject, but she nodded. "Weather permitting. Though I hope by then we might have a clearer understanding of all the… factors involved."

The emphasis was subtle but clear. Darcy bent over the surveys again, acutely aware that their deception was unlikely to satisfy Elizabeth Bennet's sharp intelligence for long. But for now, the truth about Dunbar Court—and his own role in its purchase—

must remain hidden.

Chapter Forty-One

At Longbourn, Mary met them at the door, her composure betrayed by evident concern. "Jane, Lizzy—thank goodness you have returned. Grandfather has taken quite ill. Mamma is with him now."

After assuring themselves of their grandfather's care—he slept fitfully whilst Mrs Bennet applied cool cloths to his brow—the sisters gathered in the dining room. Elizabeth related their morning's efforts whilst Kitty fidgeted uncomfortably in her chair.

"The barn at the Lodge is nearly complete," Lydia reported. "Although moving the sheep flock in spring will be a delicate business. We shall need to time it precisely with the grass coming in on those new pastures we bought from Matthews' estate."

"And the removal of our personal effects to the Lodge?" Elizabeth asked.

"Nearly done," Mary answered. "Mamma's jewellery and personal plates have been packed, along with the books and sheet music we purchased. The furniture brought with her marriage portion is safely stored, and we have catalogued all the smaller items that came from the Gardiner side—the tea services, paintings, and linens."

"We must act quickly," Elizabeth said, then sighed deeply. "Uncle Phillips warned us plainly: 'Should the court find merit in Mr Collins's petition, they may appoint a commissioner to take inventory of Longbourn, to determine which portions fall within the scope of the entail.' We are to ensure that only what cannot legally be moved remains within reach of that determination."

"I find the whole business intolerable," Mrs Bennet declared from the doorway, her hands fluttering in distress. "To be told what we may or may not remove from our own home! To have strangers poking about my cupboards and counting my linens!"

"Uncle Phillips was most emphatic," Jane said gently. "He urged that we must not allow sentiment or discomfort to endanger the legal clarity of our position. All that can be justly claimed as personal property must be removed—soon."

"I daresay if he had to pack up his own drawing room he would not speak so confidently," Mrs Bennet huffed. "Disrupting the entire household! I never imagined I should live to see such a day."

"We shall manage it, Mamma," Elizabeth said with a calm that belied her own weariness. "The more diligently we act now, the better fortified we shall be if the matter proceeds to trial."

"And the books?" Lydia asked.

"The agricultural texts purchased have already been marked," Mary replied. "Those inherited from previous generations must, of course, remain, but we have distinguished them in the catalogue."

Elizabeth glanced around the room, taking in the familiar furnishings with a pang of quiet resolve. "Let it not be said that we did not meet Mr Collins's falsehoods with clarity, order, and truth. We will preserve what is ours—and defend what remains."

"Must the portraits remain?" Jane added quietly. "Are they fixed to the walls so that they are considered part of the house?"

"Personal chattels." Elizabeth replied. "They are only hung upon the wall. They are not integral to the structure—like glass in the windows or the wainscotting; the question is whether they are to be termed 'heirlooms.'"

"As with most of the furniture," Mary continued. "Although Mamma was careful to keep the bills of sale for the pieces we purchased with the profits over the years. Those at least are ours to take."

"And Grandfather's personal effects?" Elizabeth asked.

"His personal volumes remain in his chambers for now," Mary said. "The modern agricultural texts, in particular, are clearly his personal property."

"What of the plate in the dining room?" Lydia asked

practically. "Did not some of it come from Mamma's family?"

"Only the smaller pieces," Jane explained. "The main silver service was here when Grandfather inherited. We have marked everything—Hill has been most particular about checking the dates of purchase against the household books."

"I have begun moving my dried specimens and saved seeds to the Lodge house cellar," Kitty offered. "Although I worry about transferring the more delicate specimens in this weather. The new kitchen garden beds will not be ready until later in spring, but at least the house is sound." She hesitated, then added, "Speaking of the gardens, there is something else I should have mentioned before," Kitty said, her fingers worrying at her sleeve. "About three weeks past, when I was gathering herbs in the kitchen garden, two men came to the door. They claimed to be selling farm implements."

"I remember," Jane said. "Hill turned them away."

Kitty nodded. "But afterward, I heard them talking as they walked the path toward Netherfield. I did not think much of it then—they seemed to be discussing drainage work they had performed at other estates. But they mentioned Netherfield, and they carried far more tools than ordinary peddlers would."

Elizabeth's eyes met Jane's. "They were establishing a pretence for being seen in the area."

"And the tools they carried," Mary added quietly, "would have been exactly what one needed to move the soil and alter channels."

"It makes a pattern," Lydia said seriously. "First the writ against Grandfather, then this attempt to damage Netherfield. He means to discredit our management of both estates."

"We cannot prove it was Mr Collins's doing," Jane said.

"No," Elizabeth agreed. "But who else would benefit from flooding Netherfield's kitchen gardens? Who else would have both the knowledge of our improvements and the motive to cause such targeted damage?"

"The question becomes," Mary said, "what we do with this information."

"Whatever we decide," Lydia interjected, "we must secure the Lodge property first. If Mr Collins gets wind that we have discovered his scheme, he might turn his attention there next. I will not have my sheep's spring pasture ruined because of his spite."

The sisters fell silent, each considering the implications. Through the window, Elizabeth saw storm clouds gathering on the horizon. They would need to act quickly, before winter's grip strengthened and their evidence was lost beneath the ice.

Lady Catherine de Bourgh
Rosings Park
Kent

My dear Aunt,

I trust this letter finds you in good health. The weather in Hertfordshire has been uncommonly fine this fortnight, and Georgiana progresses most satisfactorily.

It is with considerable reluctance that I take up my pen to address a matter of some delicacy. Intelligence has reached me concerning certain activities undertaken by your parson, Mr Collins which appear to be directed against the Bennet family of Longbourn. These include attempts to have Mr Bennet declared of unsound mind, and what appears to be deliberate damage to improvements recently made to their estate. Such actions seem quite beyond the resources of a clergyman whose income derives solely from his living.

I feel obliged to remind your Ladyship that, as trustee of the Rosings estate since my uncle's passing, and after the recent difficulties with the accounts of the estate which constitute the property of my cousin under the terms of my uncle's will, I maintain oversight of all financial matters pertaining to the property. In this capacity, I have observed several substantial withdrawals from the estate accounts in recent months, made without the customary explanations or documentation. I find myself unable to approve these expenditures without proper accounting.

It is my unpleasant duty to inform you that these irregular disbursements, combined with the extraordinary expenses already incurred this quarter, have entirely depleted the allowance allocated for your Ladyship's use. No further funds can be made available for the next two quarters, and then only if accompanied by proper accounting of their intended purpose.

Should it transpire that your Ladyship has any connection to Mr Collins's present endeavours, I must caution that such involvement carries considerable risk. The courts look most unfavourably upon attempts to impugn a gentleman's sanity or to damage his property deliberately. Any person found to have instigated such actions would face both legal consequences and irreparable damage to their standing in society.

Finally, I am compelled to address what I suspect underlies these machinations. If, as I fear, these actions are undertaken with the design of compelling me into marriage with my cousin Anne, I must speak plainly. Neither Anne nor I have ever entertained such an expectation, despite your Ladyship's frequent assertions to the contrary. To continue to put about such reports as established fact can only result in harm to Anne's reputation when it becomes evident that no such union will occur. The scandal arising from such disappointed expectations would fall most heavily upon Anne herself, who has done nothing to deserve such treatment.

I remain, as ever, mindful of the respect due to your Ladyship as my relation, and it is with genuine concern for your welfare and that of my cousin that I write so candidly.

Your most obedient nephew,

Fitzwilliam Darcy

"Another court filing." Elizabeth spread the legal papers across the table in her Uncle Phillips's law chamber, where Jane and Uncle Phillips examined them. "Mr Collins now claims the recent damage to Netherfield's gardens demonstrates our incompetence extends beyond Longbourn's boundaries."

"Unfortunate timing for him," Mr Phillips observed dryly, "given Mr Darcy's recent submission to the court."

He produced a thick sheaf of documents. Elizabeth recognised Darcy's elegant hand in the detailed survey measurements they had taken, accompanied by sworn statements from Bingley's steward regarding the costs of repair.

"More significantly," Mr Phillips continued, "I paid an interesting visit to Mr Stevens, the ironmonger in Meryton. It seems Mr Collins purchased a noticeable quantity of earth moving tools last month. Paid in coin rather than taking credit, which attracted notice."

"The same week as those peddlers Kitty mentioned," Jane said quietly.

"Indeed. And Mr Robinson's men found something rather telling when they examined the damaged sections." Mr Phillips produced a mud-stained tool from a bag. "This spade was buried in one of the filled-in channels. The maker's mark matches Stevens's stock exactly."

Elizabeth studied the tool. "Could Mr Collins not claim it was used by the estate workers?"

"He might," Mr Phillips allowed, "were it not for young Tobias Carter's statement. It seems Mr Collins approached him first about doing some 'landscape work' at Netherfield. The boy refused, having worked for you on the original improvements. He recognised the proposed alterations would cause flooding."

"Young Carter's testimony alone will not be enough," Elizabeth said, "And I fear for him if Mr Collins learns of it.".

"No. But combined with the purchase records, the tool evidence, and most importantly," Mr Phillips produced another document with a flourish, "--this draft of a letter found among Mr Collins's papers when magistrate Freeman ordered a search of his lodgings at the inn. It appears to be instructions he obtained to give those 'peddlers' regarding exactly which drainage channels to alter."

Elizabeth's eyes widened as she read. The instructions were detailed, revealing both some knowledge of the Longbourn land and water and clear intent to cause damage.

"Mr Collins was foolish enough to keep such evidence?"

"Perhaps pride," Mr Phillips said simply. "He could not resist documenting his clever scheme. And now that he has brought the matter before the court himself--"

"If all of this becomes admissible evidence," Elizabeth finished. "It has weight not just regarding the damage but speaking to his character and fitness to manage any estate."

"That is correct." Mr Phillips began gathering the papers. "A hearing will be set soon. We will present the full accounting of damages then. Given the extent of repairs needed and the lost productivity of the kitchen gardens…"

He named a figure that made Jane pale.

"Mr Collins cannot possibly pay such a sum," Elizabeth said.

"No," Mr Phillips agreed. "He cannot. Which puts him in a rather desperate position regarding his future interests, does it not?"

As they walked back to Longbourn, Elizabeth could see repair work already beginning on the damaged fields. Mr Collins had meant to prove their incompetence. Instead, he had demonstrated his own—and at a cost that might well force him to relinquish his claim to Longbourn entirely.

The attorney's office proved even more cramped than Darcy had anticipated, its low ceiling and musty air doing little to improve Bingley's evident discomfort. Mr Kensington, a thin man with spectacles perched precariously upon his nose, cleared his throat yet again.

"So, you are unable to provide specific details regarding the alterations to the grounds, Mr Bingley?"

"I am not a man of particulars, sir." Bingley tugged at his cravat. "Mr Darcy has a far greater understanding of such matters."

"Yet you are the leaseholder of Netherfield." Mr Kensington's pen scratched against his page. "And the testimony must come from you directly if it is to hold legal weight."

"Yes, well." Bingley shifted in his seat. "There were ditches where ditches ought not to have been. And… stones moved. Or perhaps not moved when they should have been. The technical aspects escape me."

Darcy sat rigidly beside his friend, resisting the urge to intervene. Bingley had to manage this portion of the inquiry alone, yet each halting response further undermined their position.

"I see." Mr Kensington's look suggested he saw very little indeed. "And these alterations occurred after you took possession but before your recent return?"

"I cannot say with certainty. That is, I did not notice them immediately upon taking possession of the property, but then, I was not looking for such things."

"Of course." The solicitor made another note, his expression decidedly unsympathetic. "Perhaps you might return with more comprehensive documentation, Mr Bingley—Dates, measurements, observations from your staff?"

"Yes." Bingley stood abruptly. "Certainly. Another day, perhaps. Thank you for your time, Mr Kensington."

The carriage ride back to Netherfield passed in uncomfortable silence until they had travelled beyond the town limits.

"I have no head for this, Darcy." Bingley burst out suddenly. "Drainage systems and legal testimony and property disputes. It is wholly beyond my capabilities."

"You underestimate yourself," Darcy replied, although with less conviction than he might have wished.

"I do not. The owner should manage this matter himself. Why should I struggle with an issue that shall be his concern long after my lease has ended?"

"Because it affects your tenants and your yields presently. And because you gave your word that you would address it."

Bingley waved a dismissive hand. "The word of a man who did not fully comprehend what he was agreeing to undertake."

Something in Darcy's chest tightened at the cavalier response.

"Is that to be your approach to all challenges that arise, Bingley—To withdraw when the circumstances prove more complex than anticipated?"

"Not all challenges. Merely those for which I am ill-suited." Bingley's gaze slid away from Darcy's. "I own, Caroline has suggested I might apply the same wisdom to other areas."

"Such as?"

"As you know, she has strong reservations regarding Miss Bennet." The words emerged in a rush. "Her connections, her unorthodox situation. Caroline believes I might form a more advantageous attachment elsewhere."

"And you are persuaded by this counsel?"

"I…" Bingley hesitated. "I value my sister's opinion in such matters. Her judgement is sound."

"Her judgement is concerned primarily with her own interests." The words emerged more sharply than Darcy intended. "Have you considered whether Miss Bennet's qualities might outweigh the supposed disadvantages that Miss Bingley has catalogued?"

"Of course I have. She is all that is gentle and lovely. But a man must consider practical matters as well as affection when contemplating matrimony."

"Indeed." Darcy turned to look out of the carriage window, his jaw tight. "Have you given equal consideration to the practical matter of your own happiness?"

"Happiness comes in many forms, does it not? A suitable match need not be built on grand passion. Classic beauty is not everything."

"No," Darcy agreed, thinking suddenly, painfully, of Elizabeth Bennet's fine eyes. "But neither should your wishes be sacrificed to please those whose primary concern is their own consequence rather than your contentment. Moreover, perhaps you ought to have restrained your attentions to the lady until you had sorted your thoughts on the matter. A gentleman does not raise expectations which he has no intentions of fulfilling."

Bingley fell silent, and Darcy did not press him further. He was deeply disappointed in his friend—and more than troubled—by the parallels drawn to his own situation. If Bingley could so easily be dissuaded from pursuing a woman who brought him evident joy, what did that suggest about the strength of his character? And what of Darcy's own resolve regarding Miss Elizabeth?

The remainder of the journey passed in silence, each man absorbed in his own thoughts, and neither entirely pleased with their course.

"Good God." Bingley stared at the figures his steward had laid before them in Netherfield's study. "The damage extends beyond the kitchen gardens?"

"Yes, sir." Thompson pointed to his precisely drawn diagrams. "The altered channels have undermined the foundation of the west garden wall. Come spring, the entire structure may need rebuilding. And the flooding has killed most of the root stock in the fruit trees—they will all need replacing."

Darcy examined the cost estimates. "What of immediate repairs required to prevent further damage?"

"They are extensive. And must be done before the soil has been washed away completely, sir. That is the most pressing expense." Thompson shuffled his papers. "But the damage to the kitchen gardens alone… we will be buying in vegetables and fruits for at least two seasons. The soil has been fouled in places—it will take a great deal of work to restore it."

Bingley ran a hand through his hair. "And you are certain about these figures?"

"I had Mr Williamson from the Caldwell orchard examine the fruit trees himself. And Mr Jenkins, who did the original drainage work three years ago, provided the estimates for repairs." Thompson shifted in his seat. "They are both willing to testify to the extent of the damage, should it come to that."

Darcy watched his friend pace to the window. Once the steward had gone, Bingley dropped into his chair. "You are plotting something, old friend."

"Perhaps."

"I know that tone, Darcy. What is in your mind?"

"Mr Collins holds no present ownership interest in Longbourn—only the expectation of inheritance. Yet he speaks and acts as though the estate were already his. Such presumption, combined with his recent manoeuvres, suggests a certain… eagerness to consolidate influence."

Bingley turned, his interest sharpening. "You believe he might be susceptible to pressure?"

"I believe he may consider any proposal which lends legitimacy to his position—or funds to his purse. If one were to express interest in acquiring adjacent fields—"

"Fields he cannot truly sell," Bingley interrupted.

"True. Yet men of ambition may seek to bargain with that which is not theirs to sell. He may attempt to broker terms in anticipation of what he presumes will one day be his."

Bingley's expression turned thoughtful. "It would be a perilous matter."

Darcy inclined his head. "Perilous, yes. But not impossible."

"Mr Collins does not know I purchased Matthews's estate. If he attempts to bargain with both you and Matthews…"

"He may well be eager to sell to both, thinking he can play us against each other." Bingley laughed. "Rather devious. Although will he not discover the truth, eventually?"

"Not before the agreements are signed." Darcy's smile was grim. "And Mr Collins will find himself with significantly less of Longbourn to inherit than he imagined- if any."

Bingley mused. "Even so, rather devious of you, Darcy."

"I prefer to think of it as… anticipatory estate management."

"Indeed?" Bingley's eyes glinted with amusement. "And your interest in anticipatory estate management would not have anything to do with a certain lady's involvement in these matters?"

Darcy ignored this, returning to Thompson's figures. "We should have these repairs begin immediately. The more visible the work, the more pressure on Mr Collins."

Bingley was silent for a moment. "Whilst I see the merit of your plan, I must admit some hesitation at the outlay. Would this not more properly be done by the landowner? I am only a tenant here."

"Have you already decided against purchasing?"

"I have not decided, but Caroline is far happier in town, and she is not terribly fond of Hertfordshire. She insists I ought to buy in Derbyshire," Bingley's speech echoed his sister's petulant whinges. Darcy cringed at the obvious intention of Miss Bingley to force her brother away from Miss Bennet and closer to his own estate. It mattered not to him. If Caroline Bingley took up residence on the doorstep of Pemberley, it would not advance her campaign to become his wife by a single yard. It would, however, be sorely inconvenient.

"If that is your intention, then Mr Phillips will need to contact the owner and determine whether he will pursue the action. And you ought to end your lease to allow him to find a long-term tenant. I hope you will think long and hard about the responsibilities you undertook at Netherfield, and how you see your future. In any case, I can do little more here. The next steps require decisions that only you, as tenant, can undertake."

Bingley looked up, uncertain. "You are leaving?"

"I must return to London tomorrow." Darcy's tone was even. "There are obligations awaiting me, and Georgiana cannot remain indefinitely without my attention."

Bingley did not respond but rose and walked to the window.

"I am convinced it is not so dire that I must decide today. What say you to a ride around the fields? I think there may still be shooting to be had if we engage some beaters for tomorrow."

Darcy nodded, his role as a guest compelling him to accommodate his host's entertainments. Bingley's indecisiveness did not sit well.

Chapter Forty-Two

Darcy had just settled into his preferred corner at Brooks when Viscount Eastbridge dropped into the opposite chair, brandy in hand.

"Intelligence has been circulated regarding unfortunate circumstances at the property leased by your particular friend. Netherfield, was it not?" the Viscount said without preamble. "Nasty business with flooding."

Darcy set down his paper, studying the young peer's expression. Eastbridge seemed more amused than concerned.

"We were favoured with a most singular caller this sennight past," he continued. "Fellow named Mr Collins. Came to my father with a rather elaborate scheme regarding drainage alterations."

"Did he indeed?" Darcy kept his tone neutral, although his interest sharpened.

"Indeed. The gentleman was most solicitous regarding certain 'improvements' he proposed to undertake for the protection of our interests. He expressed particular concern for the damage sustained by our northern pasture." The Viscount's mouth formed the slightest suggestion of a smile. "Yet I perceive this was but a pretext for his true purpose. He displayed uncommon eagerness to discuss potential arrangements concerning that which he anticipates will eventually come into his possession. His interest in his future inheritance was most pronounced, I assure you."

"What sort of arrangements?"

"It appears his circumstances are somewhat straitened at present. He intimated that, once Longbourn falls into his possession, he might be disposed to relinquish certain portions of the estate—at terms he described as exceedingly advantageous to the purchaser." Eastbridge swirled his brandy. "I expressed neither acceptance nor refusal, merely… interest."

"And now?"

"Well," the Viscount leant back, "It occurred to me that such negotiations might be of particular interest to you, as the true proprietor of the estate in question. Especially in light of certain irregularities that appear to have manifested themselves of late."

Darcy considered this. "Mr Collins does not know of my connection to the estate."

"No. Nor that you have documented his involvement in the sabotage." Viscount Eastbridge set down his glass. "He seems quite convinced he can still extricate himself from this unfortunate entanglement—provided he might secure a willing party to make such a prospective arrangement."

"You are willing to… maintain his misconceptions? Hold him in hopeful expectation,"

"I might be persuaded," the Viscount said slyly. "Purely to determine the full scope of his intentions, of course. Although I would need certain assurances about the eventual disposition of any agreements, he might be foolish enough to sign."

Darcy nodded slowly. Mr Collins's desperation might prove useful—particularly if he could be manoeuvred into signing away his interests before learning the true identity of his negotiating partner.

"I believe," Darcy said, "we might come to an understanding on that point."

"I thought we might." Lord Matthews stood. "I will have my man contact you with the details of Mr Collins's proposal. Although I suggest we act quickly. One cannot predict the actions of a man pressed to the wall."

Darcy watched him leave, already composing a letter to his solicitor in his mind. Mr Collins had provided them with an opportunity—one that might finally secure the Bennets' position, if handled with care.

And perhaps, he thought, resolve other matters as well.

Grandfather sat at his writing desk, the faint winter sun casting pale light across the neatly arranged papers before him. A letter bearing Mr Darcy's seal lay open, its elegant handwriting stark against the creamy paper. His brow furrowed as he reread the careful words:

"Dear Mr Bennet,

Recent developments concerning the legal actions initiated by Mr Collins necessitate urgent consultation with my solicitor and barrister in London. It is vital that you, or a suitable representative authorised to act on behalf of your family's interests, meet with them promptly. I urge your swift response.

Respectfully, Fitzwilliam Darcy"

A knock at the door interrupted his thoughts. "Enter," he called, folding the letter with deliberate care.

Elizabeth stepped into the room, Jane and Mrs Bennet following closely behind, their expressions filled with quiet expectation. Elizabeth glanced toward the letter in her grandfather's hand. "Grandfather, is there news from Mr Darcy?"

"Indeed," he replied dryly. "Mr Darcy wishes me to journey to London—or appoint someone to act on our behalf—to confer with his legal advisers about Mr Collins's nonsense."

Jane's gentle voice was tinged with concern. "Grandfather, pray, he does not expect you to travel, given the state of your health?"

Grandfather's chuckle was more of a dry rasp. "I fear my travelling days are well behind me, Jane. London would be the death of me, or so your mother would insist." He sighed, glancing toward the window where winter's chill crept steadily into the room. "Nonetheless, it is clear someone must go."

Elizabeth glance quickly at her sister before stepping forward. "Perhaps Uncle Phillips might attend in your stead?"

Mr Bennet shook his head slowly. "Your uncle's presence will certainly be necessary; however, the solicitors and barristers in London require someone vested with direct responsibility for the estate and empowered to make binding decisions."

"Please do not choose me, Mr Bennet, I could never manage such matters!" Mrs Bennet said.

"Calm yourself, my dear Fanny," he said gently, gesturing for her to sit. "You shall not be required to leave Longbourn."

Mrs Bennet exhaled in relief, sinking into a chair near the fire. "Then who, Mr Bennet? Who could speak for us in London?"

Grandfather met Elizabeth's steady gaze, then looked toward Jane, noting the quiet strength and composure both young women possessed. "Elizabeth. Jane. It must be the two of you."

Elizabeth nodded; her expression resolute. "We shall go, Grandfather. You may rely upon us."

Jane reached for her sister's hand, offering quiet support. "Indeed, Grandfather. Together we shall represent your interests and ensure Longbourn's protection."

Their grandfather regarded them with a blend of pride and melancholy. "I know you shall. Very well then," he said, holding out Darcy's letter to Elizabeth. "Inform Mr Darcy that he may expect you. You compose a pretty letter, and I shall sign it."

Elizabeth accepted the letter with steady fingers, determination lighting her eyes. "We shall depart for London as soon as arrangements can be made."

As his granddaughters left the room, Mr Bennet leant back in his chair, eyes closing briefly against the weariness that threatened. "Well Fanny, the burden of Longbourn's future, has now passed into the hands of the capable young women we raised." Despite the uncertainty ahead, this thought brought him no small measure of peace.

The solicitor's chambers in Lincoln's Inn Fields were austere, all dark wood and leather-bound volumes. Elizabeth smoothed her best muslin dress, conscious of its dated trim, whilst Jane sat perfectly composed beside her. Their Uncle Phillips shifted uncomfortably in his chair, out of his element in the opulent London office.

Mr Darcy, however, looked quite at home. He had risen immediately when they entered, ensuring Elizabeth and Jane had the chairs nearest the fire. Now he stood by the window, his bearing effortless among the trappings of wealth and power that seemed designed to intimidate country clients.

"Miss Elizabeth," he said, voice lowering as he approached her chair, "Have you brought the estate records I mentioned?"

"Yes." She withdrew the figures from her reticule. "Although I fear my calculations may need review by more experienced heads."

"Nonsense," he said with quiet firmness. "Your management of these matters has been exemplary."

Something in his expression made her pause—a warmth she had not expected. When he accepted the papers, his manner suggested respect for her work rather than mere politeness.

He drew a chair near. "Pray explain your findings to me."

This was familiar ground—drainage patterns and soil composition, yield calculations, and labour costs. Darcy listened intently to her explanations, his questions showing genuine interest in her expertise.

"Extraordinary," he murmured, clearly impressed.

"Only the application of careful attention, Mr Darcy."

"No." Elizabeth saw in his expression respect—and something more complex—in his gaze. "It is far more than that."

The arrival of the senior solicitor interrupted whatever he might have said next. Elizabeth was both relieved and oddly disappointed as Darcy resumed his more formal manner. But she did not miss how he positioned himself between her chair and the intimidating desk, as if to shield her, nor how his presence made the whole proceeding less daunting.

The solicitor, Mr Graves, settled behind his imposing desk. Darcy noted how Elizabeth straightened in her chair, all business now despite the intimidating surroundings.

"The sabotage has been fully documented," Mr Graves began, shuffling through his papers. "Mr Darcy, you have brought the surveys?"

"Here." Darcy presented the detailed drawings. "Along with sworn statements from Mr Bingley, his steward, and the local nurserymen regarding the extent of the damage."

Elizabeth leant forward to examine the documents. "The western section is worse than we initially thought."

"Indeed." Darcy appreciated her quick grasp of the technical details. "The foundation damage to the garden wall was discovered only yesterday."

Mr Phillips nodded. "And you believe these documents would be sufficient to force Mr Collins to make restitution?"

"More than sufficient," Mr Graves said. "Should the court find in our favour and given his own legal claims of waste and mismanagement. He has, in essence, invited the court's scrutiny of these very matters."

"Although restitution would prove difficult," Elizabeth observed quietly, "given his limited means."

"Which brings us to the matter of alternative arrangements," Mr Graves said.

Darcy watched Elizabeth's expression intently as Mr Graves outlined their strategy. Her quick mind would immediately grasp the implications of Mr Collins's attempts to sell his future interests.

"A rather elegant solution," she said finally. "I am sensible of some surprise that Lord Matthews would involve himself in such negotiations."

Darcy kept his expression neutral. That was dangerous ground.

"His Lordship has his reasons," he said carefully. "The legal documents are being drawn up now. We require your family's agreement to proceed."

"The entail presents a significant obstacle," Mr Graves interjected. "Mr Collins, as heir presumptive to the Longbourn Estate, has no present interest he might legally convey. His attempts to sell what he does not yet possess could be viewed most seriously by the court."

"Indeed," Mr Phillips agreed. "The entail gives him only the expectation of inheritance, not a present right to dispose of any portion."

Mr Graves nodded. "By entering into secret agreements regarding the future disposition of entailed lands, Mr Collins places his position as heir in some jeopardy. The courts take a rather dim view of such speculative arrangements."

"Then these agreements he proposed with Lord Matthews…" Elizabeth asked.

"Would demonstrate Mr Collins's unfitness to succeed to the estate, particularly when viewed alongside his actions in soliciting the sabotage. One cannot simultaneously claim concern for proper estate management whilst secretly arranging to damage and dispose of portions of that same estate."

"Assuming," Phillips said slowly, "the court accepts the connection between the sabotage and Mr Collins's attempts to gain control of the estate."

"These written arrangements with Lord Matthews," Mr Graves continued, "not just proposals but signed agreements to dispose of specific portions of Longbourn - they demonstrate a troubling disregard for both law and property. He tacitly acknowledges that the cost of repairs at Dunbar Court and at Netherfield will be his to bear."

"The court's view would be especially harsh," Phillips added, warming to the legal discussion, "given that Mr Collins has already repeatedly brought the matter of estate management before the court through his accusations against Mr Bennet."

Mr Graves selected another document from his desk. "By his own petition, he has claimed deep concern for Longbourn's preservation. Yet these papers show him quite willing to divide and sell portions of that same estate - and to a party who, he believes, has a legitimate claim for damages due to the flooding he caused."

Elizabeth's expression sharpened with understanding. Mr Collins had not only violated legal principles - but he had also revealed the fundamental dishonesty of his position.

"So, by attempting to sell what he does not possess," Elizabeth said, "Mr Collins demonstrates that his petition regarding Grandfather's management was never truly about protecting Longbourn."

"The court," Mr Graves confirmed, "would likely take a most severe view of such duplicity. Particularly when presented with the evidence of his direct involvement in damaging neighbouring estates."

"And what remedy would you suggest?" Phillips asked.

"That," Mr Graves said, with a slight smile, "depends on how much pressure we wish to apply. The law provides several interesting possibilities when an heir presumptive acts against the estate's interests."

Elizabeth's hand tightened on her papers. The next decisions would not be easy ones, but they could give her family protection against Mr Collins's machinations. He only wished he could offer more direct comfort in this moment.

Mr Graves turned to Elizabeth. "Should we not consult Mr Bennet before proceeding? These arrangements will affect Longbourn's future disposition considerably."

A faint colour touched Elizabeth's cheeks, but her voice was steady. "Grandfather spoke with Jane and me. He has… he has entrusted to us the solemn responsibility of determining our family's course in this grave matter."

Darcy caught the flash of deeper meaning in her words. Mr Bennet was far more ill than they had allowed to be known. His chest tightened at the implications - both for the urgency of their legal arrangements and for Elizabeth herself.

"The timing of his legal actions is damning," Mr Graves continued. "He files a petition claiming grave concern over

Longbourn's management yet simultaneously approaches Lord Matthews about schemes to damage Netherfield's productivity. Then, when faced with the potential consequences, he attempts to dispose, in secret, of portions of an estate he does not yet possess."

He spread three documents across his desk. "Here we have his petition regarding Mr Bennet's management, dated the third of November. Here, evidence of his involvement in the drainage alterations beginning the following month. And here…" He tapped the third document significantly, "Lord Matthews's written account of Mr Collins's approach regarding the sale of future interests, dated but yesterday."

"A clear pattern of deception," Phillips observed.

"More than deception," Mr Graves said. "The law takes a particularly severe view of an heir who attempts to profit from damaging neighbouring estates. That he would compound this offence by attempting to sell portions of his expectancy…" He shook his head. "The courts are most particular about maintaining the integrity of entailed estates."

"Might the court consider removing him as heir presumptive?" Phillips asked.

Elizabeth's posture lifted with hope at this suggestion. Such an outcome might offer the best protection for her family.

"That would be… extreme," Mr Graves said slowly. "Although not without precedent when an heir has demonstrated active hostility to the estate's interests. The sabotage alone might not be sufficient, but combined with these attempts to dispose of his future interest…" He pulled another volume from his shelf. "There was a case in '89 where an heir's actions against neighbouring properties led to an heir's removal."

"But such proceedings could be lengthy," Darcy interjected, thinking of Grandfather Bennet's failing health.

"There might be a more expedient solution," Mr Graves suggested. "One that uses Mr Collins's own actions to secure a more favourable arrangement."

"Mr Collins," Mr Graves explained, "has already

demonstrated his willingness to negotiate regarding his future interests. Rather than expose his improper attempts, we might instead… redirect them."

"Through Lord Matthews?" Phillips asked.

"And Mr Bingley," Mr Graves added. "Both have legitimate claims for damages. Both could offer Mr Collins a way to avoid public exposure of his actions, in exchange for certain binding legal agreements regarding his future management of Longbourn."

"What sort of agreements?" Elizabeth asked.

Mr Graves opened another volume. "A trustee arrangement. Mr Collins would retain his position as heir but agree to place the oversight of specific portions of Longbourn under the direction of trustees - to include Mr Bingley and Lord Matthews's representative, as neighbouring landowners with vested interests in cooperative drainage management."

Comprehension dawned in Elizabeth's eyes. The arrangement would effectively prevent Mr Collins from interfering with the estate whilst preserving his expectation of his inheritance rights.

"And Mr Collins would agree to this?" Mr Phillips sounded sceptical.

"When presented with the alternative - public exposure of his actions, lengthy legal proceedings, and possible restitution and removal as heir - I believe Mr Collins could find the trustee arrangement quite appealing." Mr Graves smiled thinly. "Particularly if Lord Matthews implies he might still be amenable to future business arrangements, once the legal difficulties are resolved."

"A fiction, of course," Mr Phillips said slowly.

"Of course." Mr Graves gathered his papers. "But one that might serve all parties' interests. Mr Collins retains his position, if not authority. The estate's management remains secure. And the neighbours' interests are protected."

"No, no," Mr Phillips interjected. "A trustee arrangement fails to address the imminent concern. With Mr Bennet's health…" He glanced apologetically at Elizabeth.

"Indeed." Mr Graves set aside the documents and thought

silently for a moment. Elizabeth's fingers worried her reticule.

"You are quite right. What we require is not management of the entail, but its dissolution." Mr Graves said. Elizabeth released a long breath.

Darcy straightened. This was more extreme than their previous discussions had contemplated—and more welcome.

"Can it be done?" Elizabeth asked directly.

"The entail might be broken," Mr Graves said cautiously, "if we can demonstrate both Mr Collins's actions against the estate's interests and his attempt to circumvent the very purpose of the entailment through these secret sales. Combined with his sabotage of neighbouring properties…" He retrieved a different legal volume from his shelf. "The court's primary concern in upholding entails is preserving estates intact for future generations. If we can show that Mr Collins's actions threaten this purpose…"

Mr Graves then set aside the weighty legal volumes, his expression solemn. "Whilst the evidence we have assembled presents a compelling narrative of Mr Collins's duplicity and intentions, we must remain mindful that the decisions of the court are never entirely predictable. Though precedent strongly favours our cause, and the equities as well, we nevertheless remain at the mercy of chance."

Elizabeth felt a chill run through her, despite the warmth of the fire. "Do you mean to suggest, sir, that our case might yet fail?"

"Not fail precisely," Mr Graves replied gently, "but we must acknowledge the inherent uncertainties of any legal proceeding. The courts, even upon reviewing identical facts, may weigh matters differently. It is my duty to prepare you for every eventuality."

Jane spoke softly, her voice steady. "What preparations, then, would you advise us to undertake, Mr Graves?"

Exchanging a brief glance with Mr Darcy, Mr Graves continued. "If the court determines that Mr Collins's allegations have some basis in fact or law—however unjustified—they may order a detailed inventory and valuation of Longbourn's assets. It would thus be prudent for your family to compile all deeds, bills of purchase, and pertinent records that establish ownership of your belongings and movable property. Such diligence may forestall distressing confusion later."

"Our uncle has already initiated such preparations," Elizabeth said, her tone resolute yet weary. "Though I had dearly hoped they would prove unnecessary."

"Let us hope so indeed," Mr Graves said kindly. "Yet prudence demands readiness. You must create an exhaustive and detailed list, paying particular attention to items whose ownership might reasonably be contested, or those we can document were brought by Mrs Bennet to her marriage."

Elizabeth inclined her head in acknowledgement. "We shall proceed accordingly."

"And the forthcoming trial itself?" Mr Phillips interjected; his anxiety evident. "How ought we to best prepare ourselves?"

Mr Graves's voice was firm and reassuring. "I will guide you thoroughly in all matters—preparing testimony, presenting documentation, and anticipating the questions likely to arise. It is imperative that witnesses remain composed and present their evidence clearly and without undue emotion, regardless of provocation."

Darcy stepped forward, his presence reassuring. "You may depend upon my continued support in all respects, Miss Elizabeth. Whatever support you and your family require is yours."

Elizabeth met his steady gaze and felt her resolve strengthen. "Your generous assistance is deeply appreciated, Mr Darcy."

"Very well," Mr Graves concluded, rising to signal the meeting's end. "We have considerable work ahead. Whilst I remain optimistic, let me caution you once more: court proceedings invariably carry an element of uncertainty. We must do all within our power to prevail, yet ultimately, we remain subject to the mercy of chance."

Outside the solicitor's chambers, Elizabeth drew a deep breath, steadying her composure in the crisp London air. Turning to her uncle, she could not completely conceal the turmoil she felt.

"Uncle," she said quietly, "is it truly to come to this? Is our entire future—the future of our home, indeed our very lives—to be decided by the judgement of one man clad in a red robe and wig, whom we have never met?"

Mr Phillips smiled gently, placing a comforting hand upon her arm. "My dear Lizzy, the gentleman beneath that wig is no ordinary man, but one solemnly sworn to uphold the law. He is bound by oath to weigh thoroughly the facts before him and to render his decision strictly according to established precedent."

Elizabeth sighed, still unconvinced. "Yet even the wisest of judges must err at times. What safeguard have we against such a misfortune?"

Mr Phillips regarded her seriously. "Should the judge's determination seem inconsistent with justice or centuries of legal precedent, there remains the possibility of an appeal. That right alone is no small matter, Lizzy. It is the safeguard of all who seek redress under the law. Our legal system—however imperfect—is founded on the principle that every person, regardless of station, is entitled to a fair hearing. Since the Magna Carta, and more firmly still with the Bill of Rights, the law has stood as a barrier against tyranny and caprice. We are not wholly at the mercy of any single ruling, for our institutions provide for correction and redress. Our government is based on the rule of law, not the whims of man."

Elizabeth nodded slowly; her eyes thoughtful as she considered her uncle's words. "Then we must trust, it seems, in the integrity of the law and the honour of those appointed to uphold it."

"That we must, my dear," Mr Phillips replied gently. "Take heart. Our case is sound, and we have both justice and precedent on our side."

Chapter Forty-Three

The morning sun filtered through the parlour windows, casting long shafts of light across the worn but well-scrubbed floorboards. Mary sat at the secretary, her pen moving steadily across the page as she tallied accounts and catalogued the remaining household items to be transferred to the Lodge. Though her posture was upright, and her expression composed, her eyes bore the weight of quiet responsibility.

Kitty lounged nearby on the settee, pretending to mend a pair of gloves, though her attention was plainly elsewhere.

"You know," Kitty remarked, threading her needle without looking down, "it is rather fearsome, the way you have taken command of the house since Lizzy and Jane left. A less charitable observer might suppose that you enjoyed issuing instructions."

Mary did not glance up. "Someone must ensure order is maintained."

"Yes, but you need not march about quoting the account book like the Articles of War," Kitty teased. "If Mr Fairfield calls again today, I shall know it is to report on your new system for storing turnips, or to hear your latest theories on composting straw."

A faint flush rose in Mary's cheeks, but she kept her voice composed. "I have simply endeavoured to maintain the expectations set by Grandfather and my sisters."

Kitty's grin widened. "And to inform Mr Fairfield that calcium-rich soil may yet revolutionise the lower orchard?"

Mary finally looked up, the corner of her mouth twitching. "If you are determined to mock my interest in agronomy, you may take over the inventory of preserves."

Kitty gave a theatrical shudder. "No, thank you. I shall

confine myself to teasing and glove repair. Far safer."

Mary shook her head, returning to her entries. But even as her pen resumed its path across the page, a flicker of amusement remained in her eyes.

A knock at the front door brought Mary's head up. Hill entered a moment later. "Mr Fairfield to see Miss Mary."

Mary rose at once, smoothing her skirt. "Show him in, Hill."

Mr Fairfield entered with a brisk step, hat in hand, and a case of papers tucked beneath one arm. "Good morning, Miss Bennet," he said, his bow deep and earnest. "I hope I do not intrude. I come with the notes from the soil survey and a question regarding your marsh drainage figures."

"You are most welcome, Mr Fairfield," Mary replied, gesturing toward the table already laid out with maps and ledgers. "I have just finished updating the records from last week's observations. Please, let us review them together."

He joined her at the table without hesitation, and the two bent over the documents with the solemn concentration of scholars examining a treatise. Their voices dropped as they entered discussion—Mary pointing out the elevated calcium levels in one sample, Fairfield offering a comparison from another estate's marshland.

Kitty looked at Hill, who had remained quietly near the hearth. With a mischievous gleam in her eye, she murmured, "And they say sentiment is out of fashion. Or should I say, sediment?"

Hill's mouth twitched at the corner, but she demurely replied, "Seems to me Miss Mary's doing fine work, no matter the topic."

By midday, Mr Fairfield had taken his leave, his eyes lingering on Mary as he offered his farewells. She returned to the secretary with a deep breath and resumed her cataloguing, the faintest smile curving her mouth.

Mrs Bennet sat beside Mr Bennet's chair in the small sitting room he preferred, updating him on household matters as was her custom each week. She had just finished recounting the details of a dinner party when she paused, seeming uncharacteristically hesitant.

"Is something troubling you, my dear?" the elderly gentleman asked.

"No, not troubling," Mrs Bennet replied, fidgeting with her handkerchief. "It is just that… well, Mr Freeman has been calling rather frequently."

"So, I have observed," he said with a gentle smile. "A fine man, Freeman. Steady and respectable."

"Yes, he is most respectable," Mrs Bennet agreed. "And the girls seem to like him well enough."

Mr Bennet reached out and patted her hand. "Frances, my dear, you need not circle the matter so delicately. I am not so old that I cannot recognise what is happening."

Mrs Bennet blushed like a young girl. "Certainly not, nothing improper—"

"Of course not," he interrupted kindly. "You are a lady of impeccable propriety. But you are also a woman still in the prime of her life."

She looked down at her hands. "It has been nearly eight years since Thomas passed."

"Indeed. My son would not have wished you to spend the rest of your days alone." The old man's voice grew softer. "Life is too precious, and too short, to deny oneself happiness when it presents itself, Frances."

Mrs Bennet looked up, her eyes filled with unshed tears. "You truly believe so?"

"With all my heart," he assured her. "Thomas would want you to be happy. As do I. As do your daughters, although they may tease." He chuckled. "I hear the kitchen has never produced so many apple tarts."

Mrs Bennet laughed despite herself. "The girls are incorrigible gossips."

"They are observant," he corrected. "And they love their mother." He squeezed her hand. "Now, when next Mr Freeman calls about some transparent matter of business, perhaps you might suggest a walk in the garden. I hear the early daffodils are quite fine this year."

Mrs Bennet's smile was radiant. "Thank you, Father Bennet."

"No need for thanks," he replied with a wink. "But perhaps you might ask Cook to send up one of those famous apple tarts. I should like to see what all the fuss is about."

The clock had not yet struck four when the sound of hoofbeats broke the hush of the afternoon. Mary, seated at her account books, glanced up as a footman approached, dismounting with practised ease. Kitty, nearest the window, let out a small exclamation. Hill entered the parlour with unaccustomed urgency, her cap askew and her cheeks touched with colour. "A London post rider, ma'am," she announced. "A letter has arrived for Mr Bennet."

At once, the household stirred. Mary rose from her place and reached for the sealed packet with steady hands. "From Gracechurch Street," she read aloud, studying the seal. "It is Elizabeth's hand."

Mrs Bennet entered in haste, followed by Lydia. "A letter! Oh, Mary, read it aloud this instant. I shall not be able to rest until I hear what she says. Perhaps the matter is resolved, and they are returning home."

Mr Bennet, already settled in his favourite chair, nodded to Mary "Read it aloud, Mary. We shall all learn their news together."

"Yes, yes, Mary," said Mrs Bennet, her voice fluttering. "Read it at once—I shall not be easy until I hear that my girls are safe in that dreadful city."

Mary unfolded the letter and began, her voice steady.

Gracechurch Street, Tuesday morning

My dearest Family,

I write in great haste to share what news I may, and to assure you—and especially dear Grandfather—that Jane and I arrived safely and are now comfortably settled at Uncle and Aunt Gardiner's. Our reception here has been most warm, and the children were delighted to see us, though Aunt has already confessed her concern over how little rest we are likely to take whilst in town.

Yesterday we attended Mr Graves's chambers in Lincoln's Inn Fields, accompanied by Mr Darcy and Uncle Phillips. The setting was intimidating—oak-panelled walls, legal tomes towering above our heads—but Mr Darcy proved a steady and reassuring presence throughout. He took care to place us near the fire and made every effort to ensure we were not overwhelmed by the formality of the meeting.

She read without interruption, but when she came to Elizabeth's mention of the chambers in Lincoln's Inn Fields and the intimidating setting, Kitty gave a small shiver.

"Lincoln's Inn! That sounds most dreadful. I imagine some grim, echoing hall filled with clerks in black."

"I do not know how they can bear it," Mrs Bennet fretted, wringing her handkerchief. "Solicitors and barristers and all those dreadful legal persons—I should swoon on the threshold."

"They will not swoon," said Mary crisply. "They are there to defend our family's interests."

…Mr Graves has reviewed the documentation pertaining to Mr Collins's petition and believes our position to be quite strong, particularly with the evidence connecting Mr Collins to the drainage sabotage and the improper attempts to sell a future interest in Longbourn. We were made to understand the gravity of these matters in full, and I confess to being both astonished and appalled by Mr Collins's boldness.

Lydia's eyes widened in delighted outrage. "So, it is true, then! That smug little toad really dared to sell what is not his to sell. I should like to box his ears."

"He is shameless," Kitty added. "But what if the court believes him?"

Mary glanced at her grandfather, then replied with quiet certainty, "Then we shall rely upon the measures we have already begun. The Lodge is ours by purchase and much has been removed from Longbourn already. Even should the court prove less than just, we shall not be destitute."

Mr Bennet gave a slow nod of approval. "Quite right, Mary. We are not without recourse."

Mary read on.

Mr Graves reminded us that the court may soon require a formal inventory of Longbourn, should the petition proceed to trial. Uncle Phillips has advised on preparing such a list, and he has emphasised the importance of distinguishing between entailed and personal property. We shall send further instruction in the event that effort begins in earnest.

Mrs Bennet gasped. "I declare it is an outrage! That man means to strip me of my very teaspoons!"

"They must determine what belongs to the estate, and what is our personal property," Mary said calmly. "Mr Phillips advised us to prepare for such a possibility."

"Well, my marriage portion and the Gardiner heirlooms shall not be touched."

Mary glanced at her grandfather, then continued the letter.

…We are to remain in London for at least a fortnight, perhaps longer, to assist with preparations and review affidavits. Mr Graves has been most diligent, and Mr Darcy exceedingly generous with his time and efforts I need hardly say how grateful we are for their support.

A silence followed this sentence.

"Well," he said at last, "we are indebted to Mr Darcy.

"Jane sends her love and adds that she is doing her utmost to remain composed for all our sakes. Pray give our warmest affection to Grandfather and reassure him that we are equal to the task he has entrusted to us. I hope he continues comfortable, and that the rest of the household is in good health and spirits. Write soon and let us know how you all fare.

Yours ever affectionately,

Elizabeth

Mary reached the end of the letter and folded it once more.

"Mary, do write to them tonight," Mrs Bennet declared. "They must know how we are managing here—and how we are keeping them in our prayers."

"They are very brave," Kitty said quietly. "I never imagined

Jane and Lizzy would go to court."

Mrs Bennet clutched her handkerchief. "Heaven preserve them from being made to speak before a judge!"

Mary gave a calm shake of the head. "They shall not. Women are not called to speak in such proceedings. Mr Graves shall present all testimony. Our sisters attend only to advise and review the affidavits."

"And they do so under the protection of Mr Darcy and Uncle Phillips," added Mr Bennet. "They are not without support. I have no doubt they will acquit themselves admirably. Let us hope the court sees what we have always known—that the fate of Longbourn ought not rest in the hands of a fool."

There was a moment of stillness in the room as each considered what lay ahead.

Then Lydia reached for her mending. "I suppose I had best finish this hem, in case they wish to inventory that as well."

Chapter Forty-Four

The Court of Chancery hummed with ancient ceremony, its vaulted ceilings echoing the murmur of gathered barristers and the rustle of parchment. The traditional call rang out, a declaration of order steeped in centuries of practice:

"Oyez! Oyez! Oyez! All manner of persons having anything to do before the Right Honourable the Lord High Chancellor of Great Britain in His Majesty's High Court of Chancery, draw near and give your attendance!"

A hush fell, interrupted only by the scratch of quills and the soft shuffle of clerks moving among the oak benches. Upon the Lord Chancellor's bench, the great mace of office lay before him, its presence a symbol of authority as he took his seat, his robes faced with miniver marking the winter session.

Before him, a Master in Chancery, his expression impassive, sorted through a sheaf of reports—lengthy accounts prepared for His Lordship's deliberation. The Commissioners of Oaths, seated in their designated area, remained poised to verify any sworn statements brought before the court.

The mountain of documents upon the bench—bills, crossbills, answers, rejoinders, affidavits—all tied in red tape, bespoke the notorious burden of Chancery litigation. Barristers in their horsehair wigs and black silk gowns adjusted their notes, whilst solicitors conferred in low voices with their clients. Mr Graves's shifted his black silk gown, the mark of having "taken silk" setting him apart from the more junior barristers in their stuff gowns.

The court officer's staff struck the flagstone, and the Master in Chancery began his formal recitation of the case.

"In the matter of Mr Collins versus Bennet, praying for relief concerning the entailment of Longbourn…"

The ancient formulae of the court rolled on, each ceremony marking another inexorable step in Mr Collins's assault.

The barristers conferred. The court noted that a member of the nobility was present as a witness and instructed that his testimony be taken immediately. Lord Matthews advanced with measured step, the clicking of his boots against the stone floor the only sound in the hush. He ascended to the witness box, took his appointed place. Lord Matthews met the courtroom's gaze with unshaken poise, adjusting his gloves as though this were a matter of mild inconvenience, rather than a case that might decide the future of an estate.

Mr Collins loosened his neckcloth. Beads of sweat had formed at his sparse hairline and were beginning to slide down his face. Hemmed in between his counsel, he shrank beneath the solemnity of these proceedings. His eyes darted between Lord Matthews's aristocratic figure and the impassive visage of the Lord Chancellor seated above.

Low chatter disturbed the chamber as the presence of a noble witness was noted. Lord Matthews, his posture as precise as his tailored frock coat, took the witness box. The clerk of the court held out the bible, and Matthews, with a nod, placed his hand upon it.

"You shall true answer make to all such questions as shall be demanded of you, touching the matters in this cause, and by Almighty God to speak the truth, the whole truth, and nothing but the truth."

"So help me God."

The Lord Chancellor's gaze settled upon him; his words deliberate. "Lord Matthews, you have given written deposition in this matter. You shall now answer further to the court's satisfaction. Pray, state for the record the nature of your dealings with one Mr Collins."

Mr Collins inhaled sharply. A nervous tremor passed through his frame. The weight of the Lord Chancellor's quill poised over parchment signalled that each word spoken here would be preserved in the annals of the court.

"My Lord, I was initially approached by a gentleman of that name who sought to discuss matters of estate improvement. Specifically, he proposed certain alterations to drainage works which he claimed would be to the benefit of the estate of Dunbar Court."

"At the time of this encounter, were you the owner of the estate entitled Dunbar Court?

"Yes, at that time I was,"

"Do you currently hold title to that property?

"I do not," Lord Matthews grimaced at the admission. Mr Collins leant toward his solicitor, whispering with visible urgency. A sharp bang of the court officer's staff echoed in the vast chamber, making Mr Collins start like a guilty man.

"And to whom did you sell this estate?"

Lord Matthews hesitated a fraction of a second. "To a holding company, recently formed—Pemberley Holdings."

Darcy's composure remained unchanged, though Jane glanced sharply at Elizabeth. Elizabeth's brows drew together. The name struck an immediate chord.

"Pemberley Holdings," repeated the Lord Chancellor, noting the name. "And is it known who stands behind this company?"

"It is not generally known," Matthews replied. "However, I believe this court may wish to inquire directly of Mr Fitzwilliam Darcy, who acted through his solicitor."

Shock settled over Elizabeth. She turned slowly toward Darcy, who sat composed and silent, offering no denial.

The Lord Chancellor looked toward Darcy. "Mr Darcy, do you acknowledge this transaction?"

Darcy rose, bowing. "I do, my Lord."

"And what was your purpose in acquiring this estate?"

"An investment in a property with excellent potential."

The Lord Chancellor narrowed his gaze. "Prudent, perhaps. But I find it notable that a gentleman with no ties, lease, or familial claim should take such an active interest in the area. You will explain yourself, sir."

Darcy straightened, his voice calm but deliberate. "I have

offered counsel to Mr James Bennet and his granddaughters, regarding improvements to that estate's drainage and agricultural efficiency. Dunbar Court is adjacent to Longbourn and the estate of another most respected acquaintance. My intent was to secure the sound management of lands adjoining those.

Elizabeth's cheeks coloured, though she betrayed no outward alarm. The explanation was careful, measured—yet to her ears, it rang with the disquieting resonance of a truth half-disguised.

The Lord Chancellor regarded Darcy a moment longer, then returned his gaze to the documents before him. "So noted. We shall now proceed with the substance of Mr Collins's claims."

Elizabeth sat motionless; her hands clenched tightly in her lap. Her thoughts tumbled—anger, confusion, something softer and more complex—all vying for precedence. Jane reached for her hand, but Elizabeth could not yet look at her.

"Lord Matthews, did Mr Collins mention any financial interest in this matter?"

"Indeed. His scheme was twofold—first, to suggest certain 'improvements' to lands within Dunbar Court, and second, to negotiate the future sale of portions of Longbourn, an estate he expects to inherit. He sought an advancement of funds for the interest in Longbourn. He was, to my judgement, in some financial distress and eager to secure immediate funds."

"My Lord, did Mr Collins at any time make reference to the recent acts of sabotage upon the estate water works in question?" asked the barrister for the plaintiff,

"Not directly. However, he betrayed an undue eagerness to position himself advantageously, as though anticipating certain difficulties might arise—difficulties which, I now understand, were of his own design."

"And did you, at any point, indicate willingness to enter into such an arrangement?"

"I neither indicated willingness nor unwillingness. I merely expressed interest in seeing his full proposal. It was my intention to ascertain the details of his intended sales and whether they might be relevant to the present issues in the area."

"To your knowledge, does Mr Collins understand the limited extent of his authority in this matter?"

Lord Matthews paused briefly, then replied evenly. "He does not. He remains under the impression that his actions remain undiscovered and that he might still extricate himself—if he can secure an advantageous agreement. According to his later correspondence, he planned to force the transfer of Longbourn to his hands through court action and then fulfil his obligations by leveraging that property."

"And you retained these letters, my Lord?" the Lord Chancellor enquired.

"Yes, your honour. Including Mr Collins's specific proposals regarding the disposal of Longbourn's east fields." Lord Matthews's accent remained perfectly aristocratic, making Mr Collins's schemes sound all the more tawdry.

"You will submit all correspondence pertaining to this matter to the court."

"As Your Lordship commands."

Lord Matthews recited the Viscount's account of their meetings leaving no room for reinterpretation. The Court of Chancery remained silent as Lord Matthews's testimony concluded, the weight of his words pressing upon the assembled company. His measured cadence had delivered a damning account of Mr Collins's eager scheming, but the process was not yet complete.

At the conclusion of the Lord Chancellor's questioning, he intoned, "Let the record reflect that the witness's statement was delivered under oath and without contradiction. Your witness, Plaintiff."

Mr Collins's barrister, Mr Forsythe, a man of middling talent and little courtroom presence, rose from his bench, adjusting the sleeves of his stuff gown as though the act might lend him gravitas. His thin lips pursed, his fingers smoothing the pages before him as he attempted to formulate a strategy of defence.

He bowed to the bench. "With Your Lordship's leave, I shall

now put certain questions to the witness."

The Lord Chancellor inclined his head. "Proceed."

Forsythe cleared his throat. "Lord Matthews, I put it to you that my client—Mr Collins—approached you with a simple proposal of mutual benefit, one that any reasonable landowner might entertain."

Lord Matthews arched a brow, glancing toward the Master in Chancery, who dutifully recorded each word. "If by 'mutual benefit,' you mean a scheme to first manipulate estate drainage in his favour, and then to dispose of lands which were not yet lawfully his, then I suppose that is one way to frame it."

A few muffled chuckles stirred among the barristers.

Forsythe straightened his shoulders. "It is not remarkable for gentlemen to seek improvements to their holdings. Is it not true, my Lord, that you yourself have engaged in such discussions?"

A slight smile ghosted across Lord Matthews's lips, a confident expression of effortless superiority. "I have indeed discussed estate improvements, sir, but I daresay I have never resorted to sabotage, nor have I sought to sell that which I did not own."

Mr Collins shrank in his seat. He fidgeted with the buttons of his waistcoat.

Forsythe flipped through his papers, pressing on. "You state that my client's financial position was strained. How did you arrive at such a conclusion?"

Lord Matthews straightened, his voice even, patrician. "He confessed it. Mr Collins spoke at great length about the pressing need to secure funds, lamenting the delay of his inheritance. He suggested that a sale of certain portions of Longbourn—which he assured me he would soon possess—could be arranged immediately."

Forsythe frowned, fumbling for an alternative line of questioning. "And yet, you did not immediately report this alleged scheme to the Magistrate?"

Matthews tilted his head, a picture of effortless condescension. "I did not. I am not in the habit of running to the magistrate over a man's desperate boasts. But as Mr Collins's actions grew more brazen, I saw fit to retain his letters."

Forsythe seized upon this. "Letters! But did my client ever explicitly confess to wrongdoing?"

The Bennet's barrister did not object—he knew well that Forsythe was digging his own grave.

Lord Matthews steepled his fingers, his delivery unhurried, each syllable enunciated. "I believe the phrase used in one of his letters was: 'It will take but a little pressure upon the court for the lands to be made mine, and then I shall be free to act.'"

A ripple of scandalized murmurs spread through the gallery. The Lord Chancellor raised one grey brow.

Forsythe visibly paled. He pressed forward with the air of a man running out of road. "My Lord, you claim Mr Collins had knowledge of the—ah—unfortunate damage to your drainage works. But do you have evidence that he ordered it?"

Matthews's expression remained composed. "The court has already heard from Mr Tobias Carter, whose sworn deposition states that Mr Collins directly sought his services for the purpose of interfering with the works. Mr Collins spoke with an intimate familiarity with the manner in which the damage was accomplished."

The Commissioners of Oaths murmured among themselves as the clerk of the court lifted a sheaf of parchment—the official deposition already entered into evidence.

Mr Collins shifted in his seat. His fingers plucked ineffectually at his neckcloth.

Mr Forsythe, now plainly desperate, waved a hand with forced nonchalance. "But my Lord, one might argue that a simple conversation is hardly an admission of intent."

Lord Matthews's smile was glacial. "Oh, I quite agree. But when a gentleman follows such a conversation with written instructions, a signed agreement, and evidence of bank payments recorded in his own name—one is rather compelled to draw conclusions."

The court erupted in a stir, the spectators murmuring not

even attempting to conceal their opinions.

Forsythe, defeated, vaguely gestured to the bench. "No further questions, my Lord."

He sat down heavily, his wig listing to one side.

The Lord Chancellor laid aside his quill, surveying the chamber with the solemn weight of centuries of legal authority behind him. He adjusted his spectacles with deliberation, then raised one hand. At his signal, the court officer stepped forward and struck the floor with the ceremonial staff, its sharp report echoing through the vaulted hall.

"This court will hear from the remaining witnesses after a brief recess. We shall reconvene at two o'clock."

The corridors of the Inns of Court were thick with murmured speculation, as figures in dark robes passed with brisk purpose, their expressions ranging from impassive to gravely engrossed in hushed conferences. Elizabeth, Jane, and Mr Philips lingered in the antechamber, uncertain whether they ought to remain standing or seek some more tolerable respite. The court recess was lengthy, and whilst none of them wished to stray far, the prospect of loitering in such a cold and impersonal space was equally unappealing.

Darcy, ever decisive in moments of uncertainty, took command of the situation. With a few quiet words to a passing clerk, and a discreet sum pressed into a waiting hand, he secured a private parlour in one of the adjacent chambers. The room was modest, yet well-appointed—furnished with a sturdy oak table and a low-burning fire in the hearth, its warmth a welcome contrast to the damp chill of the corridors. At his direction, a tray of tea and a light repast was arranged, the refreshment as much a gesture of care as of necessity.

Elizabeth seated herself near the fire, absently tracing the rim of her teacup, her thoughts too preoccupied to take more than a sip. Across from her, Darcy stood stiffly near the window, his gaze fixed upon the rain-slicked cobbles outside. His composure remained intact, yet Elizabeth—now keenly attuned to his moods—observed the tension in the set of his shoulders, the subtle flex and curl of his fingers, as though he resisted the urge to pace.

She knew the source of his disquiet.

The revelation of his purchase, so publicly spoken in court, still rang through her thoughts. She ought to have felt deceived—he had kept it from her, had let it emerge under oath like a fact of no consequence. Yet, what unsettled her more deeply was not his silence, but that it had been so unexpected, done so swiftly, nearly recklessly, at least by his meticulous standards. She had always mistrusted such boldness from men of fortune, too often cloaked in self-importance. But Darcy had risked something rarer—his privacy, his principles. He had wagered them not for admiration, and surely not for gain. He had acted with her family's interests in mind—that was beyond question, but what troubled her was the implication beneath it. He was tying himself to Hertfordshire, to the land that bordered Longbourn.

To her.

Darcy turned then, as if sensing her scrutiny. His dark eyes met hers, searching, wary.

"I hope," he said at last, voice low and measured, "that you do not find my recent decision… objectionable."

Elizabeth tilted her head, considering him. "That depends. Am I to assume you consulted no one before making it?"

The corner of his mouth twitched, although his tension did not wholly abate. "That would be an accurate assumption."

She let out a breath, shaking her head with something that was not quite exasperation. "You do not make things easy for yourself, Mr Darcy." she said. "You act as if certainty alone were its own justification. And yet…" Her voice faltered, the protest yielding to something more fragile. "And yet, I have every reason to be glad you did. You cannot know how such certainty unsettles those who have never had the luxury of it."

"I have never sought ease," he admitted. "Only what I believe to be right."

The simplicity of the statement struck her. There was no arrogance in it, no expectation of gratitude. He had not acted to impress her or to force her regard; he had done what he thought right, with little concern for how it might be perceived. How many men of his station would have troubled themselves with such considerations?

"And yet, for all your certainty, you seem rather concerned about my reaction."

He hesitated. "Your good opinion…" He exhaled, as though frustrated with himself. "It matters to me."

Her heart gave a peculiar, traitorous lurch. Rather than alarm her, it came upon her gently, that realisation—unexpected, yet wholly welcome. How easy it had become to look to him in times of uncertainty. How natural it felt to trust his judgement, to find steadiness in his presence.

She knew now, with a certainty deep in her chest, that he was steady, capable, and unshakeable in his convictions. He understood her—perhaps better than she had thought possible.

And more than that, he was precisely the man whom, in disposition and talents, she now realised she could most admire.

The thought settled in her heart, unexpected yet wholly welcome.

Darcy cleared his throat, his posture subtly shifting as though he had read something in her expression. "The recess should not last much longer."

"No," she agreed. "But long enough, I think, for a cup of tea."

Before she could speak, Jane's voice—quiet and distant—drew their attention away. She had sat largely in silence since they had entered the room, staring down into her untouched cup of tea.

"Have you heard from Mr Bingley? It is unexpected for him to be so absent," she murmured at last, her voice intentionally neutral.

Elizabeth's chest tightened at the subdued note in her sister's expression. When last they had seen Mr Bingley, he had offered warm expressions of regard and spoken in general terms of his hope that the matter might soon be resolved. But he had not been at court that day, nor had he sent word. The contrast to Mr Darcy's unwavering presence could not have been more marked.

Darcy shifted, his brows drawing together. "I have not had word of him recently."

Jane gave a small, polite nod but said nothing further.

Elizabeth studied her sister with quiet concern. Jane, who always sought the best in people, who so rarely allowed disappointment to show, had reached the limits of even her generous patience. Mr Bingley was a fool.

A silence stretched between them all, filled only by the distant sound of voices beyond the door.

Elizabeth turned back to Darcy, finding his gaze still upon her.

She reached for the teapot, pouring for them. And though no more was spoken, something unspoken passed between them—a quiet understanding, an accord that had not been there before.

The summons to return to court echoed through the corridors with chilling clarity. A clerk's voice, formal and dispassionate, called the assembly to order. Figures in black robes flowed back into the courtroom like shadows returning to their appointed posts. The great doors of the Chancery swung closed with solemn finality. Once again, the Lord Chancellor took his place beneath the carved canopy of justice, and the gavel struck.

The ironmonger Stevens followed. Long regarded in Meryton as a man whose ledgers were neater than most parsons' sermons, his reluctance to take sides in village disputes was matched only by his devotion to exactitude. He presented his meticulous records of tools purchased—entries neatly notated in his ledgers, detailing the spades, crowbars, and iron bars procured on Mr Collins's account. When asked whether such purchases were typical for a clergyman, Stevens hesitated, glancing at the assembled company before shaking his head with a scoff. No, such requests were most out of the common way. He had assumed, at the time, that they were intended for some necessary repair upon the Longbourn Estate. But with all that had now come to light, he was forced to reconsider.

Then came Tobias Carter's deposition, entered into the record with solemn gravity. The clerk of the court read aloud from the sworn document, his voice steady, betraying none of the weight of what was spoken. Carter's account was damning in its clarity—he recounted, without embellishment, how Mr Collins had sought him out, suggested a minor adjustment to the drainage of a neighbouring estate, and, when Carter hesitated, knowing the Bennets were still in residence, had sweetened the offer with coin and the promise of further employment.

A murmur swept through the courtroom, subdued at first, but rising in intensity as if the very walls bore witness to his perfidy. The murmur swelled into audible disapproval. A lady gasped; an older gentleman muttered with rancour beneath his breath. Even the Lord Chancellor, seated beneath the heavy canopy of the bench, allowed his quill to still upon the parchment before him.

Elizabeth, seated between Jane and their uncle Phillips, maintained perfect composure throughout. Her hands, folded in her lap, remained utterly still. Only Darcy, seated apart in the public gallery, just visible beyond the carved partition, noticed the tension in her grasp upon her reticule. His gaze did not stray from her.

Mr Collins rose to offer his testimony, his imperiousness withering under the judge's stern gaze. The usher stepped forward, holding out the worn leather-bound bible. "Place your right hand upon the Holy Scripture and repeat after me."

Mr Collins hesitated, his fingers twitching at his sides. He cast a glance about the court, as though searching for a sympathetic gaze, before drawing himself up with an air of wounded dignity. "My Lord Chancellor," he began, "as a clergyman of the Church of England, my word is my bond. To swear an oath is, in my case, unnecessary, as I am ever bound by the truth before God."

A silence followed, thick and expectant. Then, with a rustle of silk robes and a measured dip of his quill into ink, the Lord Chancellor addressed him. "Mr Collins, this court shall not make an exception on the grounds of personal sentiment. Whatever oaths you may take in your own conscience, here you are bound by the law as any other man. You shall be sworn."

The slight creak of the Lord Chancellor's chair as he leant forward made Mr Collins start. He swallowed, his Adam's apple bobbing, and finally lifted a shaking hand to the bible.

"Repeat after me," the usher intoned, and Mr Collins, with evident reluctance, obeyed. His voice quavered as he swore to speak the truth, the whole truth, and nothing but the truth. When he finished, he lowered his hand as though the act had physically wearied him.

The Lord Chancellor regarded him with the cool detachment of a man unimpressed. "Now, Mr Collins, you shall answer to this court. You have presented yourself here on numerous occasions, first concerning the competency of Mr Bennet, then regarding the entailment of Longbourn, claiming waste and spoilation by mismanagement. We now hear testimony that contradicts the very arguments you have put forth. Pray tell, how do you explain this?"

Mr Collins licked his lips. His gaze flickered toward his barrister, who was already fumbling through papers, and then toward the assembled court, where the rows of barristers, clerks, and spectators sat in rapt attention. He shifted uncomfortably as though his attire had suddenly grown constrictive, his voice too small for the grandeur of the room.

"I merely sought to protect—" he began, the words spilling forth in desperation. Mr Collins cleared his throat, his confidence faltering. "I have always acted in the best interest of the estate," he declared. "Mr Bennet's mental decline has been evident for years—his eccentricity well known. It was my solemn duty to ensure that Longbourn was turned over to capable hands."

The Lord Chancellor raised an eyebrow. "Indeed?" He lifted the beribboned petition from the stack before him. "You sought to protect the estate when you filed your petition regarding Mr Bennet's competency?"

Mr Collins nodded fervently. "Quite so, my Lord. It was a most distressing circumstance. I could not in good conscience stand idle whilst the estate fell into mismanagement."

The Lord Chancellor tapped the petition lightly against the desk, his expression momentarily betraying a flicker of disbelief. "The same Mr Bennet who, the records show, had that week completed a detailed survey of drainage requirements with his granddaughter? The petition to find Mr Bennet non compos mentis which my learned colleague dismissed as wholly without merit?"

Mr Collins twitched, his lips pressing into a thin line. "With respect, my Lord, such tasks are hardly proof of sound mind. A gentleman of advanced age may still go through familiar motions whilst lacking true understanding."

The Lord Chancellor gestured to the Master in Chancery before selecting another document. "Do you dispute then, that Mr Broadmore's examination of Mr Bennet was thorough? Was his report not accurate? You are surely aware of its findings- ah, I see in his summary that you were present. Do you, sir, call into question the veracity of Mr Broadmore's sworn testimony and determinations?"

Mr Collins stiffened. A flush of mortification crept from his collar to his temples "I—of course not, my Lord. But eccentricity—"

"Eccentricity is not incompetence." The Lord Chancellor's voice cooled. He addressed Mr Collins with the quiet certainty of one accustomed to being heeded "Would you like to revisit the examination? The one in which Mr Bennet not only demonstrated impeccable memory but also corrected the examiner's arithmetic? Mr Bennet, who when asked to identify the reigning monarch, provided not only his name and title but also an assessment of the legal implications of his declining faculties? Do you have evidence to contest that, when questioned on his own daily affairs, Mr Bennet detailed a meticulous accounting of estate improvements, challenged the bias against female competence, and offered insights into animal husbandry that left the examiner himself at a loss for further inquiry?"

Mr Collins opened his mouth, but the Lord Chancellor continued, his voice cutting. "Or perhaps we should recall Mr Bennet's response when asked to total a sum of coins laid before him—when he not only provided the answer instantly but remarked that it would be wholly insufficient for the drainage repairs you claim he is incapable of understanding? Or the apothecary's testimony, which confirmed that his mind is as sharp as ever, requiring only mild tonics for age's minor discomforts?"

A few chuckles rippled through the gallery. Mr Collins blanched.

"And yet, despite all evidence to the contrary, you maintain that Mr Bennet was unfit?"

Mr Collins grasped at his dignity. His voice was reduced to a quavering squeak. "It—it was a concern shared by many, my Lord."

"Many?" The Lord Chancellor's features arranged themselves into a momentary expression of incredulity. "Or just you, Mr Collins?"

Mr Collins floundered as hand rose absently to his throat as if the very air had grown difficult to breathe. "I merely sought to protect—"

The Lord Chancellor's tone could have frosted glass. "Protect whom, Mr Collins? For it does not appear it was Mr Bennet, or Longbourn. Where are these concerned many who will testify to his incompetence?"

His Lordship's fingers sorted through the damning evidence, then lifted a paper. "Mr Collins." The Lord Chancellor's measured words fell into the silence of the court. "Now I must ask you directly. Did you approach Lord Matthews regarding the disposal of portions of Longbourn?"

Mr Collins's cheeks reddened with mortification. He tugged at his too-tight cravat, his mouth working before words emerged. "My Lord, I merely sought to explore possible arrangements—"

"That is not what I asked. You are to answer the question put to you." The Lord Chancellor's voice remained steady, but the weight behind it pressed down like a stone. "Did you, or did you not, propose to sell specific portions of Longbourn to his Lordship, before you held any interest except as heir presumptive?"

"I… that is to say… certain discussions were had…"

"Answer the question, sir."

Mr Collins swallowed with visible effort. "Yes, my Lord." His voice had dwindled to barely more than a whisper.

The Lord Chancellor inclined his head. "You sought to offer for purchase property not your own after you had petitioned this court regarding Mr Bennet's management of the estate?"

"The circumstances—My Lord, I merely sought to—"

"A simple yes or no, sir."

Mr Collins's hands twisted around the crown of his hat, his throat bobbing as though he might yet swallow his own words.

"I—that is—"

"Yes or no will suffice."

A beat of silence.

"Yes, my Lord." Mr Collins expelled a lengthy sigh, his shoulders sagging.

The Lord Chancellor extracted another red ribboned packet from the pile before him. "In your petition regarding Mr Bennet's competency, you expressed particular concern about, I quote, 'the preservation of Longbourn's lands intact for future generations.'" He lowered the paper and fixed Mr Collins with an unwavering gaze. "How do you reconcile this with your attempts to alienate portions of those same lands?"

Mr Collins opened his mouth, but no words came.

"Further," the Lord Chancellor continued, "you claim deep concern for proper estate management. Yet we have before us evidence that you arranged for and directed the sabotage of drainage works and caused flooding on neighbouring property- the Netherfield estate, property of Caleb Sims under lease to Charles Bingley, as well as to Dunbar Court."

Muttering was heard in the gallery.

"My Lord, I had no direct involvement—" Mr Collins

protested weakly.

"Then explain these letters to the labourers, written in your own hand?" The Lord Chancellor, with deliberate care, held up a sheaf of documents. "Or the records of payment from your account book? Mr Stevens's records of purchase of earth moving tools by your account? Is this not evidence of your direct involvement?"

Mr Collins paled. The silence stretched, thick and suffocating, as the court's collective gaze bore down on him.

His fingers fumbled for a handkerchief, dabbing at the perspiration beading on his forehead. "There were… circumstances—"

"Yes," the Lord Chancellor interrupted, his voice sharpening. "Circumstances which seem to form a pattern. First, an attempt to examine the estate records without authority, followed by a complaint to wrest control of the estate through frivolous claims of incompetence. Then, deliberate interference with water works damaging neighbouring lands. And finally, private arrangements to dispose of property you do not yet—and may never—possess."

He set down his papers with finality. "Did you imagine the court would not take notice of such actions?"

The inked words before him, so damning in their clarity, were as a noose tightening around Mr Collins's throat.

The afternoon proceeded with the inexorability of a well-laid trap. Every piece of evidence, every witness's testimony, formed another bar in the cage around Mr Collins. His own letters to Lord Matthews proved entirely damning when read aloud.

Mr Collins's counsel rose. "My Lord, if I might—"

"You have had ample opportunity to present your client's position," the Lord Chancellor said in an icy voice. "I find myself particularly troubled by the pattern these actions reveal. They suggest not simply poor judgement, but a fundamental disregard for the very principles of estate preservation that entailment exists to protect."

He set down his quill. "The evidence of sabotage to Longbourn's drainage channels and resultant harm to surrounding estates is conclusive. The testimony regarding your attempt to sell future interests is unimpeachable. Your own letters to Lord Matthews make your intentions quite clear."

Mr Collins seemed to shrink in his seat with each pronouncement.

"This court cannot allow such actions to stand without consequence. The entailment of Longbourn was created to preserve the estate intact for future generations. Your demonstrated willingness to divide and dispose of its lands, combined with active hostility toward neighbouring properties, strikes at the very purpose of such protection."

Jane's calm, so often unshakeable, had frayed at the edges; a faint line had appeared between her brows, her fingers clutching Elizabeth's hand tighter beneath the folds of her shawl.

The Lord Chancellor's quill scratched against parchment as he made his final notes. The silence in the court grew heavier with each stroke.

"This court," the Lord Chancellor pronounced, gathering his papers, "will take these matters under advisement. I shall deliver my findings when the court reconvenes at two o'clock tomorrow." He rose, and the assembled company rose with him.

As the crowd began to disperse, Elizabeth felt the full weight of the morning's proceedings settle upon her. Her spine remained straight, but her vision blurred for a moment. Jane's hand found hers again, and they clung together in silence, amid the shifting sea of onlookers. From the corner of her eye, Elizabeth glimpsed Darcy standing in the gallery's shadows, unmoving, his eyes fixed only on her.

Chapter Forty-Five

"Miss Bennet, Miss Elizabeth." Mr Darcy approached their small party as they gathered their belongings. The formality of the court proceedings had left them all drained, and Elizabeth noticed the pallor that had settled upon her uncle's formerly ruddy complexion. "My house is but a short distance. Might I offer you and your uncle some refreshment before you return to Gracechurch Street?"

Mr Phillips, looking rather worn from the court's formality, accepted for them with evident relief. The clerk of the court bowed as they departed, the echoes of legal argument still seeming to linger in the surrounding air.

Outside, the winter sun cast long shadows across the cobblestones. Darcy's carriage was brought round first, its polished panels gleaming. Elizabeth approached Mr Darcy's grand carriage, holding fast to her sister's hand. The tension of the day had left her more unsettled than she cared to admit, although she maintained her composure with determination. Mr Phillips had already settled in the forward-facing seat, nodding his thanks. The footman handed Jane in first, then, when Elizabeth approached the step, Mr Darcy stepped forward to assist her.

"Are you well, Miss Elizabeth?" he asked softly.

She glanced up at him, momentarily startled by his proximity and the genuine concern in his eyes. "As well as can be expected, sir," she replied, with restrained emotion. "It cannot be denied that the day has been rather more taxing than anticipated."

His hand closed gently around hers as he assisted her into the carriage, the brief contact sending an unexpected warmth through her gloved fingers. "You bore yourself with remarkable composure," he said quietly, his tone pitched for her ears alone. As she settled herself on the bench, his gaze remained fixed upon her countenance, until he closed the door and joined the party in the second carriage.

The grand façade of Darcy House loomed before them, its elegant proportions and tasteful ornamentation speaking of generations of wealth and refinement. Elizabeth hesitated on the carriage step, suddenly overwhelmed by the disparity between this London mansion and her beloved but modest Longbourn.

How could Mr Darcy possibly understand the life she had chosen? A gentleman of his standing, with such extensive properties and connections, could not truly comprehend what it meant for women to maintain an estate without male protection in a society that valued women only by their connections. His words suggested… but no, she must not allow herself to misinterpret common courtesy as particular regard.

"Miss Elizabeth?" Mr Darcy stood waiting, having already handed down her sister.

Elizabeth forced a smile and spoke in what she hoped was a pert manner.

"Forgive me. I was momentarily overcome by the grandeur of your residence."

Something flickered in his expression—disappointment, perhaps? "It is no more than stone and mortar," he said quietly. "The true worth of a home lies in those who inhabit it."

Elizabeth averted her gaze when it was suddenly drawn to one of the tigers on the rear of the carriage—a young man whose familiar features caused her to study him.

"Is that not Tobias Carter?" she enquired, her brow furrowed.

Darcy nodded, his shoulders tensing briefly. "It is. I took the liberty of offering him a position after his remarkable courage. His account of Mr Collins's attempt to sabotage Longbourn's drainage system to flood Netherfield was invaluable."

Elizabeth felt a mixture of surprise and admiration.

"I hope you do not think it presumptuous," Darcy replied,

"The boy showed remarkable integrity, and I thought it prudent to remove him from Mr Collins's potential influence."

Elizabeth studied him, her expression softening. "It was most thoughtful, sir."

"His welfare concerned you," Darcy said simply. "Therefore, it concerned me as well."

The late afternoon light slanted through Darcy House's tall windows, painting golden rectangles across the Aubusson carpet. Darcy watched Elizabeth's profile as she accepted a cup of tea from Georgiana, whose hands trembled despite her determined composure. The morning in Chancery Court had left them all in a peculiar state of suspension. The Lord Chancellor's promise to deliver his ruling on the morrow hanging over them like an invisible clock's pendulum each tick bringing them closer to resolution or catastrophe.

"Miss Darcy," Elizabeth said, her voice pitched with gentle warmth, "your brother tells me you have created quite a paradise in your orangerie. Even in winter, to have blooming citrus must be remarkable."

Georgiana's shoulders relaxed a fraction. "The gardener says the lemons may fruit this year, though I can claim little credit."

"Then we are equally ignorant," Elizabeth replied. Georgiana's often solemn face broke in a small smile. "Although I should dearly love to see them. In Hertfordshire, we must content ourselves with hardier specimens."

"Perhaps…" Darcy hesitated briefly, aware of how this might appear but unable to resist. "Perhaps you would care to view them now? The afternoon sun shows them to particular advantage."

Elizabeth's quick glance carried a spark of mischief that suggested she was not deceived by his convenient pretext. "I should like that a great deal, Mr Darcy. One must seize such opportunities for horticultural education when they present themselves."

"Indeed," he replied gravely, although his lips betrayed his amusement. "A most improving pursuit."

The orangerie lay down a short corridor, its glass panels

capturing the weak late afternoon sunshine. Elizabeth's expression brightened as she took in the unexpectedly lush greenery.

"How wonderful," she breathed, examining a glossy leaf. "To have such summer scents in winter. I must confess, Mr Darcy, this makes our kitchen garden's rosemary and thyme seem rather modest by comparison."

"Herbs possess their own dignity," he countered, welcoming the familiar spark of challenge in her tone, "I seem to recall a rather spirited defence of their practical value during your last dinner at Netherfield."

"Ah yes, when you suggested that ornamental gardens spoke to a more refined sensibility." Her eyes caught his, bright with remembered provocation. "I believe you were extolling the virtues of your aunt's famous roses at the time."

"I would never dismiss the practical in favour of mere ornament, Miss Elizabeth. Perhaps my argument that evening lacked… nuance."

"Nuance?" She studied a delicate citrus blossom, her expression arch. "Is that what you would call your declaration that kitchen gardens belonged firmly below stairs, out of sight of genteel visitors?"

"You have an uncomfortably precise memory for my social failures," he observed dryly.

"Only the most entertaining ones," she assured him, her smile carrying a warmth that made him momentarily forget tomorrow's looming judgement. "Your orangerie makes a compelling argument for the marriage of practical and ornamental virtues." She meant to speak lightly, but the intimacy of the space, the hushed air between glass and greenery, lent her words unexpected weight.

"High praise indeed, Miss Elizabeth. I shall inform the gardener immediately of your qualified approval."

"Oh no, my approval is altogether unqualified. I admire the beauty as well as the practicality of the work. I hope you appreciate it yourself."

He stepped closer, drawn by the subtle interplay of light and shadow across her face. "I appreciate many things, Miss Elizabeth, perhaps not always as openly as I should."

Her eyes widened at his approach, and for a moment the air between them seemed to crystallise with possibility. He studied her expression with a persistence that exceeded polite observation. He straightened and turned away.

"How did you find your first encounter with the law's majesty?" Darcy asked, his tone carefully neutral although his expression held genuine interest.

Elizabeth's fingers touched the rim of a terra cotta pot, her expression thoughtful. "In truth, I had not expected the Lord Chancellor to show such… patience with Mr Collins's meandering testimony. Patience that spoke more to his thoroughness than any merit in the arguments presented."

"Lord Eldon is known for his careful deliberation," Darcy agreed, studying the subtle shifts of expression across her face. "His intent is to have his rulings held up by any appellate review. I was struck by your admirable equanimity when Mr Collins presumed to offer the court a most singular exposition on matters of riparian law, one which bore little resemblance to established precedent."

"Singular?" Her eyebrow lifted in a way that made his chest tighten inexplicably. "I believe the word you search for is 'nonsensical.' I will own that his citation of mediaeval water rights was an impressive feat of imagination."

"It would not be unreasonable to admire such determined misunderstanding," Darcy said, then caught the flash of genuine worry beneath her arch look. "Miss Elizabeth… the Chancellor's questions regarding practical management spoke to the heart of the matter. Your grandfather's careful documentation of improvements--"

"But will it be enough?" The question escaped before she could master it, and he saw how quickly she tried to recover her cheerful spirit. "Forgive me. I should not ask you to speculate."

The vulnerability in her voice stirred something protective in his chest, an overwhelming urge to offer comfort, to take her hand

and… He stepped back abruptly, his expression shuttering. What madness was this? Any gesture of particular attention from him now would be not only inappropriate but potentially damaging to her reputation. He was a gentleman, and she was a guest in his home.

"The law follows its own course," he said, more formally than moments before. "But your grandfather's case was well presented."

Elizabeth's quick glance suggested she had noticed the sudden shift in his manner. She simply inclined her head in acknowledgement. "Then we must trust in justice, must we not, Mr Darcy? I fear such trust comes more easily to some than others."

The subtle challenge in her words made him want to respond in kind, to return to their earlier easy exchange. She glanced up, catching his expression before he could school it to neutrality.

The citrus blossom fragrance in the air, sweet yet with an underlying sharpness that reminded Darcy of Elizabeth herself—a woman whose gentle appearance belied a formidable spirit. He lingered in the moment, unwilling to disturb the fragile understanding that had begun to take shape between them.

"Your documentation is most thorough," he offered, his voice softening despite his determination to maintain gentlemanly distance. "In my experience, the Chancellor values practical evidence above theoretical arguments."

"Then perhaps there is hope yet for those of us who prefer soil beneath our fingernails," Elizabeth replied, her smile returning with a warmth that reached her eyes.

Darcy took an unconscious half-step closer, drawn by that warmth. "Miss Elizabeth, I—"

Then the sound of voices from the drawing room penetrated their sanctuary, and reality crashed back. Georgiana's gentle laugh mingled with the deeper tones of Mr Phillips, reminding them both of propriety's constant presence.

He stepped back, his manner cooling perceptibly. He gestured toward the door with careful courtesy. "Shall we rejoin the others? I believe I heard Georgiana offer to play."

Elizabeth's expression flickered - a shadow passing across her certainty - before settling into something more measured. "Yes. Perhaps it will serve to distract me. 'The law follows its own course,' you said. After the day's proceedings, I better understand why even the most confident gentleman might pace his study whilst awaiting a Chancellor's ruling. Whose words shall the Chancellor credit? What decision did some court make a hundred years past that might determine our fate? It feels governed more by hazard than design." She paused, her eyes meeting his briefly. "We seek justice, but I fear we must in some measure be always at the mercy of chance." Her voice revealed fragility beneath the gentle teasing, betraying how deeply the uncertainty of tomorrow's judgement weighed upon her.

He could command a regiment of solicitors, direct the course of vast estates - yet here, now, he stood powerless to ease the anxiety that stiffened her posture beneath the calm demeanor she struggled to preserve. Proprieties formed an insurmountable barrier to his offering the comfort he wished to provide.

He inclined his head, acutely aware of how her presence filled the quiet space between citrus trees and they turned toward the drawing room where propriety - and safety - waited. Their arms brushed as they walked, the faintest contact, but he felt it like a spark. Neither looked aside..

The warmth and welcome of the Gardiner's home on Gracechurch Street settled around Elizabeth like a familiar melody, each note sweet and comforting after the austere performance of legal theatre they had witnessed. She toyed with her delicate china teacup, thinking of how the barristers had postured and preened in their formal dress, as if the wearing of a wig might somehow transform mere mortal understanding into divine wisdom.

"It strikes me as strange," she said slowly, "how peculiar it is that the fate of Longbourn - with all its practical concerns of soil and drainage and crops and tenants' livelihoods - should rest in the hands of men who have never so much as planted a seed."

Mrs Gardiner's eyes held a gleam of recognition. "Yet they would have us believe that only years of reading Latin phrases and dusty tomes can prepare one for such weighty decisions."

"Indeed." Elizabeth set down her cup with care. "Their grand theories faltered when faced with Grandfather's detailed accounts of field management. All their elegant citations could not match the simple evidence of improved yields."

"The law does seem to pride itself on complexity," Jane observed quietly. "As if understanding must necessarily be wrapped in layers of incomprehensible language. Yet the gentlemen have spent years studying such matters. All those hours at Cambridge, all that time at the Inns of Court…"

"Hours spent in chambers lined with leather-bound books," Elizabeth replied, challenge creeping into her tired voice. "

Mrs Gardiner set down her cup. "You noted how the Lord Chancellor attended particularly to your grandfather's documentation of yield improvements."

"Yes," Elizabeth acknowledged, her expression brightening. "And how Mr Collins's man faltered when questioned about actual field conditions. I suppose there is much to be said for hands-on experience over pure scholarship. But all those Latin phrases are nought but a convenient shield," Elizabeth replied, her exhaustion giving way to sharper analysis. "For if one cannot penetrate their citadel of language, how can one hope to question their judgement? After today's display, their mysterious realm struck me as rather less impressive than they might wish—once the ceremonial trappings were set aside, the principles seemed quite… obvious. Indeed, I dare say any woman who has managed a household budget or negotiated with a merchant could grasp them readily enough."

Mrs Gardiner's smile carried years of similar observations. "Heaven forbid we should suggest such a thing. Lest we disturb their very masculine conviction that only men who wear wigs and robes to work can truly understand complex matters. I believe they find it more comfortable to imagine us occupied solely with children and gossip."

"More comfortable indeed," Elizabeth agreed, her voice taking on an edge. "For what might happen if we were to demand entry into their hallowed halls? What revelations might emerge if practical experience were valued equally with theoretical knowledge?" She straightened in her chair, animation returning to her features. "I watched Mr Collins's man fumble through basic questions about water flow whilst quoting mediaeval precedents with perfect recall. As if knowing the date of some ancient ruling matters more than understanding how water actually moves across land."

"You found their arguments lacking then?" Mrs Gardiner asked, her expression suggesting she already knew the answer.

"Not lacking so much as… disconnected. They speak of property as an abstract concept, all documents and declarations, whilst we live with its daily reality." Elizabeth's expression softened. "Mr Darcy at least seems to grasp both worlds - the legal and the practical. His testimony cut through to the heart of matters in a way that made some of the other gentlemen rather uncomfortable."

"Perhaps because he too must balance theory with practice," Jane suggested gently.

"Yes," Elizabeth agreed, her voice thoughtful. "I wonder if they realise how much of their supposed expertise we mastered simply through necessity. After all, what is contract law but an elaborate version of negotiating with merchants? What is property law but the formal expression of what every estate manager must know by heart?"

Jane reached across and gently laid a hand atop Elizabeth's—her touch light, but steady. "Take heart, Lizzy," she said with a glint in her eye. "After all, we have survived far worse than a roomful of men in wigs. I believe I once diffused a family quarrel with less than a day's notice with two dozen guests already seated to supper."

Elizabeth laughed, startled and grateful. "A fine precedent, indeed." Shifting shadows of thought crossed her countenance as she added, more quietly, "It is strange, is it not, that so much of what we do—quietly, daily—counts for little until it is echoed by a man in court? I am not overawed by their mysterious profession. I simply wish…" She trailed off, letting the onus of centuries of exclusion hang in the comfortable silence between them.

"Yes," Mrs Gardiner said softly. "We all do. Perhaps one day…"

The words hung in the fire-lit air like a prayer, or a prophecy.

Chapter Forty-Six

In Chancery Court, the hush of anticipation pressed against Elizabeth's chest like a physical weight. Each tick of the ancient clock marked time not just in seconds, but in hopes and fears. The wait for Lord Chancellor Eldon's study of the papers seemed interminable, the rustling of parchment the only sound in the cavernous space.

When he spoke at last, his voice carried the authority of centuries of legal precedent. "The position of heir presumptive," he began, each word measured and clear, "is one of expectation, not of present right. It exists in that delicate space between possibility and certainty - a space that requires the most scrupulous attention to lawful conduct."

Elizabeth felt rather than saw Mr Collins shift uncomfortably in his seat. The weak winter sun, filtering through high windows, cast stark shadows across his features.

"This court has been presented with evidence of dereliction far surpassing mismanagement—indeed, pointing to deliberate and intentional sabotage." Mr Collins's face lifted with triumph at the first phrase, then fell with the second.

The Chancellor's voice sharpened. "Mr Collins, in his eagerness to prove himself a better steward than those currently entrusted with Longbourn's care, has instead demonstrated a profound misunderstanding of a landowner's fundamental duties."

The silence stretched, heavy with implication. Elizabeth's fingers pressed against the smooth wood of the bench before her, seeking anchor in its solid reality.

"The documented damages inflicted upon neighbouring properties - damages calculated with comprehensive accuracy - suggest far more than poor judgement; rather, a wilful determination to destroy value rather than preserve it." Lord Eldon's gaze swept the court. "Such actions strike at the very heart of what an entail is designed to protect. Therefore, I order the plaintiff, William Collins, to execute a deed of release of all present or future interest in the property known as Longbourn Estate in favour of Mr James Huntington Bennet, his heirs, and assigns. I further order…"

A rush of air escaped her, the release so sudden it left her dizzy. It was over. It was over. She squeezed Jane's hand and blinked to stop the tears from falling down her cheeks. Longbourn was theirs.

The rulings struck like a hammer on stone—each pronouncement rang with finality, each ripple reshaping the future. The entail's dissolution. The assessment of damages. The careful delineation of consequences that would follow Mr Collins's actions for years to come.

It was only afterward, in the corridor outside the courtroom, that Elizabeth fully grasped the magnitude of what had transpired. Darcy stood somewhat apart from the others, his expression neutral as he studied a document in his hands. She saw no trace of Mr Bingley among the well-wishers or witnesses. He had spoken warmly of loyalty—but had sent no letter, no message. Nothing.

"Mr Darcy." She approached him with measured steps, conscious that the ground beneath her feet had shifted. "I find myself puzzled by one particular detail. Regarding the Matthews property at Dunbar Court…"

She saw something in his look - hesitation? concern? - before his mask of self-possession settled into place. "It became clear that certain… interventions might be necessary."

"Interventions," she repeated, the word tasting strange on her tongue. "Your purchase of the estate was not, I collect, simply a matter of investment? You intentionally placed yourself in a position where a legal remedy might be sought for injuries done to your property?"

"I positioned myself where I might be of most use," he replied slowly. The space between them seemed to crackle with unspoken implications.

Elizabeth studied his face, searching for some key to unlock this perennial puzzle he presented. The same gentleman who had maintained such intimate distance in the orangerie on the previous day had simultaneously been orchestrating events with calculated forethought. His strategy had encompassed not only the advantages of a dependable neighbouring estate to benefit Longbourn and the Lodge, but the specific measures which would render Mr Collins's schemes utterly ineffectual. She could scarce determine whether to feel grateful or unsettled by such calculation.

"You have my thanks," she said finally. Her uncertain voice made his expression shift in a manner barely discernible. "However, I am not entirely sure for what I am thanking you."

His response held reserve, like a man measuring every word against unseen consequences. "Sometimes, Miss Elizabeth, the most effective assistance requires a certain… discretion." He shifted the papers in his hands. The tension in the strong lines of his face illuminated the conflict that roiled beneath his determinedly maintained reserve.

Elizabeth studied him, noting how his gaze kept returning to her face despite his evident determination to remain at a distance. Here stood the public Darcy, master of Pemberley, every inch the influential landowner—But last night she had glimpsed something else beneath that polished surface. He had moved with quiet determination to ensure this victory, even as he held himself rigidly apart from a true connection. Why exert such influence on her family's behalf whilst maintaining this careful distance?

"I suspect you would prefer I did not examine too closely the particular nature of your… assistance."

She caught a flash of the same tension that had charged the air between them again and again. The paper in his hands crackled as his fingers tightened imperceptibly on its edges, betraying the cost of his rigid self-control.

"Your understanding of the situation is, as always, remarkably astute," he replied, his voice dropped to a deeper timbre, sending an unexpected shiver through her. Something in his tone suggested an acknowledgement, perhaps, of this delicate dance they continued to perform around each other.

Mr Darcy stepped aside to allow a barrister to pass, now standing so close to Elizabeth that she could see the glittering pin in his cravat and the widening of his eyes as he gazed at her. She became aware of a sense of warmth despite the cool corridor. They stood in silence for a moment, each acutely aware of the other's presence. Elizabeth felt the burden of all their unfinished conversations, all the moments when his manner had softened only to freeze again, pressing against her chest like an ache. His actions spoke of dedication, even devotion, yet his behaviour remained a study in careful retreat.

Darcy straightened as if bracing himself against a storm of his own making, his eyes intent on hers. "Miss Elizabeth…" he began and paused, visibly wrestling with some profound internal conflict. Honour demanded he either step forward or back - this middle ground they occupied could no longer be sustained without injury to them both.

But before he could continue, Mr Phillips appeared at Elizabeth's elbow with congratulations and questions about the practical implications of the ruling. The corridor seemed to recede around them, the moment of possibility vanishing like mist. As her uncle drew her away with gentle insistence, Elizabeth cast a glance back over her shoulder. Mr Darcy did not move, but his eyes clung to her retreat with a tenderness so unguarded, it pierced her. For the briefest moment, his reserve had fallen away completely, revealing the depth of feelings he had taken such pains to conceal. Then, becoming aware of her gaze, he inclined his head in a bow of exquisite formality.

The carriage wheels churned through March mud as they left London behind. Each turn of the wheel drew them closer to

Longbourn—and to the weight of its responsibilities. Elizabeth watched the familiar countryside take shape under the soft haze of afternoon light, her mind turning over possibilities like seeds being sorted for spring planting.

"The Lodge," she said finally, breaking the contemplative silence, "might be let to advantage. Its position near the village would suit a gentleman of modest means, particularly one who values privacy."

Jane's gloved hands lay perfectly still in her lap, although her voice showed thoughtful consideration. "The gardens there are most fine; perhaps we might reserve those, adding their yield to Longbourn's kitchen garden?"

Mr Phillips tapped his fingers, his legal mind already navigating practical channels. "A partial lease would maintain greater control over the property's future use. You will want to consider the matter of access prudently."

Elizabeth caught Jane's eye, reading there the same measured hope that stirred quietly in her own chest.

"Mary will want to return her piano to the main house," Jane observed, deftly steering their thoughts toward family matters. "And Mamma… how shall we present this change in circumstances?"

"With careful emphasis on the security it brings," Elizabeth replied, her fingers absently holding the carriage strap. "The end of the entail means Longbourn's future rests solely in our grandfather's hands now. She will find that notion more palatable than our original plan of removal to the Lodge."

"Your grandfather has shown remarkable foresight," Mr Phillips noted, "in preparing you both for estate management. Few young ladies have such practical education."

The observation carried whispers of their recent conversations about women's capabilities, but Elizabeth let it pass unremarked. The landscape of Hertfordshire unfurled before them, softened by the pale gleam of a clouded afternoon—the same landscape visible from Longbourn's north pastures, and now, she supposed, from Mr Darcy's newly acquired fields as well. She thought she glimpsed the distant shape of Dunbar Court's eastern rise.

"We shall need to review the repairs again," she said briskly, squaring her shoulders against memories of politely maintained distances. "Now that legal matters are settled, we can implement all our improvements without fear of interference."

"Indeed," Jane agreed, her soft smile suggested she heard all that remained unspoken. "And such work would be materially advantaged from coordination with neighbouring estates."

Elizabeth cast her sister a warning glance, but Jane's calm reserve revealed nothing but practical consideration of agricultural matters. Mr Phillips, absorbed in his papers, appeared oblivious to the currents of meaning flowing beneath their exchange.

The familiar gates of Longbourn appeared ahead, and Elizabeth sat taller. Whatever the future held, she was ready to meet it. As for what might or might not develop with a certain gentleman of their acquaintance, she had work to do - real, vital work that would secure their family's future. Seeds would either flower or lie dormant according to their own nature. For now, the estate demanded their attention, and Elizabeth found comfort in the solid certainty of that responsibility.

The carriage halted, and the next breath she drew belonged to Longbourn. Elizabeth stepped into the familiar entrance hall of Longbourn with a sense of homecoming that went beyond mere return. The scent of beeswax and old vellum drifted into the corridor. Elizabeth stood motionless, her hand pressed lightly to the panelled door. The victory they carried with them would change everything.

"Lizzy! Jane!" Mary hurried down the stairs, her reserve giving way to genuine animation. "You have arrived at last. How did the court rule?"

Hill appeared from the direction of the kitchen, drying her hands on her apron, her expression betraying barely contained curiosity. Kitty emerged from the drawing room, and even Lydia, who had professed complete disinterest in "tedious legal matters," hovered in the doorway.

"Perhaps we might gather in the drawing room?" Jane suggested gently. "The news is best shared with everyone present."

Mrs Bennet appeared at the top of the stairs, her face pale with the strain of waiting. "What news? Is it terrible? Oh, my poor nerves cannot bear suspense!"

"Not terrible at all, Mamma," Elizabeth assured her, exchanging a meaningful glance with Jane. "Quite the opposite."

Within moments, the family assembled in the drawing room, a hush falling over even Lydia as Mr Phillips drew himself up.

"The Lord Chancellor has ruled entirely in our favour," he announced, his professional demeanour only slightly betrayed by the pride in his voice. "The entail is dissolved. Longbourn now belongs to Mr Bennet without condition or restriction."

The silence that followed lasted but a heartbeat before chaos erupted.

"Dissolved!" Mrs Bennet exclaimed, her hand fluttering to her chest. "Can it be true? We shall not lose Longbourn after all?"

"Mr Collins?" Mary enquired, her practical mind immediately grasping the implications.

"Has no further claim whatsoever on Longbourn," Mr Phillips confirmed. "Indeed, he faces substantial costs for his rather ill-conceived attempts at sabotage."

"How was this managed?" Mary pressed, her analytical mind working through the legal ramifications. "An entail is not easily set aside."

Elizabeth exchanged a look with her uncle. "Mr Collins's own actions proved our strongest argument. The Chancellor ruled that his demonstrated willingness to sell off portions of the estate directly contravened the very purpose of an entail."

"And the damage to Netherfield's grounds and gardens?" Mary persisted.

"Provided additional evidence of his unsuitability," Mr Phillips confirmed. "Lord Matthews's testimony was especially damning."

Kitty's brow furrowed. "But how did Lord Matthews become

involved?"

"A most fortunate circumstance," Elizabeth replied, thinking of Mr Darcy's strategic purchase of Dunbar Court. "His property was also affected by Mr Collins's schemes."

Mrs Bennet, who had been fanning herself vigorously, suddenly stilled. "Then it is truly over? We need never fear that odious man again?"

"Never," Mr Phillips assured her. "Longbourn is secure."

"Your father would be so proud," Mrs Bennet whispered, tears suddenly welling in her eyes. "He always said his girls were the cleverest in England."

The sisters exchanged glances, emotion threatening to overcome their composure at this rare mention of their father.

Hill coughed discreetly from the doorway. "Mr Bennet asks if you might attend him now that you have returned."

"Grandfather has been most anxious for news," Mary explained. "His health has been poorly these past days."

"Mr Phillips," Elizabeth said, rising, "would you be good enough to share the details with Grandfather? I am sure he will have questions best answered by you."

"Of course," her uncle agreed readily. "There are some matters regarding his settlement that I should discuss with him directly."

As the family dispersed—Lydia and Kitty already planning how they would circulate the intelligence in Meryton, Mrs Bennet instructing Hill about a celebratory dinner—Elizabeth caught Jane's hand.

"I can hardly credit it," Jane murmured. "After so much uncertainty…"

"Yet it is quite real," Elizabeth replied, squeezing her sister's fingers. "Longbourn is ours."

Later, as dusk settled over the estate, Elizabeth passed the partially open door of her grandfather's study. Mr Phillips's voice drifted out.

"I have taken the liberty of drafting the document as you

instructed," he was saying. "It might be prudent to review the provisions now that circumstances have resolved."

"The provisions stand," Grandfather Bennet's voice, weakened, retained its characteristic decisiveness. "Equal shares among the girls—that was always Thomas's wish, though convention prevented him from arranging it. The dissolution of the entail now makes possible what he could only hope for."

Elizabeth hesitated, knowing she should not eavesdrop, yet unable to move away.

"And Mrs Bennet?" Mr Phillips enquired.

"The North Lodge will provide her suitable independence," Grandfather replied. "With Longbourn so close, she need never feel isolated, yet both she and the girls will benefit from separate establishments."

"Very well," Mr Phillips agreed. "I shall prepare the final document for your signature. The language regarding the executrix—"

"Remains as written," Grandfather insisted. "Elizabeth has demonstrated precisely the qualities needed for the task. Jane will support her, of course, but Lizzy's practical mind will serve best in this capacity."

Elizabeth stepped back; her heart suddenly too full for comfort. The gravity of responsibility, of her grandfather's trust, pressed upon her even as it lifted her up. She moved quietly away from the door, unwilling to be discovered, carrying with her a profound sense of the legacy being placed in her hands.

I, JAMES HUNTINGTON BENNET, Of Longbourn House in the Parish of Meryton, Hertfordshire, being of sound mind although failing body, do hereby make and declare this to be my last Will and Testament.

To my beloved granddaughters Jane, Elizabeth, Mary,

Catherine, and Lydia Bennet, I give and bequeath in equal shares all my estate both real and personal of which I may die possessed, or which may hereafter become due to me, to be divided among them with that same spirit of sisterly affection which has marked their care of Longbourn these past years.

To my daughter-in-law Frances Bennet, I give a life estate in that property known as North Lodge, which lies adjacent to Longbourn's eastern boundary, together with its gardens and the small parcel of land attached thereto, that she may have a suitable establishment of her own befitting her station as my son's widow.

To Mr and Mrs Harold Hill, who have served this family with uncommon devotion these thirty years past, and whose friendship has brightened my declining days, I leave the sum of one hundred pounds each, to be paid as soon as may be convenient after my passing.

I do hereby appoint my granddaughter Elizabeth Bennet to be Executrix of this my last Will and Testament, knowing her sound judgement and practical understanding will serve to implement these provisions with wisdom and equity.

In witness whereof, I have hereunto set my hand this fifteenth day of March, in the year of our Lord one thousand eight hundred and twelve.

James Huntington Bennet (SEAL)

Chapter Forty-Seven

That evening, in the quiet sanctuary of their shared bedroom at Longbourn, Elizabeth sat at the dressing table whilst Jane brushed out her hair with steady, methodical strokes. The familiar rhythm seemed to untangle not just curls, but thoughts that had knotted themselves throughout the day's proceedings.

"You are unusually quiet," Jane said, meeting Elizabeth's eyes in the mirror. "Do you not find today's victory should bring some peace of mind?"

Elizabeth watched the candlelight play across her sister's composed features, measuring her next words. "I find my thoughts rather… unsettled. Mr Darcy's role in all this…" She trailed off, unable to articulate the complexity of her feelings about his secretly orchestrated assistance.

"Dunbar Court, the Matthews estate," Jane mused, running the brush through Elizabeth's hair with gentle strokes. "It does share that long boundary with Longbourn's north fields."

Elizabeth met her sister's eyes in the mirror. "Rather convenient, is it not? One might wonder why he would trouble himself with such a modest property."

"Unless," Jane suggested, "he had reasons beyond mere investment."

"Jane." Elizabeth's voice carried a warning, her fingers twisted restlessly in her lap. "You do noy mean to suggest…"

"I mean to say that a gentleman might arrange matters to necessitate frequent consultation between neighbouring estates." The brush paused mid-stroke. "That improvements might require careful coordination?"

"You sound remarkably like our aunt," Elizabeth observed, a

treacherous warmth blooming in her chest at the possibility. "Next you will suggest he purchased it solely to have an excuse to call at Longbourn on estate business."

"Would that be so very surprising?" Jane's gentle speech belied the significance of her words. "Given how his eyes follow you, even as he maintains such careful distance?"

Elizabeth stared at her own reflection, remembering how Darcy's expression had shifted in that courthouse corridor - duty warring with something deeper, something that had made his hands tighten on those papers as if they were the only anchor in a storm of competing obligations.

"We should not indulge in such speculation," she said finally, although her voice lacked conviction. She tied the sash of her dressing gown with finality. "The property's value is clear enough without seeking hidden meanings."

"Of course," Jane agreed, resuming her brushing with a small smile that suggested she was not quite convinced. "Those north fields catch the morning light… as if they were meant to be viewed as one estate."

"Jane!" But Elizabeth's protest held more laughter than censure, and in the candlelight, sister's eyes met sister's with a shared understanding of all that remained unspoken.

Jane's hands stilled. "He has proved himself a true friend to our family."

"He has, has he not?" Elizabeth paced three quick steps before spinning back, colour rising to her cheeks as she awaited confirmation. "He baffles me still. At times, he stands so near I could swear I feel the warmth of his regard—and then, as if a line has been crossed, he retreats behind walls of propriety more impenetrable than the Tower itself."

"Lizzy." Jane's look held gentle understanding. "Could it be that his heart wages war with his sense of duty?"

"His heart?" Elizabeth attempted a laugh that emerged rather too brittle. "I think you attribute too much significance to simple courtesy."

Jane resumed her brushing. Her eyes remained fixed on Elizabeth's reflection. "I saw how he watched you in court yesterday. As if memorising every detail of your profile whilst simultaneously forcing himself to look away."

Elizabeth's fingers drew an aimless pattern on the dressing table's surface. "Even if… even if there were some inclination…" She drew a steadying breath. "He has made it abundantly clear that any such feelings must be mastered rather than indulged."

"And your own feelings?" Jane's question floated between them like a dove seeking purchase.

The silence stretched, filled with the soft scratch of brush through hair and the distant sounds of Longbourn Street settling into evening. "I find myself…" Elizabeth began, then stopped, gathering courage. "I find myself wishing he were less honourable and more selfish. Is that not a terrible thing to admit?"

"No more terrible than my disappointed hopes regarding Mr Bingley's lack of resolution," Jane admitted with uncharacteristic candour. "He seemed everything amiable, everything kind, yet he doubted his own judgement in all things. One day he appeared certain of his course, the next…" She sighed. "He looks to others to determine his path, rather than trusting his own heart."

"We are a fine pair, are we not? Pinning hopes on men who appear determined to deny both themselves—and us—the smallest chance at happiness."

"I pin no hopes on Mr Bingley. For all his pretty words, his actions have spoken clearly. He is nothing to me now. Perhaps it is time we determined our own path," Jane suggested, setting down the brush. "Longbourn needs our attention, especially now that its future is secure. We need not wait for gentleman callers to give purpose to our days."

"No indeed." Elizabeth felt her spine straighten with renewed resolve. "Let them wrestle with their noble hesitations. We have an estate to manage."

"And if they should find their courage?" Jane's voice held a whisper of hope.

"Then they shall have to find us in the midst of our duties," Elizabeth replied firmly, Her heart gave a treacherous flutter at the thought. "I refuse to spend my days watching the drive for approaching carriages that may never appear."

The sisters exchanged a look of shared understanding before turning their attention to practical matters of the morrow.

Elizabeth lay awake that night, unable to banish the memory of Darcy's expression in that courthouse corridor. Her undeniable sense was that he was caught between duty and desire. The Dunbar Court purchase turned like a complicated puzzle in her mind, each new angle revealing fresh possibilities she hardly dared examine.

To buy property on mere speculation spoke of reckless investment. Darcy was anything but reckless. To position himself as an injured party required forethought, careful strategy, a willingness to commit significant resources to an uncertain outcome. The kind of forethought that suggested—but no. She dared not follow that reasoning to its conclusion.

Colonel Fitzwilliam lounged in one of Darcy's leather chairs, brandy glass balanced with military precision as he studied his cousin's restless movements about the study. The fire had burned low, casting shadows that seemed to match Darcy's brooding expression.

Fitzwilliam swirled his brandy thoughtfully. "Mr Collins's legal representation proved remarkably… well-funded for a humble parson."

"Indeed." Darcy's tone was neutral. "As was his sudden ability to consult several experts on water rights—not to mention the ruffians who wrecked the existing drainage channels."

"Our aunt has always taken an enthusiastic interest in managing other people's affairs." The Colonel's observation carried layers of meaning. "I suspect this particular investment may prove less rewarding than her former ventures."

"The damages alone will consume whatever funds she advanced." Darcy turned to his cousin, his expression sharpening. "Unless you think Mr Collins capable of securing such counsel through his own resources?"

"About as capable as he is of composing that rather eloquent petition without assistance." Fitzwilliam tipped his glass and, finding it empty, lifted the decanter on the table with deliberate care. "Proving her direct involvement would be… challenging."

"As would be explaining her sudden correspondence with Lord Matthews regarding drainage practices in a county where she holds no property?" There was unmistakable steel beneath Darcy's measured words.

"Ah yes, her newfound expertise in Hertfordshire water management. Most… illuminating." The Colonel's smile held no warmth. "I suspect her primary concern was never truly about drainage."

"No," Darcy agreed quietly. "Her ambitions have ever leant toward more… domestic avenues of control."

"Speaking of influence," Fitzwilliam said with deliberate casualness, "I understand Miss Elizabeth Bennet proved effective in demonstrating the practical flaws in Mr Collins's arguments. Our aunt's investment in his cause must seem rather less secure in light of such… competent opposition."

Darcy's movement, his shoulders tightening at Elizabeth's name betrayed more than words might have, although his voice remained steady. "Lady Catherine has never appreciated having her schemes disrupted by mere competence."

"Especially from unexpected quarters." The Colonel quirked a brow. "Perhaps this particular scheme's failure might prove advantageous in ways our aunt never intended."

Darcy gave no reply, but the tension in his posture deepened.

Fitzwilliam went on, his tone light but observant. "Or perhaps I should say—someone's swift and strategic response to our aunt's meddling has had rather interesting consequences."

He let the silence stretch, watching his cousin closely. "Miss

Elizabeth Bennet's understanding of the defence of her family's interests was quite remarkable."

Darcy kept his gaze fixed on the fire. "The law was clear enough."

"The law, yes," Fitzwilliam agreed, swirling the brandy in his glass. "I suspect that was not the only compass guiding you."

When Darcy remained silent, his cousin simply nodded, as though confirming a long-held suspicion.

Darcy's voice came low and tight. "Her understanding of many things is… exceptional." His reserve was betrayed by the faintest colouring at his neck.

"Just her understanding?" The Colonel pressed on. "Come now, Darcy. What truly stays your hand? Unquestionably not concern for society's good opinion. You have spent years cultivating your reputation for disdaining exactly such considerations."

"Georgiana's future prospects—"

"Would benefit enormously from a sister who combines intelligence with genuine warmth. Or did you imagine our shy girl would flourish better under Caroline Bingley's guidance?"

Darcy's wince was barely perceptible. "You mistake complexity for simplicity."

"Do I? You speak of duty, yet what duty requires you to deny happiness to yourself and your sister? Unless…" Fitzwilliam leant forward, humour giving way to insight. "Unless you fear that in choosing Elizabeth Bennet, you prove yourself less than the paragon everyone expects Fitzwilliam Darcy to be?"

Darcy shook his head. The silence stretched, heavy with admission. Finally, he spoke: "She makes me question all I believed about worth, duty—myself."

"How inconvenient," the Colonel said dryly. "To discover that happiness might require something more than rigid adherence to others' expectations."

"You are not helping."

"Am I not? Consider this a tactical assessment. What truly prevents you from pursuing her? Not society—you have never cared for its opinion. Not family—except perhaps our aunt, whose own machinations may have inadvertently brought you together. Not even duty—unless you count duty to your own pride."

"And Georgiana?"

"Who glows like a Yule lantern whenever Miss Elizabeth's name is mentioned? Who has shown more animation in one afternoon of her company than in months of refined social calls?" Fitzwilliam set down his glass with care. "If you prefer, we could continue seeking a sister for her among the ranks of those who measure worth solely by consequence and connection. I am sure my mother would be thrilled to present some worthy candidates—with spectacular dowries, perhaps a title, and certainly the docility of a lamb."

Darcy groaned. "And ovine intelligence to match." His expression shifted, as if seeing a familiar landscape from an entirely new angle. "She does make Georgiana smile."

"She makes you smile too, cousin. When you forget to maintain that impressive façade of yours." The Colonel rose to pour fresh brandies. "I warn you—a woman who challenges your assumptions is a dangerous thing indeed. Are you quite certain you are prepared for such a campaign?"

Darcy's answer came with quiet resolve. "The question is whether she'll find me worthy of the attempt."

"Only one way to discover that," Fitzwilliam remarked cheerfully. "Might I suggest fewer observations about duty and connections and more appreciation of her 'exceptional understanding'?"

"You enjoy this far too much."

"Naturally. Now, shall we discuss strategy? I have some thoughts on how to manage that particular campaign…"

Lady Catherine sat like a very angry alabaster statue, her posture rigid. Mr Collins's stumbling explanation of the court's ruling fell into silence as dead as his future prospects. Only her cane, tapping with frightening regularity, betrayed the magnitude of her rage.

"The entail… dissolved?" Each word fell like an executioner's blade.

"Entirely, your Ladyship." Mr Collins's unctuous manner had shriveled under the thoroughness of the catastrophe. "And the damages… most excessive. Beyond any hope of--"

"Spare me your financial calculations," she cut in. "I must know what my nephew said in their defence?"

Mr Collins shifted uncomfortably, aware that this particular intelligence would prove most wounding. "Mr Darcy spoke at some length regarding the excellence of their estate management. He praised their innovative approach to--"

The cane halted mid-beat. "Innovative? He used that word? In open court?"

"Most unfortunately, your Ladyship."

Lady Catherine's complexion achieved a hue of purple previously unknown to nature. "My own nephew. Publicly advocating for such unnatural arrangements. My poor sister would have been appalled by his interest in a creature so beneath his station." Her voice dropped to a dangerous whisper. "And you, Mr Collins, have managed not only to fail in preventing this catastrophe, but I find you arranged matters so that my name might be connected with your… activities."

"Your Ladyship's involvement was never--"

"Will be presumed by anyone possessed of wit enough to discern the truth." Her cane resumed its rhythm with renewed vigour. "You must, of course, seek a curacy. Some position far from Hunsford."

Mr Collins's already pallid face paled to new depths of bloodless terror. "Leave… Hunsford?"

"Surely you cannot imagine remaining as my parson? After such a display of poor judgement?" Her laugh held all the warmth of a January frost. "Lack of judgement? No, that would imply *choice*—

rather than your typical bumbling incompetence."

"But your Ladyship's generosity--"

"Has been thoroughly exhausted by your recent ventures into agricultural sabotage. You have ruined me financially and I refuse to share any further in your disgrace." The cane executed a decisive rap. "Really, Mr Collins. Hiring common criminals to destroy drainage works? Could you not at least have managed your sabotage with some pretence of sophistication?"

Mr Collins seemed to deflate further with each barb. "Perhaps if we were to appeal--"

"We?" Lady Catherine's eyebrows rose to the height of aristocratic disdain. "I believe, Mr Collins, that you have mistaken your situation most entirely. There is no 'we' in your future endeavours. I wash my hands of you. Your little entail has taken far too much from Rosings. I hate to admit it, but I was a fool to offer you help. I cannot be associated with you again. Indeed, your future lies in some remote parish where neither your name nor your rather spectacular failures need ever reach my ears again."

"But my dear Lady Catherine--"

"That is no longer an appellation you may employ." She turned to gaze out the window, her dismissal as final as a coffin lid closing. "There are several modest curacies available in Northumberland. Or perhaps Scotland. Do make your arrangements with all possible speed."

Mr Collins stood on legs that seemed suddenly unable to recall their proper function. His world of patronage and consequence had shattered like ice in spring thaw, leaving him to face the bitter truth that his attempt to preserve the natural hierarchy had instead guaranteed his own social extinction.

Lady Catherine's cane maintained its steady rhythm, counting out the moments until she would be free of his presence. That her own schemes had contributed to this debacle seemed not to have penetrated her certainty. Indeed, her only real concern appeared to be the unfortunate evidence of her nephew's progressive leanings.

"My own blood," she murmured to the empty air,

"championing female estate management. Unsuitable fascination, just like a man. The world wobbles on its axis. What next? Female magistrates? Women at Westminster?"

Behind her, the fire sputtered low, but she gave no sign of discomfort. Only the cane ticked on, steady as ever.

Chapter Forty-Eight

The late afternoon light fell softly through Longbourn's windows as Jane and Elizabeth entered, their skirts still bearing traces of soil from their lengthy inspection of the north fields. They had spent the better part of the day walking the boundaries of the estate, marking points where the new drainage channels would connect with those being constructed at Dunbar Court. Mr Robinson, their most experienced tenant farmer, had accompanied them, his weathered face creased with approval at the sisters' thorough understanding of the land's needs.

"The water will flow proper now, Miss Elizabeth," he had declared, leaning on his walking stick. "First time in thirty years these fields will not be soggy come the autumn rains. Your grandfather will be right pleased with this arrangement."

The work had taken longer than anticipated, the complexity of the terrain requiring careful consideration at each juncture. Elizabeth had lost track of time, absorbed in the practical puzzle of slope and soil and water flow. Now, as they returned to the house, the slanting light reminded her they had missed taking tea with their grandfather—a ritual he had come to anticipate even as his strength diminished.

Elizabeth was about to suggest they attend him immediately when Mary and Kitty rushed into the entrance hall, their faces bearing expressions of such alarm that Elizabeth felt her heart seize.

"What has happened?" Jane asked, immediately removing her gloves, her calm voice belying the sudden tension in her shoulders.

"He took ill two hours past," Mary reported, her manner stripped to bare facts by genuine concern. "Mr Jones speaks of decline rather than any specific malady."

"It came on so suddenly," Kitty elaborated, her animation subdued by genuine fear. "He was reviewing the household accounts with Hill when he seemed to… to falter. His hand went to his chest, and he could not catch his breath."

"Mr Jones was sent for immediately," Mary continued. "He administered a draught for the pain, but—" Her voice caught, an unusual sign of emotion from their most composed sister.

"Where is he now?" Elizabeth asked, already moving toward the stairs, her mud-spattered hem forgotten.

"In his chamber," Kitty answered. "Mamma has been with him this past hour. She would not be persuaded to rest, although she was quite overcome at first."

Elizabeth met eyes with Jane, reading in her sister's eyes the same fear that gripped her own heart. They had been so absorbed in securing Longbourn's future that they had forgotten the fragility of the present—of the grandfather whose wisdom had guided them.

"I shall change quickly and join you," Jane said, her voice gentle but brooking no argument. "You go to him now, Lizzy."

Elizabeth nodded, grateful as always for Jane's practical kindness. As she hurried up the stairs, she caught the murmur of voices from the upper floor—her mother's higher tones interspersed with the deeper rumble of what must be Mr Jones delivering his assessment.

The corridor leading to her grandfather's chamber seemed longer than she remembered, each step bringing sharper clarity to what they might now face. They had won Longbourn's security, yes—but what price might yet be demanded of them? The thought of losing her grandfather, the steady presence who had filled the void left by her father's untimely death, made her steps falter momentarily before resolution drove her forward again.

Outside his chamber door, Elizabeth paused, gathering her composure like a cloak around her shoulders. Whatever scene awaited her within, she would face it with the strength her grandfather had helped cultivate in her. She straightened her shoulders, and with a deep breath, reached for the door handle.

Their grandfather's chamber, when she entered it, held that peculiar stillness that seems to gather around sickrooms, as if the very air hesitates to disturb the occupants.

Mrs Bennet sat rigid beside the bed, her fingers working ceaselessly at her handkerchief whilst she maintained a stream of what was clearly meant to be cheerful conversation. "Such a lovely spring day, Papa. The daffodils will be quite spectacular this year, will they not? Just as Thomas always said they would be, with careful attention to the soil. He had such a way with gardens, did Thomas…"

Her voice caught on her husband's name, the wound of that loss suddenly fresh again with this new grief. Elizabeth moved to touch her shoulder, but Mrs Bennet flinched away, her composure threatening to shatter at any gesture of comfort.

"Lizzy." Grandfather Bennet's voice came weak but clear. "You have news from Dunbar Court?"

"The most satisfactory solution, Grandfather," Elizabeth replied, keeping her voice light although her heart clenched at his frailty. "All arranged exactly as you predicted."

"Good. Good." His eyes, sharp despite his weakness, moved between his granddaughters.

Mrs Bennet's fingers stilled momentarily on her handkerchief. "Just as Thomas would have wished," she said, her composure wavering audibly. "He always said the girls showed promise in estate matters. Such an unusual notion, I thought at the time, but he insisted…" She pressed the already-mangled handkerchief to her lips.

"Fanny." Grandfather Bennet spoke with unexpected warmth. "You have been most attentive these past hours. But perhaps you might rest now that the girls have returned?"

"Rest? Oh! Yes, I suppose I should…" She rose, movements uncertain, like a sleepwalker disturbed. "One must maintain one's strength in times of trial…"

Jane entered and moved to support her mother with gentle efficiency. "Come, Mamma. Let me sit with you a while. Tell me about the daffodils."

Elizabeth watched them go, noting how her mother leant into Jane's strength as if it were the only thing keeping her upright. When she turned back to the bed, she found her grandfather watching her with familiar acuity.

"She feels it all again," he said quietly. "Each loss echoing the first."

"Yes." Elizabeth settled into the chair her mother had vacated. "She need not face it alone."

His thin fingers found hers with surprising strength. "No indeed. You girls will manage. Just as Thomas knew you would."

The afternoon light softened further, wrapping them in quiet understanding as Elizabeth began to tell him of their day's work, each deliberately chosen detail designed to assure him that his legacy rested in capable hands.

Darcy stood at the window of his friend's London study, watching Bingley's restless movements with growing impatience. The spring rain painted meaningless patterns on the glass, much like his friend's circular reasoning.

"The foundations require rather extensive work," Bingley was saying, his exuberance dampened to mere restless spirits. "And the fields… well, after the recent flooding…"

"Fields your neighbour had managed to protect—through timely, careful attention to drainage," Darcy said pointedly. "The Bennet's understanding of water management proved quite reliable. If you were to work with them the matter would be quickly resolved."

Bingley's fingers drummed an uneven rhythm against his chair. "Yes, well… that is… Caroline has observed that perhaps such detailed attention to estate matters is not quite…"

"Is not quite what?" Darcy turned to face his friend, his voice carrying an edge sharp enough to make Bingley flinch. "Is not quite proper for ladies who have demonstrated more practical capability in a month than you have managed in eight months leasing an estate?"

"Now see here, Darcy--"

"No, Bingley. You spent the autumn offering marked attentions to Jane Bennet, creating expectations, winning her family's approval through your talk of estate improvements. And now you retreat because your sister finds capable women threatening to her pretensions?"

"It is not that simple," Bingley protested, although his voice lacked conviction. "The investment required…"

"Well within your means and would be considerably less had you attended to these matters when first advised. But then, attention to duty has never been your strong suit, has it? It is much easier to play the role of an agreeable gentleman than trouble yourself to master the responsibilities of your position. Far more convenient, is it not to withdraw and leave others to bear the consequences—despite the obligations you undertook—though you were eager to claim the estate when it flattered your vanity,"

Bingley straightened, stung at last to genuine emotion. "We cannot all be perfect masters like you, Darcy. I am out of my depth here."

"Indeed. You raised expectations in a most deserving young lady only to retreat at the very moment that honour and integrity might cost you something." Darcy's voice could have frosted the windowpanes. "I, however, intend to demonstrate that at least one gentleman of our acquaintance understands the value of a woman whose intelligence matches her beauty."

"You cannot be in earnest—"

"I mean to court Elizabeth Bennet openly and with serious intent." He spoke with the quiet conviction of a man no longer at war with his heart. "Having observed her management of Longbourn, I find myself rather anticipating our future discussions of estate improvement."

"Darcy, think of how such an attachment will be spoken of. A gentleman of your consequence, attaching himself to a lady with no fortune, no connections, who concerns herself with estate management? Walks the muddy fields herself and has her fingers in the soil?" Echoes of Miss Bingley's frequent disparagement of the ladies of Longbourn rang in Bingley's voice.

"Perhaps they will say that whilst some men retreat from happiness out of fear of opinion, others have the courage to recognise true worth when they find it. Society's judgement, your sisters' disapproval, whispers of the ton, - these are shadows without substance when weighed against genuine merit." Darcy moved toward the door, his meaning unmistakable. "Good day, Bingley. Do try not to let your sister's prejudices overcome what remains of your judgement."

The door closed with quiet finality, leaving Bingley to contemplate how a lifetime of cultivated amiability had quietly curdled into something perilously close to cowardice.

Chapter Forty-Nine

Some days had passed since the Chancery ruling, yet the dining room at Longbourn still bore the echo of celebration—its triumph now tempered by the shadow of their grandfather's decline. The triumph had settled into something quieter now—gratitude tempered by worry. Mr Bennet's failing health, each day weaker since their return, hovered over the household like a veil, muting laughter and sharpening every glance toward the staircase. Elizabeth watched the family interaction shift in this new light, each sister's response to their changed fortunes as characteristic as it was revealing. "The Lodge would have served well enough," Mrs Bennet said. "Yet, one does grow attached to particular views. The breakfast parlour receives the morning sun in a most agreeable manner."

"And the sheep fold at Longbourn lies closer to the main route to market," Lydia added with practicality. "If we are to increase the flock as intended, the location is most advantageous."

Jane looked quickly to Elizabeth at this evidence of their youngest sister's growing ambition. "The Lodge might serve other purposes," she suggested gently. "Mary has been studying methods of soil improvement, I believe?"

"The southern exposure offers particular advantages," Mary pronounced with genuine enthusiasm. "Given regular attention to enrichment, the kitchen gardens there will prove most productive."

Kitty dropped her fork with a faint clatter, then picked it up only to turn it absently in her fingers. Her liveliness had deserted her; even Lydia's antics failed to draw a smile. "Can improvements not wait," she asked firmly. "There are more pressing matters requiring our attention at present."

"Indeed." Mrs Bennet's fingers worried at her napkin, her

thoughts straying toward the upper floor. "Your grandfather wishes us to conduct ourselves as we normally do. He always says …" a sob interrupted her words.

"The estate requires constant attention," Jane supplied smoothly, covering their mother's momentary distress. "As does family."

"Just as Grandfather taught us," Mary declared with certainty, although her voice caught on the word 'Grandfather.' "One must consider both immediate needs and future prospects."

"Future prospects," Mrs Bennet echoed, her expression shifting between pride and peculiar vulnerability. "How pleased your father would be, to see his daughters so… so very capable. And now, you will hold all the land from here to Dunbar Court!"

"As for Dunbar Court, Mamma," Jane said, setting down her soup spoon, "Lord Matthews' sale of the properties during the hearing proved rather illuminating."

Mrs Bennet asked indifferently, "Indeed?"

"When Lord Matthews was pressed about authorisation for certain actions on the property," Jane continued with perfect composure, "he explained that his Lordship's interest had been transferred some months prior. Mr Darcy's ownership of the estate caused quite a stir in the gallery."

"Mr Darcy?" Mrs Bennet's fork paused halfway to her mouth. "Dunbar Court belongs to Mr Darcy? But how? Why…"

"A sound investment," Elizabeth managed, her look a study in neutrality that fooled no one at the table.

"How exceedingly convenient," Lydia interrupted, her smile suggesting depths of comprehension her sixteen years should not possess. "That such a particular piece of property should draw Mr Darcy's investment interest. One imagines improvements might require frequent consultation between neighbours."

"The soil composition there matches Longbourn's northern fields rather remarkably, as Mr Fairfield observed just yesterday," Mary interjected with animation. "His studies of agricultural science suggest that similar underlying clay deposits--"

"Mr Fairfield calls ever so frequently to discuss soil," Lydia said, her voice sweetened with unmistakable mischief. "Though I daresay he studies Mary even more closely than the clay content."

Mary's cheeks coloured, but she lifted her chin. "Scientific inquiry demands rigorous attention--"

"And Mr Fairfield's attention appears most rigorous indeed," Kitty managed, momentarily roused from her worried contemplation of the empty chair at the table's head.

"Civility also demands attention, Lydia—and a sister's well-earned admiration ought not be the subject of sport." Elizabeth said lightly, casting Lydia a glance that held more edge than her words.

Lydia grinned, unabashed.

"Besides," Jane added with a gentle look in Mary's direction, "Mr Fairfield seems genuinely interested in Mary's observations. And Mary's experiments with the Lodge soil have already yielded promising results."

"Whilst Netherfield stands empty," Mrs Bennet sighed, her thoughts shifting direction. "Mr Bingley's steward maintains the house, the servants were all dismissed, and I hear he has no plans to return."

Jane's even features did not falter. Elizabeth noted how her sister's fingers tightened so subtly it could scarce be marked. She stirred her soup slowly, long after it had cooled, as though unaware of the motion. "The damage from the flooding will require significant investment to repair," she said at last, her voice steady.

"Though not beyond the scope of proper management," Lydia declared. "If he had only attended to the drainage when first advised--"

"As Mr Fairfield explains it," Mary began earnestly, "the underlying soil structure--"

"Yes, dears," Mrs Bennet interrupted with unexpected gentleness. "Perhaps we might save detailed scientific discussion for your next consultation with the gentleman. He appears especially eager to share his knowledge with you, my dear. My nerves are unequal to the rigours of agricultural science."

The exchange of glances around the table spoke volumes about Mr Fairfield's evident partiality. Mary's fierce concentration on her plate suggested she was not quite ready to admit her interest.

Darcy stood at his study window, the untouched brandy in his hand reflecting the spring evening's fading light. Colonel Fitzwilliam occupied the chair near the fire, his buoyancy somewhat subdued.

"Bingley abandoned Netherfield completely, then?" The Colonel's voice held careful measure. "Rather a reversal, given his enthusiasm throughout autumn."

"His attempts to play gentry paled after his initial enthusiasm. His solicitor is negotiating termination of the lease. His more personal investment has faded as well. His sister whispered of impropriety, and suddenly female capability became an insurmountable barrier to happiness." Darcy said with rather more bite than he intended.

"Ah yes, the terrible burden of a bride who understands her duties." Fitzwilliam studied his glass with unexpected intensity. "Indeed, Miss Bennet's particular blend of grace and understanding… one could sympathise with Bingley's retreat. Her knowledge is far superior to his. Such perfection would prove rather daunting to lesser mortals."

Something in his cousin's voice made Darcy turn. "You speak with marked warmth of Miss Bennet's qualities."

The Colonel's smile held edges of what might have been regret. "Perhaps I simply appreciate the rare combination of beauty and genuine intelligence."

"I had not realised you observed her with such particularity."

"Intentionally so." Fitzwilliam's said, but volumes remained unspoken. "I would never permit anyone to think I would toy with a lady's…well, no matter now. Bingley's retreat leaves the path clear for more resolute admirers, should any present themselves."

Darcy studied his cousin's artfully arranged features. "Do you mean to suggest…"

"That a poor, battle weary soldier might appreciate serenity when he finds it? That intelligence wrapped in grace might prove devastatingly appealing?" The Colonel set down his glass. "Of course, a younger son's admiration must remain purely theoretical."

"Richard--"

"No, no, pray do not look so concerned. I merely observe that Bingley's loss might prove another's gain, were circumstances different." His smile recovered some of its light. "But come, tell me of your plans regarding Miss Elizabeth. I daresay I hope you mean to show rather more resolution than our retreating friend?"

The shift in topic carried clear warning against further enquiry. Darcy wondered how he had missed this particular undercurrent in their previous discussions of the Bennets. Yet his cousin's determinedly bright manner suggested some confidences were to be left unexplored. For now.

"I mean to travel to Meryton tomorrow," he said instead. "The Matthews property requires attention."

"A pressing concern, all at once—how curious." He said with his customary humour. "How fortunate that such matters require frequent consultation between neighbours."

Darcy pierced his cousin with a glare. "I am in possession of a minor estate which has suffered rather pronounced neglect. It is my duty to inspect Dunbar Court."

"No doubt the property shall demand your most scrupulous attention—now that it proves so conveniently situated," the Colonel mused, his offhand manner belying the sudden interest in his expression. "As your nearest relation currently in London, I feel rather duty-bound to offer my assistance in the inspection."

Darcy's eyebrow lifted. "Your sense of familial obligation grows remarkably acute."

"One must consider the broader implications of such an acquisition." The Colonel's smile held just a trace of self-mockery. "The property's proximity to certain… established estates might affect its future prospects considerably."

"Particularly now that Longbourn's future ownership may shift." Darcy watched comprehension dawn in his cousin's eyes. "The dissolution of the entail removes those ancient constraints. Without an entail, the estate may follow a path of Bennet's own choosing rather than that dictated by legal precedent. He is likely to leave the estate to his granddaughters."

Colonel Fitzwilliam leant forward in his chair, the firelight casting thoughtful shadows across his features. "A remarkable development, considering how few avenues society typically affords women for such independence."

"They have already demonstrated considerable aptitude in its management, even under the shadow of legal challenge."

The Colonel mused, not quite meeting Darcy's eye. "Military service does instil certain organisational principles that translate rather effectively to estate management."

Darcy arched a brow. "Am I to understand that your interest extends beyond theoretical considerations of land management? Perhaps to a particular manager, er manageress?"

"Your regard for delicacy, as always, is refreshingly absent." The Colonel set his glass down and straightened. "Miss Bennet combines practical wisdom with a rare gentleness of character. Such a combination proves… difficult to dismiss from one's thoughts."

"Yet you maintained your distance."

"How could I not? With Bingley's prior attentions so well known, and her situation seemingly dependent on an advantageous marriage, duty dictated restraint." The Colonel's fingers tapped briefly against the arm of his chair.

"One might forgive hesitation in matters of war, but to retreat from Miss Bennet?" He shook his head slowly, disbelief writ clear across his features. "That is a failure of judgement bordering on the absurd. She was all grace, discernment, and quiet strength—and Bingley cast her aside as though such a woman might be found upon every street in London."

Darcy did not reply at once, and the fire snapped in the grate.

"I own," the Colonel continued more quietly, "that duty has grown increasingly burdensome with each passing day."

"And now?" Darcy leant back, studying his cousin with newfound interest.

The Colonel smiled faintly. "A man's happiness might lie in directions he had not…previously permitted himself to contemplate." The Colonel's voice dropped. "Her composure in company is remarkable—a quality I once mistook for indifference. But there are moments when that composed exterior yields to something warmer."

"You believe her affections might be engaged?"

"I believe they might be awakened by the right suitor." The Colonel's expression grew contemplative. "Her particular combination of grace and capability proves rather devastating to a man's peace of mind."

"Your regard, if it existed, was guarded to the point of invisibility."

"A gentleman does not interfere where another gentleman's interest appears engaged." Fitzwilliam's voice carried an edge of self-mockery. "Now, however, I see good reason to question the wisdom of such restraint."

"Particularly now that the field lies open?" Darcy's said with careful query. "She maintains such perfect composure in company, it is no simple task to discern her particular inclinations."

The Colonel's smile held surprising warmth. "You recall she stood up with me twice that evening?"

"As she did with another gentleman, I believe."

"Ah, but when I approached for that second dance…" Fitzwilliam's expression softened at the memory. "There was a moment, just as the set was forming, when her composure faltered—just slightly, yet unmistakably. I fancied myself the recipient of a smile a lady grants to one whose attentions she does not politely tolerate but perhaps anticipates."

"You speak as one who has made a most attentive study of Miss Bennet's every subtlety of expression."

"One does acquire some aptitude for subtle signals in military intelligence," the Colonel replied with attempted lightness. "In truth, none of my campaigns has ever required such careful attention to the precise degree of warmth signalled in her greeting."

"And these signals suggest…"

"That perfect serenity might conceal depths of feeling, given the correct encouragement." Fitzwilliam's expression shifted to something more serious. "That a lady's carefully maintained public face might allow for private preference, should the right gentleman present himself."

"And you would be the right gentleman?"

"My dear cousin, not all of us can boast your particular combination of looks and fortune." The Colonel's spoke with careful lightness. "Some of us must rely on more modest attractions."

"The son of an earl, with distinguished service and excellent connections?" Darcy's eyebrow lifted. "I hardly think Miss Bennet would find such a prospect wanting. Particularly when combined with your evident appreciation of her worth."

"Worth indeed." Fitzwilliam's expression softened. "Her beauty is considerable, to be sure—but it is her tranquil intelligence… the way she manages chaos with such gentle certainty…" He caught himself, clearing his throat. "I speak only from general observation, you understand."

"Naturally." Darcy's words suggested he understood rather more than that.

The Colonel's expression shifted through several interesting variations before settling into studied neutrality. "Tomorrow, then? For the inspection? One should understand these matters thoroughly before contemplating any… strategic alterations."

"Tomorrow," Darcy agreed, noting his cousin had acquired an unfamiliar animation. "Perhaps we might call at Longbourn afterward. To discuss boundary considerations."

"Purely practical matters," Fitzwilliam agreed with suspicious readiness. "One must maintain civil neighbourly relations."

Neither gentleman felt compelled to examine too closely

how their separate paths toward happiness had somehow aligned into a single campaign.

Chapter Fifty

Elizabeth saw the hunched figure of her sister Kitty coming along the garden path. Her stride was slow and tentative. The ever-present basket on her arm was empty of herbs. The trace of tears on her face shown in the morning light when she looked up.

"Kitty, whatever is the matter?" Elizabeth said, crossing the garden to meet her.

Kitty heaved a deep sigh and chewed her lip before she stammered, "I called upon Mrs Faxon."

Elizabeth nodded, then put an arm around Kitty. "And what transpired?"

Kitty's inhalation turned into a sob. "She was kind, but she had nothing to help. 'Your grandfather is beyond the reach of my tinctures and potions.' she said."

Elizabeth gathered Kitty into an embrace. "My Jones said the same. We must keep him comfortable and be cheerful. He has lived a very long life, a good life." As much as Elizabeth wished to comfort Kitty, her own words brought tears.

"Why must everything die, and always too soon?" Kitty said through her sobs.

"I cannot answer that, Kitty, but I can promise you that love does not die. We will always have our love for Grandfather and his for us."

Kitty gave a shaky nod. "Mrs Faxon said much the same. We cannot change the course of nature, but we can give our love freely."

The two sisters, arms about one another, returned to the house.

Elizabeth and Jane sat beside her grandfather's bed in the hushed hours before dawn, his thin hand resting in hers as pale spring light began to edge the window curtains. His eyes, although tired, held their familiar acuity as they studied her face.

"You will manage splendidly," he said gently, his voice carrying all the quiet certainty that had guided their education. "Albeit, I had hoped to see certain matters settled before…"

"We are well settled, Grandfather," Elizabeth assured him, her throat tight with things unsaid. "The estate--"

"The estate, yes." His smile held fond exasperation. "I speak of other settlements. Mr Darcy's recent acquisition of our neighbouring estate suggests interesting possibilities."

Even now, his gentle teasing brought colour to her cheeks. "Grandfather…"

"My dear girl," he pressed her hand with surprising strength, "do not let pride stand in the way of happiness. Yours or Jane's."

Jane, keeping vigil on his other side, looked up at this. "You need not concern yourself with our—"

"I have spent my life concerning myself with your happiness," he interrupted with familiar asperity. "I do not mean to abandon the habit now. Or in the hereafter if I have the ability." His gaze moved between them, sharp despite his weakness. "One's happiness must in some measure be always at the mercy of chance. Joy may present itself unexpectedly. Promise me you will not let anything prevent you from grasping it. "

"We promise," Jane whispered, her calm manner wavering.

"Good." He settled back against his pillows, satisfaction briefly overcoming exhaustion. "I have watched you grow into women of remarkable capability. Your father would be…" His voice caught, then steadied. "Thomas would be so proud of you both. As am I."

Mrs Hill appeared at the door with fresh tea, her eyes suspiciously bright as she set down the tray. Her presence in these private moments went unremarked, as natural as breathing after thirty years of devoted service.

"Tell Mary," he continued after a moment, "that her scientific approach to agriculture shows true promise. And Kitty's eye for propagation will serve the estate well. Lydia's determination, properly directed has …" His voice faded briefly before rallying. "You will guide them, help them pursue their particular strengths?"

"Of course," Elizabeth managed, her composure threatening to crack.

He nodded once, satisfaction settling over his features. "Then I may rest content."

They sat in comfortable silence as dawn painted the room in strengthening light. When Hill entered an hour later, he lay in final repose, a quiet stillness upon his features, his granddaughters still holding his hands as if they might keep him with them through sheer force of will.

The women gathered in Longbourn's darkened parlour whilst the funeral procession wound its way to the churchyard. Elizabeth stood at the window, not quite watching as the sombre line of gentlemen disappeared around the lane's curve. Jane maintained perfect composure as she arranged tea things. Her eyes shone with unshed tears.

Mrs Bennet sat rigid in her chair, her cheer subdued. "Mr Hill will see all arranged as it ought," she said with quiet certainty. "He knew your grandfather's preferences in all things."

"Indeed," Elizabeth managed, turning from the window. "Thirty years of friendship disguised as service."

Mary and Kitty occupied the settee, their disparate natures united in shared grief, whilst Lydia's restless movements about the room spoke of emotions too complex for her sixteen years to fully express.

The ticking of the clock marked time's slow passage until the first carriages began returning. Mr Phillips appeared to report that all had been conducted with perfect dignity, and that father and son now lay together beneath Meryton's ancient yews. His careful account faltered only once, when speaking of Mr Hill's quiet authority in directing the final arrangements.

"They are together now," Mrs Bennet whispered, her fingers working at her handkerchief. "My Thomas and his father…"

Jane's arm slipped around their mother's waist as Elizabeth clasped her trembling hand. Behind them, Mary, Kitty, and Lydia formed a protective wall, unified in shared loss.

The March wind rattled the windows, carrying spring's early promise as the women of Longbourn gathered their collective strength, preparing to face the stream of callers that social custom would soon deliver to their door. Their private grief must now give way to public performance.

Dunbar Court, the Matthews' house stood in resigned dignity against the spring sky, its weathered facades suggesting years of genteel neglect. Darcy and Colonel Fitzwilliam surveyed the faded grandeur of the main hall, where dust sheets draped what furniture remained like shrouds.

"Rather reminds one of a charming billet I once had in Spain," the Colonel said, running a finger along a dusty window frame. "A Coruña, I believe. Although the Spanish farmhouse boasted more current furnishings."

"Peters has maintained the essential structure," Darcy replied, referring to his newly installed steward. "The interior, however, requires considerable attention."

"As does the news Peters just delivered." Fitzwilliam shifted to genuine gravity. "The old gentleman's passing… one rather regrets missing the opportunity to pay proper respect."

"Indeed." Darcy's single word carried meaning his cousin readily interpreted. "Our inspection can wait. We must convey our condolences at once."

Their arrival at Longbourn an hour later found the young

ladies seated with due formality in the front parlour, their hastily darkened gowns lending additional pallor to already subdued countenances. Elizabeth's quick glance at their entrance held none of her sparkle. Darcy noted how she straightened with no more than a breath of change.

"Mr Darcy. Colonel Fitzwilliam." Jane's perfect composure wavered only marginally. "You are most kind to call so promptly."

"We were deeply grieved to learn of your loss," the Colonel replied, his manner gentled to match the occasion. "Mr Bennet was a gentleman of remarkable character."

"He spoke often of your visit in November," Elizabeth managed, her voice steady, whilst her fingers smoothed the fabric of her dark skirts. "Your discussions of military organisation quite captured his interest."

A moment of weighted silence followed, heavy with all that could not be properly expressed in a formal condolence call.

"Please excuse me for a moment?" Elizabeth rose quickly and left the room.

Jane followed her sister's abrupt departure with her eyes, then turned back to the callers.

"I fear we are all quite emotional," she said.

Colonel Fitzwilliam shifted his chair closer to Miss Bennet's and spoke with kindness. "No one expects you to feel otherwise. I understand your loss is quite fresh. We will not impose—"

"Oh no! Please do not leave! We are all going quite distracted, having only one another for conversation. Elizabeth will be well." Jane's expression and glistening eyes mixed grief with longing as she reached her hand towards the Colonel, then stopped herself.

"Shall I see whether Miss Elizabeth requires anything?" Darcy asked.

"Yes, please, Mr Darcy. She may be in Grandfather's study." Jane said, then her attention fully turned to the Colonel.

Darcy bowed. "With your permission, Miss Bennet…"

Something unreadable passed across his expression as he stepped from the room, following the path Elizabeth had taken.

Elizabeth had maintained her composure admirably throughout the day, accepting condolences with quiet grace whilst managing the myriad details that death demands. But now, seeing Mr Darcy struck her with great confusion of mind. In the fading light of her grandfather's study, the familiar embrace of his books and papers proved her undoing. Her tears fell as her hands rested on his desk, where just weeks ago he had sat reviewing estate papers with characteristic acuity.

The door's soft click announced another presence. She hastily straightened, mortified to be discovered in such a state, but when she turned to find Mr Darcy's tall figure silhouetted in the doorway, something in his expression stopped her automatic apology.

"Miss Elizabeth." His voice held none of its accustomed reserve. "Pray, do not feel you must maintain appearances on my account."

"Indeed, sir, you need not concern yourself—I am quite well…" But the gentle understanding in his eyes undid her careful control. A sob escaped.

In two long strides he crossed to her and gathered her against the solid warmth of his chest. The impropriety of their position registered dimly in her mind but was overwhelmed by the profound relief of allowing herself, just for a moment, to be supported rather than supporting.

"I remember," he said gently, his breath stirring her hair, "finding similar comfort in my father's study after his passing. The familiar space somehow both comforts and makes the absence more acute."

Elizabeth pressed her face into the fine wool of his coat, breathing in the subtle scent of sandalwood and horse that she would forever after associate with comfort. His arms tightened fractionally, one large hand moving in soothing circles on her back.

"I should not…" she managed after a moment, but she made no move to withdraw.

"Should not what? Grieve? Feel the weight of responsibility? Allow yourself human frailty?" The rumble of his voice vibrated through his chest against her cheek. "I assure you, you have earned the right to all three."

The quiet strength in his voice, the solid reality of him anchoring her when everything else seemed to be shifting, created a curious lightheadedness. She became acutely aware of the breadth of his shoulders under her hands, the careful restraint in his embrace that somehow made it all the more intimate.

"I had not thought…" she began, then faltered, unsure how to express her surprise at this newfound gentleness in him.

"No," he agreed, seeming to understand her unfinished thought. "I believe there is much we had not thought of one another."

The moment stretched, filled with unspoken possibilities. Finally, reluctantly, Elizabeth stepped back, although the loss of his warmth felt as a physical pain.

"Thank you," she said simply, meeting his eyes.

"There is no need." His gaze held hers with an intensity that made her breath catch. "I would… that is, I hope you know you may always…" He broke off as he handed her a fine linen handkerchief.

"Yes," she replied. "I have come to know that. Thank you."

He bowed and withdrew, leaving Elizabeth to wonder if it was only grief that made her heart beat so erratically, or if perhaps there was something else taking root in the space between what they had been and what they might become.

Elizabeth remained in the study for several minutes, collecting herself. She touched her grandfather's favourite quill, still resting in its stand as though awaiting his return. The room held his presence so strongly that she half-expected to hear his voice calling for his ledgers. Taking a deep breath, she neatly folded Mr Darcy's handkerchief, tucking it into her sleeve rather than her pocket. Such a personal item ought to be returned, she told herself. The prospect of doing so sent a strange flutter through her chest.

When she finally returned to the parlour, she found Jane engaged in quiet conversation with Colonel Fitzwilliam, whilst Mr Darcy stood near the mantel, his posture rigid yet somehow conveying an air of patient waiting. His eyes found hers immediately, a silent question in their depths. She managed a small nod of reassurance, which seemed to ease some tension in his shoulders.

It was Mary who unexpectedly broke the tension. "The gardens show the first signs of spring," she said with careful modesty. "Perhaps… that is, the air might prove refreshing…"

"An excellent suggestion," the Colonel agreed with alacrity. "If the ladies would not find it too taxing?"

Jane's glance at Elizabeth carried volumes of sisterly communication before she replied. "Some gentle exercise might indeed prove beneficial. Lizzy?"

The weak spring sunshine cast long shadows across Longbourn's grounds as the small party made their way along the gravel path. Elizabeth fell into step beside Mr Darcy, whilst Jane and Colonel Fitzwilliam naturally drifted ahead, their quiet conversation carried away by the spring breeze.

"Your grandfather was a remarkable man, Miss Bennet," Darcy said, his voice carrying a new intimacy. "To have preserved his faculties so completely, even in his final days. He showed remarkable foresight."

Elizabeth brushed the black ribbon at her wrist. "His last words were of his pride in us - in what we had built together. He spoke of hope for the future." She paused, gathering herself. "I must own, Mr Darcy, there were moments in recent months when I feared that hope might prove unfounded."

"Yet here you stand, one of five mistresses of an unentailed Longbourn," Darcy replied, his steady gaze holding hers. "I should think your grandfather's confidence was admirably placed."

"You seem most approving, sir. I had thought you rather attached to traditional ways."

"I find myself increasingly convinced of the merit in… challenging established patterns." His gaze, when it met hers, held such intentional meaning that Elizabeth felt her breath catch.

They passed the old oak that marked the boundary between the original Longbourn lands and the newly secured portions.

Elizabeth paused, resting her hand against its weathered bark.

"This tree has witnessed three centuries of Bennets walking these grounds," she mused. "I doubt any previous generation gave it quite so much legal significance as we have of late."

"The law, like many rigid structures, occasionally requires gentle correction to better serve justice," Darcy offered; then added with deliberate weight, "Much like certain long-held opinions."

Elizabeth's eyes sparkled with sudden understanding. "And have you found such corrections… difficult to implement, Mr Darcy?"

"Less difficult than maintaining erroneous convictions, once thoroughly examined."

Ahead of them, Jane's soft voice carried on the breeze as Colonel Fitzwilliam entertained her with tales of his many adventures. His natural charm seemed to have accomplished what months of Bingley's vacillating attentions had not - drawing out Jane's genuine animation rather than solely her polite interest.

"You may trust my word, Miss Bennet, diplomatic relations are far more challenging than military campaigns," the Colonel was saying. "One rarely fears for one's life in a ballroom, but one's dignity is perpetually under siege."

"Your cousin seems to have developed a sudden interest in horticultural walks," Elizabeth said, allowing a bit of mischief to colour her words.

"Fitzwilliam has always been an admirer of… English gardens," Darcy replied his voice tinged with dry humour. "I believe his current enthusiasm may be more specifically directed."

Elizabeth felt the charge of all that remained unspoken—a silence at once delightful and disquieting. "And you, Mr Darcy? What draws you to survey Longbourn's modest acres today?"

Darcy drew a careful breath, as though marshalling his thoughts. Elizabeth had never seen him so visibly striving to maintain his characteristic restraint. It lent him a curious vulnerability that made her heart beat faster.

He turned to face her fully. His expression held such earnest intensity that Elizabeth felt the very air around them still. "I have learnt that Longbourn contains treasures far beyond mere acreage."

Chapter Fifty-One

Darcy measured each word with excruciating care, acutely conscious of the delicate balance required. How different these grounds appeared now - no longer a symbol of the gap between their situations, but rather the very proof of Elizabeth's extraordinary capabilities. Still, divining her feelings proved as challenging as ever.

Ahead, his cousin demonstrated the easy charm that had always eluded Darcy, drawing genuine warmth from serene Jane Bennet. There lay a lesson, perhaps, although Elizabeth would respond poorly to any attempt at studied lightness. No, their understanding had always rested on more complex foundations.

"Your grandfather showed remarkable judgement," he ventured, watching her profile with interest. "In placing his trust where others might have seen only conventional limitations."

"He was rather in the habit of seeing beyond convention," Elizabeth replied, offering neither encouragement nor rebuke. "I wonder, Mr Darcy, what prompted the observation?"

There lay the challenge - how to bridge the distance his own pride had created without stumbling into the very same errors of presumption. Her every response carried that familiar spark of intelligence but guarded now in a way that twisted something in his chest.

"I have been contemplating the nature of discernment. How a truly superior mind must be willing to… revise its understanding when presented with compelling evidence."

Her quick glance showed another feeling - amusement? Interest? - before her features composed themselves again. "A rather philosophical observation for a garden walk, sir."

"Perhaps." He gathered his courage. "I would argue that gardens are most well suited to contemplating growth and change."

The ghost of a smile touched her lips. "Have you been cultivating such changes, Mr Darcy?"

There it was - an opening, if he was brave enough to take it. But before he could frame his response, the Colonel's laugh carried back to them, accompanied by some witty observation about military strategy and marriage that made Jane Bennet's eyes dance with mirth.

Elizabeth's attention shifted momentarily to her sister, and Darcy said the flash of protective assessment in her gaze. Ever aware of her family's vulnerabilities, even now. The reminder strengthened his resolve - she deserved to know that her loyalty, far from being a drawback in his eyes, had become one of her most admirable qualities.

"I have learnt," he said with deliberate weight, "that the most valuable growth often comes through challenging our most deeply held convictions."

Her eyes returned to his face, sharp with that penetrating intelligence that had long drawn his attention, long before he had learnt to truly value it.

"That sounds rather uncomfortable, Mr Darcy."

"Less uncomfortable than persisting in error," he replied, willing her to understand the deeper meaning beneath his words. "Particularly when that error prevents one from recognising what one truly desires."

Darcy halted their walk at the small stone bridge spanning Longbourn's stream. On the other side lay the path to Dunbar Court. He was aware that his next words could alter the course of both their lives irrevocably. He had to get it right. The late afternoon sun caught the amber in Elizabeth's hair, gilding her in sunlight, and for a moment, his prepared speech deserted him entirely.

"Elizabeth." His voice emerged rougher than he intended. He drew a steadying breath, drinking in the sight of her. "Elizabeth. I can no longer tolerate half measures or implied understanding between us."

Her eyes had widened at the use of her Christian name, but she remained silent, her expression a study in restrained surprise.

"You must allow me to tell you how ardently I admire and love you." The words rushed forth now, as though breaking through a long maintained dam. "These past months have taught me that my happiness depends entirely upon you. Society's concerns about connections and circumstance seem not merely foolish now, but utterly contrary to the evidence of your extraordinary worth. Your brilliance illuminates everything around you - your wit, your courage, your devotion to those you love. You have taught me what true excellence means, and in doing so, have made me a better man."

Elizabeth's lips parted, but no sound emerged. The colour had drained from her face, leaving her complexion like fine porcelain.

"I speak now with no presumption, only hope," his hands clenched behind his back, knuckles white with tension. "Would you do me the great honour of allowing me to court you? To prove myself worthy of the treasure of your regard?"

The pause lengthened, thick with expectation. Elizabeth's eyes were wide, her chest rising and falling rapidly. Each heartbeat felt like an eternity as he waited, scarcely breathing.

"Mr Darcy." Her voice, when it finally came, held an utterly unfamiliar note of uncertainty. "In such cases as these, a lady's affections should be freely given, with neither duty nor gratitude to compel them."

His heart stilled in his chest. Was this a rejection? The world narrowed to her next words.

"And so, I tell you, with neither obligation nor constraint," she continued, her voice strengthening as a smile began to dawn across her features, "that my affections and wishes are engaged completely, irrevocably, and entirely in your favour."

The world blazed into glorious colour around him.

"Elizabeth?" He breathed her name like a prayer.

"My heart, Mr Darcy, has long been yours - I believe I was the last to know it."

Joy surged through him with an unbearable intensity. "You are certain?"

"Quite certain." Her smile held both warmth and that characteristic spark of challenge. "I suspect we shall spend years discovering how deeply we misunderstood one another—and how sweetly we may remedy it."

The subtle play of meaning in her words - acknowledging their past whilst transforming it into promise - made his heart leap.

"I look forward to every new marvel you show me," he managed, his voice rough with emotion.

"As do I," she agreed. "For I find my understanding of you grows ever more fascinating with each new piece of knowledge."

Darcy took her small hand in his, gently caressed her fingers. A gentle breeze stirred the leaves overhead, casting dappled shadows across their joined hands.

"My dear Mr Darcy," Elizabeth ventured, her fingers still entwined with his, "propriety demands I remind you that my current state of mourning places rather severe limitations on any… courtship activities."

"I had considered that circumstance," he replied curiously, studying the play of emotion across her features.

"Indeed?" Her lips curved in that particular way that always presaged some delightful challenge. "Then perhaps you have also considered that a betrothed couple might find themselves afforded certain… allowances that mere courting couples could not expect?"

Darcy felt his breath catch at her daring. "Miss Bennet, are you suggesting that we circumvent the rules of mourning through an immediate engagement?"

"I would do no such thing, sir." The sparkle in her eyes belied her serious mien. "I simply observe that a bereaved granddaughter might properly receive her betrothed in the family parlour, whilst a gentleman caller would be restricted to fewer and more formal visits. Surely no one could object to a future husband offering comfort in times of loss?"

The subtle emphasis she placed on 'future husband' sent a

thrill through him that he struggled to master. "Your concern for propriety is admirable."

"I find it wise to consider all aspects of any… arrangement," she murmured, her thumb tracing the smallest arc against his palm through their gloves. "Particularly ones of such personal significance."

The touch, slight as it was, nearly undid his careful composure. "Your wisdom continues to astound me."

"We are agreed?" The sunlight caught the amber flecks in her eyes as she gazed up at him. "That an extended courtship would be quite impractical under the circumstances?"

"Entirely agreed," he managed, wondering if she could feel his racing pulse through their joined hands. Elizabeth's eyes held his, a blend of challenge and tenderness in their depths. "I fear I have been most forward in suggesting such an arrangement, Mr Darcy." Her voice softened. "But there remains a rather crucial question that only a gentleman can ask."

She waited, her hand still nestled in his. Darcy felt the meaning of the moment settle around them like a physical presence - all their misunderstandings, growth, and dawning understanding crystallising into this single breath of time.

He shifted to face her fully, his free hand coming up to capture her other one, propriety be damned. The rough stone of the path pressed against his knee as he sank down before her.

"My dearest, loveliest Elizabeth." His voice emerged rough with emotion. "You have transformed my understanding of happiness itself. Your strength, your wit, your tender heart - every day reveals new depths to treasure. I come to you now offering you my heart, complete and unreserved."

Her fingers tightened on his, and he watched a shimmer of tears gather in her eyes even as her lips curved in that beloved smile.

"Will you do me the extraordinary honour of becoming my wife? Of allowing me to spend my life with you? Of building a future together?"

A single tear spilled over, catching the sunlight as it traced down her cheek. "Yes," she whispered, then stronger: "Yes, with all my heart."

He rose, drawing her hands to his chest, his heart pounding beneath them. "You have made me the happiest of men."

"Then we are well matched," she managed through her tears, "for I cannot imagine greater joy than this."

The distant sounds of birds and breeze faded away, leaving only the precious reality of Elizabeth in his arms, her fingers warm against his heart, and the promise of all their tomorrows stretching out before them. From somewhere came the sound of the Colonel's laughter and Jane's answering response, but Darcy barely registered it. The whole world had narrowed to the woman before him, her eyes bright with promise - not just of love, but of a lifetime of her intelligence challenging and complementing his own. Every dream he had never dared to voice was suddenly within reach.

Chapter Fifty-Two

The late afternoon sun burnished Longbourn's drawing room as the party returned, Elizabeth's heart thundering beneath her composed exterior. Mary, ever observant, lifted her eyes from her book to study her sister's countenance with quiet intensity.

"You seem remarkably restored by your walk, Lizzy," she said. "I gather your ramble was restorative?"

"Indeed." Elizabeth untied the black ribbons at her neck, conscious of the precious understanding so newly forged between herself and Mr Darcy. "Perhaps not quite as beneficial as the company."

Jane, still caught in the glow of Colonel Fitzwilliam's engaging discourse, sat near the window with her embroidery. Her needle remained motionless as she gazed abstractedly into the garden.

"I cannot recall when last I saw you smile so," Mary persisted, closing her book with a snap. "Not since before…"

The unfinished sentence seemed to hover in the air. Elizabeth's joy faltered for a moment, guilt threading through her happiness.

"Lizzy?" Kitty looked up from her own needlework, suddenly alert. "Oh! Oh, surely not…"

"What am I missing?" Mrs Bennet asked, roused from her reverie by Kitty's exclamation.

Elizabeth felt the pressure of their combined regard, save Jane's. She glanced toward Mr Darcy, who stood by the fireplace maintaining an admirable façade of composure.

"I had planned to wait," Elizabeth began, "out of respect for our mourning. But as Mary and Kitty have quite thoroughly exposed my inability to mask my feelings…" She drew a steadying breath. "Mr Darcy has offered for my hand. And I have accepted."

"Oh!" Mrs Bennet's eyes grew wide. "But this is… this is…" For once, words seemed to fail her.

"Grandfather would have been so pleased," Kitty said, giving way to genuine emotion. "He always said Mr Darcy reminded him of himself at that age."

"Did he?" Darcy's voice held surprised pleasure.

"He did," Mary confirmed. "He also suggested you should find considerable benefit from learning to smile more frequently." Her lips curved subtly. "I observe that particular fault appears to have been addressed."

"The mourning period," Mrs Bennet mused, practical concerns asserting themselves. "For a grandparent, three months of full mourning would be quite sufficient, followed by half-mourning…"

"He was more than a grandfather to us," Elizabeth interjected gently. "These past years especially…"

"Of course, my dear." Mrs Bennet's voice softened with understanding. "But consider - would he not want your happiness secured? A wedding in half-mourning, with all due gravity and respect…"

"Perhaps in summer," Colonel Fitzwilliam suggested from where he had stationed himself near Jane's embroidery frame. "When the skies match Miss Bennet's eyes."

This drew Jane's attention. She turned from her contemplation of the garden, took in her sister's radiant expression and Mr Darcy's poorly concealed adoration, and burst into delighted laughter.

"Lizzy! How long did you intend to keep this secret?"

"Approximately three more hours," Elizabeth admitted. "But Mary has quite remarkable powers of observation."

"Mr Darcy has been watching you as though you were the sun breaking through storm clouds," Mary replied dryly. "It required no great acuity."

"Has he indeed?" Elizabeth's eyes sparkled as they met her betrothed's. "How remarkably unsubtle of him."

"I find subtlety rather overrated at present," Darcy murmured, his composure cracking into a smile that would have astonished his London acquaintance. "Would June still be rather soon?"

"Three months would be more fitting, given Grandfather's particular role in our lives." Mary said.

"And then half-mourning could begin in July," Kitty calculated, her fingers touching the black ribbon on her sleeve. "Lizzy, you need not rush to grey silks merely because convention allows it."

"The question of timing need not be settled this hour," Darcy interjected, his voice gentle as he noted Elizabeth's conflicted expression. "What matters is the understanding between us."

"How diplomatic you have become, sir," Elizabeth replied, her smile warming. "I suspect society may have stronger opinions on the matter."

"Society's opinions, whilst no doubt numerous and forcefully expressed, hold no particular sway over such decisions for me," Darcy answered with steel beneath his smooth words.

"I see marriage has not yet been accomplished, yet already you champion your future wife's wishes," Colonel Fitzwilliam said with a grin. "A most promising beginning, cousin."

"A most promising beginning indeed," Elizabeth replied, her eyes glinting with amusement. "I wonder, Colonel, whether your diplomatic skills might not be better employed in other quarters than teasing your cousin?"

"You may rely upon it, Miss Elizabeth, that years of military service have taught me to deploy my resources where they might prove most effective." The Colonel's glance toward Jane held careful meaning.

"And what lessons has your service taught regarding the merits of a strategic retreat?" Darcy enquired dryly, noting the hour.

"That it often precedes one's most successful advances," his cousin returned smoothly, before turning to Jane. "I have found," his expression shifted to something more thoughtful as he addressed her, "that travel breeds a particular appreciation for one's native landscape. The gardens of Spain have their merits, but they lack a certain… English sensibility."

Jane's response, when it came, held the blend of gentle insight and careful reserve that marked her character. "Perhaps, Colonel, it is not the gardens themselves but rather our understanding of them that changes with absence."

"An astute observation, Miss Bennet." His smile suggested deeper currents beneath the seemingly innocuous discussion of horticulture. "One's perspective does tend to sharpen when viewing familiar territory through new eyes."

Mrs Bennet, observing this delicate exchange with the amused eye of a reformed matchmaker, noted the Colonel's attentions and the subtle animation in Jane's countenance. Her fingers smoothed her skirts with barely contained satisfaction, although she maintained an admirable façade of maternal indifference.

After the gentlemen had made their bows and departed - Darcy's lingering look at Elizabeth speaking volumes - the drawing room erupted into joyful chaos.

"Oh, my dear, dear Lizzy!" Mrs Bennet clasped her hands together. "Ten thousand a year! And such a fine figure of a man!"

"Mamma," Elizabeth laughed, "surely his figure is the least of his recommendations?"

"Not an insignificant one," Kitty teased, then ducked the cushion Elizabeth aimed at her head.

"I cannot think any pair so perfectly matched," Jane murmured. "His gravity complements your liveliness, and your wit lightens his reserve."

"Whilst we discuss perfect matches," Elizabeth's eyes danced, "shall we speak of a certain colonel's marked attention to a certain sister?"

Jane's blush spoke volumes. "Lizzy! We are celebrating your engagement."

"And what better celebration than the prospect of another?" Mrs Bennet interjected. "I must say, Colonel Fitzwilliam's conversation shows a decided improvement over certain other gentlemen's efforts."

"Mother!" Jane protested, but her smile betrayed her.

"To think," Mary mused, setting aside her book—a certain sign of the occasion's import, "that Grandfather's final triumph should lead to such happiness. He would have revelled in the justice of it."

"He would have celebrated the man you have chosen," Jane agreed. "He saw Mr Darcy's worth long before any of us."

"Even Lizzy," Lydia added, her eyes alight with mischief.

"Especially Lizzy," Elizabeth admitted, sinking onto the sofa beside Jane. "I maintain my blindness makes my current clarity all the sweeter."

"And what of your clarity regarding a certain colonel, dearest Jane?" Mrs Bennet prompted hopefully.

"Mamma!" Four voices chorused in amused exasperation.

But Jane's quiet smile, Elizabeth noted, spoke of possibilities yet unfolding.

The two gentlemen paused in what had once been the grand entryway of Dunbar Court, where a fine chandelier now listed precariously, dark and tarnished, several pieces missing from its once-elegant array. Dust motes danced in the late afternoon light streaming through grimy windows.

"Your definition of 'requiring some attention' rivals Bingley's of 'a small party of intimates,'" Colonel Fitzwilliam remarked, running a finger along a once-elegant side table. "I must say, the accommodations do remind me fondly of certain more rustic campaigns." He lifted his hand and brushed off a layer of dust.

"You find my temporary lodgings lacking?" Darcy grinned as he led the way toward what might once have been the library. "I am confident, the roof is entirely sound—in at least three rooms."

"How fortunate we are only two, then. I note you have chosen to maintain your own staff at minimal levels. Preparing for married life with an estate manager, cousin?"

Darcy's expression softened at the reference to Elizabeth. "I find myself increasingly appreciative of practical knowledge in matters of property management," he paused before a window overlooking overgrown gardens. "This estate has remarkable potential, although it would require dedicated attention to restore it to its former glory. And far more time than I could dedicate to the project."

"No doubt your own obligations at Pemberley would make such dedication challenging." The Colonel remained deliberately neutral.

"Indeed. I have wondered whether a man of military background—guided, perhaps, by someone acquainted with the local soil—might find in it an excellent opportunity." Darcy turned to face his cousin. "Particularly if such a man wished to establish himself within a convenient distance of certain neighbouring estates."

"How diplomatically put." The Colonel's eyes sparkled with understanding. "Would this hypothetical man's efforts benefit from the counsel of an insightful local beauty?"

"I could not speak to that," Darcy said. "However, I understand the eldest Miss Bennet has shown remarkable aptitude in matters of estate improvement."

"Indeed?" The Colonel moved to join him at the window, his gaze drifting toward Longbourn's distant chimneys. "How fortunate that military service has taught me to recognise superior intelligence when I encounter it."

"More fortunate still that you have learnt to act upon such recognition—with decisiveness."

"Unlike some of my acquaintance who required a great deal of time to acknowledge their own good fortune?"

"Thorough evaluation of merit," Darcy replied with dignity.

"So, it is to be termed thus, is it?" The Colonel laughed. "Well, cousin, should your thoughts about this estate's future prove more than speculation, I believe I might be persuaded to take up the commission. Particularly given the… strategic advantages of the location."

The garden had begun to bloom in earnest, though it felt quieter than it had in years. Kitty knelt beside the thyme beds, pulling back spent stalks and thinning the new growth with careful hands. The air was fragrant with sage and damp soil, bees humming low and steady.

Her grandfather had been gone a fortnight. His absence lingered everywhere—in the stillness of his study, the unsent letters on his desk, the way the family now relied upon her for the upkeep of the herb garden without needing to ask.

When Mr Blackwood approached the gate, Kitty did not stand. She glanced up briefly, her hands still busy with a stubborn root.

"Good afternoon," she said, smiling.

"Miss Catherine," he replied, removing his hat. "I… I was told I might find you here."

"You were told correctly." She sat back on her heels. "If you have come about the marigolds, they've taken well in the eastern beds. I can dig a few starts for you."

"Thank you," he said. "But it… was not the marigolds."

Something in his voice made her finally rise. She brushed her hands against her apron, waiting.

"I had meant to speak with your grandfather first," he said quietly. "To ask for his blessing before approaching you. But—" He faltered. "But I know he trusted you to manage what matters now.

And so, I come to you directly."

Kitty's heart beat a little faster, though her face remained still.

"I have been offered an apprenticeship in Exeter," he said. "With a physician of some reputation. I am to leave within the month. The work will be long and exacting. And I will not be free to return for some time."

She nodded once, already sensing what must follow.

"But before I go, I wished you to know—" His voice steadied. "My regard for you has grown beyond friendship. I admire your mind, your humour, your quiet strength. I do not presume to expect anything from you now, but… I hope that, in time, you might consider a more formal understanding between us. When I am in a position to offer one."

Kitty looked down at her gloves, now darkened by damp soil. She took a breath, then met his gaze.

"You are the first person who ever asked what I knew about anything," she said quietly. "Not what I wore or how I danced, but what I had studied. You listened."

He swallowed hard. "I hope always to listen."

She allowed herself the smallest smile.

"You have my permission to write to me, Mr Blackwood. On the condition that your letters include medicinal observations. Especially of the useful kind. I've no patience for men who rhapsodise about fevers and then mis-dose the laudanum."

He laughed, relief and something warmer in his eyes.

"Then I shall write faithfully. And often. And humbly submit all botanical claims for your approval."

She stepped aside, gesturing toward the edge of the thyme bed. "You may take a handful, if you like. It dries well against the headaches that come with spring storms."

He bowed, but did not reach for the plant.

"Only if I may return the favour," he said, hesitating before continuing. "I have something that belonged to my mentor—an apothecary's folding case, for samples and tinctures. It is worn but well made. I thought… you might find it useful. And I should like you to have it. As a token—of shared study, if nothing more."

Kitty blinked, startled by the quiet intimacy of the offering. Not flowers, nor jewellery, nor anything a sister might tease her over—but something that fit perfectly into the rhythm of her own hands and daily work.

"I would value it greatly," she said, more firmly than she felt. "Thank you, Mr Blackwood."

As he turned to leave, she did not watch him go at once. Her eyes returned to the soil, the quiet beds of rosemary and yarrow, the place where her grandfather once knelt beside her.

When she looked up again, Mr Blackwood was gone—but in his place, she felt something solid take root. Not grief, not quite hope. Just the steady promise of something *growing.*

Chapter Fifty-Three

April 15, 1811

Dearest Elizabeth,

The spring planting commands my presence, although my thoughts remain fixed at Longbourn. I find myself mentally composing observations to share with you throughout my days - from the particular challenges of drainage in the north field (which I suspect might interest your practical mind) to the way the morning light strikes Pemberley's windows (which reminds me, with painful sweetness, of how the sun caught in your hair that afternoon by the stream). In truth, I find the sun's brilliance a poor substitute for the memory of you.

Your most devoted,
FD

April 18, 1811
Dear Mr Darcy,

How formal you remain in closing, despite such tender sentiments preceding it! I shall not tease you over much about it, however, as your observations about drainage have quite captured my attention. We faced similar challenges in Longbourn's east field two years past. Might I suggest…

I find myself rather disturbed by how frequently your voice intrudes upon my thoughts, offering dry observations about my daily activities. The other morning, whilst reviewing the household accounts, I distinctly heard you murmur something about efficient organisation. Most unsettling, sir, to have one's mind so thoroughly invaded. I fear you have taken up tenancy in my thoughts, without first applying through proper channels.

Your own Elizabeth
(Do note my own closing's relative informality - you may consider it a challenge)

April 22, 1811
My beloved Elizabeth,

Your suggestions regarding the drainage issue prove remarkably sound. I confess some amusement at implementing improvements to Pemberley under your distant direction. Although perhaps I should not be surprised - you have been improving me from afar since our first meeting.

Speaking of improvements, I accept your challenge regarding closings, although I maintain that some degree of formality provides a necessary restraint to expression. Particularly when one's feelings run so very deep that their full acknowledgement might overwhelm the page entirely. Your more recent influence leaves me increasingly unfit for society's standards of reserve.

Yours, with carefully measured devotion,
Fitzwilliam

April 25, 1811
My dearest Fitzwilliam,

How cleverly you navigate between propriety and passion! I wonder if you realise how your reliable restraint serves only to heighten the effect of your words. When you speak of feelings overwhelming the page, my mind cannot resist wandering to less… restrained expressions of sentiment.

But perhaps we should return to safer topics. The lambing season progresses well here, although I find myself unexpectedly missing your incisive questions about our methods. One can only discuss breeding lines with one's sisters for so long before longing for more challenging discourse. The ewe who shares my name shows far less restraint than I. Were she capable of speech, I fear she would be scolding me for blushing over field reports.

Yours, with decidedly improper thoughts about agricultural discussions,
E

April 30, 1811
My dearest Elizabeth,

The spring sowing proceeds apace, however my thoughts turn frequently to a particular bloom of Hertfordshire that has taken root in rather more personal soil. Your suggestions regarding crop rotation have proved invaluable -Perhaps your practical wisdom about allowing fields adequate time to develop their full potential might apply to other matters entirely.

The steward remarked today upon my increased attention to detail in estate matters. I did not enlighten him that my newfound diligence stems from imagining your keen eyes reviewing each decision. One particularly vexing matter of tenant negotiations was resolved by simply asking myself what observation you might make about the situation, complete with that arch look you employ to such devastating effect—equal parts amusement and judgement, which no steward could survive unscathed.

Yours, with thoughts that stray persistently from agriculture, struggling valiantly to think pure thoughts of clover and fencing,
Fitzwilliam

May 3, 1811
Dearest Fitzwilliam,

How delightfully you blur the lines between estate management and courtship! I find myself equally afflicted - this morning I caught myself explaining to Lydia that whilst immediate gratification in breeding programmes might be tempting, the rewards of patience and careful cultivation often yield far superior results. The knowing look our shepherd gave me suggests I may have revealed more than intended about matters entirely unrelated to sheep. I begin to fear the sheep believe me to be composing poetry in their honour, given the dreamy manner in which I now drift through their pastures.

I must take issue with your assessment of the north field drainage - not for its technical merit, which I find sound, but for how thoroughly your detailed descriptions of water flow have dampened certain other thoughts that propriety suggests I ought not entertain.

Your increasingly impatient student of agricultural patience,
Elizabeth

May 7, 1811

My beloved Elizabeth,

Your letter regarding the lambing figures arrived today, and I marvel at how you manage to make animal husbandry sound simultaneously completely proper and utterly scandalous. I had to read your paragraph about selective breeding three times before I could focus on its actual content rather than its… broader implications.

Georgiana asked me at dinner why I smiled so at the mention of sheep. I believe I maintained my composure admirably whilst explaining that I simply took satisfaction in good estate management. She appeared unconvinced, whether by my explanation or my attempt at nonchalance, I cannot say.

Yours, with thoughts that would shock the sheep,
Fitzwilliam

May 10, 1811
Dearest heart,

I write this from the oak grove where we first spoke of estate matters - do you recall? I walked here quite without intention, I cannot regret the detour. The spring air holds such promise, does it not? Although perhaps that is merely my own anticipation colouring the breeze.

Jane suggested today that my newfound interest in comparing Longbourn's ledgers with Pemberley's might have motivations beyond mere academic curiosity. I assured her that nothing could be more natural than studying the precise figures of another estate. Her quiet smile suggested my choice of words might have betrayed me. I merely innocently calculated depreciation rates whilst imagining your handwriting in the margins.

Yours, with entirely proper thoughts about estate comparison,
Elizabeth

P.S. The sheep send their regards, although they wish you would stop shocking them. They beg you to reconsider the tone of your next treatise on selective breeding—it has left the rams unsettled.

May 13, 1811
My dearest Elizabeth,

I passed the afternoon reviewing Pemberley's east orchard, yet I confess I remember little of it. I was too occupied imagining how you might walk there, what remarks you would make about the apple grafting, or whether you would allow me the indulgence of choosing a tree to dedicate to your name.

Georgiana has noted that I now reread your letters before retiring each night. She suspects I am memorising agricultural data. Let her believe so. If she knew the truth—that each turn of phrase from your pen is more rousing than any poem—I should never hear the end of it.

Yours, entirely undone by ink and wit,
Fitzwilliam

May 16, 1811
Dearest Fitzwilliam,

The days grow longer, yet I find my patience shorter. Each morning, I consult the almanac as though it might speed your return by sheer force of will, and I now measure time not by meals or tasks, but by how many hours remain before I may justly expect your next letter. Even the sheep begin to grow suspicious of my frequent visits to the post.

All is in readiness here—Longbourn, the gardens, my sisters (who cannot seem to cease speculating about wedding clothes, menus, and the exact shade of blush my cheeks acquire when your name is mentioned). Only one thing remains out of place, and that, sir, is you.

The orchard is in bloom. I wandered there this morning and thought how well it shall suit our first walk as husband and wife. I am even prepared to overlook your preference for early starts, should you promise to share your coffee and offer commentary on my planting schemes with the same gravity you reserve for parliamentary debate.

Hurry home, my love. You are awaited not only with affection, but with considerable impatience—and more than a few plans that propriety prevents me from outlining here.

Yours, already and always,

Elizabeth

"My word," Mary said, noting another letter's arrival. "Poor Mr Darcy's courier deserves extra compensation for attending to the demands of your correspondence."

"Whatever do you mean?," Elizabeth replied evenly, Her hands trembled as she broke the seal. "We are discussing estate matters."

"Of course," Mary agreed, dry as dust. "I often blush when reading about crop rotation myself."

Chapter Fifty-Four

Kitty sat apart near the hearth, a shawl tucked about her shoulders, her workbasket at her feet. From beneath the folds of a clean muslin cloth, she drew out the small leather case—one Mr Blackwood had given her.

Narrower than a gentleman's shaving kit, it was bound in cracked calfskin with worn brass hinges. She opened it carefully. Inside, nestled in faded velvet, were small glass vials, a pair of folding steel tweezers, and a slim bone-handled spatula—tools for measuring powders and blending ointments..

She stoppered one vial with her fingertip, her brows knit, though her expression was not unhappy—only thoughtful. The fire crackled softly beside her.

"What is that?" Lydia asked suddenly, peering over the back of the settee. "It looks like something a dentist would use to frighten children."

"It is… nothing," Kitty replied too quickly, instinctively tucking the case against her side.

A pause followed. Elizabeth looked up at her sister. Mary slowly lowered her book. Lydia, whose curiosity was rarely short-lived, narrowed her eyes.

"An apothecary's case is hardly *nothing*," Mary observed, her tone neutral.

"Indeed," Elizabeth said mildly, tapping her pen against her lip. "It implies a certain… professional regard. Or something more personal, perhaps?"

"Perhaps," Kitty said, again too quickly, then pressed her lips together.

Silence stretched a little longer than was comfortable.

"I only meant," she added, more quietly, "that he respects my interest in herb craft. He said it belonged to someone who taught him. That it might be better used than put away in a drawer."

"Mm," said Elizabeth.

Kitty closed the case gently, her hand lingering on the latch.

"A practical item," Elizabeth said at last. "But not commonly left behind by chance."

Kitty stood. "Not everything left behind is forgotten."

"If a man ever gives *me* a case of bottles," Lydia declared, "he had best fill them with perfume. Or I shall assume he thinks me ill."

Mrs Bennet, dressed in the severe black of full mourning, her customary lace cap replaced by one of plain muslin, entered the drawing room. Despite the sombre attire, there was a certain animation in her step that had been absent these past weeks.

"Mr Freeman has called to discuss the Lodge garden," she announced, smoothing her black skirts. "He has brought several cuttings from his own herb garden that he believes might thrive in the eastern bed."

Elizabeth exchanged a meaningful glance with Mary. "How very… considerate."

"He has particular knowledge of medicinal herbs," Mrs Bennet continued, her fingers absently adjusting her cap. "His late wife, it seems, maintained quite an extensive collection. He thought I might find it useful, given my interest in household remedies."

"And do you plan to show him our own collection?" Mary enquired, setting aside her book.

Mrs Bennet's cheeks coloured. "I had thought to invite him to take tea in the small parlour after our walk. Hill has prepared those apple tarts he so enjoys."

"Then we must not detain you," Elizabeth said gently, noting how her mother's eyes, still ringed with grief's shadows, nonetheless held a spark of genuine interest. "Perhaps he might stay to dine with us? Jane was hoping to discuss the new drainage work near the Lodge."

"I had already extended the invitation," Mrs Bennet admitted. "I hesitated to mention it, not wishing to appear…" She faltered.

"Forward?" Elizabeth suggested kindly. "I believe a gentleman calling to discuss gardens and staying to dine with the family is the very model of propriety, Mamma."

"Particularly when that gentleman has consulted with the local parson about appropriate behaviour during a family's mourning period," Mary added. At her mother's startled look, she explained, "Mr Willis mentioned it after Sunday services. It seems Mr Freeman is most concerned with showing suitable respect."

Mrs Bennet's expression softened. "He is a thoughtful man. Not given to excessive speech, but observant. Rather reminds me…" She stopped, then continued more quietly, "He mentioned that tending growing things can sometimes ease a heart's heaviness. I find there is wisdom in that."

From the window came the sound of boots on gravel, and they watched as Mr Freeman, a tall figure in dark clothes that acknowledged the house's mourning without matching its severity, approached the door. His slightly stooped shoulders and lined face spoke of his fifty years, but his step remained firm.

"I shall join him in the garden," Mrs Bennet said, rising with quiet dignity. "Mary, perhaps you might join us in half an hour? Your knowledge of the herb classifications would be most helpful."

As their mother departed, Elizabeth turned to Mary with undisguised curiosity. "Herb classifications? I was not aware you had developed such expertise."

"Nor had I," Mary replied dryly. "I suspect my presence is required more as chaperone than botanist. I shall endeavour to prepare a list of classifications before I arrive, lest I be asked to distinguish between balm and borage whilst chaperoning a courtship in disguise."

They moved to the window, watching as their mother greeted

Mr Freeman. The gentleman's bow to Mrs Bennet carried respect. His hand lingered when she offered hers, the gesture still entirely appropriate.

"They make a well-matched pair," Elizabeth said as the couple moved toward path to the Lodge, walking close together whilst absorbed in conversation. "His steadiness seems to soothe her nerves."

"And her animation brings colour to his gravity," Mary agreed. "Rather like another couple of our acquaintance."

Elizabeth's laugh acknowledged the hit. "Must you be so observant, sister?"

"One of us must maintain objectivity amidst all this sentiment," Mary replied, her smile held genuine warmth. "In view of my own discussions with Mr Fairfield, I have discovered the appeal of botanical conversation."

Through the window, they could see Mrs Bennet pointing out something in a flower bed, her black-gloved hand gesturing with enthusiasm as Mr Freeman bent his head attentively to hear her explanation. If their heads were perhaps a bit closer than strict propriety might dictate, the earnestness of their horticultural discussion provided ample justification.

"How fortunate," Elizabeth mused, "that one may discuss soil composition with perfect propriety, even in deepest mourning."

"Indeed," Mary agreed. "We might hope Mr Freeman's discussions of herb beds maintain more propriety than certain exchanges about crop rotation."

"Did you enjoy your visit with Mr Freeman?" Jane enquired, setting aside her book.

Mrs Bennet's fingers outlined the embroidery on her handkerchief, her expression thoughtful. "I find them… not unwelcome." She looked up, meeting her daughters' gazes with directness. "I had not imagined such feelings might arise again. After your father…" Her voice faltered momentarily.

"Papa would wish your happiness," Jane said, entering with her workbasket. "As would Grandfather."

"Mr Freeman mentioned calling tomorrow afternoon to discuss improvements to the Lodge," Mrs Bennet continued. "He has some particular ideas about the front windows that he believes might interest me."

"Windows?" Elizabeth's lips curved in barely suppressed amusement. "How fascinating."

"I understand he has renovated Garver Hall extensively," Mrs Bennet replied with perfect composure, though a slight blush coloured her cheeks. "A gentleman of mature years develops practical interests, Lizzy."

"Of course," Elizabeth agreed solemnly, though her eyes danced. "Particularly when those interests align so fortuitously with a certain lady's property."

"You are impertinent, child," Mrs Bennet chided, but without heat. "I believe your Mr Darcy might understand the appeal of a knowledge of such practical matters."

Elizabeth's own cheeks warmed. "Then we must ensure the Lodge decor receives fitting attention. Perhaps you might show Mr Freeman your collection of fine china? I understand gentlemen of discernment find such displays most illuminating."

"Elizabeth!" Mrs Bennet exclaimed, her eyes crinkling suspiciously.

"Illuminating indeed." Mary said dryly.

Mrs Bennet's startled laugh—the first they had heard since Grandfather's passing—rang through the parlour like a promise of healing. "You dreadful girls," she said, her voice warm with genuine affection. "What your grandfather would say!"

"He would say," Jane said gently, "that spring brings renewal in many forms."

As she departed, the sisters exchanged glances containing equal parts amazement and approval.

"Well," Elizabeth said finally. "It seems Mr Darcy's letters are not the only matter bringing colour to Bennet cheeks these days."

Chapter Fifty-Five

The established rhythm of mornings at Longbourn had acquired a new predictability as spring advanced toward summer. Shortly after ten, hoofbeats on the drive announced Colonel Fitzwilliam's arrival, ostensibly to confer with the ladies about some matter related to Dunbar Court's restoration. By eleven, he and Jane could inevitably be found walking the garden paths, their heads bent in earnest conversation about estate matters that somehow required daily consultation.

"Do you not think," Mary said dryly as they watched the pair disappear around the hedge, "that Dunbar Court must be the most thoroughly discussed property in all of Hertfordshire. One wonders that any renovations occur at all, given how frequently the Colonel requires guidance."

"Perhaps he finds the architectural advice here superior to that available elsewhere," Kitty suggested, her fingers busy with a delicate embroidery of herbs for Mrs Bennet's workbasket—a skill she had been cultivating with unexpected diligence.

Lydia, sprawled rather inelegantly across the window seat despite frequent corrections to her posture, snorted. "Architectural advice? Ah, so that is the phrase now in fashion? I've seen how he looks at Jane when he thinks no one is watching."

"Lydia!" Mrs Bennet admonished from her seat near the window, albeit with less sharpness than formerly. "A lady does not make such observations aloud. Do sit like a young lady."

"Even when they are completely accurate?" Lydia countered, straightening her posture somewhat.

Mrs Bennet, adjusting her black cap as she returned to her needlework, merely smiled. "Some observations may be true without requiring verbal confirmation, my dear."

"And some guidance proves more compelling than others," Elizabeth added, sorting through correspondence at her grandfather's desk. "I cannot but admit surprise at Jane's sudden expertise in military-style roof timbering."

"Does this surprise equal your own remarkable fascination with Pemberley's drainage systems?" Mary's eyebrow arched delicately as she posed the question.

A rueful smile spread across Elizabeth's face. "I surrender to your logic, sister."

"Consider yourselves fortunate that your discussions touch on interesting matters at least," said Kitty, her needle flashing in the morning light. "Mary and Mr Fairfield have spent entire afternoons debating the mineral composition of soil samples. Who knew that mere earth could inspire such passionate discourse?"

A telltale flush crept up Mary's neck to settle in her cheeks. "The pursuit of scientific knowledge demands meticulous examination."

"Most meticulous in your case, if I may say so." Lydia's teasing retort was followed by a swift ducking motion as she evaded the nearby bolster Mary had sent sailing with surprising accuracy.

Mrs Bennet's gaze had drifted toward the window again, where the distant figures of Jane and the Colonel could be seen near the stone bench by the old apple tree. "They make a handsome pair," she murmured.

On the path, the Colonel's tall figure seemed to bend toward Jane as if drawn by some invisible force, whilst Jane's customary serenity had softened into something warmer and more telling in his presence. Her gaze lingered on his profile when she thought no one noticed. A certain gentle radiance suffused her features that spoke of feelings far deeper than neighbourly regard.

"The Colonel's renovations progress remarkably well," Elizabeth said. "Mr Darcy writes that his cousin shows unexpected aptitude for country matters."

"Or unexpected motivation," Kitty murmured, her eyes

twinkling.

"I still maintain he should have installed larger windows in the south drawing room," Lydia declared. "I told him the sheep pasture visibility would be greatly improved."

"Because the Colonel's primary concern is surveying livestock from his parlour?" Mary returned dryly. "Is it settled that he will remain in residence? Has he given up his commission?"

Further conversation ceased as they heard the garden door open. Jane entered alone, her cheeks flushed with more than just morning air, her composure distinctly unsettled.

"Jane?" Mrs Bennet set aside her needlework, instantly alert to her eldest daughter's agitation.

"The Colonel has asked to speak with you, Mamma," Jane said, her voice steady despite the bright colour in her face. "He awaits your convenience in the parlour."

Lydia sat bolt upright, her eyes wide. "Oh! Oh, it has happened at last!"

"Hush, Lydia," Kitty admonished, although her own expression was equally animated. "We do not know that for certain."

"Do we not?" Lydia gestured dramatically toward Jane's flushed countenance. "Look at her!"

Mrs Bennet rose with unexpected dignity, smoothing her black gown. "I see." Her voice held understanding rather than surprise. "I shall attend him directly."

When she had gone, Jane's composure finally faltered. She sank onto the window seat beside Lydia, her hands clasped so tightly that her knuckles whitened.

"Well?" Lydia demanded, practically bouncing with excitement. "Has he declared himself? Did he go down on one knee? Was it terribly romantic?"

"Lydia, pray allow Jane to breathe," Elizabeth intervened, moving to her eldest sister's side.

"He has declared himself," Jane whispered, her voice barely audible. "After so many weeks of careful conversation, of measured steps, he spoke with such eloquence, such feeling that I…" She faltered.

"That you finally understood the depth of his regard?" Elizabeth supplied gently.

Jane nodded, a smile breaking through her composure like sunlight through clouds. "He spoke of how his military career had taught him to recognise what truly matters amidst disorder, and to cherish steadiness in a changing world." Her voice softened with wonder. "He said that in all his campaigns, all his travels, he had never found such perfect composure coupled with such genuine warmth."

"How lovely," Kitty sighed, her needlework forgotten in her lap.

"Did he mention his income?" Lydia enquired, earning herself a sharp look from Mary. "What? It is a practical consideration!"

"And your response?" Mary asked Jane, ignoring Lydia's interruption.

"I…" Jane's fingers twisted in her lap. "I cannot deny that his company has become essential to my happiness. That his steady character and kind heart had awakened feelings I had not thought possible after…" She need not mention Bingley's name for her sisters to understand.

The sound of voices from the parlour filtered through the house—Mrs Bennet's measured tones and the Colonel's deeper replies.

"Mamma manages the matter with such composure," Mary said. "She has been our family's anchor these past weeks."

"She has always possessed a remarkable clarity in matters of importance," Jane said. "Her judgement regarding suitable attachments has proved infallible."

"I have not inherited her composure," Lydia announced frankly. "Whilst you all grow increasingly proper and settled, I am still utterly myself—the one Bennet who refuses to change."

"For which we are daily grateful," Elizabeth replied with affectionate irony, making Lydia grin. "I suspect even you have learnt more from Mamma's example than you care to admit."

"And the Colonel's plans?" Kitty asked. "Will Dunbar Court become his permanent residence?"

Jane's smile held quiet joy. "Fitzwilliam, Mr Fitzwilliam Darcy I mean, has granted Richard a lease with option to purchase. His military obligations are concluded, and he speaks of applying his organisational skills to estate management. He believes," her voice coloured with pleasure, "that my understanding of local agricultural methods might prove invaluable to his success."

"How fortunate that you have devoted such study to these matters," Elizabeth teased gently.

"No less fortunate than your own voluminous correspondence concerning improvements at Pemberley," Jane returned, her eyes sparkling with uncharacteristic mischief.

"Or Mary's sudden interest in soil composition," Kitty added.

"Or Kitty's detailed botanical drawings that require such frequent consultation with young Mr Blackwood," Lydia countered wickedly.

"Or Lydia's newfound dedication to sheep breeding that has nothing whatsoever to do with Mr Hargreaves' son who manages Lord Milton's prize-winning flock," Kitty retorted, making Lydia flush.

The parlour door opened, and Mrs Bennet emerged with the Colonel at her side. The gentleman's military bearing seemed suffused with new vigour, whilst Mrs Bennet's expression held the quiet satisfaction of seeing perfect order established.

"My dears," she announced, her voice steady, "Colonel Fitzwilliam has requested permission to marry your sister Jane. I have, of course, granted my consent."

Lydia could no longer contain herself. "Wonderful! When shall we order the wedding clothes? Will you have a military wedding? Can there be officers in attendance? Will the Earl of Matlock attend? The Viscount?"

"Lydia," Jane admonished gently, although her smile remained.

The Colonel bowed, his eyes seeking Jane's with an intensity that belied his composed manner. "Miss Bennet has done me the great honour of receiving my addresses," he said, his voice carrying the gravitas of a man accustomed to battlefield commands yet gentled by genuine emotion. "I have learnt to assess the strength of a position, Miss Bennet—and yours, I believe, is unassailable. I am more grateful than I can express."

Jane rose; her serenity returned although her eyes shone with quiet happiness. "The gratitude is mutual, Richard."

"Indeed," Mrs Bennet remarked with singular insight, "when genuine affection and mutual respect form the foundation of an attachment, gratitude becomes just one component of a more complex whole."

Elizabeth blinked, then smiled. Her mother, it seemed, had mastered the art of restraint, whilst Kitty and Lydia exchanged surprised glances. The Colonel inclined his head in agreement.

"Just so, Madam," he replied. Then, turning to Jane smiling. "I believe we were discussing the east fields before this… detour in our conversation. Might we resume our consultation?"

"I believe I can spare another quarter hour," Jane replied, her eyes communicating far more than her measured words.

"Only a quarter hour?" Lydia exclaimed. "But I am certain there are hours' worth of estate matters to discuss!"

"Lydia," five voices chorused in unison, making even the Colonel chuckle.

As Jane and the Colonel departed for the garden again, Mrs Bennet settled back in her chair with a contented sigh. "Such a fine match," she murmured. "Not merely in fortune, although that is certainly satisfactory, but in temperament."

"Like your Mr Freeman and you?" Elizabeth suggested innocently.

Mrs Bennet's cheeks coloured but her dignity remained intact. "Companionship based on shared interests brings particular satisfaction in later life," she replied with surprising poise.

"And in early life as well," Kitty said, her gaze drifting toward the window where Mr Hill could be seen arriving with the post.

Lydia sprung up from the window seat. "I believe the sheep require my attention at present."

"Of course," Elizabeth said, watching with amusement as she hurried from the room.

Mrs Bennet shook her head, but her expression held fond indulgence rather than exasperation. "Longbourn seems determined to thrive in unexpected ways," she said, her gaze taking in her daughters with quiet pride. "Your grandfather would be pleased."

Elizabeth felt the truth of this settle around her like a comfortable shawl. Through all their losses, all their struggles, the essence of what made Longbourn priceless remained—not just in the land itself, but in the connections it fostered and the growth it nurtured, both in fields and in hearts.

Chapter Fifty-Six

The early July sun filtered through Longbourn chapel's ancient windows, casting honey-coloured light across the gathered family. Elizabeth, in her silvery grey silk trimmed with the palest lavender, looked more radiant than any bride could hope to be. The colour, whilst acknowledging their mourning's latter stages, seemed to capture something essential about her character - that peculiar blend of practicality and romance that had first caught Darcy's eye.

"It is not, to be sure," Mrs Bennet had said that morning, smoothing the silk with familiar expertise, "what I should have chosen for my second daughter's wedding attire. But then," her voice softened with hard-won wisdom, "I suspect Elizabeth shall soon have more choices in fine fabrics than even my younger self could have dreamt of."

Now, watching Jane adjust her sister's bonnet with tender care, Mrs Bennet's eyes held both tears and triumph. The Colonel's steady gaze, following Jane's every movement, suggested that perhaps another grey silk gown might be required before the mourning period was completed.

"I suspect," Mary murmured to Kitty, "that improvements at Dunbar Court have progressed with remarkable speed, given the Colonel's frequent need to consult with Jane."

Kitty returned quietly. "I am uncertain that his extensive military experience explains his marked concern for monitoring the orientation of the flower beds. The ones beyond the bower where we cannot see them."

The sisters' exchange faltered as Elizabeth took her place beside Darcy, escorted by her Uncle Phillips. Something in their bearing - her lifted chin, his softened gravity - spoke to the absence of those who should have stood witness. The very sense of that absence seemed to add poignancy to the joy, like shadows giving dimension to light.

"Dearly beloved," the parson began, his voice carrying the weight of generations of Bennet marriages within these walls. Elizabeth's hand shook as it met Darcy's, but her voice rang clear and true through her responses. Darcy's own vows, delivered with characteristic intensity, held a depth of feeling that brought fresh tears to Mrs Bennet's already dampened handkerchief.

"I do not believe," Colonel Fitzwilliam remarked quietly to Jane as they followed the newly married couple from the chapel, "that I have ever seen my cousin look quite so… unbuttoned."

"Whilst maintaining perfect propriety in his cravat," Jane said with gentle humour. "A remarkable achievement."

"Speaking of remarkable achievements," the Colonel's voice dropped lower still, "I understand the south gardens at Dunbar Court show to particular advantage from the mistress's chamber."

Jane's answering smile held all the warmth of the sky above them. "I should be happy to offer my thoughts on the matter. For the good of the neighbourhood, naturally."

"Naturally," he agreed, his eyes suggesting thoughts far removed from horticulture.

Ahead of them, Elizabeth's grey silk caught the light as she turned to her husband, her face illuminated with a joy that owed nothing to the richness of her gown and everything to the man beside her. Mrs Bennet, watching her daughter's radiance, could not regret a single thread of any missing wedding clothes.

The wedding breakfast, modest in scale, hummed with the liveliness that occurs when long-held social barriers begin to crack. Miss Georgiana Darcy, still shy but growing in confidence, was drawn into animated conversation with the youngest Miss Bennet about sheep breeding of all things.

"But surely the wool quality of the Merino crosses…" Lydia gestured enthusiastically with her teacup.

"Lydia," Elizabeth murmured in warning, her lips curved with amusement.

"Oh, pray permit her to continue," Georgiana interjected with unexpected authority. "I have long thought Pemberley's flocks would be improved by more innovative management. Brother has been terribly traditional about it."

"Traditional?" Darcy's eyebrow rose as he joined them. "I follow a proven methodology."

"Much like your approach to courtship, brother?" Georgiana's gentle teasing drew a startled laugh from Elizabeth.

"I see my wife's influence has already corrupted you beyond redemption," Darcy said dryly.

Across the room, Mrs Long and Lady Matlock engaged Mrs Bennet in earnest discussion of estate matters - a far cry from their previous barely veiled disdain for the family's active management.

"It seems," Colonel Fitzwilliam remarked to Jane as they observed the gathering, "that successful revolution in one quarter often leads to broader changes in perspective."

"Indeed," Jane agreed, her placid smile warming as it met his gaze.

"Speaking of attention," Mrs Bennet's voice carried to the two couples. "I believe the hour grows late for travellers hoping to make good progress before nightfall."

Elizabeth felt a rush of warmth in her cheeks, whether from her mother's transparent innuendo or her husband's suddenly intense regard was difficult to determine.

"Your mother shows remarkable tactical sense," Darcy murmured for Elizabeth's ears alone. "For myself, I have been calculating departure times since dawn."

"Have you indeed?" Elizabeth's voice held that particular blend of challenge and promise that never failed to unsettle his composure. "How fortunate that estate management has taught me the value of… prompt attention to urgent matters."

Their departure, when it came, combined dignity with the quiet urgency of long-delayed longing and decidedly efficient farewells. As the carriage pulled away, Lydia's voice carried. "But Miss Darcy, you simply must come see my newest lamb!"

"I suspect," Elizabeth said to her husband as Longbourn disappeared behind them, "that we have created a monster. Or rather, two of them."

"Better sheep than many other interests," Darcy replied with surprising humour. Then, his voice dropping to a register that made Elizabeth's breath catch, said, "Now, regarding that urgent matter requiring attention…"

The carriage wheels clattered over the last stones of the Longbourn drive as Darcy drew his wife into a kiss that unbalanced decades of propriety with months of desperate longing. The grey silk of her gown whispered beneath his fingers, and he caught the faint trace of lavender at her throat. When they parted, Elizabeth's eyes danced with mingled mischief and something deeper that made his heart pound.

"I have waited," he murmured against her temple, where a few curls had escaped their pins, "to do that properly since that morning I found you on the stream along Netherfield, mud to your knees, demolishing my arguments about the proper occupation of ladies with devastating astuteness."

"How remarkably unrefined of me," Elizabeth replied, her hands had found their way inside his coat, the warmth of her touch burning through his waistcoat. "What a pity you did not make your feelings known then. I imagine, however, that distinguished gentlemen rarely propose to mud-spattered critics of drainage works."

"I was rather too occupied wrestling with the realisation that said critic had somehow become essential to my happiness." His lips followed a path from her temple to the sensitive hollow beneath her ear, drawing a sharp intake of breath. "I maintain you won that argument through sheer force of logic rather than practical experience."

"Are you suggesting, sir, that my methods of persuasion lack adequate foundation?" Her fingers splayed against his chest, and he wondered if she could feel the thundering of his heart beneath them.

"On the contrary." Another kiss, deeper this time, her soft gasp lost against his mouth. "I find your methods of persuasion dangerously effective."

"How fortunate," Elizabeth breathed, arching toward him as his hand found her waist, "that I intend to use such powers only for the good of Pemberley."

"Pemberley's good being your primary concern at this moment?" The feel of her pressed against him made coherent thought increasingly challenging.

"Among other matters that demand immediate and thorough attention," she murmured, her eyes lit with a warmth that threatened to undo every last thread of his composure. Her smile held promise enough to make him forget half a millennium of Darcy restraint.

"I wonder what the ton will make of the great Mr Darcy being conquered by a country maiden who dared challenge his ideas on estate management?"

"I prefer to see it as being utterly vanquished by the extraordinary mind that the maiden displayed." His voice had roughened as she shifted closer still. "The critique was only the beginning."

"How diplomatic you have become," she said. Her own voice had grown unsteady as his hands skirted the line of her stays through silk. "I find I rather prefer this to our early encounters."

"As do I," he agreed, drawing her into the shelter of his arms where she fit as although made for the space. "I maintain that even then, you were the most beautiful thing I had ever seen."

The carriage swayed gently as it took a curve, late summer sunlight dappling through the windows across their entwined figures. Darcy proceeded to demonstrate just how thoroughly she had conquered him, propriety be damned.

They continued north, with the rhythmic sway of the carriage and the warmth of the morning forgotten entirely in the heat of their own making.

Epilogue

As the seasons turned, the ladies of Longbourn found their paths unfolding in ways none could have foreseen that cold day when Grandfather had closed his eyes for the final time.

The Lodge

The lavender and rosemary beds at the Lodge flourished under Mrs Bennet's careful attention, their fragrance greeting visitors who approached the elegantly proportioned cottage at the edge of Longbourn's grounds. Mr Freeman's quiet proposal came, as all who knew them expected, during a discussion of herb preservation techniques one autumn afternoon. Their December wedding, modest and dignified, saw the widow Bennet exchange her black for a deep blue that brought a trace of remembered youth to her countenance.

"I had not thought to find such companionship again," she confided to Elizabeth as they walked the Lodge's neat paths. "To be valued for one's mind rather than merely one's appearance—there is a particular satisfaction in that."

Mr Freeman's extensive library relocated to the Lodge where

it joined Mrs Freeman's growing collection of fine china. Their dinner parties became renowned among the seven and twenty families surrounding Meryton.

Dunbar Court

Colonel Fitzwilliam's military discipline, combined with Jane's unruffled management, transformed Dunbar Court from neglected property to the jewel of the neighbourhood. Their August wedding saw the newly renovated manor house gleaming in summer sunshine, its grounds immaculately groomed, and its interiors restored to their former splendour.

"Organisation is only the foundation," the Colonel often remarked. "It is my wife's particular genius for harmony that truly elevated this house to a home."

Jane's gentle guidance extended beyond household matters to the tenant farms, where her deep understanding of local agricultural methods proved invaluable. The Fitzwilliams soon became known for their progressive approach to estate management, balancing tradition with innovation in ways that fostered both prosperity and loyalty among their dependents.

Netherfield Park

Bingleys' hasty departure had left Netherfield in such disarray that its owner, Mr Sim, upon returning from the West Indies, declared himself "utterly disgusted with the shambles." When Mr Fairfield, whose scientific work had begun to attract attention in agricultural circles, expressed interest in the property, the owner practically thrust the keys into his hands at a price so low that it raised eyebrows throughout the county.

“The drainage alone requires complete restructuring,” Mr Fairfield explained to Mary during one of their lengthy discussions of soil composition. “With proper understanding of underground water movement…” His voice trailed off as he realised she was regarding him with surprising intensity.

“I believe,” Mary replied with care, “that I might have some thoughts on the matter.”

Their courtship, conducted largely through shared experiments and scholarly debate, culminated in a spring wedding that united two methodical minds in perfect intellectual harmony. Netherfield’s transformation under their stewardship became a study in itself, as they converted portions of the estate into experimental fields where new scientific principles were applied to traditional farming methods with remarkable results.

Longbourn

Kitty’s marriage to Mr Blackwood, whose medical training and botanical illustrations had captured attention beyond Hertfordshire, occurred with less fanfare but equal joy. Their shared passion for propagation techniques led to Longbourn’s orchards expanding beyond anyone’s expectations, the grafted varieties producing fruit that commanded premium prices at London markets. Their combined skill in medicine and herb craft benefitted the neighbourhood.

“We are but stewards,” Kitty would say, echoing her grandfather’s philosophy. “Each generation leaves its mark, but the land remains.”

As trustees for all the Bennet sisters’ interests in Longbourn, the Blackwoods maintained the estate’s central position in the family's connection, hosting seasonal gatherings that brought the scattered branches together with increasing frequency as children began to join the family circle.

Lydia's Extraordinary Elevation

It was Lydia, ever unpredictable, who followed the most astonishing path. Her genuine interest in sheep breeding led her to an agricultural exhibition in London, where her forthright critique of a particular flock's wool quality caught the attention of their owner.

"If these are meant to be prize specimens," she declared, unaware she was addressing the Earl of Hampstead himself rather than his agent, "then I fear the standards have fallen considerably since last season. The tensile strength is shamefully inadequate."

Rather than taking offence, the Earl—a widower known for his progressive agricultural methods—was charmed by her unvarnished expertise and spirited manner. Her invitation to the 'agent' to visit Longbourn to observe their breeding programme was accepted with alacrity.

"She speaks more sensibly about cross-breeding techniques than half my land agents," the Earl confided to Elizabeth during their visit. "And does so without the tedious deference that so often clouds honest assessment."

What began as agricultural consultation soon blossomed into something neither could have anticipated. The Earl, finding in Lydia both a vibrant mind and a refreshing lack of artifice, offered for her hand six months later—to the astonishment of society and the private satisfaction of Mrs Bennet, who had always suspected her youngest's exuberance would find its proper channel, eventually.

"It is not," Lydia informed her scandalised new peers at her first London dinner party, "a matter of marrying above or below oneself, but of finding a mind that challenges rather than merely echoes one's own."

Their partnership, both personal and professional, revolutionised the Earl's already substantial agricultural holdings. Lydia's innovative approaches complemented her husband's resources, resulting in breeding programmes that eventually supplied bloodstock to farms throughout England. That she presided over these enterprises whilst simultaneously managing her social position with unexpected grace became yet another testament to the Bennet sisters' remarkable adaptability.

"I always knew she would exceed expectations," Elizabeth remarked to Jane upon attending Lydia's first formal ball as Countess. "Upon reflection, even my imagination had limits."

The Circle Complete

Ten years after Grandfather Bennet's passing, a summer gathering at Longbourn brought the extended family together—from Pemberley came the Darcys with their three children; from Dunbar Court, the Fitzwilliams with their twins; from Netherfield, the Fairfields with their solitary but precocious son; from North Lodge, the Freemans, whose advanced years had only deepened their companionable affection; and from Hampstead Hall, the Earl, and Countess with their three robust children, whose titles did little to curb their irrepressible Bennet spiritedness.

As Elizabeth stood beside her husband watching the next generation explore the gardens where she had once walked with her grandfather, she felt the circle of life complete itself with satisfying symmetry.

"He would be pleased," Darcy murmured, following her gaze. "To see how his faith in your capabilities has borne fruit."

"Not only in capabilities," Elizabeth said, her hand finding his, "but in knowing happiness lies more in challenging convention than in bowing to it.

"A lesson," he acknowledged with the smile that still, after all these years, made her heart quicken, "that has proved remarkably applicable beyond mere estate management."

The summer evening wrapped around them like a blessing as children's laughter mingled with adult conversation, the legacy of James Huntington Bennet living on not just in the land that flourished under his granddaughters' stewardship, but in the lives they had built upon its solid foundation—each distinct, each valuable, and each rooted in the belief that women's minds were as worthy of cultivation as any.

Books By Mary Alice Alexander

Clever Lass
A Most Iniquitous Affair
Discretion and Avarice
The Holly and the Ivy
Sweet Caroline
The Power of Refusal

www.maryalicealexander.com

MARY ALICE ALEXANDER
AUTHOR

Before pursuing her passion for writing, Mary Alice Alexander worked as an attorney, where she advocated for justice for children. She lives in the Boston area with her infinitely patient husband of more than forty years.

3

Printed in Dunstable, United Kingdom

84843561R00308